THOUGH WE HAVE NO MERITS

THOUGH WE HAVE NO MERITS

DICK CARMEL

Published in the United States by Treams Publishing, Highland Park, Illinois
Library of Congress Cataloging-in-Publication Data
Name: Carmel, Dick – Author
Title: Though we have no merits / Dick Carmel
Identifiers: LCCN Library of Congress Control Number: 2020905730 | ISBN 978-0-578-66746-1 (pbk) | 978-0-578-66749-2 (e-book)
Subjects: 1. Contemporary Literature & Fiction—American. 2. Literature & Fiction—Genre Fiction. 3. Religion & Spirituality—Judaism. 4. Crime Fiction—Noir/Title

www.dickcarmel.com

Interior and exterior design by Danna Mathias
Edited by Laura Dragonette

In memory of Elaine Carmel

AVINU MALKEINU, BE GRACIOUS TO US AND ANSWER US,
THOUGH WE HAVE NO MERITS;
DEAL CHARITABLY AND KINDLY WITH US AND SAVE US.

—HEBREW PRAYER—

THOUGH WE HAVE NO MERITS

———————

NOISE

ONE

THE BOY WHO WAS FORMERLY SOLOMON BERNSTEIN TEETERED
at the edge of the living room like a mourner chanting the Kaddish,
bobbing and weaving in response to the breath of his father, David
Berns, who was asleep beneath the windows. The boy weighed the risk.
If he glided across the carpet, he might retrieve the book before his
father awakened. If he failed, he faced the prospect of another tirade
against his bar mitzvah. Zolly Berns, who would have been Bernstein
if his father hadn't started up with the goyim, who'd traded Solly for
Zolly by zippering his mouth at the sign of a secret, decided on taking
the chance. It was either that or allow his father to focus on the Hebrew
book when he awakened from his nap.

The room was at the front of the building, at the head of a hallway
that traveled the length of the apartment. It was like a railroad car that
had derailed years before, when David Bernstein had abandoned his
name and his family to lead a life on the road, making them just his rest
stop on weekends, a place for turning around. The fireplace wall was at
Zolly's left as he entered, its electric hearth glowing under the red glass

chips that passed for coal. The radiator that provided the heat was at the far side of the room, under windows that faced both the street and the snow that had started off the winter. Outside, every parking space was taken, except for those blocked off by brooms and folding chairs, one of which marked the place for David's Ford.

David was lying prone on the couch that hid the radiator from view, still dressed in the suit of a salesman. He never changed with the season, only by the week, and then to an identical outfit: a four-season suit and five-eyelet shoes. He could pass for an accountant when walking the streets. On the job, his hair was slicked back by a half dozen squeezes of VO5. On the couch, his hair was askew, smearing grease across the cushions, and he was honking snores as loud as the bells on the gates warning of an approaching train. You could bang on a pot a foot from his head; Dad's eyes would stay as tight as his wallet.

Mom was cooking the Shabbat dinner, an addiction from her childhood, but Dad didn't curse, provided she lit the candles out of his sight and left the wine within reach. The book was the challenge, on the table where it was always in reach if Mom made him practice. His friends' parents had coffee-table books setting off plastic-covered couches and Leon Uris novels, but the Berns residence settled for cotton slipcovers and the Hebrew book. If it was out of sight when Dad came home, he paid the same attention to Zolly he gave to the weekend papers, which remained unopened until the garbage pickup on Monday. Even at home, Dad had his mind on the road. Zolly's family was different from that of most of the kids in his class, whose fathers took the el to work and then came home for dessert and Milton Berle on their round-screen TVs. Dad insisted that Zolly was lucky he had a radio. He had surprised them this evening by arriving before it was dark, before Zolly had a chance to retrieve the book and hide it beneath his pillow. If it was there when Dad woke up, he would demand that Zolly perform, as though Zolly was trying out a nightclub act where his father could watch and heckle. Dad didn't care about Zolly's grades, had never met a Boy Scout, and forgot every birthday. But for a guy who wasn't Orthodox, David applauded ritual. Here was how the weekends went. The smell of the soup and the chicken reminded Dad he was hungry and goosed him up from the couch and into the dining room in a tie with the arrival of dinner. Halfway through the bowl, Dad would always look up, say, "You ready?" take a few more sips, then say, "Grandpa shouldn't be disappointed," and nod at Mom as though to show respect for her father. Which of course was a lie. Respect had been abandoned in Minnesota, where Grandpa Sam resided.

"I practice every day," Zolly would say, which was usually true, to the credit of Mom, who wanted it for Grandpa Sam as well as for herself. "Grandpa says I married a goy," was Becky's answer to Zolly's complaints. She meant to prove her father mistaken.

Tonight, Dad added to his usual pronouncements. "This is your chance to hit the jackpot." He drew his metaphors from his current line of work.

Leave it to Dad to dwell on his job. He spent his weekdays selling slot machines to the Kiwanis, Lions, Elks, Masons, Rotarians, and all the other Gentile clubs within an eight-hour drive of home. If he gave Zolly a tip of ten percent of the smiles he gave to the goyim, of the cracks on the back with the open palm that declared it was all in fun, of the five grins a minute and laughter at all of their jokes, Zolly would have hidden that treasure under his pillow in place of his Hebrew book. Instead, he had to settle for a wink that supposedly showed his father didn't mean it when he said, "You want to make your Grandpa proud of his bar mitzvah boy."

Great reason to kill a couple of hours a day reading Hebrew, chanting hymns, and droning his haftorah. Zolly would have been happy if his father ever gave him a sliver of the attention he gave the gifts that would come from Grandpa Sam and the rest of their relatives during the celebration. Instead, Dad was so hung up on Zolly's getting it right that he had arranged for Mr. Kleinman to come Monday through Thursday to suffer through Zolly cracking across the tropes that measured the melodies of the prayers while he prayed to God off-key. God was one subject neither Dad, nor Mom, nor Kleinman ever discussed, except in a biblical sense. Zolly himself ignored what he was chanting—not difficult, since he detested reading the Hebrew. He could just as well have been praying to Grandpa Sam as to God.

"Learn anything new?" Waking up, Dad swung his heels off the couch and onto the floor, sitting up with the momentum. What was left of his hair was as gray as his face, which came from a career composed of cigarettes and scotch and sodas in his customers' places of business. "Not that any of it counts. The real world doesn't talk Hebrew." He moved his hand across his face, denying any expression.

"Mom says it's important." The words hung in the space between him and his father. His parents could argue on their own. They didn't need him to ring the bell. Zolly sidled toward the table, keeping his eyes on his father. The book was only steps away, facedown on the glass, half-hidden by the *Chicago Tribune* and shadowed by the wine. With any luck, his father hadn't noticed. If he had, his eyes might have filed it away as clutter.

Dad approached Zolly, exuding the smell of stale cigars and day-old whiskey. Zolly's mother had demanded that David buy a second suit. You couldn't count on the Saturday cleaner getting it bagged in the middle of the weekend. But when he came home, his suits always smelled the same. The jacket showed a week's worth of creases and the stains of eating out. The lapel sported the pin of the Kiwanis or the Masons, Zolly wasn't sure—wherever Dad had finished earlier that day. The lines around Dad's mouth and eyes all pointed down, as they did whenever he wasn't selling.

"You didn't answer my question." His father sniffed.

Zolly sniffed, as well. Dinner wasn't ready yet. His luck. His father must be smelling him. "I'm supposed to stick to my assignment," Zolly said. Which was about bringing in the harvest. The Israelites had been farmers back then, poor people who lived off sheep. Zolly tried to picture his father kicking shit off his heels in a field, but all he could manage was a man whose shoes needed a shine after stubbing his toes at the base of the bars where he bought the goyim their drinks. If the Jews had waited a couple thousand years before writing it down, Zolly might be singing about Johnnie Walker Red instead of the sea that parted for passage.

"So tell me your assignment." His father cocked his head as though he cared, as though the answer changed from week to week instead of being dependent on Zolly's birthday and the synagogue's schedule. He shrugged, stretched, and then his attention strayed to the painting that hung over the fake fireplace, an oil by an anonymous artist.

"If you paid attention, you'd remember." Zolly was tired of the weekly conversations with the same questions and the same answers.

Dad's fixation in getting the answer he wanted was what made him a successful salesman.

His father grabbed Zolly's arm with a grip stronger than Hank Sauer, the Cubs' left fielder, who could crush an orange into pulp with his hand. Some nights, when Dad was away, Zolly would close his eyes and pretend he was at the game his father had taken him to as a child. But that scene was harder to fantasize about when Dad was at home, squeezing Zolly's arm and the blood from his dreams.

"I had a rough week. Don't give me any lip." His father released Zolly's arm and moved to the other end of the room, where he leaned on the baby grand. Every living room on the block had one. Either that or a spinet, if the family couldn't afford any better. You didn't need to know how to play one. You didn't even need to know how to hum. Even if the residents were all amputees whose tongues were torn out, they had to have a piano. It took the place of a college degree and familiarity with the classics. The scene worked best when you didn't pay attention to where your elbow rested, which in this apartment involved David Berns—formerly Bernstein—leaning against the Baldwin, while continuing his inquisition. "Did you learn it any better? Kleinman costs twenty bucks an hour."

Not that it really mattered. Dad regarded each twenty as a down payment for bar mitzvah gifts to come. Even considering eight months with the private tutor, the total cost would still be less than a thousand dollars, with a lot more coming back in return. That explained where Dad was leaning. Grandpa Sam alone would cover the balance Dad still owed on the baby grand.

"Mr. Kleinman says I should learn it by heart," Zolly said.

"They going to take it away?"

"In case I lose my place."

"Which is going to be a part-time job as soon as this nonsense is over." Dad never tired of talking about his time stocking shelves at the grocery store, starting when he was twelve.

"Your sales down this trip?" If Zolly got him talking business, Dad might forget about the Hebrew.

David pushed off the Baldwin, rubbed his eyes, looked down at his hands, and blinked, as though surprised that his palms were empty, but he didn't give an answer at once. That wasn't like him. He never searched for words. He could say whatever the occasion required—a banker reluctant to return a deposit but always with ready cash in the till.

"'Down' is an understatement. My sales were nonexistent." Dad moved his eyes from his palms to the recollection floating overhead like the wisp of smoke that would have been present if the fireplace had been real. "My customers are afraid of getting hurt. They had visits from the boys."

Approaching thirteen and the son of a slot machine salesman, Zolly knew the shorthand. Calling them "boys" made the gangsters resemble a pack of kids playing pranks, but Zolly had also been to the movies. You got involved, you went to jail or wound up dead, sometimes both, like Jackie Solomon's dad, who had been an accountant for the mob until the day he was shot in the parking lot alongside his El Dorado, just because he'd substituted a decimal in place of a comma. The books always had to balance. What Zolly couldn't figure out was how any of this related to his father, a man who worked on his own and bought and sold for cash. Zolly swallowed and worked to match the expression his father usually showed, that try-to-read-me-but-don't-kid-yourself-that-you-can face. No way would he show fear to his Dad. Even eight years later, he could remember their trip to the zoo, the summer day Zolly had hidden between his father's legs upon encountering the tigers, and Dad had pushed him away.

"They're giving you competition?" Zolly said. He could straddle the truth as well as his parents. He knew the opening credits and all the dialogue from eavesdropping outside the kitchen when they thought he was asleep and spent their weekends debating their odds of survival. Whoever controlled the gambling was moving beyond the suburbs, having stuffed slots into as many saloons as the police would overlook.

Dad was finally looking away from the cracks in the ceiling, focusing on Zolly. "You're just a kid. Pay attention to your lessons."

"I'm about to be a bar mitzvah." Zolly could handle whatever it was.

"David, what are you saying?" Becky had arrived in the archway between the dining and living rooms, which were almost equal in size. The apartment dated back to the twenties, when the building had been constructed. In those days, they must have lived from party to party, moving back and forth from cocktails, to dinner, to after-dinner drinks by the fireplace while the table was cleared, then back to their seats for dessert, the host or hostess pressing their feet on the buttons under the table to summon the maid. It might have even been a butler, Zolly couldn't be sure. The swinging door from the dining room led to the so-called butler's pantry, which was the buffer between where they ate the food and the kitchen where it was cooked. These days, it was Mom who did the cooking and the serving, between sitting down to eat herself. Tonight, she had dinner on the table, the matzo balls floating beneath the steam that drifted above the bowls like smoke from the leaves of a curbside fire.

"They won't push me around." His father was proving his point by standing as straight as when he started out every Monday. He was wearing the brown suit, which meant it was an even-numbered week, the jacket misshapen from his nap, tie open at the neck and his belt unbuckled, but only a moment away from making a sale if the occasion arose.

"You're frightening the boy," Mom said. But she herself was shaking while standing in the doorway to the dining room, the color missing from her cheeks as though the stove had drained her heat away in order to cook the broth. She bunched the bottom of her apron up against her breasts. A photo of Mom and Dad was in a frame on top of the Baldwin. The only practical function the piano served was to display an array of scenes from happier times. The one that was Zolly's favorite showed Mom and Dad as newlyweds—or so they seemed to him, as Zolly wasn't in the picture. It must have been before his father lost the business he had owned when he'd married Zolly's mother, Becky—with Grandpa Sam's reluctant blessing—when they could afford the three-bedroom apartment in the six-flat building. Dad was looking at Becky in the picture. Zolly imagined how things had once been. When Zolly was frightened by his parents' weekly arguments about the danger, he would focus on the picture and imagine how things had been.

"I won't walk away from all I've worked for," Dad said. "You think I enjoy a life on the road? So I'm not your father retired in Minnesota and living off the interest on my bonds. It isn't much, but this business is mine. I mean to keep it." It was like any other time David put a string of sentences together. It was the money that got him going. "I worked hard for those accounts. I won't give them up without a fight."

"David, these men have guns."

"I'm not talking about a shoot-out."

Mom was moving toward him, the soup growing cold on the table. "Find a business to buy. We have enough. Do something safe."

"Everything I've made I put into buying more machines."

She rushed to him, exchanging the bottom of her apron for the folds of his sleeves. "What were you contemplating? Competing with Las Vegas?"

David flicked Becky away. "It made sense if they minded their own business."

"Let my father help."

The chances of that were as good as Dad kicking off his shoes each night when he got home before flopping on the couch. David managed to be a room away whenever Becky called her father. Zolly wasn't sure whether that was due to his father's envy of Sam's success or because Dad resented the Hebrew. If it was up to his father, there would be no bar mitzvah, even if it meant they remained in debt on the Baldwin.

"I intend to get even any way I can," Dad said.

"You just said you're not going up against them."

"That doesn't mean I can't go to the police."

When Zolly's parents got married, Mom had tried to keep kosher for at least a week, but Dad kept bringing home the pig. Ham, bacon, pork chops—you name it—corrupted the kitchen with tref. The way Mom told the story, it had to do with Dad's misguided appetite, but Zolly sensed a connection with keeping Grandpa Sam's visits to a minimum. Either way, it added up to a house where almost anything passed across their tongues except mention of the law. In a house of tref, the cops weren't kosher. Now, Dad was breaking the rules.

"You think the police will help when what you were doing was illegal?" Mom said. "They're going to put them away and put you back in business?"

His father was looking at the carpet where he had tracked in the mud and snow from the street. Mom waited until Mondays to clean it. He said, "I know that's too late. But I warned them what I would do."

"You . . . warned them?" His mother stroked the words behind her, gulping air between them. "You're killing me."

"I told them I would do it as soon as I got back."

"David. You're tired. Wait until tomorrow."

"I shouldn't have taken the nap." He turned to Zolly. "Save my space outside after I leave."

Becky said, "Your dinner."

Friday was the one night they ate together. Weekdays, Dad was away. Saturday night, Mom and Dad went out as though they still were dating. Sundays, Dad went to bed early, getting rest before his trips. Friday remained special, even though Dad ignored any connection with religion. But tonight, the chicken would forever go uneaten.

They heard the bang of the door as David slammed it shut behind him. It was quiet for five minutes, with the silence broken only by Zolly's mother's sobs, before they heard the bigger bang from in front of their building, followed by the sound of their windows exploding into the room, and the feel of the glass as it splintered their faces.

———————————

WORDS

TWO

Z<small>OLLY WORKED HIS CONVERTIBLE DOWN THE BLOCK THAT</small> stretches west from where Michigan Avenue empties onto Lake Shore Drive. It is a Chicago street but a New York block, peaking with high-rises near the lake, sloping through a mix of shops, apartments, and a movie theater in the middle, and then smoothing into Rush Street's bars. It would take a while to pierce the traffic on an Oak Street Sunday. With a few hours' sleep and the sun burning away the booze, Zolly figured he could handle Goldberg and crew when he got there. Afterward, he decided he should have kept his convertible's top up to blend in with the suits. Top down, sun flashing off his gold necklace, Rolex, and ruby ring, and with the scars on his face obscured by his tan, he looked like cash to the cop who pulled him over.

"License," the policeman said, his hand on the El Dorado's door.

Good, Zolly thought, *he didn't start with "sir." We can do business.* He left the twenty clipped to his license when he handed it over. An old-timer would palm it without a blink.

The cop said, "Nice picture. This what you looked like thirty pounds ago?"

Actually, it had been two years and forty pounds, which made it twenty pounds a year—some food, mostly booze. At six feet even, Zolly thought he could handle the extra weight. "I enjoy the good life," he said.

The cop said, "Berns. That Irish?"

Okay, so this one was with the ethnic unit. "No, it's short for Bernstein. My grandfather was from Russia." Ever since Zolly was a kid, he had handled it head-on. If the guy gave him a hard time, Zolly had lots of friends at the station.

"I read they're letting you people out." The cop thumbed the license, but none of the ink rubbed off. "You speak pretty good English. Been here long?"

"It's not me that's from Russia," Zolly said. "It's my grandfather, eighty years ago." It had been years since he'd thought of Grandpa Sam. The only picture he had of the old man showed him wearing a beard and skullcap. Not that Zolly minded being a Jew. It was just a missing piece of foreskin. "I've got to get to my spot. It's around the corner. Zolly's Place. That's short for me."

After the cop considered his options, he said, "I know the place. I'll stop by next week, maybe have a beer after work." He winked to show he knew Zolly had friends of friends. Then he handed back the license with the twenty still attached.

When Zolly reached his destination, he headed straight for the bar. "*Dos cervezas, por favor.*" He liked to show Pedro that he was simpatico. He also liked his beer. Pedro took two mugs from the freezer and filled them from the tap, the frost making the beer froth. Those little touches counted with the customers. Besides, with the foam, it took less beer to fill a mug. Zolly drained his first stein in two swallows. His second jug was for sipping and surveying. The regulars were clinging to their usual stools, as though a different one would demand a formal introduction. The Cubs fans were at the end of the bar, near the big TV, drinking bottled beer. If Zolly closed to take inventory, they might die of thirst unless someone introduced them to water. The other end of the bar held the gamblers, who didn't care who won or lost as long as they beat the spread. The tables were for the crowd that came to socialize. That was also where the strangers sat, trying to meet women. If an outsider approached one without cash in his hand, he was guaranteed disappointment. There was no music to fill the pauses, because Zolly kept the jukebox soft. Otherwise, it would interfere with the play-by-play. Besides, Zolly had been tone-deaf ever since the explosion that had killed his father. When anyone played a song, Zolly heard a headache. The booths were a different show, where you needed an okay from an usher—whether it be Zolly, or his girlfriend, Faith, or the bouncer, Conrad Bigman. The stars sat here: the politicians, businessmen, union leaders, and all the others who ran the ward. Booth One starred Goldberg, Civiletti, and O'Rourke.

Pedro was the result of Goldberg's advice when Zolly had bought his first bar on Howard Street, on how to defend against the ways employees stole from the owner in an all-cash business. A bartender could water down the drinks and pocket the difference or serve customers from his own bottle. To try to avoid this, Goldberg had told Zolly to hire employees with no experience, and to turn them over quickly. Hiring immigrants had earned Zolly his reputation as a liberal, which was awkward in the days the Republicans ruled. But after a while, Zolly didn't mind it. Everyone deserved a chance. If the goyim in a Minnesota town could accept Grandpa Sam, Zolly could return the favor.

He finished his beer, arose from the bar, and walked to the rear of the room, talking from five feet away. He knew better than to come unannounced. "Hey, Abie, how's it going?" Zolly waved at Goldberg, who was sitting at the near end of the booth. The top of Goldberg's head was no more than five feet above floor level when he stood. With Goldberg, the back of the booth was a necessary reference point. Otherwise, you couldn't tell whether he was sitting down or standing up. But nothing gave a clue as to whether Goldberg's skin was yellow from age, a dietary deficiency, or too many nights in a row. You didn't want to get that close.

"Zolly boy. How's it going?" These days, Goldberg's conversations were mostly grunts and gasps. He pushed Civiletti over to make room.

Zolly sat on the crack at the edge of the booth, one leg dangling down, the other swinging under the table to keep his balance. "Worse than usual. I'm under audit. As though I didn't pay enough taxes. They always want more." Goldberg perked up, still the accountant twenty years removed.

"Income tax?" Goldberg asked.

"No, they haven't gotten around to that yet. But I've got the feds, state, and city on my back."

"The state don't do audits," O'Rourke said. After moving down a list of half a dozen city jobs a step ahead of the latest scandal, O'Rourke now worked in the Department of Registration and Education and thought the state only handled licensing.

"It's the Department of Revenue," Zolly said. "Sales tax."

"You're not reporting all the cash. What else is new?" Goldberg asked.

"The problem is with what I actually do report. My income tax returns don't match up with my sales tax reports."

O'Rourke said, "Can't help you there. I don't know about num- bers." His toothpick skittered from one side of his mouth to the other, as though deciding where to land.

Civiletti spoke up. "What do the feds have to do with sales tax?" No one could deduce that Civiletti was in construction from what he wore. His pimp clothes suggested he was in a different occupation, but the bulge in his pants was the ward's street-repair contracts.

"It's got nothing to do with sales tax," Zolly said. "It's the withhold- ing taxes. The feds think I underreported the tips."

"Why don't you pool them, like everyone else on the Street?" When Goldberg slammed his hand on the table, it sounded hollow instead of like solid oak.

"Watch it, that's an expensive piece of furniture," Zolly said.

Goldberg said, "You call it antique. I call it old."

"Either way, I keep this booth available for you, so take care of it."

"Pool the tips and split them," Goldberg said. "Then you know exactly how much they were, how much to take out for taxes, and how much for social security." As he ticked off each item, Goldberg drummed his fingers, treating the tabletop as a calculator. Each tap seemed to echo.

Zolly said, "I had my waiters fill out a sheet every week. I withheld tax- es based on what they put down. I figured it was their taxes, their problem."

"As it turns out, it's your problem." Goldberg stretched his seams as he wiggled his elbows. "What do you want from us?"

"The last time we renewed, my landlord jacked up the rent so much he must have thought I was coining money." Zolly shook his head at the folly and reached for his beer, before remembering he'd left it back at the bar. "I've got building inspectors, license inspectors, liquor inspectors, police inspectors, and health inspectors. Everything needs a license. The water isn't hot enough. The food is uncovered. Keep the meat in the cooler. Sweep the floors. Look out for the rat shit. Watch for the cockroaches. Cover your garbage. They never let up." Reciting his troubles aloud gave him the pain in the usual spot, the hole that spread from his stomach up his chest and out his arms until his hands felt empty, even in a fist. Whenever he had that pain, he recalled his father dying in the street. The first loss is the hardest.

"If they shut you down for structural, you're out the money no matter who's responsible," Civiletti said.

That was where Goldberg came in. Zolly didn't care what it said on his business card. Twenty years earlier, he had been Zolly's accountant. These days, Goldberg was an arranger. Zolly was never sure which came first: the Board of Health or Goldberg, the fuckers or the egg. He edged farther away until he almost fell from the booth, even though it could have swallowed a standard restaurant stall. The seats and back were real leather. He couldn't remember the name of the Milwaukee Avenue restaurant, but he could recall the auction when he'd bought the booths. Some called it bad luck to buy fixtures from a place that had gone under, but Goldberg had turned him on to it. "Remember, value depends on whether you're a buyer or seller."

The back of the booth was stuck like moulding against the wall. To his right and behind Goldberg, the door to the kitchen occupied the rest of that end of the room. Goldberg kept quiet on the obvious. The booths left no room for tables and therefore cut down on sales, but where his privacy was concerned, Goldberg had no conscience. Waitresses and busboys paraded by. The kitchen doors swung back and forth. The four of them were cocooned by the bustle of the business.

"Okay, look," Goldberg said, while Zolly strained to hear against the noise. "We can't help you with the sales tax, but assuming the worst, all you'll owe is back taxes and interest, maybe a penalty. We can't help you with the withholding tax, either. That's federal, and you'll learn a lesson. Let's focus on the positives. Talk about what we're able to do for you." Goldberg's eyes glinted, and his pig cheeks surrendered to a smile. As he had grown up and out, his need to show off had expanded. Letting him ramble might hold down the fee. "What's with your liquor license?" Goldberg nodded at Civiletti and O'Rourke to show he'd known all along where the trail would lead.

Zolly said, "Bigman left the front door to go to the john. He just couldn't wait. While he was away, some kids entered and went to the bar. Pedro figured Bigman must have checked their IDs, so he served them. A cop walked in. You know the rest."

Civiletti smiled. Lining up the paving work in the ward meant he had made the acquaintance of City Hall, the bosses at the County Building, the construction trades, and everyone else who mattered. "When is it up in court?"

Goldberg said, "The price of these things has gone up."

"Yeah, inflation," said O'Rourke, claiming a role in the conversation.

"Whatever it takes. Just let me know," Zolly said. It was like old times. He started to leave.

"Wait a minute." Goldberg frowned just when Zolly was feeling better. "Doesn't it seem a little strange? You're a Rush Street fixture. How long since you sold the bar on Howard and moved here? Ten years? Keep a quiet place, nobody hassles you since you beat the prostitution rap. Sure, you get some beefs every now and then, but never all at once."

Zolly stood there like a waiter taking orders. "What can I tell from that?"

"Is there something else going on? Anyone asking questions?"

Zolly thought about his call to his lawyer. If there was a connection, his stomach would never get back to normal. Zolly rarely looked to the past, but at times like these he thought back to thirty years of effort. The newsstand, then the bar on Howard, now Zolly's Place on Rush. He had made it on his own. No inheritance from David. Hell, they'd even had to borrow for his burial.

"Sometimes they check when a new place opens nearby, but nothing recent," Zolly said.

Goldberg looked like an accountant whose books wouldn't balance. "Okay, if that's all there is, we'll take care of your liquor license and the Board of Health. The rest will work itself out with some interest and penalties. Now get out of here. We have real business to do."

Zolly would have known to leave without being asked. His place was a hangout because he minded his own business. Especially with these three. They came in once a week, as regular as a broad on the pill. As if none of them had his own office, Zolly needed to let them do their business in his bar and at his expense. Even worse, he had a hunch it was just a down payment.

THREE

THE FIRST THING FAITH GODWIN DID AFTER OPENING UP
Zolly's Place that Sunday was to sit down at the front-door table, which
they called "King Arthur's" but was special only because it seated six
and was in view of every passerby. Zolly said a full place winked at the
suckers stalking the streets. If he would show up on time, the place
would always be at least one man fuller. As it was, at this time on a
Sunday and even with half the day crew missing, there were still more
staff than customers. No need for Bigman, yet. The pain started earlier
on Sundays. Everyone else was home in bed, including Zolly, but she
had to show up even though her preference was to have work remain
three dreams away. She pushed back from the table, crossed her legs,
found that failed to improve either the pain or her frame of mind,
recrossed her legs, and rubbed each foot in turn. She would have to
switch to sandals by noon.

On Sunday mornings, the crew was hungover from the night before and most of them didn't show up for work. They took Sunday off
like it was part of their pay. She would as well, if it weren't for Zolly. If

she lived by herself, she would be back in bed in her walk-up on Elm, turning over, eyes still shut and thinking brunch. Of course, a turn in either direction would be to an empty bed and a blank wall. Unless she had gone home with one of the Saturday-night losers. One or two would hit on her when they got drunk enough, even though they knew she belonged to Zolly. Speaking of which, maybe she was a loser, as well. She always wound up with someone who lived for himself.

Pedro motioned to her. No matter how early Faith arrived, Pedro would be waiting. A couple of times, she had suggested that they give Pedro a key, but Zolly always refused with words he pretended were Spanish. It was better than ignoring her altogether, but not much. Pedro had lined up several drinks for a group of regulars who came in Sundays after church. Funny, how prayer made people thirsty. She walked to their table balancing the tray shoulder-high, holding her left hand out as ballast. Considering that there were eight drinks on the tray, maybe she should have taken two trips, but why make the extra effort? Faith could balance with the best of them. Besides, she was tired and walked enough as it was. That damn Zolly had better appreciate her when he finally came to work.

After serving the beer to the choir, Faith walked toward the back. The booth-lined rear of the room looked so much like a dentist's office she could smell the iodine. She avoided offending Zolly with the observation. According to him, it smelled like leather. She wondered whether being tone-deaf affected his sense of smell. As she drew near, she saw Zolly. He must have shown up when she was working a table. He was bowing while backing away from Booth One, which meant he had asked for a favor. Some of the Sunday supplicants now began to approach it as well, as though, being the first pew, it was that much closer to heaven. Faith never drew close enough to determine which of the three wise men in the booth dispensed the benediction, but she suspected it was Goldberg. His buddy O'Rourke was waving both hands like a semaphore. Either they were very thirsty, or they had saved her a seat. She preferred to vote for the booze.

Careful in her choice of fingers, Faith held one up to indicate just a minute and carried her tray back to Pedro to get another order.

"I see Goldberg and crew are here," he said.

"Yeah, this is the day for Catholics and Jews together. They're ecumenical. With all of them, God is green."

"It's a good thing they're not on your bad side." Pedro gave her the drinks, which she brought to some customers at a table along with their menus. Zolly intercepted her as she returned to the bar.

"You said you'd come right after when I left for work this morning," she said.

"Ran some errands, got stopped by a cop. No big deal. We need to talk." He nodded toward the kitchen.

"I have to take care of your friends." She walked from the bar back to the altar.

Goldberg always marked the area with his smell when his visitors sought salvation. Booth One was Lourdes. His petitioners thought they left with a cure, but the spring in their step was due to a lighter wallet. Goldberg knew everyone who mattered, which was why she resented that, after twenty years, he pretended not to know her name.

"Hello, Mr. O'Rourke. Good to see you again," she said.

"Now, Faith. I told you a hundred times. It's just Mike." He reached for her. Unlike Goldberg, O'Rourke did remember her name, but neither of them thought they needed an excuse to pat her ass. She pulled away, trying to look grateful for the touch. "If I get on a first-name basis with the customers, I could get canned," she said.

"Nothing wrong with your can, sweetheart," Goldberg said. The way his tongue worked in and out, she could have been his appetizer.

"Nice to see you again, Mr. Goldberg. You, too, Mr. Civiletti. You want your usual?"

"Nothing usual about you, baby," Goldberg said. He was reaching again.

"Mr. Goldberg, you know I belong to Zolly."

Goldberg clapped his hands together. "What's with this 'belong'?" This time, instead of locking his gaze on her, Goldberg looked around the room. That was on Faith's list of dislikes about the man. Everything was always on the cuff, but he acted as though he was entitled. This time, though, there seemed to be something special about his stare.

"I'll bring your drinks. You'll feel better." Without awaiting a response, she moved away, not turning until she was at a safe distance.

Zolly was on the other side of the bar when she reached it. Even from twenty feet away, she could see that his mouth was a wet crack, which meant he had begun to drink. When and where had that started? Although her memory was clouded about much of her 1965 Zolly—when she'd first met him at his newsstand—she could remember his dry lips and a chin that double-dared you. He still had the walk, rolling along like he was mastering the deck of a mean ship, but these days, there was a little more effort behind the thrust of each leg, and his nose now showed the liquor. Even so, he never stumbled. After she gave Pedro the trio's order, she followed Zolly into the kitchen.

Faith held her breath whenever she went in there. Too much was always going on to try to inhale it all at once. Smells papered the walls like a fast-order nightmare. Waitresses rushed around to make up for being late. The grills crackled with the impatience of well-done meat as the cooks struggled with the orders. Kitchen staff rubber-banded between the coolers and the grills. The busboys were the only ones moving slowly. Faith joined Zolly by the sink. They were shielded from some of the clatter by a barricade of plates that climbed beside them, mortared by grease and crumbs. The weekend dishwasher wasn't due until one. By the time he arrived, he would need acid.

Zolly began without apologies. "I was talking to the boys about our problems."

"I wish you hadn't."

"This isn't a good time for that," Zolly said.

In the bar, schmoozing with the regulars, he was all smiles and all theirs. In back, the act was over. The worst of it was, her friends all thought her lucky. He was the Rush Street ruler and she lived in the king's court. "It's always baseball, football, or whatever else is on the screen. Or you're schmoozing with the customers, or starting in on the drink, whatever."

Zolly's eyes were slits, so all she saw was the booze. "If I didn't want to talk, I wouldn't have asked you back here with me."

"You just want to hear yourself think out loud," she said.

"I need advice, I get bitching."

"I warn you about Goldberg, but you ignore me." She squeezed a washcloth remaining from last night's business. Its creases cut her hands. "You know how I feel. When they're not trying to get in my pants, they're trying to get in your pockets."

"They got the connections," Zolly said.

"Why don't you let the lawyer handle it? You always move sideways."

It would be nice to know that Zolly listened, but she couldn't be sure. She rarely saw inside. He squeezed his eyes and bent his head, pondering questions he never shared. He was Harpo without the curls, and he never owned the smile. He licked his mouth, which had grown as dry as the cloth. "Gershom's got me so busy I don't know if he's my lawyer or I'm working for him. I got charts on what I reported here and what I reported there. He needs copies of everything, but I doubt he reads them. He probably figures on charging by the page. If I'm the one who fills out the paper, so much the better." He wiped at the moisture that had begun to ooze above his brows. "On top of it, after the feds invite Gershom only a week ago for us to come in and talk, on Friday I get a subpoena. We didn't enlist, so now I get drafted." His face grew redder. "Maybe it's about the investigations and violations."

Or maybe, it could have been due to the heat, or he might have been driving with the top down again. "Gershom said it was unlikely a grand jury would get into stuff like that," she said.

"A law degree gives him a license to steal, not some special insights," Zolly said.

"But do you think he's right?"

"I'm hoping the boys can help."

"You told the three wise men about the subpoena?" This was not what he had promised.

"Goldberg wouldn't know anything about federal stuff. Besides, if I bring him in on it before I know what it involves, God knows what he'd charge. I just figured if he and O'Rourke could take care of the state and find someone who used to work for the IRS to get them to be reasonable, it would take a load off my mind."

They stopped talking when a busboy approached to build onto the wall of dishes. Some secrets needed a safer shield than a pile of plates, but at forty dollars a square foot, Zolly would never trade a few tables out in front for an office in back where he could close the door. If he could get away with it, they wouldn't even have a kitchen.

When the boy left, Faith said, "They're coming at us from all directions. I don't know what else you've been up to. At work, we never have time to talk. After work, you never want to."

Zolly put his hand on Faith's cheek. He never touched her unless he had an angle, but he was that way with everyone. He bent over and whispered in her ear, "Sweetheart, don't be paranoid. Things go in cycles. Right now, we're in a downturn."

Faith was about to say sinkhole was more like it when Conrad Bigman interrupted. About time he showed up. He motioned over his left shoulder toward the door to the alley. "I think you should talk to this guy."

"Now I'm the one who gets the deliveries?" Zolly waved him away.

Bigman stood fast. "Not that kind of guy. Please see him before it gets worse."

Zolly maneuvered through the kitchen like a broken-field runner, while Bigman did the blocking. Faith could see the visitor through an opening framed by the pots hanging from the ceiling. Even at a distance, it was clear the caller was shorter than Faith. He had a wispy white beard and was wearing both black hat and suit. Not karate black. He looked much too frail for a villain.

Zolly and Bigman listened to the man. Then Zolly shook his fist and hoisted the man in the air, pushing him out the door. Instead of helping Zolly with the rough stuff, Bigman began to laugh. When Zolly returned, his face was wetter than the heat of the kitchen warranted.

Faith asked, "Aren't you a little out of shape?"

Zolly wiped his sleeve across his face. "Some old guy looking for charity. They tell him no solicitors are allowed and say he should go around back. I've always got to be the one, even when Conrad bothers to work the door instead of taking a leak."

"He looked like an undertaker," she said.

"Nothing like that. He's one of them Lubavitchers. You've seen them before. The rabbis who always wear black."

"I was afraid you were going to hurt him."

Zolly passed his hand again across his forehead, pretending it was absentminded so she wouldn't notice the sweat. "These guys are a real pain in the ass. First thing they say is, 'Are you Jewish?' Today, that's the second time for me. Then they want your money. I've worked hard for every dime I got. At least the cop didn't take the cash."

"But honey, you are Jewish." Faith swallowed her acid reflux. She didn't care what Zolly said. The old man was dressed for a funeral.

FOUR

ZOLLY DROVE DOWNTOWN FOR HIS APPOINTMENT EARLY enough to find a parking spot on Plymouth Court, before the club members hogged them all for an early lunch. He winked at the no-parking signs as he passed them, turned the corner, and entered the building through the Jackson Street entrance. It was a 1920s edifice with more concrete than windows, a manor house that made its visitors feel secure. Speaking of which, Zolly had to work at not looking behind him toward the Metropolitan Correctional Center, a modern-architecture prison that peaked thirty stories high and had both a rooftop exercise court and overhead screening that discouraged helicopters and escaping inmates alike.

Dewey Gershom's office was on seven, a location that gave Zolly hope. The door was mostly a frosted window that showed shadows to the outside hall if there was movement in the office, which suited Gershom's clientele, who were happier when seen in silhouette. As he entered, Zolly considered Gershom's concerns. The feds wouldn't tell him anything. If Zolly would cooperate, they would make it worth his while. With threats, you knew the language. When they stonewalled, it was like wearing gloves while reading Braille.

It was Zolly's fifth visit this month, plus his daily phone calls. Gershom's secretary greeted Zolly with the smile she reserved for clients before their convictions and the open palm they all got. He handed her the envelope. One of the things he had learned from his father, David, was that cash trumps checks and credit cards. Not that Dad had left him anything to spend.

Gershom didn't look up when Zolly entered the inner office. He continued to write on his legal pad while shaking his head at the folly of it all. His sideburns were still long and his hair uncombed, preserving a grayscale version of the look that had made him famous. When he was young, Gershom had run radical rallies and looked the part. These days, his favorite cause was cash, but he still talked the Constitution. He remained hunched over a pile of papers, showing his clients value for their money. "I still don't have a clue. They wouldn't give me a hint before, and they sure won't now. Carney Fallen is a hard nose. We would have been better off with the interview." He finally looked up.

"How could we do that without knowing what they were going to ask?" Zolly said.

"So you could have fainted from the surprise, we could have walked out from the surprise. It would just have been an interview." Gershom kept his head down. He was used to clients kissing ass. "I would have been in there with you, feeling him out, fending him off. You would have been free to go whenever you wanted. Instead, we're going to get a fast hello and then you're going to be alone in the grand jury room with Fallen, farts and all. I'll be cooling my heels in the hall."

Zolly said, "I still wonder if I should have talked to Goldberg about it. He's helped me out of jams in the past."

"Yeah, I'm sure he fixed some parking tickets."

"He handled some heavy cases." The first had been the slip-and-fall the year he bought the bar on Howard. Unfortunately, suburbanites stumbled at the taste of sin. Back then was when he learned to do business with friends and the friends of friends.

"You're nuts to even consider it," Gershom said. "For all you know, Goldberg is what they want to talk about. It's a good thing that you called me first."

"If it's about them, I have nothing to say. I would never hurt a friend." That was due to David. Last lesson, pass or fail. His father had returned home that Friday night announcing no hoods were going to scare him. Zolly's ears still hurt from the noise that followed later, when the blast broke the picture window, and pieces of David dusted the couch where he had napped that afternoon. Afterward, the neighborhood kids had acted as though snitching might be catching. When Zolly's mother said they had to sell the house, he surprised her with a smile.

"If you don't want to rat, that's fine," Gershom said, "but he's just business."

"That's not true," Zolly said. "Did I tell you about when I almost lost my license?"

"I'm sure you did." Gershom fumbled through the file and then abandoned the effort in favor of showing off his memory. "Your bar on Rush with your hookers."

"They just hung out there."

"Yeah, they roosted like pigeons. Right?" Gershom shrugged to show he didn't buy it. The same expression Goldberg's had been back at the bar.

Goldberg had said, "Schmuck, you're charged with running a whorehouse. It's your first beef, so you won't get time, but a conviction will lose your license." Goldberg had waved his cigar as though it were a pointer and Zolly's face Exhibit A. "You think because you have a place you must own it, but you don't. You got to know the rules, the main one being taking care of your friends."

"I used your general contractor to build out my place, and I buy my booze from your guy," Zolly said.

"I'm not talking my friends, I'm talking your friends," Goldberg said. "Friends on the force, the beat cop and the squads, making nice to the lieutenant." The cigar kept waving. "Agree how much a month, pay it when the Man comes by, make sure the broads don't make noise, and things will be okay." Tired of the cigar, Goldberg had dropped it into the saucer and sunk back in the booth. Just as Gershom was now sunk in his chair.

"I don't actually know anything about their business," Zolly said. "When Goldberg talks shop, they wave me away, or I leave on my own."

"But just in case, you might want to change your mind about not testifying before the grand jury," Gershom said.

"I'm no rat," Zolly said, determined not to become another David.

"Okay, if worst comes to worst, I'll ask for Lexington if they sentence you for contempt." Gershom issued glowing reports about the Kentucky federal jail. It was soft, like the prison camps opening all around the country to deal with white-collar crime. The camps only cost half as much as armed guards and barbed wire. The fact that the men who qualified were free from physical risk was an incidental benefit. Lexington also boasted female inmates.

"We still don't know that it's about Goldberg," Zolly said.

Gershom was leaning back, hands in his lap, happy to charge by the hour. "So you think it might be one of the other things on your list. Where did I put it?" He rocked forward and reached back into the file jacket. Again, for show. It wasn't much of a list, and they both knew it by heart.

Gershom said, "We agree the federal government isn't a state sales tax collector. Okay, now for federal, we have the withholding tax. But you didn't evade payment; you just failed to collect it from your workers. That's for an IRS agent to discover, not Carney Fallen. We'd better get going. We can worry about the Health Department on the way. In case the U.S. Attorney's Office now enforces the Chicago City Code."

———————

AT THE DIRKSEN FEDERAL BUILDING, THEY PASSED THROUGH weapons scanners resembling those at every airport, although some of the visitors here were about to take longer trips than anyone at O'Hare. The U.S. Attorney's waiting room was on eight. Gershom said hello to the receptionist while Zolly sat at the far end of a room decorated to reassure visitors, with chairs upholstered the same color as the carpet, which made it hard for a visitor to know how much to bend his knees when he sat. The portraits on the walls were mostly men, mostly old, and all professional. Zolly had once read how public speakers could fight their nerves by picturing their audience nude. He tried to apply that to what was coming next, but all he could see was himself, naked on the stage.

After a long enough wait for Zolly to conjure three different speeches, none receiving applause, the receptionist called his name. Gershom led him down a hallway, passing by a series of unmarked doors until they reached the right office. Carney Fallen didn't resemble the pictures in the reception room. Instead, he looked summa cum laude. The Ivy League diplomas on his wall reinforced the impression. He wouldn't last five minutes on the Street.

Addressing Zolly as though Gershom weren't there, Fallen said, "We know about your problems with the state and federal authorities. We also know your place is a hangout for hookers. Of course, we don't enforce local vice laws, but we are concerned when they aren't enforced due to official corruption."

So it was the inspections, after all. But the reference to corruption gave the impression it was more of a Goldberg problem. Zolly smelled cordite in the air.

Fallen said, "The pandering charges were dropped several years ago, so you've been able to carry on your business ever since. We also know you host Abe Goldberg and his confederates. We'd like to discuss the coincidence." He fondled a piece of crystal that weighed down the papers on his desk, rubbing it as though it would summon the truth genie.

Gershom leaned forward, talking fast before Zolly could respond, expanding his arms to embrace the entire office. "Carney—I hope you don't mind my using your first name—surely you're not concerned about whether any of Mr. Berns's customers are prostitutes. You're not spending federal resources on that."

"Goldberg and his friends spend a lot of time at his bar. They discuss many things that would interest us."

"My client doesn't know anything that would. It would be a waste of your time and an abuse of process if you involved him in your investigation."

"Mr. Gershom," Fallen said, emphasizing the *mister* and leaning over a desk that didn't hold a single picture. "We are not involving your client. He involved himself. The question is whether he's going to make it easy or difficult for me. Of course, there is also the question of whether we are going to make it easy or hard for him."

"How easy? How hard?" Gershom asked.

"With your cooperation, we could put in a word with the IRS. We might even be able to go easier on the conspiracy charge."

Gershom dropped the charm and snapped his words like a terrier at a postman's legs. "This is bullshit. This man may owe some taxes, but there's no crime involved. He's certainly not involved in any conspiracy."

Fallen wrinkled his forehead. "The same three men hold court in his bar every week. They have a parade of visitors carving up the gambling and the vice in the ward. Maybe doing dope, as well. Berns gives them office space. They keep him from harm. No crime involved? That's for the grand jury to decide." He rose from his desk and walked to a window that stretched from knee-high to the ceiling and faced up Dearborn. Zolly wondered how much force it would take for Fallen's crystal rock to pierce the glass.

Fallen said, "We would like to go over some details with Mr. Berns before he goes in front of the grand jury. You can explain to him the advantages of cooperation."

Gershom began working on his hair. In the old days, the hippies probably hadn't minded it, but he ought to wash it now. "You're tossing pieces in the air, hoping they'll land together."

"Tell us what he's heard them talking about. Maybe your client sits in on their chats. Or, he could start." Fallen turned from the window and paused, as though what was coming was just an afterthought. "Maybe wear a wire, so we get the conversations right. Would you like to adjourn so you can discuss that in private?"

Zolly wondered at feeling no surprise that Faith and Gershom had been right all along. Maybe there was such a thing as intuition, after all. Gershom looked at Zolly for an answer, as though they hadn't discussed this in his office on every visit. A lot of his clients probably talked the talk better than they walked the walk, but Zolly had David to remember. He pursed his lips and shook his head. He was determined not to become dandruff on Goldberg's shoulders.

FIVE

"So you're a fighter, after all." Gershom jabbed Zolly's shoulder. They were headed for the elevators, close behind Fallen, so they needed to whisper. Wood moulding ran waist-high down the walls. Zolly had expected sculptures and more portraits in the carpeted hallway, but all he saw were ceiling-high doors.

"I told you I wouldn't rat," Zolly said. He was tired of repeating himself while thinking of David. When they reached the grand jury room, he tugged at Gershom's sleeve. "If I tell them I don't know anything, it won't take long, will it?"

"Tell them you don't know anything, you'll be in there forever. All you can say is your name and address if you want to take the fifth. Remember, I have to wait outside, so they get you all to themselves. Questioning you with as many lawyers as they like. The game begins with the score ten to nothing. You're the nothing."

"Don't I have a constitutional right to a lawyer?" Zolly kept hoping for a different answer.

"I told you, they let you leave the room as often as you want, so you can talk to me about any question they ask. They love it when you do that. Piss off the grand jurors some more, why don't you?"

The grand jury room wasn't designed like a courtroom. There was no raised bench for a judge, no rear section for any spectators. The architects had designed it like a carpeted arena, not expecting anyone to spit. Several of the grand jurors leaned forward when Zolly identified himself. Fallen began by asking him about his bar on Rush Street.

Zolly looked at the script Gershom had given him. "On the advice of counsel, I exercise my rights under the Fifth Amendment to the Constitution of the United States and respectfully refuse to answer, on the grounds that my answer may tend to incriminate me." One of the grand jurors leaned farther forward and glared. The others sank back, already ready to indict.

Fallen had his own script. He asked Zolly about his background, about Goldberg, Civiletti, and O'Rourke. Zolly again recited from the script, differently each time, as though the right inflection would let him go home. But this was no slip and fall case, and Fallen's suit was custom-made with its pockets still stitched. Fallen said Zolly could skip repeating the part about his rights. Ten minutes later, as Zolly was attempting to recount the session to Gershom in the hallway, Fallen approached. "Let's go upstairs before the judge."

They spent less than five minutes in front of Judge Lamont Dillon of the United States District Court for the Northern District of Illinois before they headed back to the grand jury. Gershom warned Zolly again. "Dillon gave you use immunity. That means they won't be able to use any information from your answers to prosecute you. The bad news is, if you still refuse to testify, the judge can jail you until you talk. It's not punishment. It's encouragement."

The next session took less time than the first before they were on their way back to Dillon. Gershom reminded Zolly about the judge's reputation. "When the president appointed him, the court was mostly filled with Republican judges. We were glad to get a liberal."

"Then maybe he won't be too hard on me," Zolly said.

"Dillon runs his court like a training camp," Gershom said. "I'll be lucky if I get a chance to explain. Although there really isn't much to say. He won't have sympathy for a speech about snitches and rats."

Dillon interrupted Fallen's complaints about Zolly's refusal to testify. "I'd like to hear what Mr. Gershom has to say about his client's conduct. It sounds like contempt of court to me."

Gershom pushed his fingers through the bush on his head as though searching for a crib note. "Your Honor, the Government may be technically correct, but I ask the Court to consider a Constitutional question."

Dillon had a hawk face and a nose to match, with hair snowed on his head and ears that wobbled as he listened to Gershom's speech. The only color was in his lips, which he bit as he counted to three. "I thought we had taken care of the Bill of Rights with the grant of immunity," Dillon said.

"Immunity is not enough, Judge. A witness faces sanctions from several quarters. In addition to federal prosecution, there is a risk of state indictment or civil action based on what he says. The fact that the Government will not use Mr. Berns's testimony against him in a federal criminal proceeding does not address all the Constitutional issues."

Dillon's eyes began to glaze over, now resembling any of the pictures on the wall in Fallen's waiting room. He sighed. "It is well established that we respect Mr. Berns's Fifth Amendment privilege with the grant of immunity. You are correct; use immunity only applies to federal prosecution. However, the grand jury sessions are secret, so your concern as to jeopardy in other forums is misplaced. What other rights are you asserting?"

Gershom pulled his hand out of his hair and examined his palm for inspiration. "Your Honor, Mr. Berns risks leaks from the grand jurors about his testimony. In addition to our concerns as to state prosecution, his business might be affected. Therefore, we have the issue of the potential deprivation of his right to property without due process of law. More fundamentally, this threatens his rights to liberty and the pursuit of happiness."

Fallen stood still in the silence of a sure winner.

Dillon said, "Counsel, don't waste my time. Unless you have precedents to cite, let's dispense with the rhetoric and get on with it."

"Your Honor, the cases may support the Government's position, but there are times to make new law," Gershom said. "This Court is known for its independence. I was appealing to your sense of justice."

Dillon gave that one a smile. "Thank you, Mr. Gershom, but I am here to follow established law, not to make new law. Anything else?"

Gershom was not yet out of breath. "Judge, the Government is just fishing. They want to ask Mr. Berns a lot of questions without knowing where his answers might lead. That is an unconscionable intrusion into his privacy. They need more than mere speculation to dig into his life."

Fallen was ready for that one. "Your Honor, if we don't know where our questions may lead, it is because Mr. Berns refused to confer in my offices earlier today. I gave him the opportunity to avoid any unnecessary intrusion into his personal life by going over things in advance. That was a courtesy." Fallen nodded, more to Gershom than to Zolly. "Under the circumstances, I think the objection that we are fishing is unfair as well as irrelevant. So long as our questions are germane to the matters before this grand jury, we are entitled to ask them."

They were talking about Zolly as though he were merely another case about to appear on Gershom's bookshelf, sandwiched between drug deals and sex offenders. He was a businessman. He paid taxes, at least some of them, just like everyone else. He'd worked hard to get where he was and didn't belong here instead of at his bar, calculating the crowd and the take. As a kid, he had resented it whenever David and Becky talked as though he were absent, but it wouldn't bother him now if everyone failed to notice as he slipped away. Then he felt Gershom's nudge. The judge was talking directly to him.

"Mr. Berns, I want to be certain that you understand the consequences if you persist in your refusal to testify. I can hold you in contempt and remand you to the custody of the United States Marshals until you are prepared to comply with my order."

"I understand, your Honor. But I won't talk about my customers."

Dillon's grimace resembled David every time Zolly had ever let him down. "Then I have no alternative."

It was time for Gershom to speak again. He had promised a pitch for easier time. "Your Honor, I believe it is within the Court's discretion to recommend an appropriate facility. We are asking you to direct that Mr. Berns be incarcerated at the Federal Correctional Institution in Lexington, Kentucky."

Fallen objected. "This is very irregular, Judge. We have room for Mr. Berns here in Chicago, at the Metropolitan Correctional Center. We are dealing with civil contempt. He can purge himself at any time by agreeing to testify. It makes sense to be able to bring him back before the grand jury on a day's notice."

"What do you say to that, Mr. Gershom?" Dillon asked.

"Your Honor, what is usual and what is right are not always the same thing. Mr. Berns intends to maintain his position indefinitely, so convenience does not matter."

"Even so, why should I remand Mr. Berns to FCI Lexington?"

"Because Mr. Berns is an alcoholic." Gershom paused to swallow. "If he is going to be incarcerated for a substantial period, as now appears to be the case, he needs continuing treatment. They have facilities for that there."

Fallen objected. "Your Honor, this is a sham. The man owns and operates a bar patronized by hustlers and scum. If he can handle that, I don't know what kind of treatment he needs."

Dillon considered his notes before responding. "Frankly, Mr. Fallen, I'm unclear why you object so strenuously. I see no difference between housing Mr. Berns at the MCC or at the Federal Correctional Institution in Lexington. Both facilities serve the same purpose. The Bureau of Prisons is not required to follow my recommendation, but I suspect they will." He turned to Zolly, anxious to get his agreement on the record. "Mr. Berns, should you change your mind and be willing to testify, do you understand that being hundreds of miles away will prolong your incarceration until arrangements can be made to bring you back to Chicago?"

Zolly turned to tell it to the court reporter. "Yes, your Honor, I do."

Then Fallen took his last shot. "Your Honor, in any event, I request that you direct the marshal to take Mr. Berns into custody at once. They can transport him to Lexington."

Gershom looked to see whether Zolly understood this part of the play. "I assumed that the Court would allow my client to self-report. After all, he is not a flight risk."

Fallen said, "Your Honor, we are not talking about a conviction. The man refuses to obey your order to testify. He is in contempt. Taking him into custody is automatic."

"I think that Mr. Fallen is right." Now Dillon looked like David when the punishment seemed too severe and Becky was looking on. "The marshal can transport Mr. Berns. It will save him the airfare."

As the judge gaveled the session closed and left the bench, Fallen looked triumphant. Faith was at the rear of the courtroom. Twenty years and she still didn't know when to stay away. Now she was moving toward him—maybe she had in mind some scene from one of those movies she got off on, wanting a last hug or kiss. As though she didn't know him better. Before they led Zolly away, Gershom answered the question in his eyes. "They're turning a couple-hour plane ride into a two-week trip. They'll bounce you from jail to jail, take you in hand-cuffs and shackles on every broken-down bus they have. They want to fuck with your head."

SIX

IT WAS THE EIGHTH DAY IN A ROW THAT BOWIE TRUMAN HAD stubbed his toe. It was all a ritual. Get out of bed barefoot, grope his way downstairs without turning on the lights, feel his way from the foyer to the kitchen and hurt himself on the way. It might not be a record, but he figured it was close. This was what happened when you pulled weekend duty. Here it was, only Monday, five more days before relief, and he was already limping again. Truman was a commando on a beachhead. He began to rant. He swore at the threshold of the hall that led to the kitchen, unlevel ever since they'd built the house. He cursed at himself for failing to sand the ridge anytime over the past fifteen years. When he felt his foot throbbing and bent down to touch the pain, he damned the splinter that now stuck out of his big toe, a medal for stupidity. He enlarged his epithets to accommodate his entire house, as well as the sun that had yet to illuminate the interior. Then he stopped to map his route. The kitchen was twenty feet and only two turns away. A couple of different approaches might bring him there intact. A combination that had him sidle, feel, push, and probe a passage through the minefield brought him to the kitchen without fresh wounds, pleased with his performance, before realizing that his book wouldn't be waiting for him open on the table. He had finished it last night and replaced it in the bookcase. That was what happened when you read a novel. History stuck with you, but fiction faded like a dream.

Deciding to demonstrate that one could learn from experience, after all, Truman flipped on the lights. Now he could see that his toe had left droplets of blood on the parquet all the way to the kitchen. For the first time that morning, he had something to be grateful for. Explaining new stains on the living-room carpet to Pru was a prospect that ranked near the bottom, outdone only by drawing weekend duty at the jail. Truman debated which to repair first, his toe or the stains on the floor. He decided toe first, floor next, and slippers tomorrow.

Truman bent over but gave up trying to reach his toe from a standing position. Holding his bad foot, he hopped to his favorite chair and sank into the cushion, careful not to stain the horse-patterned slipcover. Seated, he was able to cross his leg, reach his toe, and stanch the blood with a tissue from his pajama pocket. The gauze stuck to the wound like a stamp. He remained in the chair for several minutes, thinking about his wife instead of the next book. Their parents' pictures hung like "wanted" posters on the wall opposite the chair, between the bookcases. When their son, Jimmy, was younger, he would climb onto Truman's lap, look at the pictures, and want the same stories repeated. Each time Truman retold them, he had to be careful about the endings. Jimmy counted on the good guys winning, just as in the fairy tales. Pru wanted fables, as well. The stories provided structure to their lives. Accordingly, Truman made up stories about their folks and what it had been like when they were young, memorized them, and thereafter held to a single version, although Jimmy did permit some embellishment if it did not contradict the core. At times, when Pru was in another room, Truman sprinkled his stories with seeds of truth that he intended to enlarge as Jimmy grew.

"Your mom and I met in high school up in the hills. Most of the people in town worked in the mines those days. It was a lot of fun." Truman would skip the part about the men leaving early in the mornings, sitting upright as they drove to work, the shadows hiding the scars on the slopes. There was no point in telling Jimmy how they came home stooped, their bodies cramped from the slits in the hills, their skin grimed with coal. His father coughed blackness the doctors called the lung disease. Truman knew that they were wrong. The phlegm betrayed the sickness of his father's soul. No matter what Pru wanted, he would teach Jimmy that lesson later.

Truman thought about the end of his latest novel. He decided to read a psychology book next, to help understand the characters' motivations. Keeping his weight on his healthy foot, careful not to awaken his family, he walked to the bookcase and selected a text he had brought home from work the week before. In the half hour before Pru and Jimmy were due to rise, he would finish a chapter and a cup of coffee and be on his way to work. Truman had never traveled more than a hundred miles from home, yet his books let him live foreign lives like the inmates he met at work, characters choked with daily drama. At times, he searched his dictionary for an unfamiliar word that proved to be a fancy way of saying what he already knew. When Truman would talk to Stein, the shrink at work, he usually left feeling he had taught more than he had learned. Other times, Truman would talk about it to Pru. They had reenacted their usual argument just last night.

"Bowie, no matter how much you like them, they're not the same as us," Pru said.

"Who said like?"

"You know you do," she said. "They're all you talk about when you come home."

Truman paused, considering the possibility. "I don't think so. I discussed it with Stein. For once, he got it right. Interested, yes. But not like."

Pru had made the same expression her mother wore in the picture on the living-room wall. "You walk around like none of it's real. I'm afraid you'll get too close."

"None of them is violent."

"They hurt people in other ways," she had said.

"I'm teaching them not to," Truman had said. "I show them how to live."

There was movement upstairs. Pru was rousting Jimmy from bed. In half an hour, the next shift would take over. He sidled over to the kitchen and put his cup and saucer in the sink. It was time to go to work.

Truman lived twenty minutes away from the jail. The daily drive got him in the mood. It was early, well before the Lexington rush. He would let his mind wander as the grounds glided by in a slide-show of hayfields and horses. The farmhouses, barns, silos, and sheds were painted with Kentucky watercolors that were shaded differently throughout the day. In the spring, the colts licked early-morning dew that pigmented the bluegrass and danced about as though the furrows had been formed just for them. When the road curved, Truman was upon the VA Hospital. The bureaucratic brown was out of place amidst the green that stretched as far as he could see. Truman slowed as the road curved again a couple of miles beyond the hospital and his destination burned its way into view. There were hundreds of acres of buildings, fields, and chain-link fence, but it was too quiet for a city.

He drove by the dormitory at the near end of the compound. Its color mimicked the hospital, but there were bars on the windows that faced the road. A field separated the building from the rest of the compound. At his speed and distance, the grounds ahead seemed bare, but Truman knew better. Approaching closer, he could see the chalk-striped green of the baseball fields and, beyond the farthest backstop, the tennis courts and the two-story ladder that held a referee's chair perched like a lookout post. A running track encircled the perimeter of the Yard. The structure beyond was the kind that sprawls wherever land is cheap. Also brown, it was connected to smaller buildings on either side and set off from the road by a circular driveway and careful landscaping. Bushes ran its length like bristles on a brush, interrupted only by the large glass door that led inside. Truman parked his car in the lot, crossed the road and driveway, and pressed the buzzer by the side of the door. The guard in the control room pressed the button that allowed him entry. It was always easier getting in than getting out.

———

APPROACHING FCI LEXINGTON, ZOLLY LOOKED FOR GUARD towers and razor wire, but all he saw were flat roofs and a cyclone fence. Even from the outside, it looked friendlier than the federal penitentiary at Terre Haute, Indiana. The nights there had demanded too much thinking. He had been placed in one of the cells in the block that housed solitary confinement, encased in wire to deprive the desperate a chance at glass. The bulb on the wall had blazed away, depriving him of night. When the hack took pity, he plunged Zolly into a darkness that burned with memories of David. It had been years since his father had died in the explosion, but Zolly was certain he would see David's frown if he spun around fast enough.

The guard who now buzzed them into Lexington looked unarmed. And this place permitted daylight. "We'll take off your leg irons, so you won't have to slide down ass-first." They were at the head of the stairs. The taller marshal was smiling, showing tobacco teeth and ash eyes. He was the one who had talked about Jews during the drive all the way from Terre Haute.

The friendly marshal unlocked Zolly's handcuffs and delivered him and his paperwork to the downstairs guard. He had allowed Zolly to sprawl the last part of the ride. Sitting upright for hours in handcuffs and leg irons got to your back before your head. Driving past miles of freedom was bad enough, but having to do it while five pounds of iron pulled you down was cruel and unusual punishment. Zolly remembered that last phrase from Gershom but had decided not to test it on Tobacco Teeth. Zolly had said, "Thank you," ignoring the smoke that still clothed the man. Zolly had nothing against cigarettes. Back at his bar, the booze had cleared his eyes. He could use a cold one and an English Oval now, but that was two weeks behind him.

They took Zolly to a room at the end of the basement of the reception building. A footstool and camera stood by the entrance to record the arrivals. Three folding tables near the door were arranged side by side like a banquet table but were too rickety to hold much food. A schoolhouse clock that told the minutes with its hands and bonged out the hours hung on a wall. Several shelves stacked with clothing in cardboard boxes stretched beneath the clock. At a right angle to the banquet table, a single table with card chairs on either side sat ready for newcomers. At the far end of the room, several more card chairs and folding tables faced forward, toward the door. The room was ready to spring into action at a moment's notice.

Zolly's host had the kind of forehead that grows bigger from grade school on. His hairline showed he was about halfway to retirement. The sieve of his mustache muffled his voice. "You call those clothes?"

Zolly gestured at his jumpsuit. "They took away my own."

"Can't wear those to church." The guard sucked in hair at his joke.

"I wasn't planning on praying."

"Might do you some good. Course, you got to dress for it. Some inmates even wear suits and ties to church."

This was the part that Zolly hadn't heard about. There might be just as many assholes and comedians on the Street, but they stayed away from his bar. "I wear a tie to weddings and funerals. You got any planned?"

"You never know," the guard said. "Just in case, you'll want to get some sent from home. Your team will tell you what you can have. Meanwhile, we'll set you up with underwear and fatigues." The guard looked at the slip-ons Zolly was wearing and made an expression usually reserved for gristle. "Real shoes, too." As he spoke, he withdrew clothing, soap, and a throwaway razor from one of the shelves behind him. He deposited them on the table an item at a time, as though Zolly's allotment were priced by the ounce.

"Now, hop up there," the guard said, pointing to the stool.

"How about one of the chairs? I'm not one for hopping."

"Hop, climb, however. I take your picture. Hold this below your head and try to smile." His tone and accent resembled how Southerners usually sounded to Zolly, parceling out words as though they were sweets.

He handed Zolly a slate with eight numbers written in chalk on its surface. They were the numbers Zolly had been awarded two weeks earlier, after Dillon held him in contempt. The last three digits, 024, stood for Chicago. The first five figures took the place of his name. Finally, clapping his hands like an artist pleased with his latest composition, the guard directed Zolly to the far end of the room for paperwork that seemed identical to the forms at the MCC. Maybe, after two weeks, his responses should be different. Perhaps the hacks were looking for progress.

Zolly closed his eyes, too tired to think ahead. Less than an hour later, another official limped into the room holding the toes of his right foot up in the air. He was dressed like the guard: blue shirt, black tie, and the kind of pleated, government-gray slacks that never needed an iron. A nameplate clipped to his shirt pocket read COUNSELOR, as though that explained it all. He sat at the separate table by the side of the reception guard's station, put his foot up on the extra chair next to him, and began reading the files. After remaining silent long enough for Zolly's mind to wander, the counselor looked up, called Zolly forward, and waved him to sit. "I'm Bowie Truman. I'll check you in."

"I thought the guard just checked me in."

"He did the checking in part of checking in. I'm doing the checking out part of checking in. We call it an evaluation." Truman leafed through the papers before looking up again. "I see you haven't been convicted of anything. At least, not as of yet."

"I wouldn't answer questions for a grand jury."

"Good reason to keep you up in Chicago."

It must have been like this at Ellis Island, when Grandpa Sam arrived. "My lawyer explained I'm an alcoholic. The judge sent me here for treatment."

Truman appraised Zolly further. "Your eyes look clear. You talk okay, considering you have a Chicago accent. You don't have a wino's color. No shakes, either. Look me in the eyes, state your name, and tell me you're an alcoholic." But Truman looked down at his files without the demonstration. After further review, he leaned over the table and pronounced his decision. "I could have you repeat it, but I still wouldn't believe it. Let's forget the paperwork. Tell me straight."

Zolly decided to take the chance. "I don't mind a drink on occasion. And I do own a bar, so I'm around liquor all the time."

"Congratulations. They never want to admit it, but I think your denial is for real." Truman studied the papers some more, as though a new reading might provide a different answer. Then he shrugged the file closed. "I don't have to agree, I just have to accept the diagnosis."

Zolly smiled. "Then, I get to stay?"

"That was never an issue. The only question was, where? We have several buildings here, male and female. However, we have one building where we put the alcoholics. Atwood Hall, where I work."

"There are women here?"

Truman tapped the folder. "Don't be cute. You can smell it when you walk in the door."

———————

TRUMAN TURNED ZOLLY OVER TO BUTTERFLY SWEETS, A BLACK inmate from Atwood, who led the way out. After walking back up the stairs Zolly had used on arrival, Butterfly took Zolly to the glass door on the side of the lobby opposite the entrance to the building. Zolly's new sneakers already pinched his toes.

"We have to wait until he lets us out," Butterfly said. He nodded toward the guard in the glass-walled room. "That's control. They monitor everything."

Zolly turned his attention from the control room booth and the slate lobby floor to the scene outside. He remembered a story from his years at Sunday school. Moses on Sinai, looking down at the Promised Land. He put his fingers on the door handle. The rear of the reception building had more windows than the front. Considering what they overlooked, the architect's choice made sense. It could have been a country estate, if not for the fortress walls that ringed the flowers and close-cropped grass. Bushes buffered the park from the buildings. Hedges formed runways for the descending butterflies. The sidewalks crisscrossed into a checkerboard of concrete, pebbles, and grass. He expected to see an Englishman bounding about, setting up a game of croquet, as in a movie he'd seen after losing some forgotten argument with Faith.

After the guard buzzed them through, Butterfly led the expedition through the garden with a blanket roll and pillow on his shoulder. Zolly followed, treasuring the paper bag full of clothes and toilet articles in his arms. He usually breathed through his mouth, but now he inhaled through his nose to test Truman's premise. They passed a woman tending a flower bed. Zolly said, "I'm surprised they have women living here."

Butterfly broke stride. "You can do it with Truman, but don't put me on. We've got about nine hundred of each sex. Four units for women, seven for men. The women's buildings are bigger. They stretch from the main one, Women's Unit, to the other end of the courtyard. The men's units are across the way, except for Atwood. That's all by itself, across the Yard." Butterfly gestured throughout the tour as though Zolly had paid for admission.

"It must be hard to keep things separate."

"Women are always complicated," Butterfly said.

"Different places to live, work. Extra dining rooms. Why not separate joints? I think I'm getting a corn." Zolly stooped and loosened his laces.

"You'll turn it into a callus going across the Yard a few times a day. Take off some weight, too. Meet some women. Hell, we do everything together except where we sleep. We would have been able to walk up, talk to her while she was working. Women all around. Stay long enough, you'll get to work with them all." Butterfly looked back at the gardener, who was hunched over behind them. "Sometimes, even more."

They passed through an archway that joined two buildings clad in the kind of buff-colored brick they used in Chicago bungalows. Zolly could have been on a sidewalk back home, but there it was smoke, garbage, car fumes, and other city smells, instead of the flowers that lined the walk. When they entered a smaller courtyard between the two buildings, Butterfly said, "That's Women's Unit on the left. This is the end of the Main Building, on the right. When we get past them, we'll be in the Yard. Your feet will tingle in no time."

A guard stepped out of the shadows as they approached the far archway. "That's Messer. Thinks he's the Gestapo, but he's just a hack. Try to keep your cool."

Messer motioned for them to stop. "Let me see your passes."

Butterfly held out a slip of paper. "Here's mine. He's new. I'm escorting him to Atwood. I'm the unit clerk."

"I don't care if you're the unit cook," Messer said. "Everyone needs a pass unless it's free time. He should have his own." Messer's cheeks were free of wrinkles, the mark of a man who never smiled. He stared longer at Zolly than at Butterfly, making up for the lack of a picture. The hack was about Zolly's height but as thin as some suburban kid trying to slip into the bar on his first drive to town on his own. Messer jammed his finger into Zolly's chest with a dare-you look. "I'll let it go this time. But next time, be sure you carry one. Otherwise, you'll get a shot for sure."

"Is he talking about a doctor's visit?" Zolly asked as they proceeded.

Butterfly studied him a moment. "He doesn't mean disease. Though, of course, a shot could make you sick. It's when they write you up for breaking some rule."

They passed through the archway and came to an empty running track that skirted an athletic field. The cinders were worn to powder, but the track was wet, so they raised no dust as they walked a path worn deep enough to hold them in, even without the chain-link fence. Across the deserted field, there were tennis courts and sand pits sprouting benches, barbells, weights, and presses. It was summer camp all over again, but this visit might stretch into snow. "A shot is like an indictment, except the same ones who prosecute also get to judge," Butterfly said.

"Then why do they bother?"

"Oh, it's no bother. The guards take turns. Enjoy it either way. You want to stay away from shots. Messer, too."

"We're already in jail."

"Yeah," Butterfly said, "but there's jail and there's jail."

They were through the last archway. Butterfly said, "This is the Yard. It's only open for free time, when we get to play. But remember, no matter how they paint it, you're the one in jail."

Zolly was ready to rest by the time they passed through a gate at the far end of the Yard and went up the walk. Atwood Hall was a three-story block of a building at the top of a small rise, about fifty feet past the inner fence that ended the Yard. Another fence beyond Atwood separated it from the outside world. They walked up the concrete steps to an entranceway on the second floor. Then Butterfly pulled the door open and showed Zolly home.

SEVEN

CARLINO MAGGIANO WAS AT IT AGAIN, SITTING ON HIS BED IN the two-inmate room. If he got off schedule, he would disappoint his grandkids. Meeting obligations was important to Maggiano. That was how he kept his world in order. He was wearing his favorite team T-shirt, green shorts, and sandals. After too many washes and whatever Charlie Chicken did that passed for ironing, the wrinkles were as much a part of the shirt as the seams and buttonholes. The color, once bright green, was now shaded fade. Even so, the shirt still made him proud. The front said, "Fighting Irish." To dispel any doubt, "Notre Dame" was on the back. Maggiano also knew the words "South Bend," but as far as he was concerned, his favorite team was New York and their home was on TV.

He looked up from the bowl he'd formed where he sat on the edge of his bed. One of the benefits of a room to himself was the privacy it gave a guy to write his letters home, but afternoons he also found himself watching Joey Philly Friedman blink.

"Tuna, more letters?" Joey Philly was in the doorway, faking surprise.

Maggiano paused, then waved him in. Joey Philly was part of the punishment. "You know to call me Carl." Maggiano extracted his toothpick from the pocket in his shorts and inserted it in his mouth to search for any remainder of lunch. This toothpick had lasted a week and had too many flavors. Maggiano rolled it on his tongue. "Carlino, if you prefer."

Joey Philly sat on the spare bed that occupied the opposite corner of the room as a reminder that Maggiano's privacy could be invaded if he got on the wrong side of Truman. The hacks who served at Atwood knew enough to reserve the best beds for Truman to assign. Truman was Maggiano's friend. At least, as much a friend as you could be with a hack. That made the bed less a threat of future roommates and more a visitors' invitation.

Joey Philly said, "I'm your pal. You may be Carlino or Carl to the rest of the guys, but you'll always be Tuna to me." He referred to Maggiano's most recent conviction. Joey Philly should have been a TV writer instead of selling hot sets out the back of a truck. That was no job for a Jew.

"He owed me fifty big ones. Said he couldn't even pay the juice. I would have packed those cans with pieces of him if he didn't." Maggiano sniffed, remembering the smell of assembly-line fish.

"Yeah. Too bad someone opened some cans."

Maggiano nodded agreement and resumed his latest letter for his youngest grandson, full of illustrations. Every time he moved to a new line, the board on his lap shifted, forcing him to snatch the colored markers before they rolled onto the floor. Between grabs, he shielded his drawings from view. "What happened to work?"

"You're not the only one who gets a sick day," Joey Philly said. "They gave me a bed-rest slip. Just a couple of days. Not like you. Of course, you're working on your disability claim."

Maggiano stretched. "Backs take a long time to heal."

"Yeah, especially when you hurt them lifting books. You ever try it one at a time? Or, while you were at it, opening one up?"

"I worked in the library; I didn't play there." Maggiano preferred writing to reading, any day. He put his pen down onto the stack of lined paper. Three letters finished, five to go. He stuffed the drawings and the letter into an envelope, addressed it to his grandson, and tasted the flap closed. Then he flitted his tongue through barely open lips. "They should flavor these. Say, spearmint." He looked about his room, grinning as the idea took hold. "Lots of guys like scotch. What do you think of gin?"

Joey Philly had the expression dealers wear while waiting for the players to throw in their ante. "At least you won't get a lot of time."

"This is legit. Flavored envelopes for every taste. I can see the ads now."

"Probably eat them, too. At least they got no calories." Joey Philly stared at Maggiano's gut and blinked extra to make his point.

"Why don't you take your humor to the main TV room? I hear the viewers are getting bored."

Instead of leaving for the TV lounge, Joey Philly lay back on the bed, as though settling in for the night. "I'm suggesting they'll be watching. Isn't that how they caught you laundering the tuna money? Watching you wash?" He was more pleased with his humor than ever.

Before starting his next letter, Maggiano looked at the bulletin board hanging over his bed. Pictures of his grandchildren covered the board with every stage of their growth. Maggiano stretched his fingers apart and back again. Eight of them, so he had to keep his fingers in shape. One more grandkid and he would need to work on his thumbs.

He squeezed his shoulder blades together. Working out his back would have been even better, but that would involve lying on the floor. No way he would do that with Joey Philly present. Besides, the floor was always dirty the day before inspection and Charlie Chicken's visit to sweep and mop.

"Why not the whole body? Look out the window after Count clears. You'll see people in the Yard doing something called *exercise*." Joey Philly caressed the last word, pausing between each syllable. It sounded like *exorcise*, which wasn't a bad idea.

Maggiano said, "Friedman, you'd better get back to your room for Count."

"We got half an hour. You could fit in some stomach crunches."

Joey Philly was always on Maggiano about his weight, his smoking, the pictures on his board, and the letters he wrote home. The routine was as familiar as last month's Playboy the third time around and getting just as boring. Maggiano was ready to rip out some staples.

Joey Philly might be a comedian, but he couldn't read minds. "You better get another board for under your mattress."

"Joey, let me tell you for the tenth time this month—but who's counting—you're completely full of shit. Lots of guys leave in bad shape. There's no one to hassle them about what they eat or if they smoke, except for you."

Joey Philly introduced his chin to his chest. "You got me wrong, Tuna. I don't want you to get sick again. You could do the diet line. You can get healthy here, if you put your mind to it."

Maggiano put the writing board down and heaved himself upright to change the topic. He walked to the window and viewed the Yard. The cinders on the running track had been grooved into powder. With so many guys running, they had to water it down every morning or it would blow away. The tennis courts were empty, but an echo of grunts, curses, and bouncing balls remained. The weight pits reminded Maggiano to rub his groin. That proved his point. You did your time your own way. He turned to face Joey Philly. "You can keep your fucking diet line."

Sitting upright now, Joey Philly moved his hands shoulder-high and palms up. "I'm on the kosher."

"Yeah, and you're pissed that I'm there, too."

Joey Philly said, "You and a dozen other *paisans*. I give you credit for pulling it off."

Maggiano belched and crossed himself. "God bless you Jews. You sure serve good pasta."

When he heard the knock, Maggiano looked up to see a black face in the door window. Great, another visitor. Soon, there would be more guys in here than out in the main TV. Maybe he should do his writing there. "Who the hell is it?"

The unit clerk, Butterfly Sweets, entered with some guy Maggiano had never seen before. Butterfly usually flew around with too much to do, but now he was taking his time. He deposited Zolly's bedroll next to Joey Philly and looked everywhere except at Maggiano when he spoke. "This is Zolly Berns. Not my idea."

Maggiano said, "New guys go to a dorm. I had to wait a year before they let me move, and then it was to a four-man." He looked around his room. The two beds were catty-corner from each other, as far apart as the room allowed. Even so, they were joined at the toes. The blankets that served as spreads defined the difference. One was white, the other green, matching Maggiano's shirt. What the room lost in width it gained in length. Each bed boasted its own set of lockers and a folding chair that sucked in guests like Joey Philly. The far end of the room held a window that was shaped by curtains woven by Charlie Chicken and was free of bars because it faced inside the grounds. The single bulletin board over Maggiano's bed proved the room was his.

Butterfly was backing out of the room, still not facing Maggiano. "I tried to tell the hack, but we're full-up and it's almost time for Count. He flipped through the bed book and saw your two-man with only one man in it. I told him Truman was letting you stay by yourself, and the hack said fine, Truman can shuffle everyone around when he gets back after Count."

Butterfly left without waiting for Maggiano's response. Unit clerks were like that. Black or white, they bounced around because they had no balls.

Joey Philly smirked and extended his hand like he was the host. "I hope I didn't mess up your bed, buddy." Maggiano's back started hurting again.

"They call me Zolly. Sorry if I'm screwing things up." Berns was apologizing to the wrong man and in the wrong tone of voice. Where was he from? His neck didn't look red, yet he still had no street smarts.

Joey Philly said, "I'd better get back to my room for Count."

Then Joey Philly was gone and the new guy, Berns, just stood there, holding his paper bag. Maggiano decided he would have to put up with it until he could get to Truman. Skip dinner, if he had to. "If you're thinking of unpacking, the lockers by that bed are yours. Your towels and shoes stay outside. Or you could leave them in the bag, make it easier in case you move."

"It's a lot of room for what they gave me." Berns was taking inventory of the shirts and pants on Charlie Chicken's hangers in Maggiano's locker.

"That's because they don't give you much," Maggiano said. He passed his hand over his chest one letter at a time, fingering the Fighting Irish. "When they opened this joint back I don't know when, they started with civilian clothing and never bought enough uniforms to pass around. There's supposed to be enough, but khakis would put them over budget. Your hanging stuff will fill the tall locker, and your underwear and socks in the small one. Keep things in order, pass inspection."

"Looks okay," Berns said.

Maggiano looked at the floor. "I got Charlie Chicken. When he's not making the rounds at night selling stolen food, he does chores. We'll split the cost as long as it lasts."

"It took me two weeks to get here. I couldn't get near a phone to call home and get some clothes sent in."

"Most guys get to self-report." Maggiano wondered what made this Berns so special. Guys who needed the marshals to bring them in usually went to higher-level joints. This guy didn't look rough, and he wouldn't be facing a bunch of years and starting off here. Unless the marshals were there for protection. Snitches needed cover.

"Any rules on what I can have my girlfriend send?"

"We got so many our rules got rules. Ask Truman, he's the unit counselor. Matter of fact, I have to talk to him, too. Nothing personal, but I like living alone."

"I hope I'm not here long enough to be an issue."

So the guy was a short-timer. Or he thought his shyster could do magic. Either way, Berns was packaging the mattress with his sheets as though wrinkles didn't matter. He encouraged Maggiano by dropping the pillow into its case like an afterthought. Might as well make conversation. "First time down? Let me tell you, every place is different.

But some things they all got in common. You want to make your time go by as fast as you can. What you don't want is to stand out. The less the hacks notice you, the better. None of the guys will hassle you here. You'll get along if you mind your own business. Especially with me." The hacks had their rules, Maggiano had his.

The sound of the shouts outside the room echoed like a warning passed from one outpost to the next. "Count," Maggiano said. "We have to get our asses outside."

Maggiano stood just inside the doorway, waiting for Berns to proceed through first. Even though he was depending on their arrangement being temporary, he wanted Berns to handle his first Count right. Maggiano's goal was to remain invisible, even with a roommate. Once they were in the hallway, Maggiano motioned Berns to stand on one side of the doorway while he took the other. That way, the hacks could walk by, count them, and look in the room without breaking stride.

Governor Grady was standing by the door just opposite. Even though they were immediate neighbors, Maggiano rarely saw the governor other than during Count. Even then, the governor rarely spoke, but on seeing a newcomer he did have some questions. They could hear the hacks at the far end of the hallway, so the governor was careful not to talk out loud. Instead, his widened eyes and nod toward Berns said, "I see you have someone new." Raised eyebrows and a furrowed forehead said, "I thought you liked living alone." Head cocked and lips pursed, his expression asked, "Or is he an old friend?"

The hacks were almost upon them. Daugherty was in front, turning his head from side to side, pointing at each man and mumbling. Either Daugherty liked the sound of his own voice or he needed to count out loud to keep track. Peterson walked behind, carrying a clipboard and whispering. As the hacks passed, Maggiano looked at the governor and turned his head left, right, and then left again.

The men lining the hallway remained motionless until the hacks turned the corner at the other end of the hallway, at which point the floor relaxed in commotion. Grady said, "I hope they get it right the first time. Yesterday, it must have been five o'clock before we cleared. I was plenty hungry." The governor was known for limiting himself to one meal per day, mostly vegetables with high water content. Two years down, he was still flushing out the alcohol from his system.

Great, Maggiano thought, *now he wants a conversation. Hell, if he wants to know, he can ask straight up.* "I think they screwed it up in control. Between these guys phoning in numbers from all around the joint and the Southern drawls, I can see how something gets lost in the translation."

The governor let the dig at his accent pass. "I hope they've included your new roommate."

"If they hadn't, they would have kept him in reception until after Count."

Giving up on an introduction, the governor shrugged. Like any good politician, he could read between the lines.

Maggiano and Berns reentered their room. Maggiano said, "Where you from?"

"Chicago. I own a bar."

"You owned a bar."

Berns sat on what was his bed, at least for now. "You get a news flash I missed?"

"Just talking from experience. This place is a chemistry set. You report here, sugar turns to shit." Maggiano shrugged.

Berns drew himself up. "I got friends," he said.

"Got, had. They're two different words. I been doing some writing."

"I know about words," Berns said. "I gave mine."

Time to change the subject. A little more talk, this guy would drop in like Joey Philly, even after he moved. "So what's the word for you?" Maggiano asked. "Irish? German? Most of the bars in New York are Irish or German. Some, Italian. Me, I'm Italian. What are you?"

"I really don't follow a religion."

"Who's talking religion?"

"I'm Jewish, if that's what you're asking."

"That don't mean nothing. I eat on the kosher line myself. Talk to Butterfly. Have him introduce you to the other Jews. We got lots. You already met Joey Philly. I heard about, what you call ten? A ninja?"

"That's a Jap fighter. I think you mean minyan."

"Yeah. You and Joey Philly and we got Solomon Davis and Haskell Goldman down the hall. Must be a few others. Why don't you all move to a dorm. You could make some plots together."

EIGHT

Solomon Davis was on his knees, facing his bed with his head bowed down. Anyone who didn't know better would have thought he was praying. Petitioning was more like it. What Solomon was seeking was a lot closer than heaven. At times like these, you had to bend over for a client. He moved his hands between his mattress and the board that rested on his innerspring, pulling out papers like chances from a hat. "Be patient, Natron. I've got you in here somewhere." Solomon poked again near the head of the bed, this time thrusting his arm in up to his shoulder. Every time he pushed, the mattress rose to reveal the documents piled beneath.

"You sure gots lots to read," Natron said. "How do you hold all them cases clear in your head?"

"Every one of my clients is important. They each got different facts."

"You sure you keep them straight? Some gots to be special," Natron said.

That was just like a con. You did him a favor, he figured you owed him. He wanted to be your only client. Times like these, Solomon regretted not charging a fee. "You're all important to me."

Natron said, "It must keep you up nights, trying to remember which is mine."

Solomon resolved next time to arrange things before Natron arrived. "No, when it gets too complicated, I sleep on it." Solomon turned to view the effect of his words on his visitor. Natron was on a card chair near the window, leafing through the *Time* magazine he had selected from the library on top of the footlocker. He had one leg crossed over the other an inch above his knee. As usual, Natron appeared to be holding something in. He folded the corner of the page he was reading and closed the magazine. "I hope I don't give you no nightmares."

"You're a dream client." Solomon turned back to the bed. There, he had it. Natron Blades. Careful not to disrupt the dossiers on either side, he pulled Natron's file out from under the mattress. "As long as the hacks don't hassle me, we're okay." Solomon moved off the floor to the other folding chair and organized his bed as a desk, careful to keep his paperwork weighted down against the wind from the fan in the far corner of the room.

"Why would the hacks care? You cool." Natron dragged the last word out the way he did when talking to a honky.

When Solomon was done with the paperwork, Natron's file had been transformed into three stacks: pleadings, cases, and notes. The biggest pile was cases, which was touching notes like a lover. Pleadings had just been born. Solomon turned toward Natron, pen in hand, legal pad attached to his clipboard, and ready to work. "Okay, let's go over it again. You're waving your gun around when they arrive."

"Like I tell you, a water pistol."

"So you announce, 'Hey folks, this may look like a gun, but don't you worry. It can't do nothing but pass water.' You go like that?" Natron was still on the folding chair. Now he had his arms crossed, as well. "Okay," Solomon said, "you don't say that. What do you say?"

"I say, 'Make it fast, motherfuckers.'" Natron's voice was two levels lower than Solomon had ever heard it.

"And then?"

"The cops come in and I'm out the back door."

Solomon turned back to his bed and reached in again. This time, he knew the exact spot to poke. He removed his Speedy Trial notes and turned to tutor Natron without emphasizing the importance. Solomon had the kind of students who always paid attention. "We have this federal law going for us. It's called the Speedy Trial Act. It makes the government bring you to trial within ninety days if you're in jail."

"What you mean, it make? No one make the Man do anything. Specially for us folk."

"The law is for all of us. That's what the Constitution says," Solomon said. Natron was nodding to humor him. "Speedy Trial makes sense. If there's a long delay, it jeopardizes your chance for a fair trial."

"What you mean, jeopardize? Like that program on the TV?"

"No, like your witnesses could disappear."

"I knew you get mixed up, all those cases. All I has is bank workers and customers. And they be scared shitless."

"I don't mean witnesses against you," Solomon said. "Say there was someone who could be a witness in your favor. Someone who could give you an alibi."

Natron uncrossed his legs and stamped a foot. "Maybe you should read my file again. I stay patient while you do it."

"It was just a for instance. The law allows for that."

"Ain't no one like that," Natron said. "Unless I makes some calls."

"You miss my point."

"You watch how you talk," Natron said.

"I'm going to argue it shouldn't matter. Some state courts assume you have a witness, or the delay hurts you some other way. Blow the deadline, you're out of there. You have to show the federal courts you were prejudiced by the delay. We can deal with that later. The important thing is to get your papers on file."

Natron stood up and floated to the window, making Solomon wonder if he was high again. You never could tell with Natron. Sometimes, he seemed to be in the room with you, following what you said and even a step ahead. Other times, he was left or right of you but never straight in front. You had to be able to see his face to know where he was at the moment. Right now, Natron was looking outside through the glass. Only his ass twitched, and Solomon couldn't tell from that.

"This work for Perez?" Natron asked.

"What about Perez?"

"Speedy Trial. I hate to leave him when I go."

That figured. They were always either pushing product or high on the profit, maybe high on each other. "Even if we lose our motion, you're out of here in a little more than a year. It seems to me Perez gets left behind no matter what." When Natron's shoulders slumped, Solomon said, "Send him over. I've got a stack of my standard motions photocopied. All I need is to fill in the blanks." Solomon loved Speedy Trial. Ever since it had won his first case, he had charged a violation in all his motions. Like a card-carrying lawyer, he made the facts fit later.

Natron said, "How much I owe you for this?"

"Don't worry about it."

"What you usually get? Roll of quarters? Couple packs of smokes? Maybe you get fans to make the room cool." Natron raised his voice over the whir of the blades. "Where you get one like that? Must keep you nice and cool, all this heat. Or that?" Natron pointed at the Mickey Mouse clock hanging eye-level at the other end of the room. Mickey's hands were telling them they were about to miss their dinner.

"Charlie Chicken gave me that," Solomon said. "He offered to clean my room for a month, but I do that myself. So he gave me the clock. I don't charge fees. If someone wants to do me a favor, that's different. I'm glad to do you the favor."

"I don't want no favors. And I can do better than coin. I can get you green." Natron smoothed his middle and forefingers against his thumb. When he smiled, his front teeth shone gold.

Solomon said, "Wonderful, so I can wear paper money in my shoe. I had to wait two years for a single-man room. When I get out of seg, I'll get to start all over."

Natron's cackle announced he had changed his mood. When he stopped, Natron said, "We do green all the time. We gets it inside the covers of books, folks in the visiting room leaves it in the hems of the curtains for the cleanup crew, all kinds. A man need green. Take too many quarters to pay for grass. And sending out the rest is easy. We just write lots of letters home."

Solomon held up his hand. "I don't need to know that."

"I could have someone send a check to your commissary. Nothing wrong with that." Natron was looking at the far wall where it met the ceiling as he posed for the spotlight.

Solomon said, "You want to do something for me, we can talk about it later. Let's concentrate on your case. The main problem is the time."

"We all got that problem."

"Your problem is you're short. You should have made your motion at the Milan Penitentiary, instead of waiting until you transferred here. By the time they get around to deciding, you could have already served all your time."

"I'll take that chance." Natron smiled. With only fifteen months to go, he could afford to be generous.

They were interrupted by Butterfly Sweets, walking behind a man who looked about Solomon's age. "Excuse me, guys, this is a new man who's rooming with Maggiano for now. I wanted you to meet him. He's from Chicago. You've got a lot in common."

Okay, Butterfly wanted him to take care of the newcomer, maybe because they were homies, maybe some other reason. Butterfly was a good one to keep on your side. Solomon said, "Natron, let me work on this later. We're almost done, anyway."

Natron had pressed his lips shut, working them back and forth as though dealing with something caught in his mouth. He looked from Butterfly to the new man and back to Solomon, connecting the dots on the map and calculating the distance and direction of home. Then, nodding to show he understood the route, he said, "You sit here. This is where he does all his clients. Specially his own kind."

Butterfly looked at his arm, which was only a shade lighter than Natron's and allowed no mistake.

"Easy, bro," Natron said. "I just say this man you bring must be someone extra special." He gave a better-make-it-soon wave to Solomon and followed Butterfly out the door.

The new man extended a hand that felt like he had just wiped it, but not well. "I'm Zolly Berns, from Chicago," he said.

Solomon put down his clipboard, careful not to dislodge any of the papers on the bed. "Welcome to Atwood. I'm from Albany Park. What part of town are you from?"

"Near North. I have a bar on Rush and Elm." Berns was looking around the room as though counting the house.

"I used to hang out on Rush. Of course, I'm sure it's changed since then." Solomon pictured himself walking out of a bar, his hand on some showgirl's ass. They said if you couldn't make it in Chicago, you couldn't make it anywhere. He had managed to make it and lose it, which was the part they didn't talk about. "You probably need some stuff. Let's see what I have." He twirled the combination to his foot-locker and opened it. "I've got an extra mug, and this jar still has some coffee. Don't worry, I got another full one."

"You don't have to do that." The words were right, but Berns was already reaching. He had a band of pale skin around his arm. Must have worn a bracelet once. His hair, which barely rose above his scalp, was crinkled bleach. The street fat that bulged beyond his institution greens and the gut that hid his belt suggested he usually took in the sun in a seated position.

"It's a loan. Interest-free." Solomon smiled. "You can pay me back when you go to commissary. A through G go on Thursday. Your money should be posted by then."

"What money?" Zolly said.

Solomon was impressed when the new man extended his empty hands beyond his sleeves. Despite his clothes, Berns didn't look prison-issue. "You must have come in with money."

"I came in with the marshals."

Which raised more questions. Maybe there was room for this guy Berns under the mattress at the foot end of the bed, but Speedy Trial probably wouldn't work. "Okay, the hard way. No matter. You'll call home, have some sent in. You can shop next week. I'll tide you over until then. Smoke?" Solomon offered a couple of packs of Kools. "The menthol seems to help."

Berns ripped the pack open sideways and smelled the contents before removing a filter tip. His cough on the first drag showed it had been a while. Then Berns stretched and waved the cigarette toward the pile of papers, oblivious to the falling ash. "This part of your job?"

"I work for UNICOR. That's the prison industries. We make stuff for government agencies. It's their version of incest." Solomon began to stuff Natron's portfolio back under the mattress. "I sure as hell don't bring my work back here. I'm doing this for some friends. Legal documents, appeals, like that."

"You a lawyer?"

The seams in Solomon's face burrowed deeper. "I did a lot of things on the Street. Hustled, sold cars, kited checks. You don't need to go to school."

"How do you get from scams to doing law?" Berns asked.

"It ain't that big a reach," Solomon said. "What I know about the law, I've learned in here. I've had the time for it. We got law books for every circuit. We're working with older precedents, of course. Our library is a year or two behind." He waved off the thought that they were being treated unfairly. "Hell, who wants new law?"

"How do you get paid? I hear a guy can only draw a roll of quarters a week from commissary." Berns was already looking for the angles. He would fit right in.

"You got me wrong, I don't do it for the money," Solomon said.

"So you say. If you could get it, you might talk different."

Berns was pretty cocky for a guy hustling coffee and smokes. "I could get it if I wanted. I could always tell another guy in here to have his family send cash to my account, assuming he still has family. Of course, if a bunch of money orders arrived from people all with different last names, the hacks might start to wonder. But most of my guys don't have that kind of money. If they did, they would have a lawyer on the outside."

"Then it must be hard, like I said."

"That's not why I do it."

Berns cocked his head to see Solomon from a different angle. "Back home, no one does anything for free," he said.

Solomon glanced at the clock. Mickey's hands were together now and pointing south. It was time to move or miss out on chow. Solomon went for the door. "Some guys read. I never got into reading for the fun of it. Others work out. I don't think my arms ever met a muscle." Solomon leaned toward Berns to make his meaning clear. "In here, we're lucky to get a letter. I fill in for family."

Following Solomon out the door, leaving the cigarettes, coffee, and cup behind for later, Berns said, "I have this girl who works for me. She'd be the one to send me money. That's about it. Except for certain people who promised they'd watch out for us while I'm inside."

Solomon fought against the memory of his former wife and kid. "When you do time, you lose more than your freedom. We help each other out. If you're a homie, we help you out even more. That's why Butterfly brought you to meet me."

Berns had his head at that angle again. "I thought it was because we're Jewish."

"There's not many of us in here. We have to stick together."

"They have got to be your friends?" Berns said.

"I have all kinds. The best are the Italians. But if a Jew arrives, you tell him the way things are, introduce him around. I'll take you down to the chaplains so you can get your kosher card."

––––––––––

THEY WERE OUTSIDE NOW, CUTTING ACROSS THE YARD, NO ONE else in sight. Solomon walked fast to get to the dining room before they locked the doors. Berns managed to keep up, breathe heavy, and talk at the same time. "What's with this kosher line? And how does Maggiano get to be on it?"

"You know what kosher is," Solomon said. "You don't eat pork; the chickens and cows have to be killed just right. I don't know all the rules, but stuff like that."

"You've got to be kidding. That makes a difference in here?"

"Inside, we need all the difference we can get." They were passing through the administration building archway closest to Women's Unit, which was just letting its inmates out after Count. Maybe Berns would pay attention to that group and change the subject.

"So how is it that Maggiano eats on the line?" Berns wouldn't let go of it.

"How many of us do you think follow the rules outside? So if we've got a group who never met kosher on the Street but eat on the line in here, what difference does it make if a few Italians join us?"

"Why would they want to?"

"Someone sued the Bureau of Prisons a few years ago to make them let people follow their religion. At joints where there aren't enough

Jews, the BOP now serves kosher TV dinners. But with so many of us at Lexington, it's cheaper to have a food line."

"Why does that make the food better?"

They were inside and approaching the dining room. Solomon dropped his voice. "The goyim think we get higher quality, but the BOP doesn't spend more per person than on the main line. We have our own kitchen, our own cooks. The ratio is more in our favor. Like I said, not that many. Say, fifty or sixty, compared to a couple thousand. So for once in your life, it pays to be a Jew."

NINE

"You're nervous," Zolly said. The way Solomon was shifting around, the hack was sure to notice.

"If I'm not careful, I could get a shot." Most of the line was facing forward, toward the dining room, but Solomon had the hack in
sight. The column of inmates stretched from the dining-room doors
down half the length of the hall and then turned toward the library,
which they closed during dinner. Priorities were important. The hack
was walking the hall like any cop on a Sunday beat with nothing much
going on, just a stroller enjoying the sun. Occasionally, he motioned to
men and women standing side by side to get back in single file, but it
was only the gesture of a man who preferred a straight line because of
the way it looked, not because of the crowd's attempts to fondle each
other. The hall was wide enough for a jet to taxi down the middle, with
a runway buffed enough to blind the pilot.

Zolly cased the scene. "Why are we whispering?"

"We're not supposed to talk in line. They don't usually enforce the
rule, but why fart in the hack's face?" Solomon said.

A second group spilled down the other side of the hall. Most of them were bald or gray, and all were overweight. "That the kosher?" Zolly asked.

"It's the diet. They think they can get healthy here. Some have even been known to."

"So where's our line?"

"I hope they don't catch me skipping it."

Zolly looked around again for danger.

Solomon said, "I have a kosher card, but I'm about to eat on the main line. Just the one meal we'll have there before you get your card."

Zolly cocked his head. Solomon had seemed normal back at the unit, except for the Good Samaritan bit, but here he was acting spooky. Was he a food fanatic? Unlikely. Solomon looked like he only ate one meal a day. Or maybe more, but he worked it off with his nerves. Or he could have a constant case of the runs.

Solomon said, "According to Chaplain Burgess, having a kosher card and then eating on the main line ranks right below blasphemy. We call him the hack in black. He likes to make rules and then catch you breaking them. If you sign up kosher, you better not eat pig." Solomon licked his lips as though they were coated with grease. "Say you like bacon and eggs, which they serve maybe twice a year. Well, if they catch you trying to eat on the main line, you'll get a shot. Then you draw extra duty, maybe lose some good time. Even worse, they'll yank your kosher card."

It seemed to Zolly that Mickey Mouse was not confined to Solomon's room. This could even be worse than the Board of Health back home. He began to shuffle his feet from all the waiting. The line barely made a move. Only mopes stood in a line on the Street. That was what scalpers were for. Then, the line surged forward as though someone had just bought a block of seats. It took several advances, and a couple of warnings from the hack to the line in general, before they reached the doors. The line now continued down a short inside corridor that bisected glass-walled rooms on either side. "What the hell? It keeps on going," Zolly said.

"Yeah, but from here we smell the food."

Zolly's sense of smell was better developed than most and sharper since he'd stopped smoking, except for the Kools in Solomon's room. A doctor told him once that when one of a person's senses was underdeveloped, the others grew keener to compensate. That, and maybe David's big bang, explained why the music in his bar was a headache but he could smell it if his supplier delivered day-old bread. His appetite grew as they approached a serving station where inmates with white uniforms, well-fed faces, and large spoons were ready to attack all trays in range. If it had been junior high, the steamers would have been full of franks and beans, or burgers and fries. Graduate school turned out to be pressed meat, mashed potatoes, and pots of a yellow liquid that was soup from a distance but colored water up close. The servers wore mittens, which explained why the edges of Zolly's steamed meat curled from pink to gray on his plate. They entered the nearest dining hall and ate with six other inmates. The room was furnished with round tables spaced just far enough apart to avoid provocation. Its walls were painted in colors that made the diners rush through their meals. Men and women talked quietly, ate loudly, and squeezed down each mouthful. Instead of waiters pushing dessert or an after-dinner drink, the guards encouraged turnover on behalf of those still in line outside.

AFTER DINNER, SOLOMON LED ZOLLY TO A DOORWAY HALFWAY back toward the entrance hall. "The chaplains are below us. Them and the chapel and the movie theater. Who says you can't have fun in here?" Downstairs, they emerged into a hallway running at a perpendicular angle to the one upstairs. Religion had its own authority. The chaplains' suite had a waiting room and inner offices walled with windows for each of the preachers. The arrangement put them on display for the waiting inmates. Men and women occupied all the chairs and couches that filled the waiting room and ran the length of the inside hallway that ran across from the chaplains' offices. Clusters of standing inmates jostled each other for space like any night at Zolly's bar, when the women had come to make relationships and the men had come to make the women.

"Why the mob scene?" Zolly asked.

Solomon said, "Some have problems, some are sucking up. Some just want a change of scene. Some want to press against their walkies." The couple on the closest couch was huddled in the line of sight of the nearest office, but they ignored the glass. They were in the first stage of love, as evidenced by how they paid attention to each other and slid together on the cushion, his knee pressed against her thigh, happy to be last in line.

"This where they come to pray?"

"The services are across the outside hall, in the chapel. Except for us. Not enough Jews to get the chapel. We've got the room in back." Solomon led the way through the crowd to the chaplains' offices, ignoring the looks he got. A line stretched in front of one of them, while the door to the other was clear.

Solomon said, "Shit. We drew Brendan Burgess." He entered the head chaplain's office to tell him that Zolly needed a kosher card. The hack in black was dressed in gray and wore tinted horn-rimmed glasses that hid his eyes. Burgess nodded Zolly toward a seat while waving Solomon to wait outside. Then the chaplain sank back in his chair, a personnel director about to interview an applicant for an entry-level job.

"Unusual name. What is its origin?"

Zolly thought of the traffic cop. Years without anyone paying attention, now it was sprouting through cracks in the sidewalk.

"It doesn't sound Jewish?"

Burgess didn't flinch. "We have to be certain someone is entitled to eat on the kosher line. We respect a person's faith, not his appetite."

"I could show you my circumcision." Zolly would have welcomed any reaction from this man with thin lips, but Burgess barely moved his mouth.

"That is as much a medical as a religious procedure. It likely began for hygienic reasons." Burgess turned into a Bible-school cheerleader, devoting the next few minutes to chanting his admiration for the "People of the Book," while Zolly's mind drifted. It landed as Burgess said, "Federal forms don't list a man's religion. I need someone who can confirm that you're Jewish."

"Like a friend back home?"

"Like a rabbi back home."

The last time Zolly had his own rabbi was when he'd been preparing for the bar mitzvah that David's bang had blasted away. The bar mitzvah had been David's idea in the first place. He wanted to please Grandpa Sam. When David shortened his last name, the old man had been hurt. Selling slots had been David's second assault. If they had skipped Zolly's confirmation, Sam would have said Kaddish for both generations. As it turned out, he'd said Kaddish for David.

"I don't have a rabbi or attend services. But I really am Jewish."

"We are not investigating the quality of your faith, Mr. Berns, just your background. You must have someone who can confirm you're a Jew."

Well, there was Becky's funeral. Everyone else had been dead, so Zolly had made the arrangements. The cemetery had insisted on a Jewish undertaker, who had hired the rabbi. What was his name? He resurrected the memory. "There's Rabbi Lipschultz. In Chicago."

Burgess waited for more, then shrugged. "I don't suppose you have a first name. Let's see what information can tell us." Zolly listened to Burgess interviewing the operator, repeating the names and numbers of all four Chicago Lipschultz rabbis. Then he made his calls. Rabbi Three remembered officiating at the funeral of a woman named Becky Berns, unusual last name for a Jew, who had a son whose name might have been Zolly. A teenage son, with a shady look.

Burgess said, "Would you like to speak to your rabbi, Berns?"

Yes, Zolly was fine. No, he had never married. Really, he had not known the cemetery required annual payments for the grave upkeep. Sorry, he could not go into the reasons he was in jail just now. Yes, of course he knew there were Jewish services every week at FCI Lexington. He was going to attend them, for sure. Thank you, Rabbi, thank you very much. He handed the phone back to Burgess.

The hack in black filled out a form, choosing each word as though there were a shortage of ink. "This will be your temporary pass. You will get a permanent card with your picture on it in a couple of days. Keep in mind, this means you may only eat on the kosher line. We are very firm on that."

Then Burgess looked up, extending his arms like a new graduate from chaplain school. "Is there anyone back home you would like to talk to? Normally, you must call collect from your unit, but on special occasions, we can arrange for calls from here."

———

ZOLLY SHIFTED FROM ONE SIDE TO THE OTHER, IN RHYTHM with the telephone's buzz. How could they ignore it at the other end? It was eight o'clock in both cities, so the bar must be jammed by now. The phone rang six or seven times before she answered. He could hear Faith but no other customers, only the noise of the music in the background.

"It's been two weeks," she said. It sounded like a sob. "I didn't know how to reach you."

"They had me on the road. They wouldn't let me get near a phone, not even to call the lawyer. I don't think they'd ever heard of due process." Burgess's eyebrows rose above the top of his horn rims, like the mark over *mañana*. "I just got here today. How are things going?"

Rather than giving an honest answer, Faith blew her nose. For the first time since his arrival, the back of Zolly's neck began to ache. His vertebrae could have been wired all the way back to Chicago.

"The evening after you left, the Board of Health arrived. There were more inspectors than customers. After an hour, they gave me a pound of citations. They said we'd have to close until we made things right. They said they would arrest me if we operated without clearance. We've been closed ever since."

The memory of pink meat seemed to rise in Zolly's throat. "Two weeks?"

"The water in the sink isn't hot enough, so we need a booster. We need a plumber to ream out the toilets."

"How could you let it go two weeks? We don't even close for Christmas."

"There was food on the counter that should have been in the cooler, but the cold-storage temperature is too high, anyway, because of a crack in the seal of the door."

"Christ, Faith, I depend on you. How are we going to make it if you let me down?" Zolly found himself thinking of David again. Was this the way it had felt when they took away his slots?

"Our purveyors and service people aren't returning my calls."

"Someone is sending a message. What does Gershom say?"

"I wasn't able to reach him until yesterday. It's been two whole weeks."

The pain in Zolly's forearm made him loosen his grip. The phone almost fell, so he took it in his other hand and held it to his other ear, not expecting better news. Again with the crying. "He'll look into it. You said things would be okay."

"Yeah, like I knew they would drag me straight from court to jail, without a chance to line things up. As though I planned it that way. Faith, even with only a few days, I could have made decent arrangements."

"I always said we should stay clear of Goldberg."

"I can't talk that long."

"I'm afraid what will happen to us."

There wasn't much doubt what the situation would be if Faith couldn't hold it together. Try straightening things out from in here. If his favorite trio didn't help, they would lose their customers to the other spots on the Street. No chance getting it back after you lose the business. "Did you try to reach Goldberg or Civiletti?"

"They were here when it happened. Goldberg acted like he expected it. He asked when I expected you to call. He said they were counting on you to do the right thing. He said to remember you were his boy now, not David's." That last bit dated back to the grand opening of the Howard Street bar, when Zolly had drunk one too many and told the story to Goldberg.

"He didn't say anything about the inspection?"

"He just raised his hands and said he couldn't get involved. He said, 'If Zolly has a problem with the city, he'll have to work it out himself.'"

Zolly stood, talking down into the mouthpiece. His reflection in Burgess's glasses resembled every guy he ever knew who held a losing hand. "Work it out myself? How do you suggest I do that from the inside? I leave you alone a couple of weeks, now everything has turned to shit." Burgess stood as well, reaching for the phone.

"I don't know anyone who can help with the fix, if that's what you want," she said. "If your friends won't help us out, I don't know what we'll do."

Zolly wagged his free hand as though she could see it. "Be careful what you say. There's some hack listening in or recording the conversation." Burgess was still reaching. Zolly turned away, pretending not to notice. "Do you have enough money to get by?"

"The bank froze the account. There's a tax lien."

He couldn't imagine what they thought he knew or wanted him to say. "Did you talk to Goldberg about that?"

"When I saw him on the Street, he drew away. He must have thought I wanted a handout. That wasn't a bad guess. I have some cash set aside, but it's only enough for groceries."

"The hell with Goldberg. That just proves the bottom line. You have to look out for yourself." But when saying that, Zolly remembered David and wasn't even tempted.

TEN

WHEN ZOLLY AWAKENED, HE REACHED FOR HIS HANGOVER AND then for Faith before remembering where he was. Faith was hundreds of miles and a lifetime away, and his bar was long behind him. Instead of enjoying a morning after with his girl and recalculating the take, he was sober, alone, and broke, three good reasons to keep his lids clenched shut. Eyes closed, he could have anything. He could have his own business, with paying customers and cash in the bank. Eyes closed, he could be anywhere. He could be driving to work, convertible top open to the sun and the cheering crowds. He could smell the leather of his El Dorado, switch to overdrive. His Caddy rolled in rhythm to his heartbeat before hitting the pothole in the middle of Rush. His bar disappeared, in flames. Zolly gasped his eyes open to find himself parked in a room the size of King Arthur's table. The other bed was empty. He was deciding between turning over and looking for Maggiano when Solomon showed up, wearing a polo shirt, chinos, and an appetite.

"What about taking a kosher-kitchen breakfast?" Solomon said.

"Your life revolve around meals?" Zolly said.

"Thought you'd like to try out your new card."

Zolly's mouth was dry. The last time he took breakfast, maybe twenty years ago, it had been after he woke up hungry. These days, he awakened empty. "I'd rather take a shit."

Solomon shrugged. "You need ammunition for that. But you can start off light and build up to lunch. When you're ready, make yourself some coffee. There's hot water in the main TV room."

After Solomon left, Zolly was too wide awake to forget. Rather than dwell on Faith's news from the night before, he decided to get ready for the rest of the day. As soon as he could, he meant to call Gershom. Zolly showered and shaved in an empty washroom where the steam still lingered from men who were never late for a meal. He dressed and took the instant coffee in his cup to the main TV room, which was also empty. He went straight for the vending machines he and Butterfly had passed the night before. The top row would do for breakfast. Zolly clinked his borrowed quarters down the slot. Then, honey-glaze in hand, he made his way to the hot water pot.

Solomon's client, Natron, was standing nearby, one hand holding his mop, the other extended, palm open and waiting. He was wearing Levis that could stand on their own, a scat group T-shirt, and a medallion that proved he had all kinds of cash. His hair was fixed in dreadlocks that had more knots than his mop. "I hope you got something in that mug besides air. You want free coffee, go to chow. That pot by you just got water. Truman took up a collection, got it at the Kmart. No mind, glad to share. You pay next time, when this one rusts out. You got the coin, maybe I can find some instant to go with it."

"Solomon lent me half a jar." Ignoring Natron's disappointment, Zolly moved to an imitation-leather couch with authentic cracks and took a seat as Natron mopped away. CNN was reporting on some space shuttle that would go up in the fall. The announcer was excited because there was going to be a female astronaut. Zolly wondered how the man would act if the Cubs were to win the division again. He decided to start watching the news. It probably helped pass the time. Might even give a hint before the heat came down again, instead of the feds taking him by surprise. He held a bite of the roll in his mouth to sweeten the next swallow of coffee and was washing down a mouthful when Truman spoke behind his ear. The man must have seen a doctor, because now he was walking on tiptoes.

"Enjoying your Danish?"

"That's out east. We call them sweet rolls." Zolly chewed another bite to show he took no offense.

"Coffee okay?"

"I understand I've got you to thank."

Truman smiled and leaned against the back of the couch, a neighbor talking over a fence. "It wasn't convenient for the men to go to town. Seeing as you're grateful, after you've finished your meal, maybe you'd help us out." The man looked as pleased with himself as he had the day before, when he had announced his decision to send Zolly to Atwood. There were lots of cops like that on the Street, reminding you who they were, if their uniforms weren't enough. Zolly tossed away the rest of his meal.

Truman led Zolly to a closet holding a collection of dust mops and brushes that were leaning against the sink like teenage girls at a dance. Truman said, "Why don't you help Natron work on the floor. Well, he calls it working, anyway."

Zolly took the only mop that still looked ripe, filled a bucket, and joined Natron at the end of the hall. Natron watched his approach from down the hallway. Drawing close, Zolly could see that Natron's curls had beads of water at the tips. Better not get close enough for whatever was living in there to make the jump to him. "Where do I start?" Zolly asked.

"Don't give me 'do,'" Natron said. "I'm an inmate, just like you."

"I'm doing it for the Man." Zolly gestured at Truman, who was halfway down the hallway by the guard's desk and pretending not to watch.

"Don't pay no mind to that motherfucker. He just a counselor. I clean for the hack on duty. I don't know why the Man stick his nose in this business." Natron shoved the mop as he spoke, his movements smooth but his voice cracking, as though his body were plugged in but his voice was filled with static.

"I guess he didn't like seeing me sitting there and wanted me to get to work."

"Look at your hands. I bet they feel soft, too. What you know about work? You and Solomon just do with the books, right?" Natron rubbed his necklace and grinned before modeling down the hallway, head held high, knees knocked in and ass tucked tight. If he had worked in the bar back in the day and carried on like that, Zolly would have fired him on the spot. He would have enjoyed seeing Conrad throw this one in the street. Natron looked right and then left, continuing to the end of the runway before swiveling and flouncing back, removing dust from the mop as he walked. "There, you do like that."

"You must have lots of experience," Zolly said.

"Who you disrespecting? On the street, I was the man people come to see, they want to get things done. You people think you something special, but I had, how you say, lots of shekels."

If he had to hang around Natron, it would be worse than with the marshals. Zolly wondered whether his being Jewish was going to come up every day. Probably would, if he used the kosher card in front of Natron. On the Street, it hadn't mattered.

"All kinds of action, too, but janitor wasn't one of them." Natron was running on full power now. "Lots of action in here." Natron winked at his secret.

"Such as?" Zolly recognized the mistake before seeing the look on his teacher's face, but he didn't really care. He was merely feeling his way.

Natron said, "If you was to walk alongside with your bucket and mop and talk only half the way, we could get this done twice as fast."

Then they shuffled side by side, Natron sweeping left and Zolly right. After dry mopping the entire hallway, they washed the floor, Natron swabbing from the elbow, keeping the mop neither so wet as to streak nor so dry as to make him press down. Zolly followed with the bucket, replacing the water when it turned sour with fresh flow from the closet tap. On the occasion when an inmate would appear at the end of the corridor wanting to return to his room, Natron would shriek to the motherfucker not to track up his hallway or he would wipe it with his ass. By midmorning, the floor was ready for the buffer. Just as Natron was showing Zolly how to make the floor shine without having to use wax every time, Truman emerged and summoned Zolly to his office. Natron shrugged as though he had expected it all along.

———————

TRUMAN'S OFFICE OCCUPIED WHAT COULD HAVE BEEN A FOUR-man room, which helped explain Atwood's shortage of space in the inmate rooms. His desk looked like it was from grade school, except there was nothing carved on the top and the inkwell was missing. Bookcases lined every wall, overflowing with histories, dictionaries, encyclopedias, atlases, and novels. Truman was either a slow reader or a hoarder. Zolly released himself into the only chair available, ready to rise if its legs gave way. Truman leafed through a manila folder. He seemed to be searching for the solution to some puzzle he was unwilling to share. Zolly thought of the tax collector poking around in his books. "Let's talk about your future," Truman said.

As Zolly saw it, if he didn't get out of here fast, his future was probably past. He knew the source of the pressure, but he couldn't figure why Goldberg had dumped him. It didn't look like Gershom would be any help, either. That was the problem with paying a fee up front. If you owed a man, he returned your calls. Coming up with fresh cash was out of the question. With the place closed, they couldn't even afford to dust the tables. But money wasn't the issue. The problem was the price that Fallen wanted. Maybe David had paid it without a blink, maybe he'd swallowed hard. Zolly never had a chance to ask. Either way, he was no David. He decided to work out how to use Truman to his advantage. That was more important than the Reverend Burgess and any kosher card.

Truman was no longer looking through his folder. How long had he been staring? Truman nodded, gratified for Zolly's attention.

"Enjoy your work?" Truman asked.

"I got no complaints."

"You can learn from anyone, put your mind to it. Not that I recommend everything Natron has to share. You should be choosy what he teaches."

"Doing halls doesn't seem so hard," Zolly said.

"Glad you enjoyed it. I gave you a taste of what's in store," Truman said. "Every convict has to work in here. You could call it rehabilitation." He pronounced it "ree-hah-bill-i-tay-shun," his smile broader with each syllable, emphasizing the "shun." He inhaled like any standup comic before the punch line. "I call it part of doing time."

"Whatever you want."

Truman swatted the offer away. "But technically, you're not a con. You haven't been proven guilty of anything. You're here for contempt of court, which means you can walk anytime you choose to talk. You're an inmate, but you're not a convict, so we can't make you work." Truman sucked the teeth on the side of his mouth like a good old boy. "You're not here for punishment or rehabilitation. No, you're here for persuasion." He emphasized the "shun" again.

Zolly told himself that the bullshit was part of the deal. He wasn't doing it for Goldberg, and he wasn't doing it for fear; he was doing it because of David. *A man has to consider his reputation*, Zolly thought, thinking "reputation" the Truman way.

Truman inhaled and sucked again. "Most men find their time goes faster when they work. I suppose that might not apply when you can close shop whenever you want. Of course, there's another reason you might want to work."

Zolly was damned if he would ask what that was.

Truman bent over his desk. If he had been standing, it would have been a bow. "There's no rule that makes us keep you with the other inmates. So if you're not willing to work like a convict, we'll set you apart. Now, I learned from these books that 'set apart' means 'segregate.' We do have a place called that."

Zolly knew about seg. Terre Haute had been dress rehearsal. Why didn't the man just come right out and tell him he had to work? "Yes, sir. Whatever you say to do."

"Everyone gets a permanent job they would like. That makes it better for them and the staff. We have jobs in supply: the library, office jobs, work at UNICOR, all over." Truman had his hands behind his head and feet up on his desk, teasing Zolly that the chair might tip over. "But first, we have to fill our ninety-day allotment for the kitchen and the captain's detail, washing dishes, cleaning the grounds. Afterward, we'll find you a better job. Maybe take Natron's place. He thinks I don't see it, but he only works a couple of hours a day. Spends the rest of his time watching TV or planning trickery."

It was time to talk to the man, start a real conversation. Zolly could make friends with customers back at the bar; he ought to be able to manage one redneck. "It must have taken quite a while to get this collection together. Have you read them all, sir?"

"Berns, this isn't the army. Call me 'Mr. Truman.' The books aren't a collection. These are my higher education." He studied the shelves as though they held framed pictures of his kids. "I got them all from my inmates."

"I thought it was okay to have books sent in."

"Of course. We want our folks to leave improved. But you can't have more than five at a time. Messes up a room. When a man finishes a book and is done lending it around, that's where I come in. I do like to read."

Truman pushed his finger down his list as though it held lots of choices. "First, let's talk about where I'm going to have you work. You may have restaurant experience, but I don't think you'd do well in the kitchen. If your hands started to shake from your so-called alcohol withdrawal, you might drop some of the dishes."

Zolly glanced at the book on Truman's desk. The cover showed a picture of a man pointing his finger straight out, summoning the reader. It reminded Zolly of the war posters he had seen as a kid. He knew he was about to enlist, but he didn't know for what.

ELEVEN

SOLOMON STOOD IN THE MIDDLE OF THE ROOM IN HIS STOCK-
ing feet, holding his shoes and looking at pictures of Maggiano's grandkids thumbtacked to the bulletin board like targets. The air stank from
floor wax. He gestured at the glare. "You'd better take yours off, too.
Charlie Chicken was here. Maggiano would kill us if we marked up his
floor."

"I figure half is mine."

"Figures like that can jam you up. What I hear, you could be moving anytime."

"How much does this guy Charlie charge?"

"Four quarters. The same as a wing and a thigh."

"That wholesale or retail?"

"He charges a dorm the same as a one-man room. We're like the
Street. Cash is always king."

Still at the threshold, Zolly studied his reflection in the floor. One
of his regulars once told him you could tell what you would look like
in twenty years by looking down in a mirror.

According to Maggiano's floor, at least Zolly would still be alive. He shook his head. No doubt about it, he was getting a headache from the wax. "I think I'll keep my shoes on. Let's go eat."

Ignoring the sidewalk that ringed the perimeter, they joined a line of men walking across the Yard on blades of grass bending toward the food. Zolly felt for the temporary pass that Burgess had given him the night before. He rubbed his thumb across the words allowing him to eat. As they reached the archway, he said, "I start work tomorrow. I thought we were getting along okay, then Truman gives me this shit assignment."

"What kind of shit is that?"

"He has me on the captain's detail. Says they'll put me on cleanup in the courtyard or one of the buildings."

Solomon laughed. "That's not tough duty. You'll see. They got four people on every two-man crew."

"Being in here is bad enough. Putting me to work with my hands is for thirty years ago. I figured I'd get to do some bookwork, do inventory in the commissary, something like that."

"I hear you push a mean mop. Truman must have been impressed."

"You think he's okay."

"If you don't bullshit him, he might help you out when you need it. As long as it's not too often," Solomon said.

"I'd settle for just once."

"Take last year. I'm helping this guy, Watson. We need a transcript of the case for his appeal. They're supposed to let you have that stuff sent in, but writing a rule and living by it are two different things." They emerged from the archway into the small courtyard between Women's Unit and the administration building. "We go to Truman, he gets permission, gets word to the court clerk, and everything arrives in a month. Counting the exhibits, it fills a dozen cardboard boxes."

"Okay, he gets credit for volume."

Solomon raised his hands in surrender. "There's no way to store all that in Watson's room. The boxes won't fit under the bed, and he would never pass inspection if he stacked them against the wall. The hacks won't stand for it, rules or no rules. So Truman takes them into his own office and lets us keep them there for the two months I take to write the brief. Truman had to leapfrog to get to his books."

"I get the message. You can work with him."

"Work with, yes. Work him over, no. You have to listen inside the accent."

They were in the main courtyard now, approaching the steps that led to the entrance to the administration building, walking with a group going to lunch. The women's outfits would have fit right in on Rush. Half the men were dressed for the local health club, while the other half wore a wardrobe that announced their favorite teams. Boyfriends and girlfriends were walking while holding hands. Walkies, Solomon called them.

"Truman did okay my clothing list." Zolly rubbed his fatigues. They felt like starch.

"How about the telephone?"

"Most of the evening slots were gone, so I signed up to call my lawyer this afternoon. I hope he has better news." The line was longer than the night before. Although there was a staggered schedule for dinner, there was no pattern to lunch. Everyone had a chance to jump ahead of everyone else.

"Welcome to the club," Solomon said. "As soon as you get here, things back home go straight to shit. Anyone who owes you forgets you exist, anyone you owe is out to collect, and your family is on their own." He squinted at the observation. "I lost my wife the first time I went down. She stayed with me for my trial, but then she disappeared. Haven't seen my son since." Maybe that was due to who Solomon was, not what he did. If he had worked more on scoring for himself and less on helping others, she might have hung around.

Standing in line, Zolly was practicing putting his weight first on one foot, then the other, when the guard called out for the kosher cards. They became the express train bypassing the local. None of those they passed even seemed to notice them as they went through the dining-room doorway, advanced beyond inmates eating off metal plates, avoided counters heaped with today's meat and yesterday's grease, and emerged through an entranceway across the room, flashing their cards at Messer, who was working on the door today and scowling like a street cop working in the rain. They joined a line of other kosher diners in an anteroom that provided its own colored-plastic platters and utensils.

"What's with the toy trays?" Zolly asked.

"The green trays tell the hacks we're eating kosher, not off the main or diet lines. They claim it helps them spot any trading of food. I figure it's like wearing the Star of David. I told the hack in black it was a Nazi trick, but he said it was voluntary."

"You said they make us."

"The kosher line is what's voluntary."

"We sit at separate tables?"

"We eat wherever, but sometimes you feel funny being marked."

A man with sunlamp skin and hair combed back to cover his peeling head turned around. "Seeing as Solomon is too busy explaining the rules to have good manners, I'll introduce myself. Haskell Goldman.

I don't mind standing out." Haskell was the type who ran on the Oak Street Beach spring, summer, and fall and did their winters at the Chicago Health Club when they weren't in the Sun Belt. His body said thirty, his face said fifty, and he paid attention to his nails. Guys like him came to Zolly's bar every other month as a reminder to everyone else of who they were, and to remind themselves where they came from. Every Haskell Goldman Zolly had ever met was hiding between the lines.

Solomon said, "This is Zolly Berns, from Chicago via the U.S. Marshals and Terre Haute, Indiana."

Haskell assessed Zolly as though deciding how much to bid. "You don't look dangerous."

"It's a long story."

"We have lots of time." Haskell twisted around to tap the shoulder directly in front of him. The man who turned resembled any one of Zolly's grade-school teachers eager to catch him misbehaving. Haskell said, "This is Gabriel Goldstein. He sold minks on the outside. In here, he runs the shul. We call him Gabby. You'll figure out why."

"So you're the new man," Gabby said. "I heard about you from Butterfly. I'm sad whenever a *landsman* arrives. I'll do what I can to help."

Zolly was second-guessing his choice. It might be hard to avoid getting involved with these people. Then the smell of lunch came toward him from the inner room, and he remembered the pink meat. "Appreciate it," Zolly said.

Haskell gestured toward a couple farther up in line. The man was about Zolly's height. The woman had her elbow even with her companion's hip, where it rested for support. "That's Reuben Lewis and Betsy Tobias. Don't expect them to pay you any notice. Whenever they get a chance, they press together. You should see them in shul. They think they're in love."

"I heard about love," Zolly said, thinking of Faith and her sighs.

"Maybe when you were twenty, not when you're fifty. You get to an age you have to take care of business." Haskell had the voice of a man accustomed to having an assistant carry his briefcase.

Messer leaned inside. "Cut down on the chatter. Get your food and go eat." His glare told Zolly he knew him.

Haskell and Gabby nodded to Messer and turned to face forward again. When Messer stepped back outside, Zolly whispered to Solomon, "Thanks for the introductions, but I thought you didn't show up at services."

"One way or another, we get to know each other."

While they were waiting for the lovers to get their meal, Maggiano entered along with two men who looked like his cousins. The back of Gabby's neck flushed, and he started to mutter. Haskell was chuckling. Solomon put his mouth close to Zolly's ear and said, "It really doesn't matter. As long as there's enough food for us."

Zolly and Solomon reached the head of the line. The kitchen worker who greeted them was named Buddy and built like a welterweight boxer. "Solomon, good to see you. We got your favorite today." Fat chance of Conrad Bigman greeting people that way. Conrad had treated customers like an imposition. Buddy had a Cossack jaw and a nose too short to matter. What he had of hair ringed his head like a mustard crown. He caught Zolly's look. "You don't have to be Jewish. I guess it does help if you have a Jewish girlfriend." A woman walked up behind him from the kitchen. "This is Rosie. She cooks." Rosie's denims were stretched too tight to put on with ease. The way she looked at Buddy,

Zolly doubted she wanted a larger size, unless to get them off in a hurry. Any woman looked better in here than she would on the outside, but even allowing for that, Rosie was dessert. They made their way past Maggiano and his friends into a dining room where Solomon chose a table with only one diner at the other end. Zolly replayed his conversation with Faith from the night before. Since then, he had gone over the call half a dozen times, trying to recollect where she'd paused and which words she'd emphasized. Between mouthfuls, he said, "Damn, things have turned into a mess. When I left home, the only question was whether Faith could run the bar on her own, or would she need help from three guys I know. They're kind of why I'm here." He took a swallow to give Solomon time to catch his meaning. "I worried they might meddle too much. First chance I get to call home, I find they've disappeared. I have to call my lawyer." Zolly pushed his food around the tray. The gravy was still cooking the chicken breast and wetting his mashed potatoes and peas. He hunched around his serving to shield it from the man with the metal tray who was seated across the way.

Solomon put down his fork but held on to his knife, carving his words as he spoke. "Lots of guys come in here with nothing. I appreciate that you are frank. But remember, it's one thing to talk about how your family is hurting and your friends are screwing you around. It's another thing to say what got you here. You never know where your words will go."

This was coming from a guy who traded with other people's cases. Zolly chewed on chicken and thought of David. He preferred dark meat, but this would do. "I know to take care of my own business. Maybe I notice what goes on, but I only talk about my own stuff, and I'm not afraid of what I might say. They've got nothing on me. Except, of course, the taxes and the liquor license and all, but that's not why I'm here."

Solomon said, "That's what I mean. I don't want to hear about taxes. I don't want to know about licenses. You have no idea what can hurt you and what can't. Don't tell me about a beef until it's time to file your appeal." Zolly hoped Solomon had a firm grip on the knife he again was waving. He was relieved when Solomon returned to his chicken, picking off the skin as though it were a scab. "Not that I would ever rat on you. But if you get in the habit of keeping your eyes open, you won't bump into things."

———————

AFTER DINNER, THEY SAT ON A BENCH IN THE COURTYARD. Grass and flowers replaced the smell of wax. It was any other spring day, any other park. Couples were walking together with nothing but dreams of their future before them.

"I appreciate the advice," Zolly said. "I won't say anything to hurt me. And I'll work with Truman, too. It's good to know he can be a friend."

Solomon was leaning back, eyes closed, facing west, catching the sun. Zolly wondered whether he had heard him. Then Solomon said, "I got lucky Truman did us that favor. Even so, you want to be careful. He may not intend it, but sometimes he scratches." Solomon opened his eyes, selected a blade of grass, and studied it like a secret. "After all, he's the cat. That leaves us to be the mice."

TWELVE

HASKELL WAS ABLE TO KEEP A STRAIGHT FACE. THEY WERE clustered around the guard in the reception lobby with Haskell the only one talking. Zolly didn't mind when they were one-on-one. You could even learn how to make a buck. But when Haskell had an audience, he seemed to wear a mask. He carried on about nonsense and demanded full attention. Maybe he was working on an insanity plea. The control room hacks were paying no attention from behind their bulletproof window. They were focused on the closed-circuit screens, telephones, and whatever else guards need for reassurance. Only the cleanup hack and the five inmates were listening to Haskell's speech. It was the usual. Zolly remained surprised Haskell could keep a straight face, and that the hack would listen even one more time without sending him straight to seg.

"I sprayed some of that special soap on the seats. Smell for yourself." Haskell pointed to the door of the women's washroom.

"Why don't we just finish up, so you folks don't have to return after Count?" the hack asked. His nostrils were already flaring.

"But Officer, you should smell while it's fresh. I sprayed the inside. Nothing beats a sweet women's toilet."

Haskell's delivery always left Zolly awed, and Joey Philly Friedman was looking across the room, managing to stare through the entrance glass with his eyes wide open. If he were looking at Haskell and the hack instead of at freedom, Joey Philly would be blinking. The black man from Newman Unit had given up trying to figure out what these white boys from Atwood were all about. That left the new crew member, who had joined them just that day and would be leaving just that night. The minute the hack saw her, he announced he did not intend to worry about a woman working out of sight with men on his shift.

Haskell said, "You ask Myra here, she'll tell you women like to go in a clean bowl. That right, Myra?"

She might be new on the job, but she was savvy enough to play along. "Absolutely. We don't like a stinky smell." She batted her eyes, maybe to flirt, maybe to make up for Joey Philly not doing his share.

Haskell said, "I'd appreciate your putting in for some more freshener and another gallon of the scented soap."

The hack said, "I'll order it for you, but now I want you all to finish up. Count is in half an hour. Unless you want to visit back after." That usually got to them.

The reception building's lobby was mostly used by people passing through, so it held little furniture. That made the floor easy to dust, mop, and buff. The evening cleaning crew only had to do the windows once a week. Three men could handle the downstairs easy, leaving the other two for the washroom, stairwell, and second-floor hall. During the week, the day crew did the visiting room. That accounted for why the evening crew always finished early except for

Fridays, Haskell notwithstanding. By the time Zolly finished the stairs, Haskell was halfway down the second-floor hall. They stopped to empty the wastebasket in the photocopy room. Then they sat down to rest before quitting for the day.

Zolly appreciated how Haskell did his bit. He paid Charlie Chicken a quarter a day to make his bed, a dollar a week to do his laundry, plus quarters for the washer and dryer, the same as Maggiano. When Haskell wanted extra food, he bought it from Charlie Chicken. Maybe Haskell and Maggiano conspired to fix the price, maybe they paid whatever Charlie Chicken asked when he made his rounds at night wearing fried chicken stuffed in his socks. What Zolly did not appreciate was Haskell himself. All he talked about was soap and money. The women were of more appeal. Some of them were D.C. hookers or tramps from the hills, but there were also city girls with smart eyes, and country girls who smelled of hay. You didn't have to do anything about it, but you could always look.

Haskell inhaled his cigarette deep enough to clear his sinuses. Probably due to his time in the women's john. "Never thought I'd smoke generics."

"I knew something was going to your head," Zolly said.

"I could buy Kools like your buddy, Sol, if the telephone calls didn't cost so much." Haskell removed a few quarters from his pocket and fingered them in mourning. "You'd think they'd raise the limit. Ten bucks a week in coin isn't nearly enough."

"It isn't like you're buying your own soap."

"I go through half a pack a day on the phone."

"I'm not surprised. Must take that much to clear away the smell." Even walking by the women's john bothered Zolly when Haskell was on the job.

Haskell was counting the coins in his palm. "I got enough to last till Friday if I limit myself to two calls a day. Anyone who's made the papers has to be careful."

"I don't see how you make it any easier calling on someone else's time. Although if you want, I got six o'clock. Hell, all I get is that my lawyer is too busy to take my calls, and my girlfriend always complains. Occasionally, if I get through to Gershom, he tells me he doesn't know about liquor laws or whatever else is coming down. He says the feds are behind the pressure. Like I need to owe him a couple hundred an hour to tell me that." Zolly never charged Haskell for the telephone time. Zolly was content to wait for payback. But he did turn away from the smoke, wondering whether Haskell's lungs were as dark as his face.

"You told me you had connections."

"The operator says, 'Will you accept a collect call?' They answer, 'No.' So I have to write."

"Watch what you write and watch what you say on the phone," Haskell said. They also called him Mr. Spook behind his back. Zolly had read about Haskell a year earlier, when he was convicted of insider trading. Zolly wouldn't have paid attention, if it hadn't been for all the zeros. Zolly moved away when Haskell put his hand on his shoulder. Zolly said, "You don't seem to worry."

"That's because I have a system. I don't talk stocks, I talk products. I don't talk commodities, I talk groceries. I want some IBM, I talk type-writers. I want to buy some pork-belly contracts, I ask what's the price of bacon. Every visit, we update our signals. It's a hassle, but it works." Haskell traded on tips, but he never analyzed his life.

"At least you have visitors. Not that I miss them. I don't need to see Faith's face to hear the bad news."

Haskell mashed his cigarette into the tin ashtray they kept on the shelf next to the copy paper, emptied the tray into his plastic bag, spit in the tray, and wiped it clean with his rag. "You don't know bad news until your broker tells you the market turned since your last call. That's why I buy so much telephone time."

Zolly said, "I didn't catch the close today." He was studying the market with Haskell. There had to be some trade-off for hanging around this guy. Solomon was hard to figure, handling cases for free. He might have been a hustler before, but he had managed to lose his maneuvers in the place you needed them most. Haskell was even harder to figure out. One minute he was a con, the next minute a clown. It was as though he was trying to keep everyone off-balance, the same as with his health-club looks and smoker's hack. Which made Zolly wonder about the quality of Haskell's lectures.

Haskell was standing now, slashing his mop back and forth on the floor as though marking the up-moves and downticks of his stocks. "Like I can scalp from in here, trade in and out every day to catch the swings of the market? The only short-term positions I can take are when I'm on the toilet. I never know if I'll get through to my broker. His switchboard doesn't take collect calls. Besides, the hacks might catch on if I call too often."

Zolly nodded in agreement, showing his sympathy and that, if he had his way, Haskell would have his own private line direct to his room. Could Haskell possibly buy his own bullshit? "You can have my turn whenever you want. I'm sorry the phones are a problem."

"Until a few months ago, it was the best year I ever had. The unit was only half full. I could call my broker with no distractions. We didn't even have a phone list. When your time was up, you just went to the end of the line and waited to start over. Or you could buy the turn of the guy after you and get half an hour, no problem. Then they changed the rules." Haskell looked like other men when they remembered sex.

"Maybe they were going after guys like you, spending half the day on the phone."

"I think they wanted an easier time with surveillance. That means you, too. Keep calling your friends to discuss your problems, you don't need to worry about the grand jury. They'll just play the recordings of your calls."

Zolly decided to take Solomon's advice and change the subject. He didn't like the image of Fallen listening in, and he didn't know if Haskell had friends in Chicago. "I wonder how long before he lets us go for the day."

"My guess is we won't have to come back after Count."

"Our chances get worse every time you carry on about the women's john."

Haskell patted the spray bottles clipped to his belt. "Hell, it really does smell nice in there."

Zolly said, "The way you use up the perfume, you should own some stock in Revlon."

Haskell said, "What makes you think I don't?"

THIRTEEN

NATRON WAS STANDING WHERE THE DOWNSTAIRS CORRIDORS met. The main hallway ran the width of the administration building and carried most of the traffic. When you were done with eating or reading, you went downstairs. If you wanted the chaplains' offices, the chapel, the movie theater, the gymnasium, or the door to the UNICOR courtyard, that was where they were. Even if you wanted arts and crafts, which was in the side hallway, you had to take the main downstairs hallway and turn at Natron's corner. This time of day, the main hallway was quiet. The workers from UNICOR had all gone through on their way to lunch, and their forty-five minutes to eat still had twenty minutes left. When they went back to work, they would go straight from the stairs to the outside doors. At lunchtime, the chaplains were standing inside the entrance to the dining room to show themselves to the inmates who never made it to pray. The movies were for weekends. Arts and crafts were at night. The gymnasium was closed during the summer because, when the weather got warm, you did your exercising outside. There were arguments on why that was. Maybe a shortage of hacks stopped them from watching the Yard and the gymnasium at the same time. Or it could just be that guards liked to be outside. Natron's theory was they were working on a suntan. They seemed proud to be rednecks.

The side hall remained deserted, unless a hack was making his rounds. That made it the best time for Gloria Blewer and her walkie, Tommy Givens, to do it, and they were counting on Natron to take care of any remaining risk. His vantage point provided a view in both directions, allowing him to alert Gloria if he saw a hack coming from the stairwell or the UNICOR courtyard, while also enabling him to look toward Gloria and her walkie while they went at it.

Natron liked to watch. He would also do anything if it paid enough. He was the man folks came to see to arrange things, but this was his first assignment from some walkies. He squeezed the roll of quarters that Gloria had given him to pin for them and give the alert if anyone approached. Ten dollars was punk change, but every roll felt good. On top of which, Natron liked the rush.

The first time Gloria asked, he'd put her off. She'd warned him that she might go elsewhere, but Natron was not bothered at the threat of losing easy money. Gloria didn't have a logical substitute for him. Natron's new job had him working with her in the chaplains' offices. He had Truman to thank for that. Not that the man had meant to do Natron a favor when he fired him from being the Atwood orderly, but working outside the unit was giving Natron the chance to make more money than ever before. In this instance, his job made it easier for Gloria to arrange things on the spot than if she had to go running for someone else every time she had the chance for sex.

For his own part, Natron rarely acted on impulse. Back in D.C., he would warn his crew that hunger led to mistakes. That last time, he had skipped lunch before walking into the bank, handing the note to the teller, and pointing the water pistol. Always make up your mind with a full belly, he wrote his crew in D.C. afterward. What did they call them, crimes of passion? He didn't believe in losing control. That just led to mistakes. The time at the bank, he was hungry. He was lucky he was able to get outside and throw his water pistol and his knife away, or it would have been armed robbery, and the police would have come down even harder. No point in even mentioning that part to the Jew lawyer.

Natron survived by watching where he walked. Not that he was indecisive. He had smelled that stink in other folks. Instead, Natron first reflected, then decided, and only then, finally, acted. Accordingly, he had considered Gloria's request before concluding that pinning for a couple of walkies was different from pimping. Too bad they couldn't go at it in the office, but the chaplains had their rules. That was the problem. This place had shit for rules. They let people walk around the Yard holding hands but told them don't stand still or touch anywhere else. What kind of rule was that? It gave a man a constant ache.

Gloria had her blue jeans and underwear pulled down. She was bent over, holding on to her ankles and groaning like the sound of a car trying to start while her walkie pumped her from the rear. That boy did look full of high octane. Natron fondled the roll of quarters, debating whether he should buy himself some sex or maybe just a joint. He was tired of getting gummed by that toothless bitch from Women's Unit. Five more minutes should be enough, unless Gloria and Tommy offered him another roll. He would stay all day if the quarters kept coming.

Natron was still thinking about how to spend the money when he saw Berns emerging from the stairwell. He was walking slowly enough to prove he had finished one of those Jew lunches. Natron meant to tell Charlie Chicken to charge Berns double from now on. No doubt, he had the coin for it. It was a wonder Berns had ever survived on the Street. The man needed someone to show him how to use a mop, following at Natron's heels that first day just to please Truman. That Berns sucked up so good that Truman would never send him away. Natron hoped Berns would turn in to the chaplains' offices instead of coming closer. If he got too near, Natron would have to choose between stopping Berns by argument or force and returning Gloria's money. Givens was moving faster than Berns. Maybe one of them would stop before Berns got this far. No, he had seen him and was coming right over to say hello.

"What's going on, my man?" Berns said, smiling and holding his hand palm up, either for a high five or to show he had nothing to sell.

Wishing he had his knife with him instead of leaving it under a dumpster by the bank in D.C., Natron considered telling Berns he was not his man, and not his boy, for that matter, before deciding to concentrate on having Berns turn back. "Where you going? There ain't nothing down this way."

Instead of the man having enough self-respect to take the hint, Berns said, "I need to talk to Reverend Weaver, but when I saw you, I thought I'd say hello."

The way he had his head cocked reminded Natron of the first time they'd met, in the Jew lawyer's room, Berns trying to add things up and see how he could make a dollar. Natron said, "Weaver is upstairs, where you ought to be. I'm just standing here. You know better than to talk so much." When Berns failed to turn around, Natron squeezed his fists, wishing he had a roll of coins in each of them to add to their force.

Berns said, "I think I'll walk down to arts and crafts, see what's going on."

"Since when you work with your hands? If you ever went down there, you already know they close before Count."

Instead of going back upstairs to see Weaver, get more food, take a walk outside, anything else a decent man would do, Berns shrugged and kept on coming, now even with Natron, moving to get by him and head down the side hall. While Natron was deciding how to stop him without having quarters fly all over, the man had already seen what there was to see.

"What a pretty sight," Berns said. Now they were both looking at Gloria and Tommy, still locked together, him bending over her with his arms around her chest as though a piece of food was caught in her throat. Natron wondered which would wear out first. Berns looked like he hoped it would be neither.

"You ought to learn when to mind your business," Natron said. "Now you know something you got to forget. Why don't you go outside like everyone else after lunch? Spend time in the fresh air, maybe find a walkie for yourself. 'Course, you an old man, maybe you have to spend some coin to get one." Natron decided that maybe, if he only did it occasionally, he wouldn't be considered a pimp. He opened his hand so that Berns could see the roll. "Take care of some young pussy's commissary, she take care of you. Or I could set you up with a bitch I know."

Berns reacted as though Natron had said something wrong. Word was, this Berns had a place in Chicago. Probably gots lots of women there, probably misses them a lot, probably upset he don't have one here. No matter, no reason for him to be angry at what Natron said, he just better forget about the pigs.

"Why would you say that? I don't talk to the hacks. Anyone who knows me will tell you I'm okay," Berns said, with the look of a man who spent lots of time facing a mirror, practicing his innocence.

"Don't know anyone who know you. Maybe I get in touch with some folk back in Chicago, find out who you are. Word is the police want you to talk on someone. That true? Some grand jury?" Natron couldn't remember who had mentioned it. The word about a man spread like molasses on stale bread. You ate it, but never liked the taste. He should lick around, see if the man himself tasted sour.

"Who the hell are you to ask me that?" Berns said.

Berns was like a punk avoiding why he came back empty after running the numbers all day. Asking instead of answering, like to make you forget your own question. Natron said, "I'm the man standing here helping some folk while you're the man sticking your nose where it don't belong. You so determined to go this way down my hall, I figure I can ask."

"I keep my mouth shut even though I can walk out whenever I'm ready to give it up."

"Do whatever you want with your grand jury. Just be sure you don't talk to any hack." Natron was so intent on his message, he failed to notice Officer Messer until he was even with the chaplains' offices. He put his hand on Berns's shoulder and spun him around. "Go stop that hack there."

"How am I going to do that?"

"Just talk to the man while I hush up Gloria and her walkie. Tell him anything, except about them. Don't you rat."

Berns was ready to protest again, even though Messer was still approaching. Messer walked around wearing creases so sharp they would cut if he got too close. And he always got too close.

"Good afternoon, Officer. How you doing today?" Natron stood straight as a post. He knew better than to back away. Messer was still thirty feet away, but Natron started talking early. He began to shuffle, figuring to give the man the fun he wanted.

Instead of saying hello, possibly even smiling at Natron's jive, Messer kept on coming. He pointed at Natron and Berns with an index finger that resembled a pistol barrel. "What are you two doing here? Everyone else is outside, you're inside."

Natron said, "Just chatting about things, Officer." Berns kept quiet, leaving it to Natron to do the work, as usual.

Messer stopped, nodding, as though to say, what do you have behind your backs, children? Then he started up again and walked around them. All three of them now faced Gloria and Givens.

———————

GLORIA STILL HAD HER PANTS AROUND HER ANKLES, UPSET AT the interruption.

Givens was closing himself up and had something caught in his zipper.

Messer was pleased to fill out the rest of his day handing out shots.

Natron was afraid Gloria might want her quarters back.

FOURTEEN

The ads covered her dining-room table. Faith leafed through the jobs she had circled the night before, resigned to another week of disappointment, which seemed as certain as Goldberg's smell. Sundays used to be for sleeping later than usual, then sometimes going to work after a breakfast of coffee, but sometimes brunch in bed first. Even if they went to the bar, they quit early. They would grab a bite to eat, and maybe take in a movie afterward if Zolly were in the mood. They lived week to week. They never planned for the future. They just assumed they had one.

These days, Sundays were the whole weekend. They started on Saturday nights, going to the newsstand to get the *Trib*, smelling the ink, spotting the jobs, writing to some on Sunday, and marking the rest to call on Monday. The help wanted section was a paper hiring hall that let you knock on the doors without the pain. The disappointment came when you went inside.

Faith used Sundays to answer the ads that had an address but no phone number. Her letters sat stamped and sealed on Zolly's desk, next to her unemployment check, which was already endorsed for deposit. What she got from the state was enough to cover the rent and some of the food, if you didn't mind carbohydrates. Faith paid the rest of her nut with odd jobs, but she was tired of traveling so far to get them. For that matter, she was tired, period. She learned early on that the Rush Street bars and restaurants connected her to Zolly. When she approached them, they did an about-face, afraid she might breathe their way. When Zolly got out, it might be different. They might not treat him the same way. Even starting over, they both might still have a chance. She highlighted the remaining ads that only listed names and phone numbers. She would call directly from the newspaper pages. By that Monday, she had reduced her list to five appointments, three maybes, and several dozen denials. She looked in the mirror. The months she had been on her own were numbered by the growing wrinkles in her face. Failing to get a job was bad enough, but not even getting an interview was like being lapped by younger, smarter, and prettier runners.

Even with the interviews and part-time work, she was spending too much time in the apartment. Everything reminded her of Zolly. The drawer in the living-room table that served as his desk still held his cigarettes, along with his favorite pen. His single malt was still in the side bar in the dining room, a reminder they'd once had money. She kept one of the sliding doors to the closet closed because his wardrobe still hung there, except for what she had sent to Lexington back when he still telephoned. Not that she blamed him for ending his calls. She had tried to talk about other things, but what was on her mind always came out as though she were under oath. When it got bad enough, Faith would go for a walk, but even outside she had to watch her way. If she turned right and walked a block to Rush, then spun to her left and walked a couple more blocks, she would pass by what used to be their bar. It had a different name now, and when she looked inside there were football uniforms hanging like trophies on the walls, with peanut shells carpeting the floor.

This day, studying the lines in her forehead reflected in the mirror, she decided to do as Zolly had insisted at the beginning. It was time to call on Goldberg. She selected a dress, not her favorite outfit but one with a high collar and lots of buttons stitched down the back from her neck to her waist. Hard to put on, hard to take off, and just right for a visit to Goldberg. She chose a pair of three-inch heels to tower over him. Finished, she tucked a twenty-dollar bill in her brassiere, leaving five singles plus bus fare in her purse, and took off for Goldberg's office. On her way there, she told herself her fears were overstated. Sure, Goldberg had hit on her on every occasion in the bar, but it was probably only showing off for his audience. There was always a crowd around. He was showing off, for sure. He moved too slow to be for real. By the time Faith reached Goldberg's building, walking all the way there in the sweltering summer air, her blouse stuck to her back, but with her luck, it would probably make Goldberg hot instead of turning him away. A bank with public washrooms was on the ground floor of the building. She washed off as much of her sweat as possible, put on fresh makeup because, after all, she did want a favor, and rode the elevator up to his office. She would begin with some talk of the old days and work her way up to now. All those years had to count for something. He couldn't turn down the favor.

The receptionist was straight out of a centerfold.

"I'm Faith Godwin."

The Playmate punched a three-digit number and waited until it answered. After announcing Faith, she held the earpiece of the phone to her ear and frowned, a question in her eyes.

"Tell him he knows me from Zolly's Place. I'm the girlfriend." It was just like Goldberg. In person or third person, he didn't remember her name.

The waiting room was furnished like the office of an expensive plastic surgeon, with tables covered with magazines whose readership were the "before" and whose illustrations supposedly were the "after." Faith began to read, losing herself on the beaches of Cannes and the streets of Montmartre. That was why she failed to hear the secretary leave at five o'clock. Ten minutes later, she did hear Goldberg's voice summoning her, loud enough to penetrate his closed door and her reverie.

The inner office held a show desk as wide as the biggest booth at Zolly's Place, adorned with telephone, calendar, empty mail trays, and a pen and pencil set. The area behind the desk was large enough for Goldberg to swivel as many times as it took to get dizzy, or with half a turn, he could stop at a back credenza wide enough to serve six hunched-over drinkers. But Goldberg's chair was empty. Behind the credenza, the windows overlooked downtown. From up this high, the Loop looked friendly.

"Faith. That's it, right? Good to see you, dear." Goldberg was at the far end of the office, which, like the reception room, looked straight out of a men's magazine. His couch wore the skin of an animal that had been stretched to fit four cushions, with enough leftover skin to cover the back and arms of the couch. The animal's head hung on the wall, its eyes looking down. An oil canvas by an artist who did sport scenes in paint thick enough to show he had sold lots of pictures hung next to the head. "Come over here. We have a lot to catch up on." Goldberg made an effort to wave.

"I'm sorry I dropped in without calling. I appreciate your seeing me." She decided not to mention the day he'd avoided her on the street. Instead, she chose a chair five feet away.

"By me." Goldberg raised his eyebrows, daring her to disagree.

Faith aimed for the farthest corner of the couch, remembering Goldberg's pats and his smell from the days in the bar. He was eating more garlic these days. "I don't know where to begin," she said.

"Start wherever you want." He patted the cushion next to him. "We're old friends."

Faith stayed where she was. "I don't know how much you know. You were there the night they shut us down, but I haven't spoken to you since. You must have missed my messages."

"I didn't know." He was sliding closer.

"They covered our floor with peanuts," she said. "We used to buff it every week."

"You were always my favorite," he said.

"I looked through the window when I walked by our old bar. The booth is gone. It was Zolly's favorite."

"I always found it hard to move around." Goldberg was still sliding.

"Zolly hasn't been able to reach you, either," she said.

"I got a couple letters. My receptionist won't take collect calls. No matter how many times I tell her, she turns them all away." He was a snail, inching toward her on the couch.

"Our bank account is frozen for the taxes. I don't have enough money to live on. Zolly says it's too late to save the bar, but we're hoping you might help me get a job. Nothing fancy, just so I can support myself." She was out of breath when she finished her speech but tried not to inhale, as Goldberg was now up against her.

"We don't want you to suffer. Neither one of you." He was moving his hand on her shoulder, squeezing the back of her neck to console her, sliding his hand down to the buttons. His face twisted in concentration as he fumbled between her back and the animal's skin.

His momentum took her breath away. She tried to keep her composure and use the right words. "You're Zolly's friend. He's known you twenty years. I thought that would count for something."

"If you would bend over and cooperate, that would count for something." Grunting with the effort, he reached across with his other hand and placed it behind her neck, pulling her head forward toward his lap. She lost two buttons as she jerked away and ran out of the room, working on how to tell Zolly.

FIFTEEN

AFTER DINNER THE FOLLOWING FRIDAY, WHILE THE SUN WAS still high above the cyclone fence, and as the walkies paraded around the park, Haskell led Zolly and Joey Philly to pray. They left their jobs early to do it. On Friday evenings after dinner, the crew had to dust, clean, mop, and buff the visiting room in addition to their regular chores. There was work enough for all five of them. The warden insisted that the place look right for the weekend visitors. Friday evenings, the hack even sniffed. Nevertheless, it didn't trouble Haskell to abandon his spray bottle early. Announcing they had to get to services on time, he led the charge for shul. The first few times, Zolly questioned Haskell about leaving the other two guys to do all the work on their own.

Haskell said, "You worried what the goyim will think? Or you got a conscience, suddenly? Like you don't play every angle for all it's worth?" That was Haskell, attributing his own traits to the world at large. That was how most men disregarded their virtues and excused their sins.

"These are our friends. It's not like stiffing a stranger," Zolly said.

"You think a guy's a friend just because you know him. That's a guarantee of disappointment. It's almost as bad as thinking you know a guy just because he's a friend."

While philosophizing, Haskell managed to abandon their detail earlier every week, even though sundown grew later as the spring progressed. Zolly never questioned him again. Ultimately, he reached the point where he could follow him without looking back. He persuaded himself that he had a lot to learn from Haskell. Not just the details on how the market worked. Haskell managed to be a success at everything he did. He was one of the few guys who managed to hold things together while he did his time. But pleasing him was not the only reason Zolly went to services. He participated for the same down-to-earth reasons that had once led him to link up with Goldberg. Introductions to men and women from all over the institution could only help his future moves. Zolly worked the shul the way he used to work his bar.

Haskell led the flight past the inner offices to the room at the rear of the chaplains' suite. Friday nights, the Muslims held their services at the chapel across the hall. A swarm of Gentile inmates buzzed around the anteroom, flying in and out of Weaver's office as though he were passing out sweets. That explained why he failed to glance at the three of them as they flew by. When Weaver pulled weekend duty, the Jews ran their shul unscreened. Its door had the usual Lexington window, allowing a view inside to a room with a lectern facing four rows of eight chairs each. The wall behind the lectern was hollowed across by windows facing a courtyard surrounded by buildings. In other times and places, the cabinet next to the lectern would have been an ark holding the Torah. Here, the cabinet held prayer books that the chaplains locked away the rest of the week. The bookcases lining the other walls were empty. The table across from the door was big enough to hold union pamphlets, placards, and sign-up sheets, reminding Zolly of when he'd worked as a kid and had to pay dues when he entered the hiring hall.

Services would start in ten minutes. Including the three of them, there were about twenty men and women spread out among the seats. Most of the chairs were in sight through the outside windows, which provided a view to the hack with binoculars in the building across the way. That arrangement gave Weaver the excuse to leave them alone. But the architect had never met their leader. Anxious to pump up attendance, Gabby arrived early every weekend to arrange the lectern and cabinet so that they blocked several chairs from view.

Gabby spread his arms open when he saw them, nodding at Haskell and Joey Philly and making a big deal of Zolly. "Good Shabbat, great to see you." Besides being greeter on the kosher line and congregation president, Gabby was also Zolly's employment coach. "We wondered when you'd get here. We already have a minyan, but it wouldn't be the same without you."

While Haskell and Joey Philly headed for the far end of the room, Zolly said, "I wouldn't miss it for the world. Who's leading?" Although he knew the answer, he hoped for a surprise.

Gabby nodded toward Adlai Sachar, the druggist from Detroit who always skipped the English. Adlai was working at his prayer book, practicing the important parts. He didn't understand the Hebrew, but he could pronounce the words as he raced through the prayers. "With Adlai leading, we'll get done in no time flat."

"Did Rosie bring the cake?" Zolly asked.

"Buddy says she's on the way. She was putting the icing on when he left."

"I'm surprised he didn't stay to lick the pot. Of course, she probably gave his tongue a workout already."

Zolly considered dessert a fair trade for thirty minutes of boredom. Every Friday evening, the kosher kitchen made a treat. Some nights it was cookies, either oatmeal or chocolate chip. Other nights, Rosie managed to bake a cake. It could be angel's food; it could be devil's food; Rosie went both ways. They kept these specials off the line. Everyone agreed there was no way the Italians were going to get in on this one. "They'll probably send some more of that grape juice, too. You would think they'd make it a different flavor every now and then."

Betsy Tobias, who had first dibs on the seats that were blocked from view, and who needed two chairs sitting down and help getting up, chose to offer her opinion with her hand on Reuben Lewis's hip. The loose part of her other arm jiggled from the elbow as she gestured like a queen. "You boys, always thinking about the goodies, forgetting why we're here. You need to remember that pleasure comes with patience."

Zolly had a habit of clearing his throat at the sight of the younger couples walking about, holding hands and pressed together. If Haskell were around, he would remind Zolly who he was. "Forget about a walkie. You may think young, but you're just an old fart like me. We get women on the Street because of what we have, but here we all start at zero."

Zolly thought Haskell was off base in giving advice on the world at large. Just because he was an expert on stocks didn't mean he knew about life. Like most rich guys, he thought he had all the answers. If he wanted to ignore the women, he could. Zolly intended to enjoy. It was high school all over again. He continued to clear his throat to relieve the stress, but there was no need to with Betsy and Reuben.

Before Zolly could work Betsy's patience and jiggly elbow into the same sentence, Gabby said, "We're all pleased to greet a new arrival. This is Darla Fine." He gestured toward the woman at his side as though introducing a new car to the press. Gabby loved introductions. They were his next favorite, after announcements. This time it was more of an introduction-announcement, allowing him to exploit both skills, so he said it loud enough for the congregants by the refreshment table in back to hear.

Zolly agreed with Gabby. Darla had hair the color of a Minnesota shiksa and cheeks that showed embarrassment. He thought she glowed, before deciding it must be the overhead lights burnishing her skin as though they, too, were glad to see her. Haskell and Joey Philly, in the next row over, were also paying attention. Haskell stared at Darla's chest, perhaps for the latest tips. Darla ignored them, speaking only to Zolly. "They told me to see someone named Gloria about getting a loan. No one told me we had services Friday nights."

So, it was "we," indeed. Despite what Haskell said, Zolly decided to make the effort. "You came to the right place. You'll feel right at home." His words tasted like B-movie dialogue. "The Inmate Welfare Fund will lend you twenty-five bucks to tide you over. When you get money sent in from home, or you earn some at your job, you are required to pay it back. Just what you borrowed. They don't charge interest." He was droning like an accountant when he wanted to hum like a lover.

"They gave me a toothbrush and paste. I could use some cosmetics, but I'm not able to shop. They didn't tell me to bring any money. I'm dressed like an army recruit, but this is all I have." She showed a smile that proved she could do without brushing her teeth for weeks, too, before it might matter, and that makeup would spoil the scene.

Haskell walked over next to them, having surrendered his favorite chair near the place for cake. "You look just fine, Miss Fine. I'm Haskell Goldman. If the Welfare Fund gives you any problems, I can help you get a loan. Or anything else you need." He shoved in between Zolly and Darla.

"Thanks, but my husband will send me some money along with my clothes."

Zolly put his hand on Haskell's shoulder and moved around him. "That must be hard, leaving a husband behind."

"I have a little girl. I miss her already."

Haskell said, "I'd be glad to give you company."

Darla shrugged, giving him the benefit of the doubt. "They explained about walkies in Women's Unit. I appreciate the offer."

"There are all kinds of ways I could do you some good."

"Such as?"

Although he stood shoulder to shoulder with Haskell, Zolly wondered if Darla had forgotten he was there.

"Lots of ways," Haskell said. "I could show you around. Tell you what to watch out for, where to get things. Like that."

"What could you help me get?" she asked. Zolly tried to think of how to tell her that Haskell spent too much time on the phone to know any sources.

"Whatever you need."

"Can you help me get out of here?"

"It all depends what you're here for," Haskell said, pronouncing his words as though articulation made them special. "I could talk to my lawyer."

She looked down at her hands, which were clasped as though they held her sentence and she were reading it aloud. "I had a lot of pain after my daughter was born. One thing led to another."

"It usually does," Haskell said.

This was the guy who was always saying forget it, considering their age and all. The guy who only talked stocks and smells. Zolly debated telling Haskell he was calling in his IOUs for all his telephone favors, before realizing he hadn't kept count. What was the problem here? Some blonde he never saw before. This was exactly what he avoided on the Street. He was prepared to tell Haskell he could have her and to tell Darla good riddance when he heard the rapping.

Gabby rapped his knuckles on the lectern. "Before services, let's have a quick business meeting." That surprised Zolly, because Gabby was supposed to wait another couple of weeks, when Zolly would be in a good position to make his move.

Reuben Lewis asked what kind of business. Betsy Tobias proved she could keep her hands still and her mouth shut.

"We need to get behind one of ours to replace Gloria in the chaplains' offices," Gabby said. After too many shots, she had been transferred to Alderson, a higher-security, all-female prison, leaving the office shorthanded.

"What opening?" Adlai always had his head in a book, which explained why he never knew what was happening. If he had been more alert on the Street, he would never have filled prescriptions allegedly written the day before by a doctor whose obituary was three years old.

Gabby said, "They need a new clerk for the Welfare Fund. I say it's our turn. We should maintain a unified front. That's why I invited everyone here."

By now, all the chairs were full. Several latecomers leaned where the cake would be if Rosie ever arrived, including some men Zolly had never seen before who were standing in the far corner, wearing faces straight from "wanted" posters. Solomon gave Zolly a thumbs-up sign while nodding at the strangers. He believed in the Chicago credo, "Vote early and vote often."

Zolly acted innocent. "Do you have anyone in particular in mind?" If it had to be voted on now, he wanted to move things along. He had been working for a month for the job.

"We need to agree on our man. I think it should be you. Anyone else can make a nomination before we vote. Whoever wins, we make it unanimous. We go to Weaver before he picks someone else. We tell him it's our turn."

"Weaver? I thought Burgess was head chaplain," Adlai said.

"Weaver runs the Welfare Fund. Burgess would just as soon close it down."

"Why should they pick one of us?" Here was Betsy Tobias, the pragmatist. Too bad she failed to see the connection between her food and her fat. She took her hands off Reuben in order to stall the vote. "If you think there should be a quota, shouldn't they pick a woman?"

"The main thing we have going for us is religion. We have three clerks; we have three major faiths, Catholic, Protestant, and Jewish. One of each of them should be in the office. The main chapel clerk, Judy, she's Catholic and a woman. That's two for one, so we got you covered, Betsy." Gabby looked pleased with his closing argument.

"They've got Natron on cleanup. I hear he's a Baptist, and I know he's black, so he gives them another two for one, in case there's any liberals. That leaves Jewish, as in Berns."

"I don't know how you figure," Adlai said. "You could just as well say the three major religions are Catholic, Protestant, and Muslim. According to my count, there are a lot more Muslims than Jews."

"Would you like me to leave the room?" Zolly asked. "I wouldn't want you to hold back on my account. Why don't you nominate the Ku Klux Klan, while you're at it?"

Adlai removed his glasses, patted his yarmulke, and kissed his siddur. "You don't have to take it personal."

"You want to be fair, why don't you vote for Betsy Tobias?" Zolly asked.

Betsy kept her hands off her walkie's thigh. "I don't have the time. If you want the job, Zolly, you got my vote. Reuben's, too." She raised his hand.

"The Muslims may have more, but Gloria was one and she struck out," Gabby said. "Now it's our turn." He slapped his hand on the lectern to wake up his jury. "Besides, Terman will be here Monday. I can ask him to intervene."

Terman was the rabbi from the temple in town. Not that he presided there. According to Gabby, "presided" more accurately described the car dealer who served as its president. "Worked" was the word for Terman. He had a contract to visit the Institution four weekdays a month. Weekends were for his own temple's services and Sunday school. Even during the week, Terman's visits were shorter than a Torah reading. He would meet with one of the chaplains, speak briefly with any Jewish inmate who had lined up an interview in advance, and then be gone. As Gabby explained in detail to anyone who would listen, it was the same as everywhere else. Terman's temple wrestled with big shots and short money. He visited sick congregants, officiated at funerals, counseled couples, and managed his obligations. The Jews in jail were lucky they got any time at all.

"You think we should go for it this Monday, instead of waiting?" Zolly had a couple more weeks before his ninety days were done.

"If we're going to wait, why am I here?" Solomon asked.

"Nice to see you, whatever the reason," Haskell said. "I hope you enjoy the party." He winked at Joey Philly and received a chorus of blinking in return.

Zolly said, "I'm supposed to work on the cleaning detail another couple weeks. I thought this could wait." He directed his explanation to the group but kept his eyes on Gabriel Goldstein.

"I want to party, I can go to commissary and entertain my friends in my room," Solomon said. "I'm asking why I'm here."

"I think we'd better act now. Weaver won't want to wait. Besides, I want Terman to help, and I'm not sure how much longer we'll have him. From what I hear," Gabby said, referring to his cousins who attended Terman's temple and supplied him with his gossip, "some of the people in his temple don't think that he should see us. You know, they're Reform. They want to get along."

There was the tapping again. This time, it was Adlai, insisting that a report on Terman and the vote could wait until after they prayed.

Solomon and his friends started to shuffle about. They hadn't expected a full night at this. Betsy and Reuben remained where they were, hidden from the outside windows and the small glass pane in the door. Haskell remained next to Darla. Adlai began his usual droning. There were periodic murmurs as the inmates joined in response.

Anticipating the vote, still campaigning for the job, Zolly was louder than the rest. He thought back to when he was a kid and he took his Hebrew lessons, before David turned rat.

"You do this for your grandpa."

"I don't see why I have to, just because you did."

"It ain't nothing to me, but I'm not going to piss off the old man." David had had that weekend look about him, ready to drop the subject and watch TV.

"All my friends are outside playing. You never go to services."

David had turned away from the game, wrinkling the couch in the process. He put his beer down, careful to place it on the newspaper instead of the shag. "Do as I say until your bar mitzvah. After you're a man, you don't ever have to open a book again."

Forty years later, the book open, Zolly was trying to keep up with Adlai. He wondered how Grandpa Sam would feel if he could see him now. He'd probably be glad, after all, that David had changed their name. When Zolly participated, the services went faster, but they were also harder. Even in English, every paragraph was a challenge. It was like reading the Illinois Dram Shop Act on the liability of bars for accidents after the drunks left the bar. However, he did want the job. As he prayed, he glanced from the pages to see the impression he made on the congregation at large. That was how he happened to notice, when they stood at the end of the service as Adlai recited his chants, that Betsy and Reuben stayed seated. The open book above Reuben's thighs rocked in rhythm with each move of Betsy's hidden hand.

SIXTEEN

MAGGIANO WOULDN'T STOP. THAT WAS THE TROUBLE WITH asking for advice. When you didn't ask, most people swallowed their opinions. Let them know you wanted it, they became your partner. Zolly decided to take it all in. If he let Maggiano ramble, he might finally get an answer.

"Another thing," Maggiano said. "People see you going in there so often, they begin to wonder."

"You think I should worry? I figure the chaplain can handle it."

Maggiano continued writing. After a couple more lines, he said, "People get concerned." He reached for another ballpoint.

"You think he'll keep a hard-on?"

"Guys start to wonder, next thing, they worry."

"I'm not alone," Zolly said.

"So, you're a team. You could be giving someone up together. You gotta talk in the open. You want to visit Truman in the hallway, or he stops by to see us, okay. Cookies and tea with a hack in private is different." Maggiano continued working on his letters. "You shouldn't go out of your way to make people concerned."

Zolly understood Maggiano's attitude. Hell, he shared it. He shouldn't have to share the story of David to prove he was okay. "If we're such buddies, why is he so pissed?" The last two days, when they'd passed in the hall, Truman hadn't broken stride, which was unfair. It wasn't Zolly's fault Truman had been on vacation when the job had opened.

"We're talking how it looks," Maggiano said.

"It's a study group. We don't talk about the joint."

"How would people know that?"

"If they bothered to read the bulletin board, they'd know what's going on. If not, the door is always open."

"What's in it for you?" Maggiano frowned at his letters, his words an afterthought.

Zolly needed to get the conversation back to the meeting he was about to have. "I asked Solomon before I signed up."

"He say a psychology class would be better than the right pills twice a day?"

"He says guys think it will help them get paroled."

"You need to get convicted first." Maggiano signed his name with extra force and started the next letter.

"Solomon says classes don't mean a damn for parole."

"Then what are they good for?"

"A hack earns extra money if he leads a self-improvement class."

Maggiano looked up, flexing his fingers as usual. "I get it, you want to help Truman earn more bread. That's why we have all those Anonymous clubs. AA, GA, NA. They ever run out of letters?"

When Maggiano returned to writing full-time, Zolly reexamined his reasons. Solomon had given him the idea when he'd first arrived at Lexington. It would do him no harm if Truman became a friend. At first, their group met on Saturday mornings for an hour, before Truman changed the sessions to afternoons in order to accommodate Zolly. Eight or nine of them sat around the table at the front of Truman's office, near an open door. Any inmate walking by could hear them talk philosophy. It made sense, back then. He decided to ask again. "You think I should offer to give the job back?"

"Sure, if he's such a good friend," Maggiano said.

———————

Whenever they were one-on-one, Zolly let Truman do the talking. Zolly was that way with everyone, planning his words while the other man babbled. This time, it was Truman silent and Zolly talking, his words gushing out before he had a chance to cap them. "I wasn't trying to go around you. You were on vacation. When I told Chaplain Weaver I needed to finish my ninety days on the captain's detail, he said he could get me off sooner. When I said you would have to okay it, he promised you wouldn't mind."

Truman hadn't changed his expression, but his voice rose. "Did you consider coming to me directly? Or do you let Weaver do my talking?" He pointed at the directory, then pushed down on his desk. "Do you think he forgot my number? I've been back two days, but my telephone hasn't rung." His fingers pressed and relaxed, in rhythm with each word. "I was going to set you up in supply, make sure we always had first call on wax." The inspectors visited every week before

Zolly went to work, with the warden leading the charge as he poked at the beds with his yardstick, fingered for dust, chose which lockers to move to see the color beneath, and scraped for rust in the showers. The unit manager and inspection hacks scurried behind the warden, taking notes. Truman and the Atwood hack followed at the rear as they received the praise or the blame. Every inspection Thursday, the building smelled from the wax Charlie Chicken stole. Truman wanted a more secure source of supply in case Charlie Chicken were trapped crossing enemy lines.

"I wasn't trying to get around you," Zolly said. "The chaplains needed help."

"I'm just your counselor. I wouldn't want you to go out of your way to help me."

Zolly could now be talking to a stranger. He tried a reintroduction. "I'd do anything you wanted. If I knew you were against it, I would have turned down the job. You were away. I had no idea." He was speaking on impulse, yet it sounded rehearsed. He should have practiced innocence with Maggiano.

"You like the chaplain so much, maybe you should sleep over there," Truman said.

It was time to follow Maggiano's advice and whisper, "I didn't mean to work around you. I'll tell the chaplain I don't want the job." It was a risk worth taking to salvage his relationship with Truman. Zolly hoped Truman wouldn't get into a pissing contest with the chaplain.

Truman stopped rocking. He looked over at his bookcase. There was a gap on the top shelf, probably from the book on his desk. Then he turned his attention to Zolly and waved off the apology. "I hope you'll be happy in the chaplains' offices."

"I wasn't aiming to get happy. I'll transfer out of the job, if you say."

"I already said okay. And I know you like to pray. After all, that's why we changed the schedule of our classes." Truman plucked a paper from the pile on his desk. "This is this week's lesson plan. You can attend after Sabbath services, tell us what you learned." During their weekly discussions, Truman hadn't hidden what he thought of religion. Zolly hadn't read all the spines of Truman's books, but he was sure that none was a Bible. Truman leaned forward. "You're my first contempt-of-court charge. Let's play cards. I'll deal." Truman picked up an imaginary deck and pantomimed the motions. "I'll bet you're a man of principle." He seemed serious, but you never knew. He hid his hand like a poker player whose opening bid was low to deceive the suckers.

Zolly decided to play it safe. "I'm not sure what you mean by 'principle.'"

Truman wagged his forefinger as though Zolly hadn't anted up. "Most men get here because of their greed. Some call it their addiction." He paused, ready to debate the distinction if Zolly insisted. "But you're here by choice. There's no other explanation. You must be here on principle."

Zolly remained uncertain how to react. Truman was always ready to pounce if you answered wrong. "I don't know about principle."

"I know your file. You're here because of some code you live by. That's principle."

"There might be other reasons."

"Sure. You could be afraid of what will happen if you talk. Maybe someone sends money to your commissary account or supports your family. The money might stop. Threats or rewards. I don't like those choices. If you're not seeing my bet, I get to read your hand how I want. I've decided it's principle."

While Truman raked in his imaginary chips, Zolly considered the possibility. Principle was what philosophers talked about while they avoided life. So why was he here, after all? Friendship with Goldberg? Not anymore. Loyalty? That should work both ways. Okay, it was because of the decision he'd made long ago, when David was killed. Zolly never saw himself in the car. He saw what happened after, when he and Becky had to move away. He could handle being a Jew. What he couldn't handle was being David. "I'd like to start reading myself." He looked at Truman's books.

"Don't change the game." Truman pushed above the top of his desk. "Even you admit you need something outside yourself to guide you. That's why you pray, right?"

Zolly studied the shelves again. "None of your books are about religion. In our psychology class, what do you say? 'We have a sickness of the soul.' Isn't that what the chaplains are for?"

Truman lifted the book he had been reading and splayed it on his desk, laying down his hand. "There's a difference between religion and spirituality." He liked to carry on about philosophy, politics, religion, and other topics people with good sense avoided. The man should have gone to college and got it out of his system.

"You want us to see with our heads instead of our hearts," Zolly said.

"Read this book, for starters. This French guy writes about a man who rejected God for intellect." The dust from the volume floated in the air, ready to infect any true believer. While Truman watched, Zolly leafed through the book about a man running from religion. Truman probably kept it as an antidote.

Zolly said, "What should I believe in? I've lost everything without being convicted of any crime." For the first time, he recognized it hadn't begun with the bar. His losses had started with David. Zolly had been on a losing streak ever since. The bar on Howard, his move to Rush Street, the life he had shared with Faith—they were all sucker bets that had led to bigger losses.

"That doesn't mean you're innocent," Truman said. "You hang with that new girl whenever your friend Haskell isn't there. But your file says you have a woman waiting back home. Innocent? You get to decide that on your own. What I'm asking is whether your heart's pure. Are you really a true believer?"

Zolly made fewer phone calls home these days. When Faith asked about it, he said it was the cost. He had to close his eyes to remember what she looked like. She was now a sputtering spark, while he could see Darla's glow from across the Yard. He spoke down to Truman's book. "All I need to do is agree to talk. But I'm still going to do the right thing."

Truman rose out of his chair. "Then you do live by a code greater than yourself."

———

WHEN ZOLLY RETURNED TO REPORT ON HIS VISIT WITH Truman, Maggiano was on his bed, still writing. Zolly wondered if he was mentioned in any of the letters. And if he was, whether by name, number, or religion. "It went okay," Zolly said. "I took your advice and apologized. He said I could keep the job. Then he talks to me about prayer and starts philosophizing. Hell, he even brought up Darla."

Maggiano traveled the pen along his fingers, manipulating it from his thumb to the end of his hand and then back again, finger to finger, until it returned to a proper position. "Did he mention your friend Haskell?"

"In passing. What he doesn't know is that Haskell acts like I'm not even in the game, leading Darla on. Sure, he can get her some drugs, he tells her. But he actually has a better chance of getting her Chanel No. 5, assuming he can spare some from the women's john."

Maggiano put the pen down and rubbed his hands together. "You never know. He does work in the visiting room."

"So did I. That doesn't mean there's drugs under the cushions, or that I could have carried them out."

"You have an even better chance now. Ask your friend Natron. But be sure your friend Truman doesn't overhear that conversation."

"Natron's been nothing but trouble. Haskell let me down. Truman's just a hack I use."

"You've done a great job so far. What else has he done for you?"

"He made me a fireman. I have charge of this end of the floor." Zolly hesitated at the question on Maggiano's face. "I do think he wants to take care of me."

Maggiano said, "They wanted to transfer me to Renaissance in case I get sick again. Said guys with heart trouble should be near the hospital."

"After all our planning for my talk with Truman, it wasn't about the job," Zolly said. "He started with what he's reading, why I'm here, like that." Zolly frowned. Hacks lived in a different world.

Maggiano again studied the pen between his thumb and fingers, seeing how his words would look before he said them. "He gets into a man, wants to live inside us for a while. When I got here, I would have laid money he never saw an Italian before. These days, he could have been born in Brooklyn and graduated from Erasmus." He studied Zolly, the pen and paper finally forgotten. "But we can't let any of that matter. Remember what you have yet to learn. The difference between us and Truman is we went to different schools."

SEVENTEEN

The end of June gave Zolly another reason to get to work early. Even on weekends, he was up and out before the sun rose high. Maggiano had managed to hustle some fans at the start of the summer. For a while, their room had cooled from well-done to medium, but now they sweltered no matter what. Maggiano said you got used to it, but all he did all day was sit on his bed writing letters and scratching his ass. You could do that in comfort with the fan blowing right on you, but try moving around in this heat. The chaplains' office space was air-conditioned, which was why Zolly headed for work before the sweat settled on him like dew on dead meat. At seven in the morning, Zolly was already leaving for breakfast when Truman entered the room. He stood silent inside the doorway, moving his gaze back and forth several times from Zolly, dressed for action, to Maggiano, still in his shorts and T-shirt. Truman liked to wait until you took notice. Sometimes he never said a word and would depart in silence, leaving you wondering. This time, he had something he needed to say.

"Good morning, Mr. Maggiano. Hope I didn't disturb you."

Maggiano grunted and reached over to pull on pants that were creased sideways from being draped overnight across his locker door. Charlie Chicken had been there the previous day to do the floors, but this was Thursday, and Charlie only ironed on weekends. "No problem, Mr. T, I was about to head for chow." Maggiano struggled as he cinched his belt.

"You might want to try the diet line a few weeks. A change of pace would do you good." Truman turned back to Zolly. "Glad you're dressed. You've got visitors."

Zolly waited for Truman to explain how he had visitors at this very moment, before breakfast, on a workday when the visiting room was closed, when he had no family, when he and Faith were on the outs and, having no more business, he had no more business associates. He had never even bothered filling out a visitors list.

"According to control, they're lawyers," Truman said.

The last time Zolly had called, all Gershom wanted to know was when he would get another payment. He timed the calls to the second for his invoices and added on the telephone charges. Zolly doubted Gershom would come all this way to grab his commissary account. Gershom was a realist. He didn't expect payment, he just liked to keep track. "I'm not expecting a lawyer," Zolly said.

"You may not be expecting, but you're getting. My guess is they're from the U.S. Attorney's Office. Probably some of the prosecutors from your file. Control called me to take you over. Maybe they're doing a survey on federal prisons. Or they could want to see if you've dried out." Truman looked at Maggiano, including him in the joke.

"Do I have to talk to them?"

"You have to see them. Talking is something else. For one thing, you can demand to have your lawyer present."

"No way he'd come down here. I can't even afford to have him meet them in their offices." Zolly said the last part to himself.

Truman put his hand on Zolly's shoulder. "I may just be a glorified guard, but in here, what I say goes. Whenever you say the word, we'll end it."

The Yard held no echo of David's car exploding, but yesterday's dust still hung in the air. Zolly didn't feel like breathing, anyway. He tried to figure out whether the visit had anything to do with his recent call to Faith. There was no way to tell whether the hacks had listened to their conversation or passed it on to the feds. The BOP and the U.S. Attorney were both in the Department of Justice, but Solomon said it was like the major leagues. The rich guys who owned baseball might be sergeants at arms, but their teams were at civil war.

"Why? I've been here for months."

Truman shrugged. "Who knows? Maybe they had some free time, wanted to see Lexington in the heat. It could be they had to work other files here before yours." They had reached the Women's Courtyard. Truman had Zolly's elbow, encouraging him to keep up. "Maybe they came because it has been months since you got here. They don't send a man like you here and then forget all about him. The whole idea is to remember." There was no way details of the case would have descended to Truman's level, but he was experienced enough to make a good guess.

As they went through the archway, Zolly recalled their last class. Truman had talked about the light at the end of the tunnel. It sounded nice, but if you thought about it, lights and tunnels didn't do you much good in getting out of a jam. What Zolly saw in his own tunnel was federal lawyers shining a light in his eyes. The problem was, the feds thought he could give them something, but he knew nothing about the business Goldberg had with Civiletti, O'Rourke, or anyone else who approached their booth. He could tell the feds what Goldberg liked to eat. Namely, everything. Or how Civiletti got hoarse when Walter Payton raced down the field. Even from a distance, he could see it pissed Goldberg off when they were talking business and Civiletti was watching the Bears on TV. But whenever they were together, unless Zolly had a problem of his own, they said, "Zolly, would you scram, we got business we got to do."

Assuming he wanted to walk out of Lexington bad enough to talk, what could he tell them? How long Goldberg and his crew had had customers? What day of the week they dropped by? Who they saw? How much time they spent? How much money they spent? The last part was easy. It was all on the cuff. When you got right down to it, they were just connections who charged him for favors, plus they wanted a place to meet and eat for free. How could that help the feds? It wasn't likely that Goldberg and the boys were worried about his talking. Not when they'd refused his calls and let him lose his bar. And the way things had gone with Faith proved it even better. It must mean they figured he had nothing on them, or were counting on him not to talk, no matter what. Maybe they were showing their muscle. Or it could be they were challenging him to prove he was different from David. Okay, the feds thought he had something to say, and Goldberg had given him lots of reasons to do it. The question was, do you get to rat when your shorts shrink and squeeze your balls?

They were in the courtyard, approaching the administration building. "Don't worry, it will be okay," Truman said. He patted Zolly on the shoulder, his touch reminding Zolly of the time when David took him to the zoo, when he was too young to know the depth of moats or the length of the leap of lions. That distant day when Zolly had pushed his way between David's legs. He could feel his father's hand and hear him say, "You're safe with me." At least David didn't take Zolly with him in the car eight years later. Zolly wondered how long the feel of Truman's hand would weigh upon his shoulder.

Truman said, "Remember, you can leave whenever you want."

The visiting room was large enough to hold more than a hundred inmates with visitors. Even so, some Sundays there was only standing room. But this Thursday morning, at the end of June, Zolly could see the scratched leather on every chair, and that the floor was still scuffed from that week's visitors. A few of the seats were bleeding stuffing from some kid's pencil wounds. There were tracks on the tables to mark where the toy trucks had collided. Haskell and his crew wouldn't cover up the damage until Friday.

There were two of them, sitting at either end of a row of three butcher-block chairs. The middle chair was empty for Zolly. The visitors had their legs crossed, ready to take whatever time it took. Fallen wore the same kind of suit as before. He must have had one for each day hanging in his closet. His shirt was clean, unless the necktie with the diagonal stripes was hiding some stains. He wore the same kind of shoes as the rabbi at Becky's funeral, laces and dots across the toes. If this guy ever went into private practice, he could model at Marshall Field on the side. The other fed who had hovered in the grand jury hallway with crumbs on his coat was there, as well.

"Have a seat," Fallen said, nodding at the middle chair, every bit the maître d', Zolly every bite the meal. "It's been a while, thought we'd drop in and see how you're doing."

"You could have asked my lawyer."

Fallen shrugged. "Mr. Gershom claims he doesn't hear from you. Do you owe him any money?"

Crumbs, whose name turned out to be Cully, was sipping a soda from the machine. He said, "Berns, I hope this doesn't turn out to be a waste of time. If we had come last month, we could have seen the Derby. Now, we count on you to make the trip worthwhile."

"This wasn't my invitation," Zolly said.

Cully said, "The grand jury's term is going to end."

"We can always get an extension," Fallen said.

"The judge won't extend it indefinitely. At best, we might go out a year from August." Cully noticed Zolly again. "How does a year from August sound to you?"

"I can take whatever you have to give."

Fallen said, "That might not be necessary." He opened his briefcase and reviewed a yellow legal pad full of notes. Lawyers needed to write it down to make it real. "Let's start with how often they came."

"We already know that. Once a week. Like the NFL," Cully said.

Fallen turned sideways to face Cully. "That's why I'm starting with an easy question. We'll see if Berns answers truthfully about what we already know. Then I'll move on to what we don't know, at least all we want to, such as who would come to see them, how regularly, how long his friends would stay, like that."

"And what he knows about their visitors." Cully was up to asking questions himself.

"Don't mind me," Zolly said.

"You don't bother us," Fallen said. "After you answer these questions, we'll discuss some other help you can give us." He turned for the first time to look at Truman, who was standing nearby. "There's no need for you to stay, Officer."

"No bother. Prison rules." Truman cocked his head as though it were the next guy's fault. "But I won't get in your way." After winking at Zolly, he walked to a couch across the room and sat down with his paperwork.

Fallen removed a tape recorder from his briefcase and made a show of turning it on before placing it on the table between them. He cleared his throat to show that so far this had been dress rehearsal. "Mr. Berns, you've suffered a great deal. You're under separate investigations by the Internal Revenue Service and the Illinois tax authorities. You have problems with the Chicago building department, the health department, your bank, and your landlord." Fallen didn't bother to glance down at his pad as he ticked off the points. "Your business is closed. You've been here several months and face a much longer incarceration, all because of some friends who aren't grateful. I'm here today hoping you've seen your civic duty and are now ready to help us. If you'll cooperate, we'll show our appreciation."

When Zolly cleared his throat, they looked at him expectantly. His knee hit the table as he stood. He had decided on the way over, but his exact words surprised him, echoing something he had said in shul. "None of you can save me."

EIGHTEEN

AFTER COUNT CLEARED, ZOLLY WENT TO THE MAIN TV ROOM to wait for chow. The regulars were cushioned in their favorite chairs, picking away at the leather. Some were talking baseball, but most had their eyes on Lou Dobbs on TV. They meant to vote Republican when they got out. Zolly turned to Solomon, who was leaning next to him against the back wall. "Truman did such a good job with his TV schedule committee, they ought to cover the whole day. Keep Butterfly busy an hour longer," Zolly said.

"That still won't get you a seat when we're waiting for chow."

"Maybe not," Zolly said. "But at least I wouldn't have to watch CNN every evening. It spoils my appetite. Not everyone wants to hear about the market. Besides, half the time, I have to hear Mr. Insider chipping in with his review." Zolly pointed at Haskell Goldman, who was sitting in front with Tommy "the Tax" O'Brien. Zolly had abandoned the market lessons when Haskell started hitting on Darla.

"Okay, so talk to Butterfly. Better yet, tell him you want on the committee. The whole idea is to avoid pissing contests in the TV rooms. Of course," Solomon said, "if Butterfly had to type a full-day schedule, he might put in for overtime."

"That's all I need. Truman's got the whites, the blacks, the Puerto Ricans, and the rednecks trying to agree on what to watch. Instead of arguments by the hour, it's fights by the week."

Zolly often waited in his room until the unit was released for chow so that he could avoid Lou Dobbs and Haskell. Today, he had no choice. He wanted to see the shrink before he left for the day. That was why Zolly was standing next to Solomon in a room full of men who wanted to be first and watching Haskell suck up to O'Brien.

What Tommy owed the IRS was enough to bail out Zolly. If Haskell weren't around, Tommy would be debating the room on where to open his next car dealership. Zolly considered warning Tommy to watch out or Haskell would wind up with the franchise, but he decided not to bother. Better that Haskell screw Tommy than Darla.

CNN began a feature on a Jewish broker charged with giving inside tips to his customers. One of the men in the last row said, "Haskell, he one of yours?"

Without turning toward the source of the comment, Haskell said, "I don't deal with tips from brokers. Sooner or later, they all get one wrong."

Tommy the Tax said, "The way I see it, Haskell, the market is for insiders and fools. You've been at it a long time, and you're no fool."

At this, the audience left Lou Dobbs. Whenever Haskell talked the market, he got more attention than MTV. "There's nothing wrong with insider trading if you're the one inside. That's the American way."

IT WAS STILL BOTHERING HIM. ZOLLY WAS USUALLY AT LEAST A second ahead of whatever came out of his mouth. This time, he was a day behind. On his way back to the unit from the visiting room, Truman hadn't mentioned Fallen and Cully or what Zolly had said to them, which was just as well. This was too heavy for amateur psychology. Which was why he headed for Dr. Stein when the hack at Atwood let them loose for chow. It was the second time in a week that Zolly had surprised himself. That wasn't the way it was supposed to go. He should be able to calculate before he spoke and consider how his words would sound. These days, he was hearing whatever he said at the same time as everyone else. It was bad enough when he'd defended his new job to Truman, but at least back then his words made sense. Both Truman and he usually knew exactly what he meant. This time was both different and alarming.

The psychologist's office was on the second floor of the main building, next to the clinic, across from the hospital and a floor below the Renaissance unit. Zolly had never visited the hospital. He didn't get up early enough for sick call. Besides, that was for aspirin and off-duty permission slips, not chats. That was why he had waited until the end of the day.

Jacob Stein was leaving his office, wearing a jacket buttoned from his neck to his waist.

Zolly said, "Doc, if you have a minute, I'd like to ask you something."

Stein could have passed for one of the doormen who pinch-hit at Zolly's bar between college classes. He looked like a PhD and talked like a thesis, but he was the best that Zolly could do. Stein said, "You're the man who is here on the contempt charge, aren't you?"

No surprise that Stein recognized him. The first time they met, even though Stein had taken notes for half an hour, he had asked the first couple of questions without looking down. He used questions for conversation. You had to justify yourself with every breath. "The very same. I was wondering if I could have a few minutes of your time."

"Do you have a pass? The guards usually telephone first."

On the Street, shrinks were known to hold your hand. In here, they liked to squeeze it. Zolly said, "It's after Count, so we have free movement."

"That allows you to take up my time without an appointment?"

They were walking down the stairs, Zolly talking fast, Stein trying to escape. Zolly said, "I was hoping you could help me. Something I said yesterday bothers me. Usually, I don't worry afterward, but I've been reading some while I've been in and it's started me to thinking."

They were outside. The light remained as bright as midday and the heat lingered with it. Several inmates were already walking off their chow. A few had claimed a bench. "Reading sometimes does that," Stein said.

"I had a visit from some government lawyers. They had the same questions as those that sent me in. You know, what we talked about when I first got here, and you interviewed me."

Stein started to move away. The first time they met, Zolly had been an assignment. Now, he was an interruption.

Zolly said, "Instead of telling them no, I said something really weird. I told them they couldn't save me. I don't know what I meant by that."

Stein stopped and turned to face Zolly. His expression suggested this might be worthwhile, after all. They found a place at the corner of the courtyard, near the toolshed that was set close to the Barnett unit. The bench was on the edge of the lawn. The nearby grass was as green as envy when the walkies paraded by the bench. "What do you think you meant?" He was again answering questions with questions.

"Maybe I'm homesick. Maybe I'm lonely. Maybe I just need a woman. Maybe I'm too old to have one." Zolly looked over at the walkies and cleared his throat. "Why are men and women serving time together here?"

Stein followed Zolly's gaze and worked his lips, glad to lecture. "Occasionally, things continue beyond their time, for so many generations that we forget their rationale."

"Yeah, tradition," Zolly said.

"That's for sociologists and theologians. I call it habit when people maintain behavior even after its reason has passed. Religion is a good example." He grimaced. Stein had the beginnings of a beard, but he kept it trimmed away from his sideburns and had the habit of wearing light-colored clothing. "Consider the rules observant Jews must follow: observing the Sabbath; men and women praying separately; all the other regulations. Habits that left the reasons behind. Keeping kosher was important in ancient times, when conditions were unsanitary, or it set the Jews apart to avoid assimilation. Today, it is an anachronism."

"Okay, today we pray together, granted. But why are we in jail together?"

Stein connected his fingertips. "This started as a hospital for narcotics addicts. When addiction was criminalized, we joined punishment with treatment. After a while, they also sent people here with other illnesses—particularly, other addictions, such as alcoholism. So we became part hospital, part prison." Stein looked at his watch and shifted in his seat.

"Okay, but why men and women?"

Although Stein was talking to Zolly, he was looking into the distance. The whole courtyard was his lecture hall, but the audience, except for Zolly, was indifferent. "We didn't have enough female addicts to warrant a separate facility. Furthermore, in the Kennedy and Carter years, they thought they could rehabilitate offenders by simulating society in a controlled environment. It also eased the sexual tensions." Two lovers walked by, as though on cue.

"You don't agree."

Stein moved his hands apart. "Rehabilitation is a farce. We're done with permissiveness. That's why President Reagan was elected." He pointed at a couple walking by them for the third time around the Yard, but not looking tired. "We're not idiots. We know where the hand-holding leads." Stein stopped, ready to tie it all together. "But I don't think you require a woman in order to be saved."

"Is it religion? Is that what I was asking about?"

"I'm not the one to speak to about that," Stein said. "You should visit with Reverend Burgess. I believe we save ourselves. But you didn't come to ask how to be saved."

"Then what did I want to ask you about, the weather?"

When Stein began to stand, Zolly raised his hand. "I'm sorry. Why did I?"

Stein settled back. "You want to know what it is about yourself or your situation that makes you feel you can't be saved. Your comment troubles you, not the answer." Stein looked pleased to be maintaining control.

"Okay, then what made me say it?"

"You weren't inclined to discuss your situation when we first met. As I recall, you refused to testify before a grand jury. I have no interest in probing into the subject of their inquiry. However, I wonder at your refusal to answer. I'm certain it wasn't political. Did you refuse to answer due to fear?" Stein studied for Zolly's reaction.

There was no way Stein could know about David. Besides, that wasn't it at all. Zolly wasn't afraid of dying; he was afraid of living after. "No, I'm not worried about the danger."

"You were talking about your freedom."

"I can get that by agreeing to talk."

Stein removed a handkerchief, pressed it against his face, and returned it to his pocket. He was a man who would be careful about what he threw away. Stein said, "The answer is obvious, but it will mean more if you get it yourself. But I will give you a hint. Think about your purpose."

"You mean, my job in the chaplains' offices?"

"That might get you there, but it goes in a different direction. I suggest you concentrate on why you are here."

The man was still posing riddles when Zolly wanted answers. That was the problem with words. "You mean, grand reason? Is that what's going to save me? How about helping others? There's this guy in my unit who helps men on their appeals. Should I be a good man, like him?"

As Stein stood, ready to leave, it occurred to Zolly that Solomon might have peace of mind. Zolly said, "There are a lot of good people in here."

Stein said, "I disagree. They may be nice guys, but they are not good people. They take from society."

ON ANY OTHER FRIDAY MORNING, NATRON WOULD HAVE stayed in the unit, taking his time at getting dressed. He worked evenings Fridays, cleaning up after the Polaroid picture–taking by an inmate cameraman at a dollar a copy. The customers could send their purchases home; sometimes, it was photos of individual inmates to remind their families what they looked like, but it was mostly the lovers who wanted their pictures to add to their memorabilia. It surely was a pleasure seeing all the walkies smile. Weaver oversaw the finances.

Natron also cleaned up after the Jew services. Their room wasn't too bad. They put their own books away and had Weaver lock them up. Must be some hot secrets in them books. They did leave crumbs on the floor, but there was leftover cake to make things even. It was the pictures that left a mess.

Due to his evening hours, Natron didn't have to report for work on Fridays until noon. If he skipped breakfast, he could sleep late, get dressed relaxed, draw water for his coffee, and go for a stroll in the private yard that ringed three sides of Atwood, where there was plenty of grass and shade to lie around in. It was a holiday, if you didn't mind fences. This Friday, instead of a pleasant start to the day, here he was, doing extra duty for Messer. That knife-in-pants had given him four hours' work in the courtyard instead of handing out a shot. It was kind of Messer to play Natron's hand, but the hack hadn't been aware of that when he gave out the work. No way Natron would give Messer credit for a favor when he thought he was handing out punishment.

"I hope she's on time," Julio Perez said. He was squatting, waiting for Natron to push the butts into his pan with the broom. Every few feet, Natron had to wait for Perez to maneuver to a new spot. Perez didn't like to get up, so he moved on his heels and toes, sidling forward like a duck. When Messer had handed Natron the broom, all he'd said was, "Help Perez." Cleaning the courtyard was Perez's regular job, which was what first gave Natron the idea.

"I tell you," Natron said, "right before lunch. Five minutes off schedule, it won't work." Natron wondered how Perez had ever made it on the Street, looking over his shoulder so much. The man had pointy ears from all that twitching. "Perez, if you relax, maybe you hold that pan steady when I push." Natron looked at his watch again and calculated. After all, he could count dime bags in his head. If he allowed five minutes for every sidewalk square, they would reach the corner by Barnett when Mandy Streeter arrived. Natron had considered doing all the work by Barnett to begin with but had thought better of that idea. No need to make it obvious. He decided to stick with their plan to do the entire courtyard at a pace that would reach Barnett just in time. So he began with Perez at the end farthest across from the storage shed. He meant to reach the spot half an hour before lunch began, the courtyard empty except for them and Mandy, a couple minutes before the man came in sight. Everyone was somewhere else at work, unless they had a late shift like Natron that left their Friday mornings free to do whatever they pleased. What Natron pleased this Friday morning was to have things work out the way he'd first told them to Perez, reciting his notes real slow because Perez needed to turn every sentence from English into Spanish before he understood.

"You like to work for Messer?" Natron really didn't care about Messer or know how to talk except in D.C., but he did enjoy seeing Perez try to talk as he scooted along the walk.

"What kind of question? He run the job like any cop you ever see, looking for dirt instead of how things shine." Perez was still on his knees. His ankles must have been tired.

This was the perfect extra duty. If Natron had gone too far, it would have been a shot for sure. He had to bend the rules just right, so that even a prick like Messer would only give him extra duty. "Why don't you stand up, empty that pan?"

"If I get up now, I'm standing to rest. I don't bend over again until I catch my breath."

Here it was, not yet noon. A man from San Juan shouldn't need a shower so soon. "You take all the air you want. She'll be another fifteen minutes," Natron said.

"How do you know she'll come? They might not let her leave."

"They don't lock the door at Women's at lunch, only after Count. She'll scoot across the courtyard when we need her."

"She won't have a pass. Why do you think she take the chance?" Perez said.

Questions like that made Natron wonder why he had ever teamed up with Perez. He could have done better with someone from D.C., but he had started with this man and now he couldn't lose him. Besides, Perez had the courtyard for his regular shift, and this wouldn't work without his help. "No pass will be the least of Mandy's problems. When this is over, she'll go straight to seg."

"Then why is she doing this?"

"Like I tell you," Natron said. "Her homeboy is my good friend. She gets out next week. If she spends it in seg or in her unit, it don't matter none to her."

Now they were down the last stretch, drawing closer to Barnett. By moving his head with each pass of the broom, Natron could see in each direction without showing off. No one was watching while they worked their way down the sidewalk, a square at a time, sweeping, shuffling, and cleaning until they reached the storage shed. No one cared when they tried the door without waiting for the hack. As Perez had promised, Messer had left the entrance open.

The shed was larger than a few brooms and brushes required, which made it the right size for their plans. There were some shelves at the far end with lots of open space between them and the door. There was even a drop cloth on the ground to keep it clean for Mandy.

"That man be sorry he ever messed with me," Natron said, licking sugar off his lips at the thought. There were all kinds of ways to handle folk. It depended on where you were and what you had going for you at the time. This was proving as fine as a line of coke drawn so neat you best hold your mouth closed and your nose puckered.

It was eleven twenty, ten minutes in advance of early lunch, five minutes to go before the man would walk out the door into the courtyard, no more time before Mandy should be heading their way—which she was, by the look of the figure leaving Women's Unit just now and moving under the portico.

"You stop worrying, she's coming along just in time. Now be the time to pray no hack look our way the next few minutes," Natron said.

When Mandy arrived, out of breath and shiny already, Natron opened the door to the storage shed, pushed her inside the room, followed her, and pulled the door behind, leaving Perez standing guard outside.

"Take your clothes off real fast," Natron said.

Mandy said, "What you in here with me for? Something else in mind?" It was too dark to be certain, but the crack at the doorjamb let in some light, enough to suggest Mandy had her mouth in a circle.

"Don't you get no ideas, girl. We got no time for that. I want to see you fixed just right, so do it fast." Mandy had already begun unbuttoning when he closed the door. She was out of her shirt and was taking off her pants, unhooking her brassiere and posing like a model.

"My panties, too?" She was whispering, as though someone might be waiting on one of the shelves in the shed, about to overhear if she spoke too loud.

"You take everything off and be lying on your back when he come in. We won't get to try again." He pushed her onto the cloth. He doubted it was the first time that Mandy had felt cement beneath her ass.

Natron knocked once on the door. When Perez answered with a double knock, Natron opened the door and slipped outside, leaving the door open just a crack. Squinting at the light, he looked back toward the reception building just as the man left reception and tracked toward Atwood. Natron began to holler for his attention. Natron pounded on the door to the shed when the man turned. "I think we gots someone locked inside, sir. You best come quick." The man came running toward them, the ring of keys that opened all the locks at Lexington dangling from his belt.

"What's going on here, Blades?" The man was already fumbling for the key. Natron wondered how they always knew which one to choose. It must be a code. Long keys for tall doors, short keys for fat doors, maybe green ones for outdoors and red ones for indoors. Maybe someday a black hack would tell him how and why. No matter; when the man turned his long, short, green, or red key, he would be setting the bolt, not unfastening it. The door was not shut tight, so it would swing open when he pulled, but when it closed behind him, the latch would click and lock. That was the last part that had to be done before Messer came by to pop the cake from the oven.

"I thinks someone's caught inside. You best have a look," Natron said. He fought for the face of a hero as the man turned his key, first to the left and then, without pausing to consider the situation, back to the right. When he entered, Natron and Perez pushed the door closed behind him. They could hear the man fumbling around, not able to see anything just yet in the dark. Natron looked back toward the administration building in time to see Messer approaching, as regular as a morning crap, ready to secure their tools so they could leave for lunch.

When Messer drew near, Natron said, "Officer, when we tried to pull the door open to put our brooms away, we hear all kind of hollering. It sound like a party."

Messer ran the last few feet to try for himself—just like a hack, never trusting an inmate's word. Finding the shed locked, Messer used his key for access and flung the door open, allowing the noon sun to light the scene inside.

Mandy was on her back, the man inside her legs. She looked like a horse lying there, the man on her a jockey, bucking up, her legs cinched around his waist, refusing to let him loose. Truman stopped struggling when he was bathed in the light. When he looked up, his face showed the pain of a favorite finishing last.

NINETEEN

Zolly had the Chicago paper on his lap. Rosie knew he liked to read the news from home, so she passed it to him whenever she could. Despite last year's first-place finish, the season was already over. That was the Cubs for you. With fifty games to go, it was wait till next year, but the crowds kept coming. The Cubs were smack and their fans were hooked. The Bears were already into preseason, so there was something else to read about if you got hold of the Chicago paper. You would never know football existed if you read the Lexington journals or listened to the local stations. Instead, Kentucky covered basketball like Betsy Tobias smothered a seat. You did have the cable, but the game was usually the Yankees or Braves. So here it was, dinner done, and if you were born Midwest you wound up sitting outside, enjoying the breeze from the walkies.

Gabby said, "Have we found a rabbi yet?" He was next to Zolly on the bench, looking over his shoulder. Not that Gabby cared about the Cubs or the Bears or any other team, but he would eat off your plate if you let him.

"I'm not on the employment committee," Zolly said. Gabby missed schmoozing with Rabbi Terman, but the main reason Gabby asked was in order to pass it on. He was the daily bulletin.

"You're there every day. You must have typed up a letter, a memo, something." The first time Gabby failed to take no for an answer he had wound up getting married, but he never learned his lesson.

"I work strictly on the Welfare Fund," Zolly said. "There's no way they'd share that with me, or even the clerk typist. All she gets to type is the hymns they're going to sing, or the schedule for church. Stuff like that." Judy was okay even if her face had more holes than the Cubs' infield. Zolly was sure she would say if she knew.

Gabby said, "Who handles the important stuff? Do they send it to a typing service in town?"

Zolly gave up reading halfway through the box score. There was no way he could concentrate with Gabby over his shoulder. Zolly saved his books for his room, but you would think you could read the sports pages outside without losing your place. With Gabby around, Zolly did more talking than Jack Brickhouse on a bright day at Wrigley Field. He folded the newspaper on his lap, saving it for Solomon.

Their bench was in the middle of the courtyard. Gabby always found him there because Zolly wouldn't hide. You had to pay for everything, even when they hid the price tag. Ever since Adlai had spoken against him the night they voted, Zolly owed Gabby for shooting the chazan down. Zolly mostly paid his debt with news from the chapel and by listening to bulletins from Gabby's other sources. Although it was weeks later, the departed rabbi remained Gabby's favorite topic. How the temple made the rabbi give up the job, because although some members wanted him to continue the visits, others thought even once a year was a scandal. Zolly was tired of it. Terman had always spent half his visit talking to the hack in black, and the other half getting ready to leave. They had started handling things on their own back when the rabbi was still on the payroll. The problem was that the High Holidays were approaching. Gabby had put himself in charge with no one to second-guess him other than Adlai, who didn't much care so long as he got to daven. So here was Gabriel Goldstein, acting like Moses and treating Zolly like his Red Sea scout.

"Gabby, if I knew what was going on, I'd tell you. I could probably get it out of Weaver, but he never knows anything until he hears from the hack in black. I did ask Burgess a few weeks ago, but all he would say was that the new fiscal year began in July. The job didn't pay enough for any of the rabbis in town."

"The money isn't the issue. I told you that," Gabby said, clearing his nostrils. He used his nose to herald significant events. "They would just as soon we weren't here."

"Me, too," Zolly said. Then they watched the walkies.

When Congressman Manning and Governor Grady sat down at the other end of the bench, Zolly looked twice to be certain before he poked Gabby in the ribs. Those two usually walked twice as far to sit alone, being politicians and all, but the benches were filled with the spillover from the Yard. Everyone was outside, hoping for a breeze, except for die-hard New York or Atlanta fans. But by the look they gave them, it appeared they were happy to visit. Besides being pushed to share a bench by the crowd, Manning and Grady had something to share.

"Evening, Guv. Good to see you, Congressman Manning." Gabby was the official greeter, even on a bench.

"Hello, boys," Grady said. He knew Gabby from the days they had lived in Barnett. He knew Zolly from across the hall. Grady had on his running outfit, which included the Reeboks he flashed on the track and jogging shorts that made up in cost what they gave away in coverage. Grady's gut was flat from pissing all that water he drank on his diet. His chest was bare because he pumped iron daily and wanted to show the results.

"He's getting in shape for another race when he gets out," Gabby said, talking into Zolly's ear.

"I wonder how he'll handle the song," Zolly asked.

"About selling the state contracts? He's counting on his voters going deaf," Gabby said, insensitive as usual to Zolly's musically challenged condition.

Even though Gabby's telling a joke was as unusual as the Cubs in first, Zolly didn't see the humor. "If you want laughs, you ought to take lessons from Manning."

Congressman Manning didn't share in Grady's protein powder. In fact, he looked like he rarely ate anything at all. His hair matched his body. Strands pointed everywhere, including a few tumbling over his forehead to make his voters feel at ease. Manning must have been a star in every court he had ever tried a case. He still lived the part inside the joint, walking the courtyard every evening and nodding to everyone like a senior law partner greeting his clients.

"What's he going to teach me?" Gabby asked.

"I hear Manning had a different story for every campaign dinner," Zolly said. "He ran for Congress as regular as a commuter train. You ever hear the one about when the envelopes fell out of his campaign manager's pockets? The cash spilled presidents all over the floor."

"Yeah," Gabby said. "Men were yanking their Johnsons to get at the Jacksons." That made it two for Gabby that day.

"Congressman, you got a new one for us?" Zolly asked.

Manning knew them both. He greeted constituents when they arrived and knew their names forever. He had a politician's way of shaking hands, grasping and simultaneously pulling away. Having his hand out was what had landed Manning here. Zolly had seen the 60 Minutes tape of Manning and the FBI version of an Arab sheik. Abscam. The sound of the word *scam* reminded Zolly of home.

Grady said, "You see Truman lately?"

"I take his class Saturdays," Zolly said. "I haven't seen him since."

"If you have to deal with that bastard every week, you'll get a kick out of this," Grady said.

Zolly understood why an inmate might hate Truman. If you reached for an edge, he'd break your arm. But if you looked him in the eye, you could deal. As it was not his job to set Grady straight, all he said was, "Fill me in."

"A couple of the guys decided to teach him a lesson." Grady rubbed his hands as though he had just counted the money and found none of it missing. "You know Natron Blades?"

"Not if I can help it," Zolly said.

"He's the cleanup at the chaplains' offices."

"I work there."

Grady said, "Before that, he was a unit orderly. Until Truman kicked him out."

"Natron has a way of aggravating friend and foe alike," Zolly said.

"Truman turned the screws on Natron. They say, what goes around comes around."

"Who says?"

"They screwed right back," Manning said, beating Grady to the punch line.

"You talking about people in general, or Natron?"

That was when they pointed to the storage shed and recited the story. Gabby listened so hard he almost fell off the bench. Zolly sat still, taking it all in without moving, staring at the shed as they spoke. The hole was in his stomach again, growing, absorbing him as he listened.

"She's buck naked when Messer rushes in, sees her climbing all over Truman. Small audience, big show," Manning said.

"That's entrapment." Zolly's stomach turned into quicksand.

"Entrapment landed me in here. And it yanked Truman right out," Manning said. "They say hacks never get prosecuted, but that used to be true of congressmen, as well."

Manning and Grady made lots of noise with their story. Zolly nodded, trying to move the muscles in his face to show he was joining in. He tried to envision Truman on top of the woman, but all he could see was the man in uniform, his desk adorned with his wife and son, his shelves wearing books like sergeant's stripes, his class at attention, with Zolly, for once, at ease. Zolly brushed his palm across his shoulder, but there was nothing there—no stripes or bars or reassuring hand. When he listened for the bugle, all he heard was Gabby blowing again, capturing the moment and preparing the evening news.

TWENTY

"I'M GLAD YOU FINALLY TURNED OFF THE FUCKING FAN," ZOLLY said. He was lying on his bed, all his clothes on, enjoying the breeze through the window.

"Yeah, this way you don't have to talk so loud when you interrupt," Maggiano said. He was up early for a Saturday morning, already in his writing position with piles of paper at his side.

Zolly said, "This time of year, we could forget the Cubs and concentrate on football."

"That was good? Gets cool, people aren't thirsty. It lets them watch TV at home."

"You'd think, but we got business even when the heat stopped driving it in. Sunday brunch was standing room only." A Bears game on the big TV had made Zolly's Sundays sing.

"Isn't it time for you to go pray?"

"I score enough points Friday nights," Zolly said. Services no longer summoned him with the air-conditioning, and Zolly was no longer campaigning for a job. These days, his week ended on Fridays with evening services and the picture-taking of the walkies that turned his grape juice sour. No one should take snapshots at a wake.

The previous night, Zolly had read the English all the way through for the first time ever. It had started that summer, when he started trying to get the sense of what he was saying. Adlai noticed the change in Zolly right away, which was impressive on its own, considering he rarely paid attention to anything beyond the end of his nose, which Zolly reckoned meant twelve inches. "Berns, are you auditioning for my job?" Since then, it was the same question every week, right before the concluding prayer. When Adlai made a joke, he carried it around like his favorite pill.

Zolly would say, "No, I'm trying to make the services go faster," or, "I might as well learn what this is all about," or, "I'm trying to take my mind off your drone." He never admitted he was searching for a prayer to satisfy Truman.

"What do you go for?" Maggiano was talking into the flap of his envelope.

"What do you think?"

"I think you're full of shit. If you go on and on in there the way you do in here, they'll kick you out on your ass."

Zolly's gaze took in the room, the outside grounds as seen through the wire mesh stuck to the back windowpanes, the grass of the grounds, the striped baseball field, the stone walls separating the Yard from the inner walks, the sky, even his recollections. In sum, he saw the disappointment and the dreams. If he squinted, he saw David. "This is the first time I'm sorry about what I didn't do."

"He's a hack, you're a con. I thought I set you straight."

"He was good to you. You said so yourself."

Maggiano put his pen down. He talked better with his hands. "Okay, but that was then. Maybe if he had asked me for something, I would have done it. But he never asked." Maggiano's expression was impassive, but his tone was jealous.

"If a man is truly your friend, he shouldn't have to." Zolly wondered whether Maggiano would give up half the bulletin board if Zolly had the pictures to fill the space.

"You think he's a friend and not a hack, okay, then do it without being asked. But what is it you'll do?" Maggiano shrugged the question and raised his eyebrows, as though Zolly was beyond hope, as well. "You going to the lieutenant? What are you going to tell him? He'll want the particulars." No longer shrugging, Maggiano squeezed his eyebrows together, brushing the top of his nose.

"I wouldn't give them up," Zolly said.

"So you say."

"What would you do? If you wouldn't rat, but you wanted to do right?"

Maggiano shrugged again, returning to his work. "If it was a friend, I'd take care of the guys on my own."

The thought of hurting Natron had some appeal. Having the guy around the office was a pain. It would be nice if Natron lived in Barnett and worked nights, but even if Zolly could arrange it, that wouldn't help Truman. Perez was just an afterthought. Zolly looked at his Rolex, which had once belonged to David. He never took it off except to shower and hid it in a different spot each day. "I've got to get going."

"It's too late for chow," Maggiano said. "You going to the lieutenant? You already said you don't pray Saturdays."

"Yeah, but we got something special going on after."

On his way to the main building, Zolly concentrated on the committee, taking his mind off Truman's disgrace and exile. The chaplains were opening the chapel to let them plan for the High Holidays at the end of the month. According to Gabby, "We got no rabbi, so we need to do it ourselves. Just like on weekends."

"Why the four of us?" Zolly asked.

"Adlai, Joey Philly, and me because we've done our whole bit here. You, because you work in the office. Make sure you get it all down." That made Gabby, Adlai, and Joey Philly the Board of Directors, and Zolly the recording secretary.

He had been in the chapel when Natron was cleaning up, but that was just in and out, passing on a message, not long enough to even push a broom. Zolly had never been there when they were holding church. It took enough energy just to go to the Jewish services. That was why, after six months, he had the time to look around. The chapel could have held ten rooms the size of their shul. The stage at the far end had steps climbing up from the floor. There was a carpeted platform on top of the stage that held a lectern and microphone. Standing two levels above the congregation, the preacher would tower overhead. Evidently, the authorities wanted to hold him high, keep him safe from the audience in case it turned mean. There were enough seats between the stage and the rear of the chapel to hold several hundred worshipers, doing whatever Gentiles did. The Jews would never fill it up. Even with a full turnout, the chapel would look like happy hour, but where the drinks were marked up instead of half price. But it was either this or standing room only in the shul.

The first thing Gabby did was to hit the stage with the palm of his hand. The sound reverberated like a bowling ball lofted in an empty alley. "There'll be more of us up there than down here," he said.

Joey Philly said, "Maybe we could invite the Italians." He blinked at his own idea.

"Why don't you shut your eyes and go to sleep? We'll wake you in time for Succoth," Gabby said.

Adlai said, "No problem. We can move the platform and lectern off the stage to the middle of the room. Everyone will surround us."

"What kind of arrangement is that?" Gabby asked. He walked toward the center of the chapel, in case there was something Adlai had seen that he'd missed. "You want people praying to your tush?"

"That's how the Sephardim hold their services," Adlai said.

"Sephardim?" Zolly asked. Then he looked away, hoping no one had heard him. They were just borrowing the place, not buying it. He was ready to head for home.

"I'll explain." Adlai was glad to lecture. "The Sephardim go way back. They're the Jews from Spain. They pray different from us. They turned left when we turned right." He paced back and forth. "They don't believe the reader should be up front. They put him in the middle. It's more democratic."

"I get it. Shul in the round," Zolly said.

"This is a holy time. Everyone will depend on us to make it special." Adlai looked sorry he hadn't moved the pulpit already. "I think we should divide things up, assign each person a piece to say."

It was quite a performance for a man who usually looked down. Adlai was holding on to a mahzor. If they got lucky, he might start reading it to himself. Zolly realized it was unlikely he could get out of typing a script, but he thought he should try. "How do we know who will be here? I say we wait until everyone shows up before we worry who says what."

"The chaplain sends a notice around to all the units," Gabby said. "Just walk up and say you're Jewish. Everyone will turn up. It's an excuse to get off work."

Joey Philly stopped sulking and backed Adlai's idea. "We got to do this right. Let's make a list of all the Jews we got."

"Hey, it's not like we have a telephone book we can go through," Gabby said. "And I don't think control will cooperate." He looked the way he had when Adlai talked Sephardim.

"No problem," Joey Philly said, talking faster than his blinks. "Between us all, we can name every Jew at Lexington. Then we decide who does what."

There was no way to avoid it. Zolly handed a sheet of paper to each of them. Gabby started writing as though he had his list memorized. Adlai wrote with a careful upstroke, the way he must have done when he was pushing pills. Joey Philly blinked between each name, which made him take the longest.

"Okay, everybody ready?" Joey Philly asked, ignoring the fact that the other three were looking at their watches.

"We been thinking paper airplanes, letting your eyelids do the wind," Zolly said.

"Write down when each of us reads his part."

Zolly said, "Thanks for the advice."

When in doubt, they included a name rather than leave it out. There would be few enough as it was. When they finished, they had fifty-five names, including their own. Then they went through the High Holiday prayer books. Zolly lived memories of David while the committee did their work. The last time he had looked at these prayers was the month before his bar mitzvah that never was. Whenever he thought of the Jewish New Year, he thought of sitting shiva in a house of mourning. He would prefer Auld Lang Syne any day of the week.

There were plenty of prayers to go around. When they were done, they had divided the services into fifty-five sections. Adlai starred, but they left big parts for all the other attendees. "That ought to keep them happy. Everyone gets a chance to be a big shot," Gabby said.

Zolly was tempted to state the obvious. Inmates weren't shy. Inflated egos helped explain their incarceration, but this was taking long enough as it was.

"Okay, Zolly, can you type the script without our hanging around?" Adlai asked. "We need three columns. Put the page number and the first few words in column one. Column two is for the name of the reader."

"What goes in column three, the name of their walkie?" Zolly asked.

"If you feel the need. But then, you'll need a column four, because there I want you to put down the last part of what to say, so the person will know when to stop. You got that?"

"I'll work at it." Between Adlai, Gabby, and a fifty-five-person list, they would be there forever.

Joey Philly said, "Okay, Adlai, who is going to sing? Your voice is an electric razor. One that needs some oil." This he said without a blink. Like looking out beyond the fence, he could do his insults open-eyed. Adlai davened in a monotone, droning even the parts set off from the rest of the page and obviously meant for singing. Zolly hoped Adlai wouldn't argue, but that was like hoping the chaplains would let the cameraman take pictures of walkies holding hands and create dissension back home.

"We'll sing together. The ones who know the tune can carry along the rest." Adlai thumbed through his prayer book, proud of his insight.

As usual, Gabby objected to anyone else's idea. "We're planning everything so careful, now you want we should wing it? We have to practice together, so we can lead the way." He pointed at his open mahzor. "Turn to page two seventy-one. Let's start there." Then Gabby blew his nose, which should have been their warning.

As soon as Gabby began to sing, Adlai waved for the lifeguard. "Are you drowning? All I hear is gurgling."

"What kind of comedy act is that?" Joey Philly asked.

Gabby stopped for air. After exhaling, he said, "That's how it goes. If we still had the rabbi, he would tell you I got it right."

"If it went that way, every shul in town would close. You're making it up as you go." Joey Philly's eyes remained wide open.

"You guys wouldn't know the tune if it was in the top ten. By you, the Hit Parade is the mob at work," Gabby said. He was walking in different directions, taking several feet before he turned and headed another way, talking as much to the empty seats as to them. He stopped and pointed at the group. "What do you know about it? This is the way we sing it back home."

"No wonder so many landsmen in Boston converted." Adlai removed his glasses, itself a warning sign. "I don't have much of a voice, but here's the melody." Adlai proceeded to buzz at different levels, like a plane taking off but never leaving the ground. They let him continue longer than Gabby, out of spite.

"Enough. You guys listen to me," Joey Philly said. He made a fist when Adlai protested. Joey Philly yo-yoed his voice up and down as though he knew where he was going. Zolly sensed his tune was different from the others. Even if Joey Philly picked notes at random, it still made for variety. Zolly was ready to go home, but Adlai and Gabby objected.

"Friedman, I don't know how it goes in Philadelphia, but that's not the way they sing it anywhere else." Spit flew from Gabby's mouth while Joey Philly ducked. "If we can't do this right, everyone is going to wonder what we did all year. What do you say, Zolly?" Gabby wiped his mouth with his mahzor, leaving a streak down its back.

Zolly had anticipated the question when they began taking turns. "You all sounded okay. Really, I'm no authority." Look at these guys, arguing over how to sing some prayer. Next thing you knew, they would want to hear him sing. He looked down at his writing pad, ready to finish his notes.

"Yeah," Gabby said, "we sounded okay, but even I'll admit we each sung it different. You don't need to be a maven to help out."

But Zolly didn't know how it should be sung. He barely even remembered the name of the prayer, and since he was tone-deaf the melody was as foreign as the words. He must have sung it once or twice, preparing for his bar mitzvah. Okay, maybe the prayer did reach God, and it meant something to Him. Or if not to God, then it had meaning for those who sang it. He could accept that. But what difference did the melody make? This wasn't some rock song. He looked up from his notes. "What the fuck. No one is going to give a good God damn."

All three of his fellow committeemen stood silent for the first time since he had known them, each with a different expression. Adlai kissed his mahzor and peered at Zolly over its top, as though he had just spotted a goy. Joey Philly blinked so fast the only way Zolly could tell he was watching was the way his eyeballs moved beneath the lids. Gabby's countenance suggested he had found a new definition for betrayal. Gabby was the one who motioned to the others and led them out of the chapel, leaving Zolly to straighten up.

He rearranged the chairs. He placed the lectern back on the stage. He put the microphone back on the lectern. When the chapel was in order, ready for the Muslims, for the Catholics, for the nondenominational Protestants, and for all the Gentile hymns, Zolly returned to the offices across the hall. He went in back to the shul and replaced the books in the cabinet that Weaver had left unlocked. That was when he looked down at his own mahzor, the pages still open, and read the prayer in English. Not the entire prayer; it was too long to read without wiping his eyes. Just the concluding lines:

"Avinu Malkeinu, our Father, our King, be gracious to us and answer us, though we have no merits; deal charitably and kindly with us and save us."

As he read the words in English, not knowing how the Hebrew went or trying for a tune, Zolly copied Joey Philly, blinking like a fool.

BOOK THREE
FCI LEXINGTON, SPRING 1986

MUSIC

TWENTY-ONE

TIME FOR LUNCH. DARLA WATCHED THE COURTYARD FROM THE steps of the administration building. Even though the snow still lay on the ground, some of the garden had already leached through. For the first time in weeks, men and women were walking without a destination. Even inmates her own age were moving in that half skip that comes with spring. Some had unzipped their jackets. The ones holding hands had removed their gloves. As they skirted the empty bushes, she recalled her arrival, when the tended yard had reminded her of home. At that time, remembrance had pricked her like a thorn. The wounds now healed, her blood now thawed, she was ready for flowers again.

"How many times do I need to tell you?" she said, pulling her jacket tighter. It was not yet the season to take it off. Her clothing allotment limited her to just one jacket, but her gabardine had worked out fine, except for when it felt like Cleveland. That was when Zolly would lend her his coat and shiver on her behalf. He was already ten minutes late when Haskell snuck up behind her.

"You already eaten, or are you waiting for someone?" Haskell sat by her as though next to her or the empty bench nearby made no difference. That approach might have worked when he was starting out, selling stocks and bonds with the youth that pinch-hit for cash, but it was in doubt now that he was middle-aged and measured his wealth by rolls of quarters. "I already ate myself. But I'd be glad to keep you company." Haskell was a man who took no as an invitation to try again in a different way.

"You might want to walk it off. They say exercise gets your blood moving."

"Other things do that better. I'm still working on it for you." Haskell was a handyman asking for payment in advance.

"You deliver, I'll come across," she said. "Until then, you're just another loser."

"I'm working with someone. He has a contact who goes in and out of the visiting room without inspection. Just give me some time."

"I thought the judge already gave you all that you could handle."

Zolly arrived out of breath and Haskell walked away. He knew better than to stay in reach.

"Ten minutes late and I had to put up with him," she said.

"I told you at breakfast," Zolly said. "I had to go back to the unit when work let out for lunch." He had moved faster last fall, but he had gained back all his weight. The other women had warned her against taking up with an older man, but Zolly had kept Haskell at a distance. After a couple of months, it had grown into a routine. Zolly would try to feel her up while saying they could just be friends. She would say a few words about her husband and then watch Zolly flinch. For a while, Haskell had her conned, but with Zolly, there was no doubt. By his own admission, he could never get her what she wanted. Besides, Zolly could leave at any time, like frosted breath exhaled over the fence. "I owed Charlie Chicken from last week. This month is my turn to pay for the room. I was short until now." Zolly tried to pay his way through everything, but without the money to pull it off. If Haskell was an imported brand, Zolly was beer on tap. He even wheedled her to bring the soda or some other treat when they walked at night.

They proceeded to the end of the line at the dining room. It was a longer wait than usual, because the word about today's lunch had spread. Today, they served the same meal on the main line as on the kosher—although, allegedly, made from different animals. It was one of those franks-and-beans meals that reminded Zolly of home, natural casing enclosing a dog that popped when you bit. He didn't talk much while eating lunch. Zolly did like his food. The kitchen was out of rolls, so they settled for white bread and the spicy mustard that might have been the start of Joey Philly's blinking. Five minutes after they were seated, Darla was only on her third mouthful while Zolly was already on his second dog. He had better slow down. They didn't serve seconds, and there was no way she would give him hers. "Say something. Anything but sex, food, and business. You're getting to be like Haskell," she said.

"I told you, I can't get you any drugs. I wouldn't even do that on the Street. By now, you shouldn't need it."

At least he didn't try to con her like Haskell. But after this long together, he still failed to understand. Darla said, "I don't miss it the way I did when I came in, not the way I still miss my family. But everything seems so dull." She pictured the world after popping a pill or smoking a joint. When her mouth began to water, she understood how Zolly felt about his food.

"I got something else that would make you feel alive." Zolly did the best Cary Grant imitation possible with mustard on his lips.

"You'll have to come up with something better than charm. Let's talk about Chicago."

Mouth still full, he said, "You know I don't like to talk about home."

There was no way he would consider it if they didn't get beyond this stage. When she saw that there was no guard nearby, she put her hand on his knee long enough to make him swallow. A little more effort on his part, she might do more.

Zolly sipped his drink to keep his sandwich down. "What do you want to know?"

Five months of meals, trips to the library, walks in the Yard, and workouts in the gym, he was finally talking. She needed to know it all to see which button to press.

Ten minutes later, he said, "So when I refused to testify, the judge sent me here until I was ready to answer. And that's not the worst of it."

There were four other inmates at their table. Darla had seen some of them around the Yard. They were paying no attention to what Zolly was saying, and none of them even seemed to notice her. That was a welcome change from being hit on. Between her time with Haskell and when Zolly was with her, she was always in some game younger men played that involved her being the ball. With Zolly around, most of them thought she was his walkie and left her alone. "I knew about the contempt part," she said. She also knew the rule against discussing what you did to get here, which meant, she supposed, that she had become his exception.

"I counted on my girlfriend to run my place while I was in here. I counted on some friends to help me," he said.

"What's her name?"

"Faith. She's out there."

"So Faith's not dead."

He told Darla it had been months since he had heard from Faith. He claimed it was as though she had never existed. He told her this with a steady voice, looking into her eyes the whole time while the food stiffened on his plate.

"Why didn't your friends help?"

"I didn't have a going-away party like you." He began to eat again. "The hell of it is, I don't have anything to give the feds."

She tried to imagine what it was like to have someone else involved. Her crime was on her own. When her sentence was over, it would be over. When Zolly finished his second sandwich, she decided to offer him hers, after all. "You don't look scared," she said.

"That's bullshit. I never let anyone muscle me." Zolly always acted as though he had something to prove. The problem was, he was only proving it to himself. By now, he should have known who he was.

Their table was empty. The hack was moving toward them from the far end of the room. She put down her fork. "Didn't that counselor, Truman, muscle you?"

Zolly must have seen it coming, because he merely wiped his mouth. "It doesn't matter anymore. I mean to stay the course."

After lunch, they picked their way along the puddled walks with dozens of other men and women, some holding hands, others just walking, all of them draining every minute of their midday break. "Okay," he said. "Your turn. I've waited long enough. All you do is say no and tell me you want drugs."

"What brings women to Lexington?" She could have been talking to herself or reading the title of one of the shrink's studies.

Zolly nodded. It was all in fun. "I'd say drugs bring half of them here. Some were users, or pushers needing cash to feed their habit. Some have other addictions, alcohol, maybe gambling, or some of the manias."

"Okay, we're crazy."

He waved his arms around. "Not maniacs. Manias. You know, kleptomania, pyromania, different manias. And some are here just because they got greedy." He stretched. "Maybe we all just had bad luck."

They reached the end of the Yard near Women's Unit, after passing by the reception building. "Okay, I showed you mine, you show me yours," he said.

"In a way, I guess those reasons all fit me," she said. "I swiped my doctor's pad and forged some prescriptions. At the end, I put out for any pharmacist who wouldn't make an issue over the doctor's signature. I wound up losing my husband and kid." For the first time in a month, Darla felt her son in her arms. He was bruised from a fall. She was kissing it better. Her husband looked on, awaiting his turn. "You could say I betrayed them both, but in my own way I've been faithful. I won't do you unless you help me score. Nothing less than that will make me." They sat on a bench by a bush that once grew roses. "You were talking about this Faith. How did she let you down?"

She expected disagreement. Instead, he drew himself up. "She tried to keep things going, but the minute they arrested me, all hell broke loose. After they shut us down, they put a lien on my bar and held a sale." He used the same tone as when he raced through what he wanted the next time she shopped at the commissary.

She tucked her hands beneath her thighs and leaned against the back of the bench, her face turned toward the sun. "Going to services helps," she said, feeling the light through her closed lids, talking to the sky. "Then it doesn't hurt so much." Friday nights she sat next to Zolly, ten rows removed from Haskell.

"When I first got here," Zolly said, "it seemed a good way to get along. You know, make my way, get to know the people. But now, somehow, it also makes me feel less empty."

She kept her eyes closed to let him feel that he was talking to himself, maybe being honest.

"I practice on my computer every chance I get," Zolly said. "I do the Welfare Fund books and correspondence and use it for our services. We learned at Rosh Hashanah that a printed program gets everyone to take part, so I'm going to create our own Seder for Passover. We'll have special food, a banquet table, and paper plates. They're giving us one of the small dining rooms to ourselves. We're inviting the Jewish staff."

Here he was, talking about food again. She doubted he'd gotten that excited about matzo and roasted chicken when he lived on the Street. "I'm sure they'll be thrilled to be there," she said. "Tell me about your computer. Do you pray on it, as well?"

He didn't see the humor. "I pray lots," he said. "I've had a bellyful of praying here."

"Is that how you feel about it?"

"Okay, maybe not a bellyful. A bellyful would end my hunger."

"Or give you a stomachache," she said.

TWENTY-TWO

THE LAW LIBRARY WAS THE LAST PLACE ZOLLY WANTED TO BE on a movie night. Reading had its place, but on movie nights he wanted popcorn and Clint Eastwood. Instead, he was helping Solomon do his research. Life was simpler on the Street. Whatever you wanted or needed, your cash made the introduction. It was, "Here you are, thank you, sir, would you like another?" After it went in the register or your pocket, no one kept track. But favors were different. You had to pay them back.

The room resembled his high school library, except that here the bookcases filled the walls end to end and floor to ceiling, pushed so tight in place it was as though the hacks had run short on paint and didn't want to show bare walls. Not that the shelves were in surplus. They staggered under their load, overflowing into stacks of books on the floors around them. The middle of the maze was stuffed with couches, chairs, and tables piled high with newspapers and magazines jumbling about the wood. There was a private office for the staff in one corner, but they barely showed themselves. The prisoners ran the place.

The inmate librarian sat on a platform behind a desk at the end of the room, across from Zolly. The word was he had been a state prosecutor on the Street. Five feet higher, he could have even been a judge. The chairs beside the librarian's desk were filled with clients. Some would sit there every chance they got until the end of their bit, hoping to get out even one day earlier. They would have been better off with Solomon.

Zolly was reading the fine print in a Federal Supplement decision when Joey Philly found him. "Why don't you give your eyes a rest, look at the big picture? They do it with sound and color these days. The word for it is movies." Joey Philly said the last word like a cow.

"I'd rather sit with you guys than here. If I don't take notes, I lose what I read two paragraphs before."

"You spend your time on jobs for Solomon when you're not working that broad. You shouldn't forget your friends. The last few flicks weren't the same without you." Joey Philly rubbed his eyes.

"I'm not avoiding you guys—at least not most of you—but I promised Solomon I'd help." Zolly tore out a page from the book, marked his place, put the volume on his two-cushion couch to reserve it for five minutes later, and stood to stretch. "I may be seeing Darla, but I'll be working while we visit."

"It's Haskell. I see you guys avoiding each other in the kosher line. That's not healthy," Joey Philly said. "You don't look where you're going, you could trip on a meal."

Zolly considered explaining about Haskell and his promises of drugs to Darla, but that would be ratting out the guy. If Haskell got no closer than the other end of the main TV room, Zolly could handle his presence. "The first few months I'm here, he jokes about walkies whenever he sees them, then a girl comes to shul and he gives me the elbow."

"We'll be in our regular seats," Joey Philly said. "We'll save you the one by the aisle, next to me and Maggiano. We'll put Haskell at the other end."

Zolly had second thoughts when Joey Philly left. On the Street, the movies ranked between a doctor visit and buying clothes, but he was a fan of them at Lexington. They took his mind off Darla's pulling away whenever he got too close. But if he went to the show without her, she made him eat his meals alone. It was Darla or the movies. That made it no contest. Besides, it would be easier to find the precedents he needed when the library cleared out and he didn't have to compete for a place to sit. He was back at work when Darla entered. Everyone kept reading, talking, and milling about the books when they should have caught their breath. She was a color TV in a black-and-white world. He moved his papers to make room.

"I had to pick up my package at Receiving. My new clothes came in," she said.

He had focused on her face and failed to notice what she was wearing, even though she had talked about the package all week. The men had a limit of one change of clothes per year, but women lived by different rules. According to Darla, this shipment made up for the confusion on her arrival. Viewing her profile, Zolly was happy for last fall's shortage. He no longer had to work with the hints of her winter clothing. Her slacks and blouse confirmed his fantasies. She leafed through his book. "Are you considering going into law?"

He marked *United States v. Sawyer* with a scrap of paper and closed the book. "I'm helping Solomon on a motion. We're looking for a case with the kind of facts that put this guy in here, but with a different ending."

Her lips were still pursed. Darla was not one for fine lines, unless she was inhaling one up her nose. However, instead of expressing disapproval, she said, "I think it's great that you're helping a friend. Maybe someday, you'll do something for me." She moved closer. She had made it clear for months that she was not his walkie. Now, with her thigh pressed against his own longer than a coincidence, he might earn a different ruling. She said, "Do you have a lot more work? I thought maybe we'd take in the movie."

The first few months after she had arrived, Darla had been resolute in her refusal to attend, explaining she didn't want to deal with his hands in the dark. Zolly knew better than to question good fortune when things were finally going his way. He put his paperwork into the Federal Express envelope that served as his briefcase and went downstairs with Darla. The theater was on the ground floor below the library, located at the other end of the hall from the chaplains' offices, presumably because the staff wanted sin and salvation set as far apart as possible. Once they passed the door that led to the UNICOR courtyard, they could see the crowd outside the theater. Lexington was a lot like the army, mostly lines and waiting. In this case, one of the lines awaited the movie. The other was for the popcorn.

The inmate Junior Chamber of Commerce, Women's Branch, owned their own popcorn wagon, purchased with the profits from their operations. The women sold the bags for the price of a load of laundry. It was thirty minutes before showtime, but the oil was already crackling beneath the kernels, making the place smell like date night.

Darla stepped over the fake butter that spattered the floor and led him into the theater. Joey Philly, Haskell, Maggiano, and a few of his Italian friends had seats in the second row but had left the aisle seats empty. Up front was a poor place to watch, because the screen was set so low the heads of the people walking in front obstructed the view, but it was the best spot to get to the john or the popcorn. Tonight, one bag would have to do, because Darla chose seats in the middle of a row halfway up from the screen. Inconvenient if you had to take a leak, but promising privacy. The way Darla was digging in, he doubted the sack would last beyond the first corpse. The hacks assigned to watch that night were already patrolling the aisles. Once the movie began and the theater went dark, the guards' flashlights would be lap high.

She said, "I've been too hard on you. You're a nice guy, even if you don't know what's what. You should get friendly with some people who know their way around. Like Natron. Sometimes, you can be too picky."

"I get enough of him in the chaplains' offices. I don't want to have anything to do with him after work."

"That's because he doesn't have anything that you want. I've been talking to Natron. He can get me something I want. You say I'm what you want, so if Natron gets it for me, he's getting it for you, like osmosis. Do you know what that means?"

"Sure. When you absorb something by contact."

She pressed against him again. He looked around to see where the hacks were. "You never wanted to see the movies with me before."

"Keep your hands to yourself."

It took a moment before he realized that Darla was Faith twenty years ago, when her hair was still light. He said, "I'm not promising."

"But I am," she said. "I like you better than Haskell, but you've got to play by the same rules." She put her hand over his, holding it immobile on his knee.

He knew that Haskell had tried to bullshit her. For his part, he had been straight with her from the start. He never made a promise, not to Faith, not to Darla, not to any other woman. If you never made a promise, you never let a person down. As the theater lights dimmed, for a moment he thought of David on the couch, telling him a story. The good thing about the movies was they didn't have to matter. But Darla counted, and he wanted her to know. "It's going to be hard, sitting next to you without a touch."

"Work on it," she said. "Consider Natron, and how you can work together. You'll enjoy it more when you earn it."

The guard was at the end of their row, moving his flashlight from one lap to the next. Darla removed her hand, and they watched Clint Eastwood's portrayal of Dirty Harry.

TWENTY-THREE

HERSCHEL YITZCHAK RABINOWITZ. HERSCHEL YITZCHAK Rabinowitz. Zolly practiced the name a word at a time. The first part was easy. If you thought of a candy bar, you had it. The middle and last names were harder. He broke them into syllables, each a separate sound. Then he worked at joining the sounds together. Even that way, the name was a climb. By the time Zolly reached the top of the mountain, it was time to return for Count. During the ten minutes he awaited Count back at the unit, he repeated the rabbi's name like a mantra. By the time Count was finished, Zolly's head was clear. Later that evening, he finally caught up to Gabby. "Have I got news for you." Dinner done, they were placing their trays on the conveyor belt to the dish room. Half their food remained.

"About the crap they served tonight?" Gabby had taken to complaining at every meal, as though when free he had been Julia Child's best friend, and now he missed her dearly.

"You'll forget all about it when I tell you the news."

"You think I forgot what we used to eat? We should have meat three times a week. Don't say it doesn't matter. That's what they're counting on. Apathy. Next thing you know, we'll be getting TV dinners."

When Gabby got started, he was a pinball pinging from thought to thought. Zolly put his hand on Gabby's arm. "I have something more important than food to talk about."

"If they serve us junk food, people will drop off the kosher line." Gabby paused, antenna twitching, hoping more news was coming. "Go ahead, if you insist."

Zolly said, "You won't have to bitch secondhand anymore."

"We got a new complaint department?"

"The Rabinowitz department."

Gabby's ears pointed up. "You trying to aggravate me more?"

"Aggravation is spelled, 'Herschel Yitzchak Rabinowitz.'"

Gabby worked on it silently for a moment. Then, the name under control, he repeated it with the same expression he'd had when describing their recent meals. But when they met the new rabbi on his first visit the next night, Gabby had nothing but good things to say. It was the biggest turnout Zolly had seen since the first day of Rosh Hashanah, and louder than a boxing match. Gabby started things off. He began by telling the rabbi about how he, Gabriel Goldstein, furrier to the stars, had organized the services, the great job Adlai Sachar, the druggist, was doing in leading them, the attentiveness of the chaplains to the needs of the Jews, and the religious growth they had experienced in their weekly classes. He mentioned that Zolly had been doing a good job with the typing, even though he was not a pro. He continued until the rabbi's open mouth sagged.

By the time Rabinowitz rose to respond, the audience was impatient for the main event. Following the introduction, he stood silent a moment, allowing them to take him in. Rabinowitz had a head of hair so thick it merged into his beard, which, in turn, filled the pits on his face like a lava flow. Zolly deduced that the rabbi must have traveled through hostile territory as a kid attending the yeshiva, because his nose had more bumps and twists than the card at a boxing match. Somewhere en route, Rabinowitz had learned to defend himself, as he had all his teeth, and not even a sumo wrestler could have moved him against his will. When the rabbi's voice boomed out, the surprise was his pitch. He could have been a radio announcer selling Sabbath specials. His opening feinted in several directions, leaving the group uncertain where he was going. After showing off his footwork and a few jabs that didn't draw blood, he punched his words, coming at them with lefts, rights, uppercuts and hooks. When he was done, a few of the more emotional even applauded. Later, Solomon said Rabinowitz reminded him of the announcer who used to do the fights at the Rainbow Arena. Every sentence was a knockout.

In conclusion, Rabinowitz said, "Never forget that we are the People of the Book. We have been chosen to live as He has commanded." Rabinowitz had taken care throughout not to use the name of God. It took Zolly a while to catch on. "You can honor the Master and do His work, even here." The longer he spoke, the more Joey Philly blinked. By now, it hurt to watch at length, but they all turned toward him when the rabbi asked, "Do you have a question?"

"I think you're saying we can do something for God while we do our time," Joey Philly said. "But what is He going to do for us? I don't think He even knows we're in here. Everybody else out there has forgotten us, why not Him?" Joey Philly was one of the guys who never received a letter.

The rabbi began to answer Joey Philly in Hebrew before catching himself and withdrawing a siddur from the velvet bag at his side. He read from the middle of the book. "Antigonus of Sokho received the oral tradition from Simeon the Just. He used to say: 'Do not be as servants who serve the Master to receive reward. Rather, be as servants who serve the Master not to receive reward.'" Rabinowitz held his finger on the place, in case there were further questions.

Reuben Lewis surprised everyone by wanting to know who those guys were. Usually, the only answers that interested him came from Betsy Tobias.

"Simeon was a member of the Great Assembly, which received our law from the prophets, and he passed it on to Antigonus." The rabbi's tone suggested Reuben might do better if he moved away from Betsy. "We study Torah, worship, and are kindly because these are the principles on which our world is based. We do not do it with the expectation that we will get anything in return."

Solomon was also ready to disagree. "I do things for guys for free, except, if they want to do something for me in return, I don't object. Are you saying I'm going about it the wrong way?"

"Of course not. We are not taught to reject reward." Rabinowitz thumbed to a different place in his siddur and read again. "All Israel has a share in the world to come, as it is said: 'Your people shall all be righteous; they shall possess the land forever.' But we are not making trades or bargains, according to *Ethics of the Fathers*."

"That what you're reading?" Solomon asked.

"I am reading from the daily prayer book," Rabinowitz said. "The same siddur you read from every Shabbat. *Ethics of the Fathers*."

"Not me," Solomon said. "I don't do shul. I came because Berns said I should. But that does make sense."

At the end, only Haskell was unimpressed, even though he posed as a regular at shul. "I don't want you to take this personally, Rabbi. But I think we could use a little input from another viewpoint. Maybe a little less Hebrew. Even with the Reform rabbi, Adlai read in Hebrew. That was bad enough, although Adlai repeated a few prayers in English. With you, we'll be lucky if we understand a single word."

Rabinowitz stroked his beard with pink hands and sparkling nails. It made sense. After the beard, he would return to stroking the prayer book. He said, "We pray in Hebrew for a perfect expression of the thought. Also, using the language of our forefathers attunes us to the spirit of the words." He sat there, an impermeable rock, Haskell's arguments splashing against him without a drop of doubt.

Haskell said, "We appreciate your being here. Your support will help. But we have all kinds of Jews here. Orthodox. Conservative. Reform. They say, put two Jews together, you have a shul. Add one more, you have dissension. One more, some break away and form a second synagogue. We also have some like me, agnostic and proud of it. The chaplain will look to you as the authority. You'll be one-sided. Being a Lubavitcher and all." Haskell pronounced it properly but said it with a sneer.

The rabbi leaned forward, anxious to clarify his point. "There is only one way to be religious, but more than one way to be a Jew." If he had been Greek, he would have been Socrates instead of Herschel.

"Of course, there's more than one way to be a Jew. Just look at me, and then look at Gabby, or at Berns." Haskell looked pleased with his props.

"And if I look, what would I see?"

"If you need to ask, you must be blind." Haskell had made his fortune with his wits, not his personality.

"Then you think there is only one way to see," Rabinowitz said. "You question that I have only one way to look at things, yet you think there is only one way to see."

Haskell swatted that away. "Look, see, what's the difference?"

"Look is an attitude, a way we go about things. See is how we perceive ourselves, our world, and our relationship with the Almighty."

Zolly's hand was cramped from keeping up. His report might miss something important. "Wait a minute," he said. "I'm losing track of where we are."

Gabby jumped in. "Where we are is easy. The Federal Correctional Institution, Lexington, Kentucky, where we're learning to be better Jews. Isn't that right, Rabbi?"

If he'd expected a compliment in return, Gabby was disappointed. Rabinowitz made a face. He said, "No such thing. Learning to be a good Jew, an observant Jew, yes. But not learning to be a Jew. We were born Jews, we are Jews, and we will die Jews. What we are about now is learning how to live as Jews." He leafed through several pages. When he found what he wanted, he reached high, arms open, almost embracing the ceiling. The sun gasped through the stained, multicolored windows engraved in commemoration of saints. They became ecumenical with Rabinowitz there. "'Where there is no Torah, there is no proper conduct; where there is no proper conduct, there is no Torah. Where there is no wisdom, there is no reverence; where there is no reverence, there is no wisdom. Where there is no knowledge, there is no understanding; where there is no understanding, there is no knowledge. Where there is no bread, there is no Torah; where there is no Torah, there is no bread.'" He closed the book. When he cleared his throat, you could hear the angels roar.

Betsy Tobias took her hands off Reuben Lewis long enough to ask, "You really think that's going to do us any good? We've got enough trouble looking out for ourselves."

Rabinowitz swallowed at this question coming from a woman. "We study, we attend services, and we follow the dictates of our faith. We have six hundred thirty Commandments, not just the ten on Moses's Tablet. 'As we live according to our laws, then they shall become us and we shall become them, and we shall truly see with our souls.'" He turned toward Joey Philly again. Ignoring the blinking, Rabinowitz said, "The time to begin is now. The place to begin is here. As it is said, 'If I am not for myself, who is for me? If I care only for myself, what am I? If not now, when?'"

Zolly considered this. He had avoided thinking about it long ago. This was a lot different from davening. Saturdays, he just said the words and read the English to avoid being bored. This guy was asking them to deal with it all day long, every day, from morning to night. He might even want their dreams. *Wait until the hack in black reads this one. It's been bad enough with him enforcing the kosher rules as though he couldn't stand the smell of pig. Now, Burgess is going to be grading us on everything we do.* He gave up trying to write it all down. It would be good enough to give Burgess the flavor of what Rabinowitz said. A taste was enough.

After the rabbi left, the group returned to their jobs. When the chaplains' offices were clear of visitors, Burgess stopped by Zolly's desk. "Quite some man, Rabbi Rabinowitz."

"Yes, Chaplain, we're lucky to have him." Zolly was transcribing his notes, the rabbi's words turning into electronic dots on a computer screen, less threatening as they flickered.

Burgess said, "Luckier than you imagine. We normally enter into one-year contracts at the start of the fiscal year, but we couldn't find a local rabbi this time. We learned that Rabbi Rabinowitz's group was sponsoring his attendance at a number of nearby prisons. Even though we're well into the year, we jumped at the chance to get him." The hack in black put his hand on Zolly's shoulder, as though about to bestow a blessing. "He represents what is best about your people. He respects what tradition means." Zolly shifted under the chaplain's hand. The hack in black continued, "Of course, if you had followed your rules, you wouldn't be here." He withdrew his hand and winked.

TWENTY-FOUR

IT WAS ONE OF THOSE KENTUCKY STORMS WHEN THE THUNDER squeezes in sideways. The rain slashed against the library windows, threatening the glass. The weather exploded the inmates indoors, where runners and walkies sought shelter in the legal section. Clusters of inmates fingered law books like children learning marbles. Zolly was at his research again. It served a dual purpose: one, it might get the guy off; and two, the time might go by faster if his inmate client could clutch at the chance he might go free, allowing the man to do his time motion to motion instead of all at once. Solomon disagreed, likening it to a gambler playing the lottery when he was short the rent. He called that the hardest time of all. Zolly reviewed the notes on his current client's appeal. Clyde was from the hills, coal mining country, one of those places where the sun shines on the back of your neck. Clyde had been hunting for deer when they caught him with his double-gauge. It was out of season, making it bad enough, but not a federal offense. Clyde's greater mistake was mouthing off to the game warden. When they ran a background check, his conviction for driving under the influence ten years earlier made his carrying the gun a federal crime. The rumor was that the judge had been moved to tears when he gave Clyde the one-year sentence. It was not so much the time, but what Clyde would have to give for the rest of his life, when the leaves were underfoot, and his dogs were wanting to run.

The research made Zolly's time move faster, as well, even though his friends thought he could leave whenever he wished. He considered explaining about David. He wanted them to know he was different, that he meant to be a proud memory, but they would probably get the wrong idea. If he told them that David had been about to rat out the guys who had muscled him out of his slots, they would figure he was like his old man. Tell them he hated David for it, they would consider him disloyal. Describe the explosion, they would look for the fear on his face. He would prove who he was by example.

Zolly was removing the volume of the United States Code that prohibited felons from having guns when Darla arrived. By then, the place smelled like a cellar because everyone who had entered was wet. Zolly wanted to stand away from them, but with so many seeking sanctuary, remaining dry wasn't an option. Instead, he focused on where they could sit. The library usually brought him luck. He now spent hours there with Darla, close enough to memorize her scent. It wasn't as good as at the movies, but sometimes he could press against her for a good ten seconds before she pulled away. When the library closed for the ten o'clock Count, he would return home with an ache between his legs. But today, his luck was bad. They couldn't find a single empty seat, much less two together, certainly not a couch where they could sit side by side. They wound up standing by a bookcase choked with atlases and maps. Zolly and Darla paged through the books in the order they were shelved, standing there, leaning against the stacks while the hacks looked on and the rain lasted. Finally, while resting between Portugal and Puerto Rico, Zolly said, "We need a better place. Maybe outside."

Darla said, "It's raining."

"It isn't always raining. We could walk in the Yard. We wouldn't have to worry about the hacks."

"Who's worried?"

"You know what I mean. Are we touching, breaking one of the rules." He let the back of his hand brush against her arm as he re-shelved the book, bringing his knuckle to his nose with the movement.

"You want to hold hands. That's very sweet, but I don't think so."

"You make it too big an issue. The hacks don't care, and no one else will notice."

"Do you think you're the only one who takes inventory? Everyone notices everything. We hold hands, next thing you know, we'll be walkies."

He thought about it. Each breath introduced a different Darla. "What's wrong with that? It only says something about two people, like going steady, or being engaged. It says that we're together."

When an inmate looking for Poland nudged them out of their place, they moved across the room to stand by criminology. There was no seating there, either, but compared to travel, punishment was empty. Darla said, "We're not in high school, you skipped college, and we don't have sex. Other than that, you hit it right on the head."

"What about Clint Eastwood?"

"That was when I hoped you'd help me out. But you chose not to, or chickened out, or for whatever reason didn't, though. And frankly, my dear, you don't make me high. All I get from you is reality."

The skies grew quiet as dusk approached and the streaks on the windows filtered the remaining light that was straggling into the room. Zolly took her elbow and moved Darla past the hack and toward the door. There was no one else in view as they echoed down the hallway toward the entrance to the building. Outside, walking through the courtyard, they passed branches bent with buds as small as teenage tits. When they reached it, they owned the Yard alone. Zolly considered his options. She wanted him to get involved in some scheme with Natron. Exactly what, he wasn't sure. If he asked, it would be a step closer to commitment. Natron was bad enough already, hanging around the office and vacuuming when Zolly was at work. Talking to the man would be worse. But there was more involved than Natron. Darla wanted something Zolly always stayed away from. He had his reasons on the Street. In here, he sensed that his reasons were different, but he hadn't figured out in what way. She was getting to be like Rabinowitz. The thinking was starting to hurt.

"Reality?" He kicked a pebble in their path and watched it skitter through the fence. "I used to think I knew what was real. Now, I wonder if anything ever was. I see a fence, I think of the zoo in Lincoln Park, when I was outside, looking in."

Darla said, "We're not animals in cages whose keepers do their thinking. We make choices."

They were at the corner of the Yard where the outside lawn and the street beyond were at their left, and the Atwood fence forced a right turn. "Such as?" he asked. She was probably going to give him the choices again. If he could put up, she would put out.

"Choices like a normal life, choices like being with my husband, making all this up to him." Darla looked ten years older than he had ever seen her before. "The parole board's next month. I've got a chance to go home if they give me the low end of my guidelines."

Here she was, changing again. One minute it was hints of sex, the next, dreams of riding high, the next, the housewife in disguise emerging. Zolly said, "This is the first I've heard of this. We've just begun to know each other."

"What difference does that make?"

"I thought, maybe, we could become closer. You never know what could develop from that." He was trying to come up with arguments without making commitments. For twenty years, he'd never said anything to Faith that she could throw back at him if he backed away. "Sometimes, certain things are meant to be. I don't know about us, but we haven't given it a chance. That's all. I just want to give it a chance."

She took his hand, interlocking their fingers. "I think the word you're searching for is relationship. You probably never used it on the outside. It's a long word, but that's not what makes it hard, and even when you learn to say it, that doesn't make it true. Be honest. Aren't you really looking for sex?" When her mouth formed the words like candy droplets, and she squeezed his hand so hard he thought his heart would give way, he wanted to envelop her, absorb her until her blondness soaked his body. "Like I told you," she said. "I won't give it away like I do my commissary. If you want to be my walkie, you have to get me what I need. That's a choice I get to make. And you'd better do it fast, in case the parole board votes for me."

They skirted the moat the rain had formed by the gate in the Atwood fence. Darla asked, "What about your choices? How about your girlfriend back home? How about the choice that you make every day? Anytime you want, you can leave. I don't get that choice unless the parole board sends me home. If you make that your choice, all I can do is wave goodbye. Assuming you'd even look back."

"I could never walk away from you." His promise erupted. The words made it real. "I want to be with you. Any way you want."

She put her hand on his cheek. "I like spending time with you. We'll just have to find a way to be together during the day. As friends, unless you can do better for me."

They had almost come full circle when they reached the tennis courts. Terry Barker was already there, giving lessons to a girl half his age, the balls bouncing lower and the water splashing higher with every volley. As her shirt grew wet, the shape of her breasts thrust in rhythm with her strokes. Terry was a good example of why the courts were placed as far back from the road as possible. He was in his forties, but he had the tan and muscles of a man whose sole employment was himself.

Darla said, "I could work in the chaplains' offices. They approved Judy's transfer to Pleasanton to let her be near her family. If you think you can handle it, sponsor me for the opening. Besides, Natron does the cleanup there. One way or another, maybe I'll get what I need." She moved closer with that, brushing against him as they watched the man with muscles score.

———

THE NEXT MORNING, ZOLLY SPOKE TO WEAVER. LET HIM DEAL with Burgess. Weaver had the center office, next to Zolly's desk. Zolly watched through the window that separated their desks. The back wall to Weaver's office, with just a few windows, faced a courtyard that separated the chaplains' offices from arts and crafts across the way. It was all windows knee-high to ceiling and wall to wall. Weaver was hunched over his ledger sheets. When he stretched, Zolly tapped on the window and the chaplain waved him in.

Weaver's office would have made a bookkeeper happy, with two adding machines on his desk and a calculator between them. Accounting textbooks lined the credenza behind him, studded with papers that marked the spots that had him stumped. From the look of it, he had a lot of puzzles yet to resolve. A gooseneck lamp stood on the corner of his desk, the end curved so low Weaver had to duck beneath the bulb. Maybe that was why he stretched so much and welcomed any visitor. He would have been at ease pumping gas or teaching freshman English. Whenever inmates came around, they found their way to his office. Making you feel at home was the best thing a chaplain could do for a man.

Zolly took a seat in front of the desk. If it had been Burgess, he would still be standing. "Chaplain, I hear Judy is leaving," Zolly said.

Weaver rocked forward with question marks for eyes and placed his palms on either side of his ledgers. "We asked her not to say anything until we had someone to take her place."

"She didn't tell me that. But that's why I've come to see you."

When Weaver tilted his head, he looked a lot like Burgess. "It's an important job. We don't give you anything other than the Welfare Fund to work on. That's why we rely so much on our clerk. We don't want applications from unqualified people."

"Chaplain, I'm recommending someone who is well qualified. She's an excellent typist." Zolly wasn't sure about the typing part, but he knew Darla had strong fingers.

With his eyebrows furrowed, Weaver was an even better impersonation of Burgess. "I know that you don't walk with anyone, Zolly. I admire that. A man your age doesn't want to act foolishly."

"That shouldn't be an issue. We're just friends."

Weaver glanced at the container that rested in the corner of his office from one weekend to the next, between the poses of the inmates. It was full of instant-developing film that Zolly would put inside the week before. It cost four dollars a roll, and they charged a dollar a shot. Not as good a markup as he used to make at his bar, but enough to make loans to indigent inmates. "We may have another opening soon. When Joel leaves, there's no reason his job can't be filled by a woman. Would your friend be interested in that?"

That was not what Zolly had in mind. Joel only worked part-time, on Friday evenings in the offices and a couple of hours Saturdays and Sundays in the visiting room. Friday nights, Zolly would attend services. Afterward, there would be a crowd around when he helped count the photo money. That would not put him alone with Darla. "She's really looking for something full-time, Chaplain. Besides, the box and all that gear might be too heavy for her to lug around. She's got a slender build." The last part was true, although Zolly suspected that if Darla used the same strength as when she pushed him away, she could carry the box across the visitors' room with three visiting kids hanging on.

"I share Chaplain Burgess's doubts about having men and women work together. It may lessen the tension, but it also causes a greater strain. I'm concerned that with the two of you working in the same office, you'd be tempted to take chances."

Zolly saw his chances slipping away at the same speed with which he had lost his bar. "Chaplain, it's not as though this would be a change in your practice. If we've had Judy working here, why is that okay?"

Weaver gestured toward Burgess's office. "We started with Gloria working with Judy. We had some doubts when we hired you to take Gloria's place. I decided to give you a chance because your community sponsored you. Chaplain Burgess respected my wishes because I am in charge of the Fund." Weaver moved his hands from one pile of papers to another, as though each were a separate set of reasons. "Judy works for both of us. And there's another difference." He lowered his voice as though it might not hurt if he whispered. "The two of you already know each other."

That was when Zolly understood how Gershom had felt when he'd pleaded with the judge. He himself was searching for the words he hadn't known he would need when he entered. "I've done everything you've asked of me. You even let me count the money. You can trust me."

Weaver leaned back, his expression suggesting he had just discovered an error he would have to call to the head accountant's attention.

TWENTY-FIVE

THE LETTER CRINKLED AGAINST THE SIDE OF ZOLLY'S LEG AS HE walked to work. He knew bringing it to the office was a risk, considering that Darla's desk was only a few feet away, but it was less hazardous than reading it the previous day, when everyone had witnessed his triumph. Immediately after the four o'clock Count, they had clustered around the hack. Mail call was for readers and watchers. The regulars got to hear their names. The rest got to envy the stars. Zolly was there, just being sociable, when the hack announced that Zolly had mail. He'd resisted opening the envelope all night. It was either bad news or worse news. It could be legal news. Maybe they'd returned an indictment. He could be up on charges. Fallen had hinted that was coming. Hell, it was someone else's taxes. They ought to change the law, make each person accountable for his own. Withholding taxes made every boss a federal stooge. But it could be even worse. If they indicted Goldberg, it might be immunity all over again. None of his research dealt with back-to-back contempt of court. It would be nice if Gershom had bothered to let him know, instead of using Faith to deliver the update. Or it could just be Faith, bitching about her past and present. She could wait a day. He didn't want to deal with issues or think about the Street.

The next morning, when he brought the letter to work to digest in privacy, Natron was across the hall, cleaning the chapel. Darla was on her weekly run for Burgess. Zolly doubted that every unit needed its own copy of the coming Sunday's hymns, but her journey would give him the silence he needed. He removed the envelope from his pocket and smoothed it out with his ruler. Just a look at the curves she made writing his name reminded him of trouble.

"Dear Zolly." *Why does mail begin that way? If your name is on the envelope, you already know it's for you.* "I haven't written in so long because I know how bad things are for you. I didn't want to depress you any further. I figured if you needed anything, you'd write, or call collect. I'm sorry I have to send this letter."

She was an intruder. He could see Faith watching for his reaction, ready to dart away if he made a sudden move. Why was she so scared? For a moment, he was with her again, meeting her out on Howard. She had been his first waitress. Those were the days they'd had sex from every angle.

"It's hard to believe things could get worse," she wrote. "You know I went on unemployment compensation as soon as they closed the bar, but the extended benefits have run out. I haven't been able to find a full-time job on the Near North. They say you can always get work waiting tables, but everywhere I go they want to know about my last job and then they turn me down. Maybe I should settle for the suburbs." Faith working on the North Shore made an interesting image. She would have to wear thick stockings and gray her hair. "I did find some odd jobs, temporary work I could hide from the unemployment, so I was able to earn extra income on the side, but now that isn't enough, and the cash register money is gone." Zolly reached for his pocket, but all he felt was quarters.

"I'm not getting any help from your Booth One friends. I always knew O'Rourke was full of shit, but I thought you were right, that Goldberg and Civiletti would look out for us for their own good. I hope you don't blame me for running away from Goldberg. Is there anything you can do? Maybe you know someone you can send me to see. Or if you have anything stashed away, can you help me get at it? I hope you're fine and that everything is well with you. Love, Faith. June 14, 1986."

At least someone loved him. It was hard to believe that she still did. Faith had been with him all those years. She was always on call when the rest of his world was sick. Every day, when he told himself he was on his own, she was right beside him, letting him believe that lie. How the hell could he help? Civiletti had stopped sending money to Zolly's commissary account the month after he reported. Then Faith went and brushed off Goldberg. Not that he blamed her, considering the man's weight and smell, but now there was no chance he could get them to do anything for him. The money was long gone for legal fees. Whatever he could do would have to come from here. He could earn more working at UNICOR but would miss out on being with Darla. Zolly closed his eyes, but when he opened them the same words scolded him from the page. Then it came to him. He looked through the window until he saw Weaver stretching and then entered the office. Afterward, he wrote her back. It had been months since he had last written anyone, which had been his final plea to Goldberg. His words cut a swath across the computer screen:

"Dear Faith, I picked up a weekend job to earn extra money. It won't be much, probably only ten or fifteen dollars a week, but it should help you out a little. I also volunteered to be the weekend cameraman. They were looking for a replacement for a guy named Joel who got released a couple of weeks ago. He worked out of our office, so I had an in for the job. The chaplain was about to hire another man who works here cleaning up, until I explained how much you need the money. I start work tomorrow. I hope you're well. Zolly. June 18, 1986."

He considered adding "Love," but that might make her nervous.

———————

VISITING HOURS BEGAN WHILE SATURDAY MORNING SERVICES were still underway, but Weaver had reassured Zolly he could bring the camera box back over afterward. That meant Zolly had to resume attendance at Saturday worship, which was just as well because, in another couple of weeks, the summer heat would compel it. Besides, if this was what Weaver expected, it was part of the job description, even if he didn't get paid for the time.

After shul, Zolly went into Burgess's office to get the camera box. The hack in black was on the phone when Zolly entered the room. Zolly swept the box into the air as though swinging a golf club and then, in the downswing, waved at Burgess while leaving. The box held only the camera and extra film. Later, it would also contain the proceeds from the sales. The clasp of the box was locked, but Weaver had given Zolly the key. It felt as strange as a third hand in his pocket. Zolly had never seen an inmate with a key or chewing gum. Anything that could open a lock or plug one up was reserved for the hacks. In the hallway, he unlocked the box and hid the key beneath the film. He walked across the courtyard with the metal case banging at his side. Entry was through a door from the courtyard into a room where the guards did pat-downs and body searches before and after visits. On seeing Zolly with the camera box, this Saturday's hack waved Zolly in without a touch, not even looking for any bulges. Zolly was tempted to flash the key but resisted the impulse and left it nestled beneath the Polaroid packs.

The room looked different than it had during Zolly's last visit. A year earlier, when the feds had come unannounced, Zolly's first impression had been it was furnished with the leftovers from a Goodwill going-out-of-business sale. The imitation leather on the seat of his chair was cracked; the fake tile floor also cracked; the curtains were gray and frayed on the inner windows that faced the Yard, as well as anyone walking past; and the painted walls were smeared with food stains from the vending machines. It was a secondhand room for the thirdhand remnants of society's failures.

This time, however, the room was no longer empty. The furnishings showed the same abuse, but the place was a terminal echoing hellos and goodbyes. Next to the visitors' entrance, lines led from vending machines to microwaves that smelled of burnt popcorn and melted pizza. Zolly knew the routine. He went from one group to another to offer instant memories. The usual poses were arms around shoulders, holding hands, looking at the cameras, and sometimes at each other. Weaver entered each sale in his book while Zolly snapped away. After a couple of hours, they had almost a hundred dollars in coins and paper money, enough for commissary loans to the next four impoverished arrivals. When Weaver waved him home, Zolly took the box and returned to the entry room. The hack didn't even bother inspecting the metal container for contraband. No wonder Natron had wanted the job.

He was returning across the Yard to the chaplains' offices when Natron and Perez approached. "I see you get the job," Natron said. "Real juicy. I put in for it, but they turn me down. You got the chaplains figuring I'm only good for pushing a broom. First, you suck up to Truman, now it's Weaver. You got a slick way about you, Chicago." Spit flew from Natron's mouth, while Perez looked on the ground for trash.

"I need the extra pay. But I never said a word against you."

"You folks always want the cash. If you so short, you should have talked to me." Natron winked at Perez, who batted his eyelids back.

Zolly said, "I need to bring this back to the office."

"We'll ride back with you. We want to talk."

Zolly picked up the pace.

Perez said, "We like to trot, too. We have a deal for you. You can trot all you like. You can be the horse and earn some carrots. You like the juice?"

Zolly said, "Thanks, but I'm carrying enough of a load already."

———

THAT EVENING, NATRON AND PEREZ PAID A VISIT AFTER COUNT, announcing they wanted to talk to him alone. Zolly was surprised when Maggiano agreed to leave, given that he was the senior in the room. When the three were alone, Natron said, "You shouldn't have run away. You don't want us to have bad thoughts."

"Nothing like that. Hell, I've known you since I got here. We even work together. It's just that I needed to get back to the office and return the box before Count."

"You got it all wrong. My man Joel used to keep the camera box under his bed overnight, handy when he went back to the visiting room next day."

"What difference does it make to you?" Zolly said.

"How long you been here, a year? Don't disrespect me. Now you say, what difference? Say you take the box back to your room, all locked up, everything inside real safe, and only you got the key. What good is that to us?"

Zolly doubted Natron could identify a rhetorical question if it bit Perez in the ass. "Maybe you want me to take some private snapshots."

"I do like a man with a sense of humor," Perez said, looking over his shoulder at the closed door behind him.

Zolly knew what was coming. If you wanted them bad enough, and had the money, you could get all the drugs you wanted. Darla told him all the time. Zolly had stayed away from that on the Street. He certainly didn't want to start in the joint, where the price was always double. Being clean meant he didn't have to worry about the piss tests that occurred at random every evening, when they called a few men to the lieutenant's office. Some guys were invited so often they drank water before every Count so that, if they received the summons, they wouldn't take too long and miss out on chow. Zolly felt comfortable staying as dry as a Supreme Court case. He said, "Neither of you is laughing."

"We were thinking again about you being our horse," Perez said.

"I sure as hell am not going to bring the box back to Atwood. The first time there's a shakedown, the hack would make me open it up. And even if I could carry something out of the visiting room, I've got to bring the box to the office. I turn it over to Weaver first thing Monday morning. We open it, he counts the film and the money, and stores the box in his office. Even if I could carry something out, I couldn't get to it." Zolly had watched Gershom one time before he hired him. The man hadn't stood still, arguing to the jury while fingering his hair, making faces as he said his words, pointing, gesticulating, and knifing the air with the side of his hand. He had italicized his arguments and underlined their depth with a hoarse voice and a sweaty brow. Zolly now tried to match that with his own angry audience.

Natron dismissed Zolly with a wave of his hand. "When Joel was nervous about the hack in his unit, he brought the box to the office, just like you. But first thing Monday morning, before he got around to counting with Weaver, he took the smack out of the box and onto his desk."

"You think I'm going to put it in my drawer?"

Natron smiled again, as full of answers as Alex Trebek. "That what you got that mother-fuck computer for. Gloria tells me it's mostly air inside. Lots of room for coke. We collect it when we need it."

Zolly admired the idea. There was no way a hack would ever open a computer. They were afraid of breaking it. But he would not join in on the scheme. Natron was a walking target.

"You say you needs the extra cash," Natron said. "That's why you take my job. You think we have this talk if you kept your nose out of my business? But you charge right in, like that time with Gloria in the hallway." He paused, showing the gleam in his eye. "We can even pay you with green. You could send it right out to your lady. Just slip it inside a card, send it out for her birthday." Natron stopped again, and then resumed as though his next argument had just occurred to him. "We might even let you keep some yourself."

"I'm not a user, and I'm certainly not going to start selling it."

"From what I hear," Natron said, "it can help another way. Darla been talking to me."

Zolly had looked away every time he saw Natron speaking to Darla in the office. Back when it was Haskell had been bad enough. Those days, she had been a fantasy, one step closer than a magazine foldout. Now she was the one who shared Zolly's meals and work hours. She read her book next to him when he worked for Solomon at night. She eluded his touch a second slower each week. She had no business even looking at Natron. Wishing Maggiano were there to back him up, he said what he had wanted to tell Natron all along. "She tells me if I don't get it for her, you will. I'm telling you to stay away."

Natron shook his head at Zolly. "I could have supplied her if Weaver gave me the job. She knew it, too. But since you suck up to Weaver, you get to arrange her supply. If you won't do it for your old friends, or for the green, then do it for that honey who's ready to lick it off anywhere you put it."

It wasn't the risk that bothered Zolly. Contemplating it further that night, he decided it was because wanting Darla was no excuse. What was wrong with rats was they let people down. Weaver had trusted him. Gabby, Adlai, Solomon, and all the others had pushed him for the job. He'd be letting them down, just as he had abandoned Truman.

TWENTY-SIX

"Are you angry at something I did, something you did, or just pissed off in general?" Zolly said.

Solomon was picking at his fingers instead of his food. His lunch would have to wait. He rubbed his hand across his chest, staining his shirt in the process. "UNICOR's got me working a new line of picture frames at work. Like anyone's going to look at any pictures long enough to notice how it's framed."

"You cut yourself with your saw?"

"I stopped to blow my nose and took off my gloves to do it. The damn sawdust gets in everywhere." When clearing his nose, Solomon had neglected the rest of his head. Traces of sawdust were spread across his hair like sprinkles on a cake. "When I went for a load of wood to bring by my machine, I forgot to put my gloves back on. These splinters are driving me nuts." He mopped his hands with a rag. "After lunch, I'm going to see the PA."

Zolly pointed at Solomon's tray. "You're missing out on the advantage of eating early." The room held only a few other men and women with excuses for skipping the line.

"Try sucking blood," Solomon said. "See how much appetite you got. Why are you eating early?"

"To keep up my strength."

The rabbi's visit was scheduled for an hour later. When Rabinowitz departed every Tuesday, he gave Zolly the points he wanted to cover in the next week's lesson. Just jottings, not even notes, scrawled on pieces torn from other documents. It took the following week to separate the rabbi's writing from shopping lists and his wife's reminders. Every Tuesday, Zolly raced to complete the outline before their meeting, consoling himself with the thought that this way it would be fresh in his mind. He reassured himself he was not procrastinating. During the week, he also practiced Hebrew.

"You may be taking things a bit too seriously," Solomon said. "After all, you're not King of the Jews. Your job is typing up memos for the Welfare Fund and keeping track of the records. This religion stuff is extra duty that doesn't get you anywhere."

"My overtime gets your legal briefs typed."

"I appreciate your good work." Solomon finally attacked his food. "There's a big difference between that and all the mumbo jumbo."

"Yeah, privilege against self-incrimination and res gestae are ordinary English phrases everyone understands. But when we do anything that involves religion, it's bullshit."

"I try to do right by my fellow man. You need the words to do it."

Zolly himself worked on words all the time. There were so many ways to say the same thing. He changed his sentences midstream these days, undecided on which bait to bite. He used to work on what he would say while the next guy was talking. Now, he found himself listening to his own words as they left his mouth, analyzing his meaning, assessing the other guy's meaning, evaluating how what he himself said would be understood. He would second-guess himself after the most trivial conversation, thinking how he could have expressed himself better. Every morning, before he read Truman's word-of-the-day book for its current selection, he would review the words he had learned to that point. He played at making as many as possible fit in a single sentence. And once a week he worked on Rabinowitz's words, as well.

At the office, Zolly considered this week's Scriptures portion, about the destruction of the Temple by an enemy army. They were still wrestling with the loss of a building a couple thousand years later. He hoped he could get over losing his bar sooner than that. He sat at his computer, ready to fill the screen with words. Glancing away, he saw the hack in black huddled with Weaver in his office. The window framed their movements like a TV screen. He watched as they worked and tried to decipher their poses and the mumbles that breached the glass. The office had a June fiscal year. They were reviewing next year's budget. Weaver had moved the books to the edge of his desk, to allow space for the paper spread out before him. Burgess was huddled over Weaver's shoulder while they worked on the ledger sheet. Burgess would point and Weaver would erase, then Burgess would speak and Weaver would write. Occasionally, Weaver would look up at Burgess and move his head side to side before looking down again. Then Weaver would crumple his current effort, toss it into his wastebasket, and they would begin again. They might have had a year-end surplus and needed some ideas how to spend it. While waiting for Weaver to wave him in, Zolly began his own list, which included a stereo, extra camera, and another computer. After another half hour of wasting paper, Burgess left the office and walked over to Zolly. That was a surprise, because Burgess usually left him alone. The Welfare Fund was a special project of Weaver's. Burgess himself spent half his time hating it and the rest of the time ignoring it. Maybe this had to do with the Jewish services, which was Burgess's project.

"Berns, I'm afraid I have some bad news for you people." Burgess might have been afraid, but the corners of his lips were turned up like a cat's mouth after slurping cream.

"What's that, Chaplain?"

"We're not able to renew Rabbi Rabinowitz's contract. Today will be his last visit." Now Burgess was opening his mouth wide enough to show a wet-chalk tongue.

"I don't understand. I thought . . . I mean, don't you think . . . he's been doing a good job?"

Burgess put on his father-knows-best face. "I'm sure he's been doing a fine job. I've enjoyed my chances to chat with him after his meetings with you people. But we just don't have the funds to have him again next year."

"But last year, we had money left over. We were scrambling to spend it. That's when we ordered the VCR." Zolly covered the notes he had typed for spending any surplus.

Burgess arched his back. "You have no idea what our situation was last year. Besides, last year has nothing to do with now." He stretched out the last word, making it a cat noise.

Zolly worked at a response that Gabby might approve. "The other groups have someone to lead their services. We've never even asked for that. Can't we just have the rabbi meet with us during the week?"

Burgess bristled. "We're not going to provide separate clergy for every single group. If we did, there would be no end to it. We have Catholics, Baptists, Presbyterians, Lutherans, Methodists, Muslims, and, oh yes, you Jews. This institution has two chaplains. Anything more is a bonus." He rubbed against Zolly's desk. "You shouldn't look at a rabbi as something you're entitled to. You people represent less than five percent of our population."

By Zolly's count, that made it three "you peoples." Seven more and they would have a minyan. He said, "Isn't there some way we could continue with the rabbi through the end of the summer? So we could prepare for the High Holiday services?"

Burgess took his time answering, posturing concern. After considering alternatives, he clapped his hands in discovery. "Ask the rabbi if he wants to visit as a volunteer. I suppose we could approve that." Burgess rubbed his hands together again, then turned and walked away before they reached his mouth.

Zolly was eager to share the news. Gabby always arrived ahead of the rest of the group. In order to report the evening news, Gabby had to hear it first. When he arrived, Zolly said, "This is the rabbi's last visit. Burgess says they can't afford him in next year's budget. He probably wants to save the money for some candles or a bunch of semiautomatics. I had to talk him into letting Rabinowitz come for free."

Gabby shrugged. "It will be hard for you all without a rabbi," he said, sounding more like a country boy than one from Brooklyn. "You all will have to study harder. I'm sure you all will do okay. Sorry I won't be here to help. This is my last year down, so I get to attend the shul in town on a pass. I'll be gone in early December. That leaves it up to you."

Zolly wasn't surprised that Gabby would deliver his own news as though it were an afterthought. It was standard Gabby, quick to distribute the next guy's gossip but covering his own under a double layer of noise. By itself, Gabby's absence wouldn't pose a problem, but it would follow Adlai's pending departure the month before. Haskell would be no help, and Joey Philly blinked. The rest of the group were just watchers.

When Rabinowitz arrived, Zolly was waiting at the door. "They tell me your contract won't be renewed."

The rabbi nodded. "This is my last visit." His beard hid his expression. Zolly had to lean forward to hear Rabinowitz say, "I was sorry when Chaplain Burgess told me they couldn't continue our arrangements. He did say I could visit on my own, but my only income is from jail visits. I'll have to replace this job at another institution. I'm disappointed for you."

"Disappointed" was a word that struck out when it pinch-hit for saddened. He might as well have said the store was out of bubble gum, you'll have to settle for Juicy Fruit. Zolly hadn't missed gum before. Now, his jaw was aching. The feeling spread across his body. It became hard to breathe. After all this time, the words still wouldn't be right. "I never thought I'd look at things this way. Hell . . . excuse me, Rabbi . . . I hadn't been to services for forty years before I got here, excepting when my mother died."

"The saying is, 'Man plans, God laughs.' I know you'll carry on after I am gone."

"But I won't be able to talk to you. I need to know how to apply what we're studying to my daily life. You say to live by the Commandments, but I don't know which ones fit this thing I'm working on."

Rabinowitz's shrug said it was a needless concern. "Work on the Commandments. Study the Torah. I know you've been reading *Ethics of the Fathers*. Your answers will come from our teachings."

This was his last chance for specifics. Zolly asked, "What do they tell us about being loyal when it hurts someone else?" There wasn't time to talk about Goldberg, Civiletti, and O'Rourke. Faith alone would take an afternoon. And there were no words for Truman.

"If you are loyal to the right thing, hurting someone else will not be an issue. You will come to see this. But now, our session should begin."

"I'm worried about our group, too. We have the High Holiday services just a couple of months away. Adlai went home last month. Gabby took over, but I just learned he's going to attend the shul in town. Without a rabbi or a cantor, I don't know what kind of services we can have." But he knew what kind. Fifty-five portions unsung and a group of kosher-line diners just filling time between meals.

Rabinowitz put his bag on Zolly's desk, removed his handkerchief, and wiped his face, the white cloth flashing hope against his beard. "They will be fine. I have heard the improvement in your Hebrew during our sessions. You are praying at services, as well?"

"Sure. I daven all the time. It's coming back to me. But even if I'm able to participate, we still need a cantor."

"Then you shall be the chazan."

"You think I can lead the services?"

Two weeks before his bar mitzvah, Zolly had still been learning his part. Grandpa Sam was flying in for the occasion. And David was snoring on the couch, while Zolly tried to get it right. After fits and starts, Zolly had cleared his throat and chosen a different octave. He was unable to hear himself as others heard him. Even though he had been tone-deaf ever since the explosion that had killed his father, he could tell the difference between E flat and E sharp if he felt his way there. He could approximate the tune but was always ten beats behind. When Zolly chanted, it was a game of catch-up. Sometimes, his hurry even turned his voice into a screech. This time, David had opened one eye, squinted, and waved Zolly out of the room.

The rabbi raised his hands, as though bestowing a blessing. "You can read Hebrew, you pronounce it properly, and if the words are unfamiliar, daven slowly."

"Even so, they'll just be words in a language I don't know. I can't say them properly without understanding them." Maybe that was it. He should have memorized the English. That might even have pleased David.

The rabbi smiled. His sideburns squeezed against his eyes. "The meaning will come to you."

Zolly doubted that. After the rabbi left, Zolly realized that learning the melody was even less likely.

TWENTY-SEVEN

FALLEN WAS THIRSTY AS USUAL IN A PLANE, WHEN WATER wouldn't do and soda left him dry. When the air grew thin and his nose grew fat, Fallen needed scotch. It was probably due to his sinuses. At ground level, the malt seemed to stuff them up, which was why he drank bourbon on the Street. Up in the air, though, Johnnie Walker Red was Drano. The stewardess brought their drinks at twenty thousand feet and climbing. The overhead lights demanded he stay in place, but there she was, serving booze as though there were no connection between his throat and bladder. When the thirst was overwhelming and you couldn't leave your seat, catheters were the only solution. Fallen considered asking the stewardess permission to go to the john, before remembering that the seat-belt sign also limited traffic down the aisle while the serving carts blocked the way, not only in order to keep the passengers secure. If he went to the rear of the plane to relieve himself now, it would be Cleveland before he could return to his seat. Fallen crossed his legs, bumping his tray upward before it settled in place for his drink. At least you got above the clouds pretty fast when you flew out of National Airport in D.C. No airline wanted to make a senator wait.

Seats over the wings made it hard to carry on a conversation due to the noise of the thrust of the jets, which was why Fallen had bought his tickets early. He looked at socializing the way he regarded water. Probably necessary, but still a nuisance. He avoided both by sipping scotch and writing opening statements and closing arguments, crafting speeches like a flight plan until they soared. Right now, though, Fallen only focused on his drink and squeezing his knees together.

He timed his gulps with the feel of the engines shaking the side of the plane. He took a sip each time an unfamiliar tremor shuddered the floor, letting the liquid roll across his tongue when the vibration drilled up through the seat and swallowing as his ice pounded with the beat. The movement melted the cubes.

"Do you ever wonder?" Cully hollered in Fallen's ear.

"About what?" Fallen pushed the tray into the rear of the seat in front of him and uncrossed his legs. Maybe Cully could help take his mind off his immediate needs. He smoothed his trouser creases back in place, forming a bend in the cloth at his knee. He liked that they called him the Suit behind his back.

The veins in Cully's forehead quivered as he spoke above the drone. "Why do you think he doesn't get it over with? On a scale of one to ten in the joint, he'll be lucky to make it to two."

"He's going to be a zero if he doesn't cooperate."

"You got to get him to speak at all before we can move on to cooperation. It's been over a year. Our superiors want results."

Cully wasn't telling Fallen anything he didn't already know. The home-office bosses had their heads in the clouds in Washington, comparing the bottom line with a budget some bureaucrat tore off an adding machine without even looking at the prices. The accountants needed postgraduate work on the Street. Information came harder in Chicago the deeper you dug. When you were done, most of the holes were dry, but Washington expected a gusher every time. They would all be rich if the Strike Force could drill it on command. Fallen focused on the drink draining down his throat. The scotch had cleared his nose, but his bladder had paid the price. Cully was adding to the pressure rather than relieving his concern.

"Besides, we're not just pushing him to talk, we're insisting he read our script," Cully said. "We should have gotten Judge Dillon to okay the bug, or pressured Berns beforehand to wear a wire. All we've got is a tape we can't use. We should have gone by the book."

There he was, talking about the bug again. When they had planted the recorder in the table at Zolly's Place, all Cully had done was cluck his concerns. But that tape was worth more than anything Berns might have known. The problem was getting it into evidence. "Since when did you get religious?" Fallen asked. When he wasn't busy with his hands, Cully was giving him an argument. Fallen funneled the rest of his drink down his throat. "What's wrong with a script?"

"Usually, when we get a guy to tell it our way," Cully said, "he's also telling it like it is, so it doesn't matter if the narrative is firsthand truth. We're just packaging it so it will play better. There's justice to that."

Fallen banged his glass onto the armrest. A cube flew out, landing in the pocket of the seat in front of him. "First it's religion, then it's conscience, then it's truth, and now it's justice. Listen, my friend, this is none of the above. We're only cleaning up scum." He'd have to use that one in a closing argument sometime. "We're going after the men who make it possible. It's not enough to arrest the ponies who smuggle the drugs across the borders."

"Then who?"

"It's not the packagers, the dealers, or the pushers." Fallen paused his speech. The problem was TV. Words were no longer enough for an audience that insisted on action. They had to see it to believe it, but the Rules of Criminal Procedure didn't allow him to use a tape he'd planted in a barroom booth without the okay of the owner, or of some judge. "It's the Goddamn fixers who set it all up, who hide the crime, that's who," Fallen said.

Cully understood, or agreed, or cared about something besides his next promotion. "You must have been quite a sight, clean-cut guy like you working for the DEA," he said.

Fallen said, "Growing a beard, letting your hair get shoulder-length is only part of it. You don't live long in disguise." He closed his eyes. Now he was a full-color image, smelling like weed after a year on the job. He moved his legs together, apart, together, apart, a few inches each way, while controlling his bladder.

"How come you didn't get hooked?"

"I never forgot who I was." To this day, Fallen knew who he was. He was courtroom-tall with hair the color of the Oak Street Beach in the sun at noon, every strand still dry. He had the face of an outdoor jogger that he had earned as an indoor drinker. He starched his collar to stand high on his neck and hold his head like a trophy. His whiskey voice soothed his juries. He would never wilt in the heat.

"All this would have gone down easier if you had taken the time to get a court order. We wouldn't have to play kiss-ass with this guy."

Cully looked down, talking into the magazine in his lap, evidently figuring Fallen couldn't hear his mumble.

He should tell Cully that sometimes you learned to read lips when you worked on the Street. Even in profile. Fallen said, "We never could have obtained an order fast enough. By the time we could have shown Dillon why a wire was needed, the deal would have gone down. Better late than never doesn't always work."

How could he lay it all out so a jury would understand? How could he show them his motives were pure, if it ever got that far? He wasn't looking forward to some prosecutor, in a criminal case against him and Cully, arguing to a jury: "These men were supposed to stop crime, not commit their own crimes. If those who are sworn to uphold the law violate the law in the name of justice, our democracy is doomed." The special prosecutor would probably say it better than that. Fallen figured he himself could rise to the challenge if he were on the other side. He held his head back for the last drops of his drink and then placed the cup in the back pocket of the seat in front of him, which still held the cube. He looked over his shoulder and saw that the stewardess had disappeared into the galley, or wherever it was they hid from the passengers most of a flight. He visited the washroom at the rear of the plane to relieve both his mind and his body. When he returned, he was ready for Cully.

"I'll let him know what we need and show him the alternative," Fallen said. "If he still refuses to talk, I'll go for criminal contempt and an indictment."

"We'd never be going after him if it weren't for Goldberg and Civiletti. Who cares about withholding taxes?"

"But it is about Goldberg and Civiletti." Fallen drove his words above the noise. "They had the connections. They were the ones who got the cops to admit to a fake mistake, or to violating some technicality, so that the charge would get dismissed. The rot starts and ends with three in a booth, and Berns can help us get them."

"That's a compelling plot. Do we write the dialogue, too?"

Fallen said, "How long have you been helping me prep witnesses? I don't have to write a script; all I have to do is have him say it his own way, but in words I understand. I'll let him know each time he says it wrong. After a while, he'll figure out what to say and how to say it."

He turned toward Cully. "Okay, you be Berns." He nodded to make the man feel at home. "Now, what's on your mind?"

"How do I get out of here?" Cully said.

"By describing in your own words, Mr. Berns, what you did about the recording device hidden inside the table in your booth."

"I don't know anything about that," Cully said, too much into his part.

"Mr. Berns, you paid off the health inspector every time he came. Bribing a public official is a federal crime. Again, tell us what you know about the recording device." Fallen wagged his finger.

"Oh. The bug. What I know."

"What you know."

"One time there was a bug in my bar. It was in the table in Booth One at my bar."

"Yes, and did you know about that device at the time it was placed there? By the way, I do think we have some discretion on the bribery charge."

"Yes. I knew before it was placed there."

"And did you give permission to have the recording device hidden in the booth?"

"Yes. I gave permission."

"And to whom did you give that permission, Mr. Berns?"

"I gave it to you, right?"

Fallen said, "If you say so, Mr. Berns. If you say so."

TWENTY-EIGHT

ZOLLY SAW THEM AT ONE OF THE TABLES NEAR THE VENDING machines. Cully was working his way through a pack of gum while Fallen inhaled his cigar. The way they worked their jaws, they might as well have been eating dinner. After Cully wadded his current mouthful onto a leftover pizza plate and started on his third stick, Zolly decided to get it over with. "This my annual visit?" Being with these two reminded him of Truman, but the guard at the far end of the room was just another hack.

Fallen mouthed his cigar as though it might yield milk. He was wearing a tan summer-weight suit and two-toned loafers. He could have just returned from inspecting his summer farm. The fact that his shoes were clean didn't prove otherwise. Zolly knew from the last visit that Cully was the one who shoveled. When he leaned forward, his gut hung over the knee-high table that rested between them. "We can help you with visits. In fact, you won't need to worry about visits. Once you're free, you can see anyone you like."

"After sixteen months, you think I'm ripe?"

Fallen waved the idea away. "After sixteen months, you don't get to walk out of here just because you agree to talk."

"Isn't that what it's all about?"

"There are some other things we haven't covered."

"You got me buried so deep I can't see air."

"Like paying your taxes." Fallen patted his briefcase like the flank of his favorite horse.

"It's no crime if there's no intent," Zolly said.

"Did Gershom tell you that? I hope he didn't charge you extra. Or was it some jailhouse lawyer?"

"I'm willing to take my chances."

"How about payoffs to get a pass from the inspectors?" Fallen patted his case as though it held five pounds of crimes.

"I'm not saying I know anything about that. But if I did, that's state, not federal."

"Corrupting a public official is a federal crime," Fallen said. He was moving into high gear now, wheels spitting rubber. "We could probably also get you on conspiracy to help them evade income tax if they failed to report the money you gave them."

Zolly slumped in his seat and closed his eyes. He missed the chaplains' offices already. He could be doing magic on the computer, watching the Welfare Fund divvy up the money. At the job, morning melted into night. "Why can't you let me do my time?"

"That's the point. You're not doing your time. You're doing someone else's." Cully drained his mouthful of Juicy Fruit saliva and started chewing again.

"Who says Goldberg or Civiletti have any time to do? Maybe they do, maybe they don't. What I do know is that I don't know anything about what they do."

"We'll be the judges of that." Fallen moved his cigar from one side of his mouth to the other, careful not to spill the ash on the floor that had just been burnished by the weekend cleaning crew.

"If Goldberg did me a favor now and then, you'll go after him on that? I'm not saying he actually did, but they certainly weren't big league."

Fallen patted his case, again judging by the weight alone how much he had left to bid. The first time they had met, Fallen was Ivy League. Two trips later, he now was Colonel Sanders. He said, "We don't want you to talk about what Goldberg and Civiletti did for you. Let's focus on what they did for others."

"I told you I don't know anything about it."

This time, Cully removed his gum and held it between his forefinger and thumb in order to make his point. "They came into your bar once a week, same day, same time, same booth. You're telling us you don't know what they did when they got there?"

"They could have bled all over the booth, I wouldn't have noticed," Zolly said.

"For this you're here sixteen months?" Cully shifted his belt from under the edge of the table. The top of his buckle looked bent.

"I don't know whether what I could give you would hurt them or not. For all I know, my saying they met might be enough to put them away."

Fallen pondered his fingers, pressing them together like a pyramid, his outstretched thumbs forming the base. He looked through the opening as though framing a mug shot. "It's not who, what, where, and when. That wouldn't be enough."

"I'm not saying I would, but if I did, that's all I could do. It would have to be."

"You'll give more." Fallen opened his briefcase and extracted the top document. "I hear you've been doing extra typing. You probably have seen some papers like these. They may help you understand."

Zolly accepted the pages with the grace of a kid getting a sweater for Christmas when he had counted on a video game. The paper was heavier than the bond the chaplains used when they tried to increase the budget. Some government lawyer must be trying to impress the judge by the feel of the goods. In this case, it read custom-tailored, as well. According to Meekins, Murphy and Meyers, Esquires, the feds had planted a wiretap without the Court's permission. "If I get this right, you put a bug in my bar."

"The Board of Health would never allow that. Unless you had Mr. O'Rourke involved." Cully could chew gum and tell a joke at the same time.

"They were never in my place unless it was full and plenty noisy. You'd have to put it right under their noses." Zolly put the pleading down and hit the table. "There."

"Why the sound effects?" Fallen asked.

"That was my first piece of furniture. I bought it at a sale when I got started." Zolly fondled the wood that separated him from Cully.

"In case you haven't heard, it's been at auction again," Fallen said. "Back taxes."

Zolly slumped and looked at the drapes on the outside wall. They were pulled wide open, allowing daylight to illuminate the room. The curtains covering the windows that faced the courtyard were closed to shield the sight of the walkies from the guests. He wondered whether the guard would let him end the visit whenever he chose, like Truman had the year before.

"The important thing isn't where we put it," Cully said. "The important thing is why." He plucked a hair from his nose like a punchboard prize.

"You want to know what's going on, is my guess. Or you got some leftover recording tape," Zolly said.

"We couldn't have done it without your okay."

"What the hell do you mean?"

Fallen mashed the remains of his cigar into the ashtray that had jumped above the table when they told Zolly about the bug. He lit another cigar, again ignoring the Clean Air Act. "I'll spell it out for you, in case you haven't digested the motion. Morry Meyers says we didn't have permission from the judge. He's right on one thing. We can't bug private property without an order."

"Which you failed to get," Zolly said.

"Or permission from the owner," Cully said.

"Or your case is over," Zolly said.

"Bingo." Cully's thumb was upright, forefinger pointing at Zolly.

"You want my permission."

"We had it." Cully turned toward Fallen, who was staring at his smoke. "You told Mr. Fallen it would be okay; otherwise, we would have asked the judge to allow it. That's what happened, right?"

"Before the subpoena, I'd never talked to you guys in my life."

"You been here so long, your memory is hazy." Cully was now a nephew reminding his elderly uncle. "Go back to your unit, think back. Memory's a funny thing."

Fallen blew out smoke and rocked forward. "Don't even think about waiting this one out until the grand jury session ends. If you refuse to talk, we'll yank you in one last time and get you on criminal contempt, besides your other crimes. And add on five years for perjury if you lie about the bug."

TWENTY-NINE

INDEPENDENCE DAY. MAGGIANO WAS TALKING HOPE AND wearing freedom. Cool in a red-and-white polo and blue walking shorts, his day was bagels for brunch with eggs cooked to order, followed by the barbecue to come in the Yard that night. After Count, they would celebrate their softball squad's game against the team from town with hot dogs, hamburgers, chicken, chips, corn cooked while still on the cob, soft drinks, and ice cream sundaes. On July the very Fourth, they got dusted by the smells.

Last year, two meals that size in a day had torn the last notch in Zolly's belt. This year, he was adding a notch at a time every month after the visit. The next time Fallen came, Zolly would need suspenders on his way to the room. Their window was cranked open enough to admit the smell of flowers. Considering brunch versus picnic, he announced he would save his appetite. Maggiano accepted the decision without going half-mast on Zolly. He was all flag when he walked out the door.

After Maggiano left, Zolly listened to the silence. The breeze played across his face. He was starting to doze when the door opened again. For a moment, he thought it was Maggiano, returning to heckle or pass gas. Then he realized it was someone else, who walked without a bounce. At first, all he saw was the form's shadow against the wall, advancing toward the window and blocking the morning sun. When the figure moved farther into the room and was illuminated by the light passing through Charlie Chicken's curtains, Zolly could make out Natron, tossing a softball bat from one hand to the other as though undecided whether he was a right- or left-handed hitter.

"Morning, Mr. Zolly." Lower than usual, Natron's voice grated like a twelve-wheeler on a gravel road.

Zolly used the time it took to reach for the lamp on the footlocker to decide on his own change of voice. He chose soft-spoken and sincere. "Good morning, Natron. What's going on?"

Natron kept moving the bat back and forth between his hands.

"I hope you're not still pissed off about that camera box," Zolly said, careful not to laugh. He had faced tougher than this every time some hood wanted to place another jukebox in his bar.

Natron twirled the bat upward toward the ceiling, catching it spiraling down. "Why should I be pissed at a box?" Natron let the end of the bat hit the floor, proving it was made of metal. "Ain't no box ever disrespect me. Not like some peoples I know."

"I don't diss you, I just don't want trouble." A couple times a year on Rush, not so regular as to become a feature but often enough to make a point, when someone had coasted when he should have stopped, or burned hundred-watt bulbs when the rest of the Street was on dimmers, there was a broken window or a four o'clock fire, depending on the offense. Zolly had always managed to look the other way.

"For a man who don't want troubles, you been looking real hard. You embarrass me with Darla, and you shame me with Perez." Natron was punctuating his charges with raps of the bat on the floor, making extra work for Charlie Chicken. "When Joel was here, I promise the lady I help her out. He leaves, I make a move myself. Then you jump on the job and suck up to Weaver. How he taste? Good as Truman?"

"I told you, I needed the money."

This time, when Natron raised the bat, he brought it down on the iron end of Zolly's bed, the noise cascading around the room. Hearing the last sound of David, Zolly flinched before controlling himself again.

Encouraged, Natron sat on the end of the bed and raised his voice to speak above the sound. "Don't you talk money to me. I give you a chance for that." He leaned forward, close enough to show he hadn't brushed his teeth that week. "Perez thinks I'm a fool. He says I should have fixed you so you couldn't work. Then I get the job for sure." He tapped the end of the bat against his foot, which was encased in a thick-soled boot despite the Lexington summer. "I'll ask you one more time. Do you want to be my friend?" Natron tapped the bat on the floor again, the thuds as varied as a xylophone. "I thinks friends should show they friends. What you think? From what I sees, you not a friend. You plays with Truman, you sticks your nose by Gloria, you takes her job, and then you diss Perez and me."

"You've got me wrong." Zolly could shuffle with the best of them when he was caught beneath the covers. "I'm as stand-up as they come. I do right by my friends."

The bed groaned when Natron twisted his body to face Zolly head-on, this time strumming the end of the bat. "Now you playing a tune I know. Maybe I hear from some of your friends in Chicago. Maybe they says you supposed to be showing you won't talk. 'Course, they don't know about you with Gloria and the hack."

"I didn't say anything."

"What you hears about Truman? Anything you wants to pass on?" Natron poked Zolly with the handle end of the bat. "You be a good little doggy. We don't want you changing into no rat."

"Dogs get hungry, they need to eat. You should pet your doggie every now and then, remind him you love him." He could do better if he were out of bed and holding something himself. Zolly tried to grin the bat away.

"A doggy get spanked if it piss on the floor," Natron said, twisting his lips without smiling. When he stood, the bed bounced in relief to be rid of the load. He tossed the bat to Zolly. "You keeps good hold of this for me. Real tight, like your life depends on it."

———

ZOLLY DECIDED ON BRUNCH, AFTER ALL. HE HAD EVEN LESS OF an appetite than before, but he wanted to discuss the visit. Lexington was the kind of place where showing muscle earned you a spot in seg or a pass to a higher-level joint. The possibility wouldn't bother Natron. Anyone with less than a year to do was considered short. With only a couple months left on his bit, Natron could almost slip under the door. Zolly needed ideas on what they would do to him if he had a beef with Natron. He decided to look for his friends. Maggiano might still be around. If not, Solomon. Even Gabby sometimes had an idea in the middle of a speech.

Brunch mornings were a good time to shower. After the unit cleared, he was sure to find a stall with a curtain and all its hooks and faucets that opened wide enough for water hot enough to burn and let him make friends with his hand. He stood there, inhaling steam thick enough to let him see whatever he wished. This brunch morning, as the mist sprayed about, he saw his bar on a day when the tourists came early and filled the tables, making the regulars stand, drinks in hand, bitching about Bigman at the door. They parted a path that cut through the crowd until it reached the booth. Looking down the aisle, Zolly could see his group sitting on their throne. When their phone rang, Goldberg answered. It was Natron calling. They never would have found him on their own. Somehow, someone gave him their number. Natron was always looking to make a single dollar become a bundle.

THIRTY

MAGGIANO WAS STILL EATING WHEN ZOLLY GOT THERE.
Considering what the brunch involved, Zolly was impressed that
Maggiano had even made a dent. It was a meal that could have come
straight from the Ashkenaz on Morse Avenue except, of course, there
was no lox. To make up for it, there were three kinds of juices and kosher-kitchen eggs, not the precooked scrambled you scooped as though
it were some chicken-based, soft-serve ice cream, but eggs made to
order. Instead of toast, today they had bagels baked so fresh the crust
was still growing brown on the plate, the butter melting through the
cracks and softening the dough. The potatoes were sliced hash-brown
style, cooked with strips of onion for flavor.

Zolly sat across from Maggiano. "I see you got my share."

Maggiano pushed his plate toward Zolly and shrugged. "I heard
you weren't hungry. That was you in your bed, right?"

Zolly pushed the food back to Maggiano. "Celebrating anything
extra?"

Maggiano took care to chew all he held in his mouth and swallow it with juice before answering. "We got a new crew. The hack in black caught Rosie on the prep table."

"He resents her sitting down?"

"He resents the way she had her legs wrapped around Buddy. He was pounded in so tight he couldn't pull free. I got a question for you, since you're studying so hard. By your rules, is the table still kosher?"

Zolly helped himself to the remaining half of the bagel. "By your rules, our room no longer is. Natron paid a visit."

"I hope you told him we're not buying," Maggiano said.

"Someone paid him to drop by."

"What for, besides hello?"

"To see if I'm a stand-up guy." Zolly debated again whether to mention David. These guys had a hard enough time swallowing his reading. Family history would give them heartburn.

Maggiano rubbed his thumb on the bridge of his nose. "How about some eggs?"

———

LATER THAT AFTERNOON, ZOLLY LAY ON THE GRASS WITH THE others. Joey Philly was distracting them by moving his attention from the game to the scene beyond the fence, blinking and staring as his gaze moved in and out. Haskell joined them midday, meaning he had finished his calls to his brokers, or the hacks had caught him again. There was usually telephone time open on holidays. Most of the inmates wouldn't spoil a good time.

"We made a nice move yesterday." Haskell was out of breath, meaning he'd scored big. With Darla no longer an option, he got his highs from the market. "Of course, if I were home, I could have done a lot better. I like to go in and out."

Maggiano said, "First you have to find the broad."

"I'm talking stocks." Haskell puffed up at having his morals challenged.

The game took Zolly's mind off the issue for a while. The governor and the congressman were working the sidelines like a political rally. The town team always got the fans riled up, trotting onto the field as though they owned it and wearing uniforms that never saw a slide. Even though elected officials were involved, the crowd wanted revolution. Notwithstanding the mood of the mob, the visitors beat the locals 15 to 10 while the Jay Cee Women sold popcorn to tide the fans over from brunch to dinner. Manning and Grady finally shut up and returned to their units to nap.

Afterward, Zolly's group lay there as though they themselves had run the bases. Maggiano propped up his head with his hand, elbow on the ground, facing the far end of the Yard. Haskell was looking up at some trading tape he must have spotted in the sky. Joey Philly had his eyes closed, thank God. A crew of kitchen helpers worked in front of the archway to Women's Unit, dumping hot dogs onto tables, chipping meat into patties, stripping corn silk from the cobs, and dumping charcoal on the grills. Zolly tried to remember how he had celebrated the Fourth when he was home. Celebrated wasn't really the word for it. Handling the crowd was more like it. Holidays were like an extra Sunday but without Goldberg and crew, which meant Booth One could turn a profit. Best of all, he didn't have to think. These days, every week that went by brought Zolly closer to needing to make a decision. That was the hard part. Not being closer but needing to decide. Coming in to the joint, his decision had been set. Going out, he was having doubts. The prospect of doing time, real time, where he didn't have the key to the door, was decidedly unappealing. Goldberg and crew with their new friend, Natron, were the other side of the issue. Then there were memories of David and Truman and Rabinowitz leaving, one way or another. Three men who had made it under his skin. Zolly didn't know where to scratch.

Solomon approached, chomping on a Baby Ruth. "Natron came to see me."

"Appeal?" Maggiano asked.

"Not very," Solomon said.

Zolly folded his arms. "I suppose, as long as he was there, he took the chance to mention me."

Solomon removed a couple of double-As from his pocket and began rolling the batteries in his hand. "When Joel left the camera job, Natron thought you'd take his deal."

"I never promised."

Maggiano said, "You been here how long?"

"I still get to enlist or not," Zolly said.

"If you don't want to play, you can always watch from the sideline." Maggiano pointed to the chalk that still marked the path from home to first. "No one is making you do that job."

"I need the money." Zolly ate a hot dog, tasting meat juice for the first time in months.

"They made you an offer. Now they're both pissed off. You got to be in or out," Solomon said.

Maggiano said, "You can't be a stand-up guy lying down."

"What's with them?" Zolly asked, pointing at the batteries, trying to change the subject.

"Natron gave me these for my Mickey Mouse clock," Solomon said. "Called it a down payment on my fee. He knows I don't say no to a favor. That's what it's all about. But Natron thinks, if he doesn't charge, you don't do favors."

"Like letting me type his motion?"

"You don't get credit from Natron for what you did for me."

"I'm not looking for a fee. If we need to match up, we're even for the coffee." Zolly looked at what was left of the grass between home and first. How had things gotten so complicated? He had come on his own. If things looked different now, that was the problem with doing time. No matter how many layers deep it was buried, he meant to bite on the truth. "I'm doing right," Zolly said.

"You're hung up on words," Maggiano said. "You got to live it. You think it's all written down in the good book and you can forget what you learned on the Street."

"You'd let them down?"

"Who?" Maggiano asked. "Like me, or Natron and Perez?"

"Gabby, Adlai, they pushed for me."

"You still buying their votes?"

Zolly said, "Weaver, Truman. I won't let them down."

Solomon delivered the closing argument. "Your conscience is good in the abstract. But put it to the test." He took a prosecutor's pause before cutting for the heart. "Take Betsy Tobias and Reuben Lewis. Are you any different? I don't think so. Given the chance, trust wouldn't stop you from *shtupping* some broad in the shul."

THIRTY-ONE

HER BACK WAS A CLUE IF HE NEEDED ONE. THERE WAS NO POINT trying to talk behind her while she played solo on her keyboard. Anything she had to say was moving across the page at ninety words a minute. She moved her head side to side, hiding her lyrics from view. From just a few feet away, he had no idea whether she was acting Mrs. Robinson or writing Mr. Rogers. Maybe this 100 percent, I've-got-to-work routine was because of the hack in black. The problem with that theory was Burgess, who was visible through his window and paying no attention. After staying silent long enough for Darla to do an encore, Zolly tried again. "It was gunshots. First Natron comes by, letting me know that now he's an enforcer. Then Maggiano's surprised the bullet hole's so small. After that, I'm still bleeding when Solomon picks at the wound. All that time, you're not there."

Her fingers continued clicking rows of type across the paper, growing the fence higher each time she hit the carriage return. As she inserted another sheet, she said, "I can't turn my headaches on and off."

"We could have spent the day together. Besides, you're the one who got Natron started."

"We spend every day together. Maybe not enough alone." She turned to face him.

That was how she was. He could talk half an hour and never get her full attention, but when she had something to say, she wanted his immediate reaction. "You keep mixing the signals," he said.

"Wishful thinking is for adolescents. I never should have taken this job just because you're here," Darla said.

He caught his breath. "Natron's a coincidence?"

When she stretched overhead, she tensed her breasts and she knew it. Then she put her hands back in her lap with fingers locked together. "There are no coincidences, just distractions. I'll clear up your confusion. I have a husband and kid. When I get out of here, I'm going back to them. When you get out of here, which could be any minute, you'll testify and start all over. You and your Faith."

He would have been better off if he had never told her about the grand jury. All she needed to know was that he had a bar. Things were tight now, but when he returned to the Street, they would be easy. He could do without Faith if he had to. The complication was that he had met Darla after meeting Truman and attending services. "If your husband and kids were important, you wouldn't have wound up here to begin with." He reached to pull back the words, but she swiveled around and returned to the noise that told Burgess he could read his newspaper again. Weaver watched them through his own office window. That was their deal. When Burgess looked down, Weaver took over. Zolly gestured toward the courtyard behind the chaplains. Draped windows hid the binoculars in the building across the way.

"We should put on a show." Darla moved the keys like the guy at the bar who had played piano Saturday nights, knowing Zolly could feel the rhythm even if he couldn't identify the songs. After a few riffs, she stopped and swooped around. "You know the price of a solo." She was back to Natron again. These days, their conversation usually got there from any direction. They could be talking the weather or the latest scandal at Women's, but sooner or later it was Natron. Their conversations were a maze with a lot of openings but only one exit.

"Why do you even talk to Natron?" Zolly asked. "He's on me all the time."

"Maybe you'll have someone else on you when I tell him you've changed your mind." She held her mouth open to signal her end of the deal.

Zolly thought about the husband, the kids, and the forged prescription pads. "You don't know how much I want you." The ache returned to his groin.

"What are you going to do about it?"

When he made his announcement, he was uncertain whether it was because of the pain or Natron or the advice from the guys. "I'll do whatever you want."

She leaned toward him, his promise flushing her cheeks. "Your credit's good with me."

He had thought about this day since the moment he met her. He could still smell the introduction and feel her breast whisper past his arm when she turned to say hello. He had maneuvered for this moment, imagined it when they were together, written dialogue when they were apart, acted it out when alone in the shower. He was as ready as the day he'd taken the fifth. Entering Weaver's office, Zolly said,

"Could I have the key?" He gestured in the direction of the john at the back of the suite, next door to the shul. The washroom was reserved for the chaplains and the inmates who worked in the office. It held a toilet, sink, supply cabinet, and the only frosted window in the offices.

Weaver looked up, nodded, and gestured toward the single key that lay on the corner of his desk, separate from the ring looped about his belt. That made it easier to identify for his own visits, and also available to anyone else. If Weaver had gone by the book, he never would have handed a key to an inmate. If Weaver were the hack in black, he would have handled everything himself except for Zolly's private parts.

Immediately after he entered the washroom, Zolly flushed the toilet once and then again. He improvised under the sound of the rushing water, tearing a strip of tape from the roll he had pocketed when he left his desk, opening the door, turning the handle to absorb the latch inside, and placing the tape over the slot, so that when the door closed it wouldn't lock. It was the Truman trick turned inside out. Each chaplain had visited the washroom within the previous hour. It was unlikely either one would return before Count. Even if one of them needed a last leak, his jangling keys should hide the missing click. Magic is misdirection.

When Zolly returned to his desk, he said, "I set it up. Tell Burgess you need to be on the Out-Count." Sometimes they stayed late to do extra work, sometimes to eat early. The chaplains treated it as a perquisite of the job.

Weaver didn't bother to look up, shrugging off Zolly's request as though he were relieving a kink. Burgess was taking longer with Darla. The hack in black was moving his head as though the noise from her typewriter were still bouncing around his room thirty minutes after the fact. Darla made Zolly proud. She stood without argument, ready to catch the next bus if Burgess insisted. Back at their desks, after Burgess departed for the day, she said, "He told me if I paid more attention, I could finish my work during regular hours. He didn't even ask about you."

"I'm glad they trust us," Zolly said, smiling at the absurdity.

After alerting control, Weaver told them he would return after Count cleared. When the door to the suite locked behind him, its click was an invitation. Zolly said, "We need to move fast." He motioned for Darla to follow him.

"Now?"

"What better time?"

"Maybe after I talk to Natron. Maybe after he delivers. Maybe after you deliver."

"You said my credit was good."

"You're a man of principle. You tell me so every time we're together, when you're not trying to get in my pants." She was so close behind him he could have been teasing her with a trail of cocaine.

He opened the washroom door and pointed at the latch, taped flush inside the jam. "We have twenty, maybe thirty minutes."

"As though that presented a problem."

"You don't know my reputation," he said.

"Are we talking current events or history?" She drew her thumb down the side of his temple as she cupped his ear with her mouth. She was already unbuttoning her blouse with her other hand. The mirror behind showed her shirt slipping off her shoulders, his fingers tracing the path of her spine down her back. She had her hand outstretched toward him. Zolly brushed against the cabinet where

Natron stored his mops. He then pulled off his pants and shorts and sat on the toilet, an actor awaiting an entrance. His star removed her clothes beat by beat, hinting at the climax. The clock next to the mirror already showed 4:20.

"Are you happy with our deal?" he said.

She unhooked her brassiere, curtsied, and resumed her presentation as though she had never been reluctant. His erection grew as Darla disrobed, removing more garments than the event demanded. Maybe that was her routine in the examination room, waiting until the doctor entered so she could distract her audience while she stole a prescription pad. When she was naked, except for the panties and jeans that draped around her ankles like an afterthought, she advanced toward him, heel to toe, legs together, holding a secret between her thighs. When she was in reach and he placed his thumbs upon her breasts and pressed upon her nipples, her legs unlocked to straddle him. She was about to seal the bargain when Zolly said, "Just a minute."

She again began to press down.

"I hear something," he said. His belt buckle scraped against the tiled floor as he sidled away from the toilet while hitching up his trousers. When he reached the door, he stuck his head out the stage entrance, a doorman sensing danger. He peered toward the front of the suite but didn't see anyone. He looked to his left into the locked shul at the lectern overseeing the chairs, all in order, wide enough to pray, close enough to the lectern to listen. Then he heard the sound again, coming from the front of the room. Although the doors to the cabinet beside the lectern were closed, he could sense the books piled inside, awaiting the Sabbath. The siddurs seemed to sigh.

"What is it?" she asked.

He turned and looked at Darla, standing there in prelude, clothing draped about one leg, poised for the finale. He wondered whether she'd held that pose when she was last with her husband, announcing her betrayal, watching him go limp.

THIRTY-TWO

THERE WAS PLENTY OF TIME TO READ THESE DAYS. ZOLLY WAS stretched out on his bed, clothes on, shoes on, a habit that had made Faith nuts. It was dusk. You could see about the room, but that was it. The ceiling light was off, Maggiano having gone to the main TV room. The gooseneck lamp that one of Maggiano's Italians in the electric shop had custom-made for ten quarters was arced across Zolly's shoulder, providing light enough for the message. He held the book so that a paragraph at a time was lit. The maneuver helped him focus. He had more time to read these days, because he no longer walked with Darla. At work, their silence made more noise than their keyboards ever did. Sometimes he caught Burgess and Weaver both staring, stunned that their clerks were producing twice as much paper as before. Darla dashed Zolly's hope that she would walk again with Haskell. Instead, she was sharing lunch with Natron or talking to Perez. When she did look Zolly's way, her eyes were a foreign language.

He was reading a prayer book he had slipped inside his shirt weeks earlier, leaving the shul a siddur short. Inspired by Rabinowitz's lectures, he was reading *Ethics of the Fathers* an ethic at a time. If they measured decency by the drop, Zolly meant to drink a double shot. It was a great twist for a title, ethics and fathers. As best Zolly could recall, David had never even said the word or anything like it. Maybe the big bang had cut short his plans for an inspiring bar mitzvah speech. Not that David never gave a speech or anything else. His slots had put out the best returns, but that was because the jackpots attracted the crowds. Even though every player ultimately lost, it made for happy gamblers. The approach scored with the clubs. Hand signals, ruby rings, and fezzes could get you going, but quarters were what bought you friends. Zolly figured he was good for an hour before Maggiano returned. He could finish another paragraph, maybe two, depending on how long he stopped to think. "Run to perform even a minor mitzvah and flee from transgression; for one good deed draws (in its train) another good deed, and one transgression leads to another; for the reward of a good deed is a good deed, and the reward of sin is sin." Zolly was glad he hadn't read this passage on the Street. Ethics would have cut his style.

Good deeds. There were the jobs he'd given the Cubans. That should count for something. So what if there was a hidden agenda? The effort did good. Okay, besides that, what else? There were the charity rabbis he'd driven away and the payoffs to the cops. The hookers who'd hung around and attracted the extra drinkers. Not loving Faith. Those were the transgressions. Maybe he should close that chapter and start to write a new one. The problem was, too many guys had their fingers in the book, making it hard to turn the page. The hall was quiet. Most of the inmates were in the main TV room with Maggiano. The melody that came from the far end of the hall was an irritation, not a distraction. Songs were words that someone set to noise.

An hour and a passage later, Zolly closed the book and hid it in his bed, deciding to walk the unit. There was a *Miami Vice* rerun drumming up the stairs. Zolly went to the first floor and peeked into the main TV room. The Cubans were driving a Mustang across the screen, radios loud enough to hear across the Bay. Don Johnson was following, weaving like a tourist. When they reached their destination, the music vanished while the pushers did their business. The crowd cheered when the Cubans wheeled away through the stall-filled streets and the peddlers' fruit went flying. The inmates weren't rooting for the bad guys, resigned to who always won. No, they were cheering for the pink shirts and stucco rings.

He went back upstairs to the guard's station. Zolly had lost his zest for flash ever since Clint Eastwood. Besides, the hack on duty was a homie. Most of them were locals, not having much to say, but holding your interest. The first time Zolly had heard talk about a "turnkey," he thought it was Thanksgiving dinner. When the control room hack mashed a button, Zolly heard potatoes. Truman taught him that slang sprang from sounds and moves, the push of a thumb, the jangling keys.

After a while, Zolly was ready to drink his discussions straight. When Hack Chicago stood watch, Zolly could get high on memories of Cadillacs and sirloin steaks. They had an ongoing debate about the Cubs and Sox, Luke Appling and Ernie Banks. In Chicago, they measured success by the generation. Hack Chicago had started at the Chicago MCC, traveled south to FPC Marion, and then on to FCI Lexington. He explained that the new camp at Oxford, Wisconsin, would not turn around his life because he hated cheese. He was aiming for Atlanta, where they served fried chicken and Cuban cons. Tonight, he had a hard-on.

"What turned you north?" Hack Chicago asked.

"You know I'm for the Cubs," Zolly said. "I go below Van Buren, I get dizzy."

"You probably started out okay. Your mama must have loved you."

"If she knew from baseball, it would have been Wrigley Field." Becky had had a hard enough time dealing with the slots. If she sat in the bleachers, she would have been blistered by the bets.

"You probably prayed as a kid. Then you wind up here."

Zolly stopped at that one. The hack was probably still sore about Zolly's remark about 1984, when the Cubs won the division. "I asked were the Sox in the league last year, is all. It wasn't personal."

"What you said is that it proved the Sox don't have a prayer. When you mix religion and baseball, I take offense."

Hack Chicago seemed serious. South Siders had thin skins. "I take my religion straight," Zolly said.

"You going straight is the idea. Pray all you like, it's just talk until you do it."

"I always liked Richie Zisk," Zolly said. It was the latest Sox name that had caught his attention, for understandable reasons.

"I know you like the Z's. Maybe you should catch some." He seemed happy at the thought of Zolly napping, when the smell of burning leaves moved their way.

They ran through the main TV room to the front exit looking for the source. The smoke was seeping from the room holding the new heating and air-conditioning system.

"Christ, let's get everybody out!" Hack Chicago said.

The nonsmokers in the room began to cough; even the two-pack-a-day generics took notice. Zolly directed them to follow him. By the time they reached the end of the hall, it was full of smoke and cursing men. While the hack chose the key, Zolly volunteered to get any inmates who remained upstairs.

Hack Chicago said, "You'll burn your ass. They already know about it."

"I'm the fireman," Zolly said.

The second floor was as quiet as during a *Miami Vice* commercial. A song came from the room reserved for music videos at the end of the hall. Zolly didn't know the tune, but he had heard "'Cuz You Make Me Smile" enough to frown at this singer, who was answering a question no one had even asked. Zolly was removing his fireman helmet from under the bed and turning toward the sound when his roommate ran up to him.

"Fire!" Maggiano repeated the word several times, using different inflections and waving his hands for accent.

"I'm getting my hat," Zolly said.

Maggiano tried to pull Zolly toward the fire exit stairwell at the other end of the hall.

Zolly drew away. "I have a job to do."

Maggiano stood in the doorway, ready to argue, before spitting on the floor, turning, and leaving Zolly with his hat. Zolly abandoned his book beneath his pillow.

Wisps of smoke were now invading from the main stairwell. Zolly decided to start at the far end of the hall, next to "'Cuz You Make Me

Smile," and work his way back from there. When he reached the MTV room, a black woman was on the screen, already in the chorus:

"I know that you're sending
The happiest ending
With nights we're together
That will last forever.
'Cuz when you just hold me
You never do scold me,
There is no denial
You do make me smile."

Arms extended and pressed against her breasts, she offered samples to an empty room.

Zolly turned away from "'Cuz You" and moved back down the hall, checking every room. He found a few inmates, oblivious to music, smoke, or any other stimulus, who were daydreaming of better times, but most of the rooms were empty.

The stragglers staggered after Zolly, tasting ash by the time they reached the center hall stairwells. Zolly proceeded alone to the other end.

"Fire! This isn't a drill. Get out now!" he told them.

However, when Zolly returned to the center lobby, ready to check the first group of rooms again, several men emerged from the stairwell spuming phlegm. The first one to finish coughing said, "The hack jammed the lock. We need to leave another way." He began to heave.

Zolly led them back to where he started. The MTV room was quiet. It could be that the woman and her friend had finally got it on. She sure did sing enough about it. About twenty men were at the fire escape just beyond, banging on the door. Failing to shake it open, they hammered against the window until Zolly warned them that the glass was lined with wire. The smoke crushed at them, making their legs heavy, as men who avoided guards like death were yelling for the hack.

Flames reminded Zolly of no cash flow and overdue loans. The last fire he had seen was across the street the night the Greek restaurant ran out of money. His hat slipped over his forehead. The melting point of plastic was an issue that needed research. "I'll try to get back to the desk to phone for help," Zolly said. To hell with the rules against touching the phones reserved for the guards. He felt his way back toward the hack's station, moving in a semi-crouch, bumping around clumps of smoke. By the time he reached the desk, he had his eyes closed. Even if they had been open, he wouldn't have been able to see. He felt for the telephone that automatically reached control. "I'm an inmate. Berns. We have a fire at Atwood."

"We know."

"We can't get down the stairwell and the doors to the fire escape are locked. The guard is still on the first floor."

"Help is on the way." The control room hack could have been announcing the time.

Zolly replaced the phone and opened his eyes to test them. The smoke was less solid now, swirling as though the leaves were catching their breath. A shape approached through the smoke. If it hadn't moved, it would have blended better, but the shape formed before him, floating above the floor, turning to a tapping, scraping sound that congealed into Natron, his bat a waving ember.

"I said to hold on to this." Natron moved closer, wielding the bat, the cloth across his mouth obscuring his voice. "We don't like guys who never take a swing."

Zolly considered returning to the group at the fire escape end of the hall, but Natron was blocking the way. The stairwell was all smoke now, and the other end of the hall was too far to hold his breath. There was probably air closer to the floor. Zolly was making plans for it, ignoring Natron and his bat slicing toward him through the fog, when the keys clanked up the stairs. As Hack Chicago emerged from the stairwell, shrouded by the end of his journey, Natron backed away wearing smoke camouflage and silence. "We've opened the downstairs door. Tell everyone to hold his breath and get outside," Hack Chicago said.

Zolly ran back to the inmates clustered at the fire escape. They made their way down the center stairs, through the burning air, and out the door.

Smoke was escaping from barred and unbarred windows alike. Groups were stretched across the Atwood grounds. Tommy "the Tax" O'Brien was describing his escape to Haskell. Solomon was worried about his bed full of files. Charlie Chicken was going from group to group, poking inside his clothes when he stopped. Zolly sat beside Maggiano on the grass beside the fence.

"That was some scene in there," Zolly said.

"Think you're a fucking hero?" Maggiano kept his voice low. "You move in on me, big shot who don't need to wait for a two-man room. Then you tell me how you know this guy, that guy, what a stand-up guy you are, meanwhile your so-called friends don't do shit. But you're okay, you tell me." Maggiano was clenching his fists as he spoke, releasing them when he paused. "Next thing I know, you're in the chapel. Suddenly, you got religion. I figure, you're probably working some angle. Gotta be that, I'll keep hanging with you. Then I never see you except for Count or bedtime. Tonight, you say, 'Fuck off, I can take care of myself.'"

"I had a job to do. Then Natron is at me."

"I forget, I do get to see you when it's that guy. Hear about it, too."

"I'm calling control, he comes at me with the bat."

"You look like you managed to duck."

Zolly sagged against the fence. "I've done the right thing since day one."

"You ain't done right by me." Maggiano turned away.

When Zolly looked in the same direction as his roommate, he saw the Institution Fire Brigade coming across the Yard. Instead of a group of inmate firemen who were all hats and no tools, these were guards and civilian staff members, equipped with firefighting paraphernalia, trundling their wagon across the Yard. The cart lurched when it bumped second base. By the time they reached Atwood, the hacks were breathing hard as the inmates cheered them on. Lieutenant Johnson was leading the team. He had a mustache that made you wonder about his teeth. He could have stepped right out of 1890, rubbing his eyes at modern times. "Okay, let's see what the hell is going on. Where are the Atwood firemen?"

Zolly and a couple of other helmets answered. Maybe this was what his prayer book was all about. Zolly wondered whether it had made it through the fire.

"Now you get a chance to shine," Johnson said. He led them into the building and opened up the heating room. The furnace was crusted too well-done to last to winter.

Johnson said, "Break the glass and get that hose." He pointed to a fire-colored box hanging on the wall. When Zolly tried to take it, the nozzle singed his hand. Holding the canvas portion, he extended the hose to Johnson, who was putting on his gloves. He had probably learned those moves back in guard school. One of the other hacks turned the handle to squeeze the water through the hose and foam out the flames. The fire hissed before disappearing into the debris that was gathered beneath the furnace in a room that was always locked away from the inmate cleaning crew. After a few seconds of water, Johnson abandoned them, fleeing from transgression, leaving Zolly and crew behind to do their minor-mitzvah cleanup job.

THIRTY-THREE

ZOLLY GOT THE PUSH BROOM, BEING SENIOR ON THE CREW. Two other inmates took turns balling up the debris while a rookie followed with the mop, needing instruction with every swipe. Zolly decided against playing the part of Natron. He refused to swish his ass. Giving a man the wrong idea was Natron's way of setting you up. He wore his skin loose until the game began, when you found he was steel inside. Zolly had grown away from games, whether on the giving or receiving end. That was why he locked his knees as he pushed through the basement, careful not to brush against the boiler and give off further steam. The outside of the furnace still glowed, as though it resented the crowd after being alone so long. He decided to name it Maggiano. By the time Zolly was finished, maybe Maggiano would be safe to touch.

"How do we get that fucking crap out from under?" It was the new man, showing off.

"Maybe with your hands," Zolly said, "if your mop won't move it."

Debris was concealed beneath the furnace like kids playing hide-and-seek. The new man pried out what he could with his mop and then, rolling up his sleeves, reached under to pull the rest away. The remains were mostly newspaper that smelled like melted fish. As Zolly pushed the mess toward the door, it became the ghost of news, the date at the top shining through like the engraving on a tombstone. How had yesterday's newspaper slipped into a bolted room in time to start a fire? Giving the question too much thought probably wasn't a good idea. Zolly pushed at the pulp with his toe and watched yesterday disappear.

When they were done with the cleanup, the hack outside directed them to the gymnasium in the main building. It had been closed since March. By August, salt would cake the walls. As the room had no windows, it soon smelled of winter sweat. The center was bare. Everyone sat in a line that snaked among barbells and treadmills, wound around the basketball court, and then reached back toward the door. There was no beginning or end. Everyone wanted the middle. The awareness there would be no winners tonight stank across the room while the hacks called for each of them, minutes between each summons, in nonalphabetic, non-numerical, palpably disjointed order.

Most of the men leaned against the walls, some with their eyes closed. Their theory was that the innocent would doze. Others talked as low as drunks counting lost chances by the swizzle stick. Others posed, such as Natron, pursing his lips, bulging his cheeks, and fluttering his eyelids across the room at Zolly. Natron turned to look straight down the wall at Perez, who was also smiling, blowing kisses, and looking as though he were about to sink the winning shot.

It was an hour before Zolly's turn. When they called for him, Natron stiffened his body as though about to rise. Then he sank back, waved his hand, and showed his gold front teeth.

"Sit down, Berns." Johnson was in the gymnasium cubicle where they taped up sprains. The room was outfitted with leftovers from re-doing the clinic three wardens ago. Zolly had the choice of an extra chair or the examination table that separated him from Johnson. The lieutenant didn't seem to miss his desk, probably because there was no piss-testing needed tonight. Rumor was, he held specimens in his drawer before they went to the lab. Rumor also was that Johnson always smelled of piss. Tonight, his uniform was dry, but it still bore streaks of soot. Ash also marked his forehead. What was the holiday that Bigman used to observe? Something sad about that day. Maybe that explained the expression on Johnson's face when he opened the top folder in his pile, or maybe it was because the room reeked of wounds. "I see you're just visiting our institution. Any reason you'd start a fire?"

Zolly said, "I'm the guy who called control for help. Almost choked in the smoke."

"Maybe you were trying to be a hero. Some have started a fire for less reason." Johnson flipped the folder closed. "According to the guard on duty, you were talking to him when the fire began. That makes a good alibi."

"You think I need one? I cleaned up the shit in the furnace room, you're welcome very much."

"You have an idea who might be involved?"

"I have an idea you inhaled too much smoke." Zolly thought better of it when the ash on Johnson's forehead began to turn to red. "If someone started it, I don't know who."

"We can't treat it like a prank. Maybe you noticed something un-usual. Besides the fire, of course." The mark on Johnson's forehead was fading now. He adopted the tone the hack in black used to put a peni-tent at ease before he sent the man to seg. "You're a smart man, Berns. The only one who can leave whenever he wants. If you knew, you'd tell us. You'd have nothing to fear."

"If I knew."

"You're a fireman. You were everywhere during the fire."

He leaned toward the lieutenant. As he spoke, Zolly pictured the words leaving his mouth as though they were passing across his com-puter screen, a phrase he could delete by mashing a key. He considered his siddur, assuming it was still alive beneath his pillow. He could hear Maggiano, telling him to abandon his post. He could see Natron, ad-vancing with the bat. He pictured yesterday's newspaper. He was tired of wrestling with ethics. "Whoever did this risked a lot of lives. If I knew, I'd tell you who."

JOHNSON WAS A WARM-UP. THE REAL INVESTIGATION BEGAN the next day. The inmates returned to their rooms and spent the day washing soot. The rooms closest to the furnace qualified for paint, an off-white that bore as much kinship to the institution green as a stand-up guy to a rat. The air pained Zolly's nostrils, forcing him to inhale through his mouth and let burnt pigment line his throat. He went to the washroom sink several times an hour. When he gargled, he leaned back and closed his eyes, seeing Natron every time. The agents who arrived that afternoon were wearing lettermen shirts from the FBI.

They carried cases of equipment and no expression. Although the area around the front door was roped off, it was obvious from their mere presence, as well as their movements in and out of the furnace room and the look of their apparatus, that they were looking for the cause.

"I doubt if this one started on its own," Zolly said.

"Don't go nosing around to find out." Despite his earlier warning, Maggiano was no longer making fists.

"I'm not asking who did it. I'm just saying."

"For a guy who don't talk, you say a lot." Maggiano was at his letters again, talking down as he lectured.

"I didn't say anything," Zolly said, even though if Maggiano had died in the fire, he still wouldn't understand a snitch.

"There's nothing you can do now except learn what you don't want to know." Maggiano had salvaged some crayons and was drawing again, as well, mostly using blue and green, staying away from red. He didn't look up when the FBI called Zolly in for questions. He just shook his head at his drawing, guarding against disappointment.

———

IT WAS ZOLLY'S FIRST VISIT INSIDE UNIT MANAGER RICHTER'S room. You could see the light shining under the door when you passed his office, and sometimes hear the radio, but for most of the inmates Richter was just a rumor. His office was another clue to the double-deck bunks the new men used. Richter evidently needed lots of room to stretch. His sanctum was grade-ten walnut and artificial leather instead of gray posts and blue bedding. He was absent, probably listening to Lawrence Welk at home or visiting with the warden. Johnson was also missing, probably washing up. There was no percentage in hanging around the FBI.

It was odd that they'd called in the feds. Usually, the BOP handled its issues in-house. The wall behind Richter's desk displayed framed pictures of him posing with other men. According to Butterfly, Richter managed to tell you every other sentence about the politicians he knew. This was the first time Zolly had seen the proof. He was trying to separate the governors from the senators when the agent spoke, telling Zolly to close the door and inviting him to sit.

"Are you a drinker, Berns?" The agent was dressed like Fallen, but you had to lean forward to hear his questions. If there was an FBI etiquette school, they'd skipped the diction course. That could be their way. You had to lean forward to hear, so it must be important. Zolly and the agent were at a table equipped with a water pitcher, several glasses and cups, a carafe of coffee, sugar, sweetener, cream, spoons, a notebook, and a tape recorder whose whirr reminded Zolly that if this was a party, he was dessert.

"Sure. Water. Coffee. Occasionally juice. Sometimes even milk."

"I didn't ask if you were a comedian."

"I like one every now and then. I used to own a bar."

The agent brushed his cuff, appearing to notice the extra dust still floating from the fire. "I understand you're at Atwood because you're a drinker."

"That's why they put me here."

"But that isn't in our paperwork, except for your presentence investigation report. The PSI comes in two parts. The first part is straight. Of course, the other part is bullshit. The defense section." The agent flipped to the next page and winked, just one of the guys. "When I reached the part about your lawyer's request, I began to wonder. It should be mighty hard for you to do time without the booze, but you don't seem bothered. You're not going to AA and you never went to sick call, not even when you got here. According to the shrink, your arrival test didn't show any symptoms. So tell me, are you a drinker?" He adopted the tone of a man asking about the weather with no intention of going outside.

"I can take it or leave it."

The agent nodded. "So, are you a pusher?" His voice changed slightly, showing he would pay attention to the answer.

"Where did that come from? I don't do drugs, I don't sell drugs, I stay away from drugs. I've passed every piss test." Zolly talked faster than before.

The agent looked up from the book. "I didn't ask if you were a user. You're not exactly flush with cash." He pretended to be studying his notes. "I see you took an extra job."

"That's right, so I could send some money home."

"I understand there are higher-paying jobs. Couldn't you earn more at UNICOR Federal Industries than from both your jobs combined?"

"I was trying to strike a happy balance." Zolly decided against bringing Darla into it. Why piss off Natron even more?

"I'm asking you if you sell certain substances."

That was just like a cop, talking like he knew where he was going when he needed you to lead the way. Every time the health inspectors came by, they would start by asking about business, what's good on the menu, how about this weather? It was only after wasting your time they would open the cooler door to see if the meat was spoiled. "I don't know from substances," Zolly said. The clock showed almost four. "It's getting late."

The agent waved it aside. "I get overtime."

Zolly said, "I have to get back to my room for Count."

"They mentioned that when I asked them to send you in," the agent said. "You ever hear of the Out-Count?"

Zolly didn't show any expression, unwilling to commit himself. It was probably best to let the agent go on, show Zolly what he was getting at, than to leave the room wondering.

The agent said, "We were talking side businesses. What do you know about selling things to eat?"

"If you mean food, there I am a user, but not a pusher."

"Then you do buy from the other inmates?"

Great, now he was asking about Charlie Chicken or one of the other cooks. Maggiano would never forgive him if they had to do their own floor. "Sometimes I buy a piece of food," Zolly said. "What does that have to do with it?"

"It depends on what else they were selling, and what was their source."

"I don't know why you care, but I do know about food. And I buy some on occasion." Zolly stopped. "But if you're asking me from who, forget it."

"We already know about Charles Jenkins. I'm asking about anyone else who has food or drink to sell."

"You mean booze? Is that what this is about?"

The agent held a half smile. Zolly could be an old friend, with a relationship that could improve with dialogue. "Let's talk about booze."

"You could have asked me to begin with."

"How about homemade brew?"

"What does that have to do with the fire?"

The agent considered the question long enough to appear he might even answer. "Do you know an inmate named Natron Blades?"

"I know a Natron. He works with me at the chaplains' offices."

"How do you get along with the men here?"

"No problems."

"You sure? This is a level-one institution. You shouldn't run into any physical problems, right?" The agent assumed the pose of an old friend. "You haven't had any concerns or threats, have you? Mr. Fallen and I are concerned."

So it was Fallen again, after all. The feds were here because of the fire, but maybe not only because of the fire. Zolly said, "I don't know Natron from any booze."

"You'd tell us if you had trouble?"

Zolly helped himself to the glass of water.

The agent nodded, keeping his voice level—maybe a statement, maybe a question. "You don't know about the yeast, and you don't know about the juice."

"We get orange, pineapple, you name it." Zolly thought it was a poor substitute for wine, but it was the symbol that counted.

"How about grape? You haven't had grape for a while, have you?"

"Every Friday night. They save it for the Jewish services."

"You must say a lot of prayers."

"Pardon my asking, but what the fuck do you care?"

"Considering they check out a couple gallons of juice a week. A locked room makes a good storage place, don't you think?" The agent's smile looked surprised to appear on his face.

Zolly thought about the tiny cups for the juice after services and Natron, always hovering around the door, acting as though he only wanted some cake. That was Natron for you. Swishing left and charging right. "What does yeast have to do with juice?" Zolly asked.

The agent relaxed his cheeks and added to his notes. "We can prove Mr. Blades had a sideline."

"I don't know about that."

"He wouldn't deliberately start the fire, would he? It destroyed his inventory." The agent was talking to himself now in two voices. The high pitch, probably Natron. The low tone, undoubtedly Fallen. When the agent shrugged Zolly out of the room, he said, "I'm not certain we have enough to prosecute, but I doubt you'll see him again."

Zolly was happy with the news. He would have been even happier if he weren't known as the last person questioned before the hacks led Natron away.

FAITH REACHED FOR HIM AS SHE HAD EVERY MORNING SINCE he went away. Every time she looked across the kitchen table to Zolly's empty chair, whenever she ordered Chinese for one, each drink she had alone, she smelled his aftershave. There was pain no matter how long she slept or in what position. When they'd had the bar, that was part of the deal. When it was yours, ownership was a salve if your body was sore. When you worked for someone else, you bandaged the bruises with cash. Not that she was ungrateful for the work. She just wished it could have been closer than a bus ride and two transfers away. After months of looking, it took Evanston to find a job where Goldberg, Civiletti, and O'Rourke became a foreign language. She felt the pain as she sat up in bed and reached for his latest letter, the one she reread each night before she went to sleep. The fact he was writing improved the chance he would return to her one day. The money reinforced her hope. What did he think she did with an extra fifty dollars a month? She made more than that Saturday nights serving steaks in the suburbs. But this was the closest Zolly had ever come to commitment. She was happy for that, for being able to keep their apartment, at least for now, and for having Sundays off, when the phone on the nightstand rang.

She heard the breathing before she said hello. It was that way every time. Let it ring, pick it up, say hello, and have someone puffing in her ear. The phone looked the same as ever, pink to match the sheets, but these days it stabbed her with an intruder's calls. It had begun months earlier on weekday nights when she got off at eight. Now, the breather was stretching out the calls to late at night, early morning, anytime, whenever she might be off guard. Helter-skelter wore her down. Instead of banging down the phone as she usually did, she listened to the sound, minutes it seemed, before she spoke again. She knew the danger in pushing him, assuming it was a man. She had never heard of a woman who made such calls, but she wanted to provoke the next step, whatever it might be, anything to reach an ending. "You're out of breath. Is this how you get it hard?"

His response was more breathing, this time in faster bursts, as though suppressing a laugh. Then his tongue made the kind of noise her mother made when caramel was stuck on her dentures. Faith hung up, gently this time. If he could change the routine, so could she.

They were listed under Zolly's name in the telephone directory, so the breather hadn't chosen her from that. He was probably a crank who had chosen their number at random. No point in telling Zolly about it. Faith was trying to limit the bad news to a couple of items a call. She thought about changing their number, but in his last letter Zolly had said he would phone her soon. She would tell him today if he called. If she didn't hear from him, she would change the number and let him know by mail. She went into the bathroom and took off her pajamas. There was no point in wearing nightgowns these days. Before she stepped in the shower, she considered herself. In the days when Zolly was there, the reflection in his eyes was all that mattered. Now, she had to rely on a mirror to remember the way Zolly knew her. Her breasts were still pointed the way Zolly liked when she pressed into his chest. Her walking took off the mileage other women her age put on. Her pleasure stopped at her face. At forty-five, her features were still defined, but no matter how much cream she used at night, morning showed another hairline fracture from the earthquake in their lives.

Sundays were the hardest. They used to lie in bed, read the paper, and sometimes go to brunch, unless she took the early shift. Now it was the day she moved fast to avoid remembering, when she bought groceries for the week. On July and August Sundays, she sometimes wore the slacks outfit that would always put Zolly in a better mood. It might be too heavy to wear today. The yellow looked summer, but the fabric felt fall. She held it against her body and then decided, to hell with the heat. What would she do after shopping? At best, groceries took only an hour. Add twenty minutes, half an hour to get there and the same time back, but that still left most of the day. She could call Conrad Bigman after she got home. Maybe they could get together for a bite later. Conrad was still working on Rush and had his Sundays off. She could invite him over for dinner if they had a good price on steaks at the Jewel. Conrad wouldn't get the wrong idea. She was almost out the door when the telephone rang. It might be the breather. Or, it might be Zolly. She had to pick it up.

"Bitch. Cunt." The voice was masculine, flat, and free of accent. So this was how the breather sounded.

"What do you want from me?" She stared into the mouthpiece as though his face might appear through the holes if she looked hard enough.

"You know."

"I have no idea. Can't you leave me alone? I'm sorry for what I said before." That was when it occurred to her for the first time that the caller might not be random.

"Just remember, it can always get worse." This time, he hung up first.

If she sat down, it might be hours before she could rise again. Then Sunday would be gone and all her plans with it, leaving her alone to clean Zolly's comb and smell his cologne. She stayed standing as she dialed Conrad's number.

"Faith. I called a couple times, but your machine wasn't working."

She decided against telling Conrad she'd turned off the machine these days because she didn't want to play back breathing. "I was wondering if you'd like to come over for dinner. I could pick up a couple of steaks."

"Sweetheart, if I had only known. I have plans."

She could hear the traffic outside his window. Conrad lived in an Old Town low-rise where the tourists started early. Then she heard the sounds of a second voice and him mumbling in reassurance.

"Say hi to Zolly for me," he said.

She assured him she would. There was no reason to tell him today would be her first chance in months.

Faith left the apartment and walked west on Elm toward Clark. The Jewel was a few streets over and a block north, up on Division next to the Sandburg Village apartments. Any other day, such a walk would be passage from serenity to noise. But on a Sunday morning, with the stores shuttered and the bars closed, it would be a small-town stroll. Considering how early it was on this particular Sunday in the middle of August, she was surprised at how many bathing suits and jogging shorts were already heading for the Oak Street Beach. The break in the weather made amends for June and July. Elm Street was the Gold Coast without the glitz. It was twice the length of most Chicago blocks, stretching from Lake Shore Drive to State Street without any interruption, past boutiques and doorman buildings. Not a single shop or restaurant fought for parking spaces, and the high-rises hadn't yet invaded. Instead, there were trees in the parkway and private cars at the curb. Elm was lined with turn-of-the-century homes, some single-family, others subdivided, as well as an occasional mid-rise. The buildings would have been brownstones on any New York side street. Here, they were the color of Midwest brick. Faith was so busy enjoying the sight of familiar surroundings and people whose faces she knew or thought she knew that she didn't spot Civiletti at the southeast corner, where Rush surrenders to State. He could have posed as one of the walkers if he weren't standing still. He could have passed for a shopper out to get the newspaper, if he weren't already holding one, still folded, watching her approach. By the time she recognized him, it was too late to turn away.

"Mr. Civiletti. I haven't seen you for a while." Did he know about the skirmish with Goldberg? Men liked to talk, and those three were always together. It was best to act natural. This might really be an accidental meeting. There was no way to be sure.

Civiletti didn't respond, at first. Another minute and he would just be another scab no longer drawing blood. But instead of letting her pass, Civiletti threw his *Trib* into the basket on the corner and began to walk away, before looking back after several steps, saying, "Maybe you should leave it off the hook."

It was the second time that day that she lost her strength. The closest bench was a few blocks south, on a sliver of grass where Rush met Chestnut, but it was the wrong direction from the Jewel. Then she considered the coffee shop. She didn't expect to see the owner. Joe was always there when they closed the bar at four and were hungry enough to put up with him balancing plates of food from his hand up to his shoulder. Yet he was there now, even this early, smiling as though he had seen her the night before instead of a year ago.

"How is it going, Faith?" Joe had already started the eggs.

"Since Zolly went away, it's been downhill."

"You should have come by. I thought maybe you went away, too. I don't mean away, but away, away." He covered his stutter by beginning the bacon.

"I haven't had much chance to eat out. Not the money, either." Here she was, crying on the shoulder of the man they always shooed away.

Joe motioned for Faith to take a table by the window facing Rush. It was later than they used to eat, and Zolly wasn't there. Other than that, it was a return trip home. When he approached with her meal, Joe was carrying the plates in both hands. All those years, he had been showing off for Zolly. Joe missed him, too. "It's on the house. After all, what are old friends for?"

THIRTY-FOUR

ZOLLY WAS UNABLE TO DO HIS LAUNDRY FOR FIVE DAYS straight, so he stayed indoors on this August Sunday that dared you to inhale its steam. The bags next to the machines were proxies for inmates otherwise standing in line, the honor system at work. Zolly believed in honor, but he never got a turn before Count and time to go to dinner. By the end of Count, Charlie Chicken was already there, handling four bags for a quarter apiece.

"You'd have a better chance during the week," Charlie Chicken said.

"I've been wearing the same underwear two days in a row. My roommate is upset."

"You want to play, you got to pay."

These days, in order to continue sending whatever he could to Faith, Zolly stood behind Charlie Chicken in every laundry line. If he stayed at it long enough, the other guys would run out of quarters. His other reason for remaining behind was to make a telephone call home. He could jump in the booth if a man on the list failed to show.

Even sitting upright, his knees hit the opposite wall. He rested his elbow on the telephone table, propping up his head, eyes closed, trying to remember how she looked.

"Some problem?" he said when he reached her. Of course, it was a problem. Easy had ended a couple of years ago.

Her voice was a whisper. "I've been getting calls. Heavy breathing."

This was why he preferred to write. You could put a letter in your pocket halfway through and read the rest later. "It could be some crank who got your name from the phone book, or maybe a clerk at a store where you gave your ID."

"Do you still believe in coincidence?"

"What I believe is another discussion. Let's not waste the time." Just once, it would be nice to talk old times. When he discussed it with the guys in here, it was a monologue. Faith could confirm that once upon a time they were at the top. Instead, her letters were all downhill and this call was slaloming out of control.

"I ran into Civiletti. He let me know he was waiting for me."

"Did he say why?"

"He talked about your coming home."

Fallen's image replaced what he remembered of Faith. If you worried about everything, once in a while you were right. "Hold on. You know our calls are monitored. Sit tight. I'll call back."

After Count, Zolly went to Solomon's room. Usually, there were stacks of paper resting on his bed. This time, Solomon's blanket was as tight as an unpaid hooker. Instead of a *Good Housekeeping* patch, there was Solomon, standing by the window, taking in the evening fog. He was smoking a cigarette and dressed in clothes that announced he had dropped a few quarters on Charlie Chicken. His pants were pressed as sharp as Maggiano's. His shirt had creased sleeves and a collar ready for an ascot.

"You sick?" Zolly asked.

"I'm on vacation. I'll begin again Columbus Day."

Which was still several weeks away, but Zolly could appreciate the concept. Holidays were good marking points for doing time. Instead of week to week or month to month, they lived celebration to celebration. "I hope the judges took your schedule into account when they did the court calendars."

"Would you like a smoke? It might calm you down." Solomon extended the pack as though it were a cup, a coffee jar, anything else he was always ready to share.

"If I take one, I'll need another," Zolly said. "And please don't tell me about side money with Perez."

"I'll always keep you in smokes. After all, you're my typist."

"You know I already quit. That's one of the few things I don't miss."

"Like your girl back home?"

"You think you know how to push my buttons. Press again. Matter of fact, we might be getting back together. I've been getting letters since I started sending her the money from my job."

"Sometimes they're grateful, sometimes they just want to keep it coming. Remember, *tuchus affen tisch*."

What did an ass on the table have to do with cash on the line? Besides, it wasn't just the money. Back then, Zolly would have been cynical. These days, he thought differently. Considering what Faith had lost because she'd staked her future on his prospects, she was entitled. "I've been writing her, she's been writing back. Things are better between us. She's under a lot of pressure. We should have set money aside for hard times before this happened."

"Yeah, a guy needs fuck-you money." Solomon jabbed his middle finger into the air.

"I should have made sure she was taken care of by these guys before I went away. I made too many assumptions." He should have discussed it with them, gotten it in writing. The judge hadn't allowed time to do it in person, but Gershom could have handled the job. It would have improved his chances of getting money sent in from outside. Two weeks out of contact, by the time Zolly reached Lexington, everything was lost.

As Solomon exhaled the last drag from his cigarette, he reached for the smoke in the air as though he could bring it back. "It's like this." He opened his hand to show Zolly it was empty. "It's nothing you can get hold of. We can't worry about outside. Here is where we do our time."

"I can't just leave her hanging out there. Today, I hear she's getting threats." Zolly repeated the conversation, hoping Solomon would gain insight from the detail. Solomon had a way with words.

"So they don't want you to give them up. Can you blame them? No one wants to go down, and it looks like you're the key."

"I couldn't give them up if I wanted to, which I don't, but I've got to tell you, they're hard to figure. You'd think if they were afraid of what I might say, they would help out. A little commissary would have been nice. A job for Faith would have been nicer."

Solomon started another cigarette. At the rate he was burning up his commissary, he would have to cut his vacation short. "Yeah, and if they'd saved your bar, that would have been even nicer. Did you ever consider why they didn't?"

"Sometimes that eats at me more than anything. It's like they're forcing me the other way."

"Maybe that Hebrew is messing up your mind. If they wanted to commit suicide, they wouldn't need your help. You ever think, they might be afraid to make their situation worse? The feds see them giving you money or Faith a job, they might call it evidence of guilt. By keeping hands-off, they're showing they have nothing to fear."

"Hitting on Faith the way Goldberg did, scaring her to death, how does that figure?"

Solomon caught the ash before it hit the floor. "Maybe you'd overreact. If you went wild, it would put a shadow on whatever you said. Or it could be that Goldberg is just a hard-on prick." Solomon examined the palm of his hand with a suspicious look, as though it might have held further answers before the breeze from the fan blew the ash away.

Zolly said, "I've got to call Faith again. I want to know exactly how they sounded. Maybe that will help me figure it out."

"Do you always lose your head under pressure?" Solomon asked.

"I told her to shut up and I'd get back to her."

"That part's fine," Solomon said. "But when you ask me how to keep it private, you lose me. Did you forget the phone in the chaplains' offices?"

———————

WEAVER WAS THERE THAT NIGHT. "CHAPLAIN, I HAVE AN EMERGENCY back home, but I couldn't get on the phone today."

"You should have come right over. We can help you make your call."

"I was too confused to think straight."

Weaver handed Zolly the phone and left the room. After a moment, Zolly remembered how to place a call that wasn't collect. "I'm in the chaplains' offices. What else did Civiletti say?"

"That doesn't matter anymore."

"I rush over here, pull strings so I can call in private, and it doesn't matter?" Every time until now, at least Faith was consistent.

"They called again this afternoon. Right after you hung up. This time, it was Goldberg. He made sure I knew who it was. He told me the grand jury term is about to end, that you would be called back to testify. He says the authorities have been threatening you with charges if you don't cooperate. You didn't tell me that." She sounded as though someone were in the room with her, his hands about her throat.

"It's the same old same old. It didn't scare me then; it doesn't scare me now." If threats had bothered Zolly, he wouldn't have been able to hold on to his newsstand long enough to buy the bar on Howard. You paid for a busy corner on the Near North Side with the size of your balls.

She said, "Goldberg wanted me to know things would go worse if you cooperate. There's more involved than what you might or might not have overheard. He said, 'Ask Zolly how he feels about loud noises and the smell of smoke.'"

THIRTY-FIVE

"Lookie here. You studying for your equivalency? Or you teaching the class yourself?" Natron was in the doorway, looking up and down and side to side as though choosing which two-man room he wanted on his first day back. He moved into the room without any floating or fluttering and took the chair Maggiano used for a table. Seated, Natron pushed his heels against the floor to scrape away from the bed. "Where's your roommate? Doesn't he like to read with you?"

"He's watching the show in the main TV."

Natron swiveled to a different angle, put his heels on Maggiano's bed, and crossed his legs, leaning back, digging the rear legs of his chair deeper into the floor. "I don't care if he's taking the place of Don Fucking Johnson. I come to talk to you. You could welcome me back, ask how I am, where I been, like that." Then he rocked back and forth, marking the floor with each pitch of the chair. Charlie Chicken would want full price for a do-over.

"We just had it shined for inspection. Maggiano will be pissed," Zolly said.

"He can piss a red stream in Biscayne Bay, won't bother me none." Natron swung his feet off the bed and rubbed his boots against the floor, digging deeper grooves.

Zolly knew he should have thrown Natron out of the room by now, but if he had gained the man's respect, that wouldn't be necessary. He had begun behind Natron's swish down the hallway and had never managed to catch up.

"After what happen, Charlie Chicken should know to stay away," Natron said.

"Lots of guys work for quarters." Zolly fought to keep his voice steady.

"Lots of guys suck dick for money. That don't mean they suck you."

"Do laundry, clean the rooms, stuff like that," Zolly said.

"Not as many as they used to be. Some of those boys were with me on my trip." Natron tallied Zolly's sins on his fingers.

Zolly considered kicking out the legs of the chair when it was on a backward rock. Natron would be too busy posing to notice Zolly's move. If he timed it right, that might end his problems, but another Natron was sure to follow. At least he knew what this one looked like. "I see you came without your bat tonight," Zolly said.

"I can get it, if you like." Natron cracked his rock mid-swing. He was about to rise when the guard looked in. It was turning into one of those nights Zolly would be lucky to read two pages.

Hack Chicago squinted at the book and at Natron, trying to find him in the pictures that cataloged the rooms. "I haven't looked at the bed book today."

"Look again, Officer, maybe your eyes get tired."

"You haven't been around for a while," Hack Chicago said.

"I been around there and around there, just not around here. I only have a couple of weeks left before they let me go for good. Kind of you to ask, Officer." Natron spit the last few words.

The guard considered Natron a moment before shrugging the remark away. An experienced hack considered which issues warranted the paperwork. "Berns, stop by my desk when you get a chance. I want to talk to you."

After Hack Chicago left, Natron said, "Congratulations, you got another hack boyfriend. Your mouth must be getting tired, come to think of it. The last I see of your mouth was in the gymnasium, headed into your meeting with Johnson. Next I know, I'm on the bus to Milan with a few other folk. 'Course, you wouldn't know anything about that."

"They questioned all of us that night."

"I'm more concerned with answers than questions," Natron said.

"They could have moved you guys because of your profiles." Zolly wondered whether Natron knew the word.

Evidently he did, as he rubbed the side of his face, getting out of the chair and walking over to look in the mirror hanging over Maggiano's footlocker. "You talking the shape of my face or my color? It look okay to me." Natron skidded his shoes back to the chair.

"We wondered, but the hacks never said. Tell me." Zolly closed his siddur and slid it under the pillow.

"Probably ask Perez each Friday, right before the pictures," Natron said. "Well, now I'm back to answer in person. What you like to know?"

"You tell me."

"Nice of you to ask. They take me back on the system," Natron said. "You know about that? Riding along in handcuffs and leg irons on a rickety bus that be illegal to carry schoolkids? Touring every joint along the way? It take longer, make you appreciate Milan even more when you get there." He had his hand on his cheek, still rubbing at whatever he had seen in the mirror. "I did get to make a couple calls along the way. After that, my lawyer made them stop. See, I has just a couple more weeks to do. I got back troubles. Sent here to begin with on account of my back. You probably don't know about that. It feels better now." Natron smiled, generous with forgiveness. "My lawyer says they are bouncing me around to punish me for what I didn't do, and they can't prove. He told me private, doing that attorney-client privilege Solomon talks about, the judge won't interfere. My lawyer calls it 'BOP discretion.' See, they even got a word for how they fuck you over. But he gives it a try and they buy his talk. Figure too much bother, me having so little time to do. So they bring me back. But the ride did me some good."

"I'm glad to hear it," Zolly said. If he encouraged more of this crap, he'd see whether the rest of the story affected him.

Natron paused, trying to identify where he left off. "I got to consider your turning up every time it—what's that word Solomon uses—inconvenient? That's it. You're inconvenient. So like I say, I make some calls. Friends in D.C. to tell them my back is hurting, about the bus ride, my lawyer who's holding my cash. While I'm at it, we talk about you being inconvenient. Ask them to make some contacts. You know, folk know other folk, they can get the word on people, like that."

Zolly said, "It wouldn't be the first time you made some calls on me."

Natron proceeded, undeterred. "When I call back from my next stop, I get the word on you. They are lots of folk who worry about you, important folk. Will you do right by them? They say, long as I be headed back, would I mind checking it out. The way I sees it, the best answer to them is how you are in here. Not too good, seem to me. Inconvenient." Arms folded in judgment, Natron continued rocking, formulating his report.

"Who do you think you're kidding?" Zolly asked. "You've had a line to Chicago for months. How much are they paying you for the bullshit you send back? I haven't done a damn thing that might be wrong, except turn you down on the smuggling. I don't owe you any apologies. You owe me for the aggravation you've caused my woman back home." Waving his hand forward, Zolly was a wizard casting his curse.

Natron stopped rocking. When he leaned forward, the smell of the road drifted across the space between them. "You talk big for a fat old man who's always ducking. We gots more to discuss and I don't want no interruption. We need a private meet."

"About what else?"

"We gots to get things clear. So I can do a proper report. If I get things wrong, I be glad to correct them. Say tomorrow morning, behind breakfast call. I'll meet you by the Women's archway. After everyone go to eat. No one be passing through, we can have a quiet chat."

After he left, the room ached with Natron's aftertaste. Zolly figured he had to do it. He should have handled Natron the first time, after what he did to Truman. Let a guy like that get away with it, next thing you knew he was muscling you out of every line and messing around with Darla. But a second opinion wouldn't hurt, in case his emotions were overpowering his judgment. He considered waiting for Maggiano, but the current cops-and-robbers TV show had just begun. He decided to see Solomon instead.

The hall was as quiet as the night of the fire. He peeked outside the doorway, intending to avoid Hack Chicago. Zolly was in no mood to discuss the Goddamn Cubs. Solomon was in his room, holding a pipe and wearing a Lake Geneva outfit that combined drawstring pajamas with buttermilk slippers and a velour robe a Pierre Cardin fan had donated the day he got out. Solomon also played the country squire in his greeting. "Ah, my typist. Are your fingers enjoying their rest?"

Zolly sat. There was a lot of room on the bed these days. "You forget I have another job. It's called working in the chaplains' offices. Sometimes I have to do it, along with my work for you."

"I don't mind, as long as I get my share after my vacation is over," Solomon said. He pinched off the end of a filter tip to smoke the cigarette raw.

"You remember Natron?" Zolly said.

"The Speedy Trial Act. I hear he's back. I guess they didn't grant our motion, after all." That was standard Solomon. He measured his victories by every permanent disappearance.

"I think the motion he has in mind is another swing of his bat. He thinks I'm guilty of something. Hell, he thinks I'm guilty of everything, beginning with the hack catching Gloria in the act. He figures I took away his camera job and got him the blame for the fire. Now he's trying to set me up as a rat with some hitters in Chicago."

Solomon gave a tut-tut laugh, the same sound lawyers make in English movies. These days, Solomon was all barrister. "Clients suffer from paranoia when they first visit. If they pay attention, they leave with reality."

"Does that make you their lawyer or their judge?"

"Many of us get to act as judge. Some of us get paid, some don't." Solomon gaveled what was left of his cigarette into the ashtray on the sill.

Zolly looked at the wall. Mickey's hands were ten hours away from his date. Maybe if Solomon talked fast, he could make the meeting on time. "We have an appointment. He set it up for the entry to Women's, after breakfast call."

"That's a good time and place. Except for when Freckles got sucked." The previous week, the hacks had caught the Alabama broker with a D.C. streetwalker earning some quarters on her knees.

"So I should be worried." Zolly considered what to take with him, to counteract the bat. "What should I do?" Zolly asked. Maybe Solomon would pretend he was a client, give it to him straight.

"Philosophers have pondered the issue over the years. What to do prompts deep analysis."

"Yeah, and a lot of bullshit, too." This was a wasted visit.

Solomon put on his solicitor smile, the kind lawyers who don't go to court are happy to provide. "We do what we have to do. In your case, it's to meet Natron after breakfast call tomorrow, at the entry to the Women's Unit yard." Solomon waved Zolly out of the room as he slipped out of his robe. He slept a lot on vacation.

Hack Chicago spotted Zolly as he returned to his room. "What about those Cubs?"

"Fuck the Cubs," Zolly said, swinging his fists as he kept on going.

———————

HALF AN HOUR LATER, MAGGIANO RETURNED, WAVING HIS hands, as well. "Those motherfuckers. They called an early Count right before the end of the show." All his blood was in his cheeks, leaving his fingers sticks of chalk.

"*Miami Vice?*"

"They wouldn't interrupt *Murder She Wrote.*" Angela Lansbury ranked just below exercise on Maggiano's list. He kicked off his shoes. When he clapped his hands, Zolly tried to avoid the flying dust. "The Cubans were bopping down the Intracoastal with bags of coke flying out the boats. So they're diving in, treading water with bags overhead, calling for a rope. Don Johnson's yelling at them to drop the bags and grab hold if they want to be saved, and then the hacks call Count."

Zolly was careful to show sympathy for Maggiano's disappointment. They were on better terms now that the memories of the fire had cooled. Zolly could remove his fireman helmet from under his bed and hang it on the bedpost once more, marking the room so that the Angel of Death might pass. "You want to know which they wound up snorting, coke or water?" he asked.

"Yeah, like that." Maggiano tore off his shirt and threw it on the bed, stalking about the room, sorry for the Cubans.

"It was just a rerun. That's all they have on in the summer. They'll probably show it again when it goes in syndication."

Maggiano took off his trousers, folded them at the crease, and hung them on a hanger in his locker. No point in wasting quarters. He scratched the hairs on his back and his hand came away slick. "Think I'll do a shower after Count. They better call it pretty soon, seeing as they insisted on an early start." He removed the rest of his clothes, wrapped his towel about him, and sat on his bed. They weren't required to stand for the ten o'clock Count. "How'd you spend your night? Practicing your Jew again?"

Now that Zolly knew the meaning of tact, he understood what Maggiano lacked. "I had a visitor. Natron's back. No bat this time. Just a message. Says he heard from some folks back home. Now he wants to meet."

Maggiano furrowed his eyebrows. "He wants a meet. Why didn't you say so?"

"I talked to Solomon because you were at *Miami Vice*. He says to do like Natron says. Be by Women's Unit after breakfast call."

"You can get all the Jew advice you want. One thing sure. You can't snitch."

Zolly leaned back on his bed and closed his eyes. There were times he wondered whether David's story hung over his head like the prologue to some Biblical epic, condensed for the slow readers. "Hell, I've been muscled by worse." He considered mentioning the cigarette machine vendor back in his ward. Having to put up with a trash-removal monopoly was bad enough. He was damned if he would rent a machine when he could buy one. He opened his eyes to see Maggiano studying his towel, which was wrapped around his stomach as though it were Scripture.

Maggiano said, "You can't rat on him, but you can't meet alone with him, either. You might have been able to take care of yourself two years ago, but Natron is straight from the Street. He probably bought a shiv from the kitchen. He'd carve you up like a Charlie Chicken patty." Maggiano crushed the wax paper left over from last night's treat.

"So what does that leave?"

Standing up, holding one end of the towel, Maggiano allowed the rest of the scroll to unravel and fall from his body, letting Zolly witness truth. "That leaves me."

THIRTY-SIX

MAGGIANO WAITED UNTIL THE NEXT MORNING TO SHOWER. HE liked to be fresh for a meet. Zolly was sleeping. Next time, he would have to charge for the service. He was the first one to reach the shower room, allowing him his choice of stalls. While soaping himself, he pictured his moves the way he had when he was young. He looked at it as insurance against surprises. When you thought it out, you saved the split second it took to lose a battle. Even as a kid, when he looked like he should have been at work on the docks, Maggiano had won his fights with his smarts. He had graduated early into working with his head. Scams involved fewer risks and lower sentences. It had been a long time since he had used his muscle.

When he was done, his heart began to beat at the thought of the sweat yet to come. He toweled himself dry in front of the mirror. The scar across his chest was the size of a surgeon's hand. Other than that betrayal, he was sixty going on fifty. Take off twenty pounds of kosher food, he would be ready for some pasta. Right now, he was going to make a meal of some black-eyed peas. Not that Natron ever did anything to him. But

Zolly was his roommate. If Zolly lived down the hall, Maggiano wouldn't have even blinked. Then he thought of the scuff marks. And ruined floor. Maybe it was personal, after all. He approached the sink to sight his razor properly. It was hard to edge a beard with the damn disposables the commissary sold. The hacks thought, no point in encouraging a bloody beef. He hoped they had done as good a job counting the utensils in the kitchen and that Charlie Chicken limited carryouts to food.

It was more than an hour before the meet, but the thought of it gave him an appetite. After getting dressed in the dark, Maggiano talked the hack into letting him leave for breakfast with the early-worker shift. Dawn was breaking overhead, revealing a Kentucky sky crossed with clouds as wet with promise as the legs of a teenage tease. The Women's archway was in a shadow where the walls formed corners and the doorways carved niches. Twenty feet long, it was deep enough for a meet or a blowjob, depending on your choice of muscle. Farther beyond, in the main courtyard, the grass still grew, and the flowers bloomed, proving the benefit of ten-cent-an-hour gardeners and plastic hose. This would be where they would take pictures for the postcards if business ever dropped. Maggiano waited for Haskell on the steps to the Main Building. They could have walked over from Atwood together, but he wanted to study the archway uninterrupted. When it was business, you needed to look at things from different angles. He was considering the oblique view when Haskell arrived.

"*Paisan.*"

"Landsman," Maggiano replied. They were working their way up to *buon giorno* and *shalom*.

As they entered the kosher kitchen, they could hear the fried eggs spattering in the inner room. Haskell said, "Glad we got here early.

I'll pile the eggs on some buttered toast. Even better than at the Stage Deli."

Maggiano was also from New York and knew the restaurant. "Yeah, but none of that, what do you call it, matzo brie?" He pronounced it like an Italian version of French cheese.

"You can get that, too, if you ask the cooks."

"Not no more. There's no Jews left on the morning shift. Not with Rosie gone." Before they left, she and Buddy had used up all the chicken fat on their personal pleasure. Maggiano could almost taste the matzo, dipped in egg batter and fried to a burnt-grease brown.

They sat at a table for four by a wall in dining room two. It would probably remain empty all morning. The main line was serving oatmeal, and word would get around. Maggiano said, "You know that guy who hassles my roommate?"

Haskell stuffed his mouth with another piece of toast that was swimming in yolk and butter. "The *schwarzer* with the bat?"

"He walks into our room and tells Zolly to come to a meeting this morning. Half an hour from now. Over in the archway, after they call Atwood for chow." Maggiano looked at his watch.

"Is Zolly going to show?"

"I wouldn't let him do that. He may be a religious fanatic, but no one can call out my family. You know what I mean? He's a lover, not a fighter."

"You give him too much credit," Haskell said. "When he had the hots for Darla, I gave him room but he struck out royal. Then he walks around angry. Misplaced hard-on, I call it. If I hadn't gone out of my way to make up, he'd still be walking by me. I don't know whether Natron has a beef or not, but Zolly is no ass man."

"You miss my point. I don't give a shit if he scores or strikes out, he can't handle heavy stuff. He's not even smart enough to be scared, but that don't make no difference. I'm going to take the meet for him. Besides, that Natron prick ruined our floor."

Haskell's egg caked icing on his last crust of bread. He nodded. "I used to take positions in the market for some relatives who didn't know squat. You've got to watch out for your own." They left their dishes on the wash line and went outside. The rest of the Atwood inmates were approaching across the courtyard. Haskell wished him luck.

Maggiano said, "I make my own. Always have, always will."

WHEN MAGGIANO ARRIVED BACK AT THE ENTRANCE TO THE Yard, the archway was already empty. Moving without a sound, except for his stomach working on his meal, he found the darkest niche and waited, bouncing on the balls of his feet. Natron arrived a few minutes later, cracking his knuckles and flexing his fingers. At least he wasn't carrying a bat. There was no telling about a knife.

"Looking for someone?" Maggiano asked.

Natron squinted into the darkness. Making out Maggiano, he said, "Yeah, but I was hoping for your roommate. You here to hold his hand? I was wanting to meet alone."

"You are meeting alone. But with me, not him. You mind?" Maggiano approached and stood within a few inches of Natron, breathing egg into his face.

"Any other time. But this time, I wants the Hebe."

"We don't always get what we want. Sometimes, another man's wants are stronger. Like right now, my wants are for you to give me a roll of quarters," Maggiano said.

"Why I want to do that? A roll don't come easy."

"Easy or hard, makes no difference to me," Maggiano said.

"Supposing I had a roll, why would I give it to you?"

"To fix the scraping. Next time, take off your shoes."

Natron drew himself up and backed away, raising his hands palms-forward at the claim. "Where do a roll come from? Charlie Chicken only charge a buck. How come the other nine?"

"It's from the aggravation that's grumbling in my stomach. Now, tell me why we're here."

"Why you is here, I still don't know. You could get your floor fixed without coming all this way. Maybe Charlie Chicken will do us the favor."

Maggiano nodded as though Natron were making sense. "I do like favors. More important, what brings you here is what I'm asking."

"I come to see if your roommate is a rat."

"You won't find that answer in here."

"From what I see of what gone down, his town folk are right to be worried."

"From what I see, you're the one to be worried. You rough up my floor, now you want to start on my friend." Maggiano advanced again and inserted two fingers into the nostrils of Natron's nose. He raised his hand upward, forcing Natron to rise until he was on tiptoes. As Natron raised his hands to defend himself, Maggiano pushed them away with his free forearm. "I see any steel coming out of your pocket, you'll be breathing through your eyeballs. Now, you listen very careful. The man's my roommate; that makes him a friend of mine. Do you understand?" Maggiano was spattering pieces of food into Natron's face, cleaning his teeth with his tongue as he talked. "It's like he's family. Remember that, as though your life depended on it."

Careful not to tear anything, Natron nodded, and Maggiano released his nose. With his extended fingers still forming a *V*, Maggiano wiped them, front and back, across Natron's chest.

THIRTY-SEVEN

AFTER LABOR DAY, IT WAS EASY. MOST OF THE MEN HAD DONE their wash before the weekend. There was reason to get dressed up. After depositing a week's worth of clothing and twenty-five cents, Zolly went to breakfast. Haskell was already there, alone at the table closest to the kosher kitchen where the men with the biggest appetites ate. But all he had on his tray was a cup of coffee. That was Haskell, showing off.

"Did your roomie send you to pinch-hit?" Haskell asked. Zolly looked around but was unable to see anyone else he knew. If he sat elsewhere, it would insult the man. Not a bad idea in the abstract, but they might meet again on the Street. Besides, Haskell had probably done him a favor. Knowing Darla would stoop to Haskell had helped Zolly make his choice. Then, too, Haskell had already apologized. Another opinion wouldn't hurt.

"I got up ahead of Maggiano," Zolly said. "I have to dry my laundry before work." Zolly sat across from Haskell and began on his Cap'n Crunch.

"First, you come to breakfast; next, you do your wash. New habits, after all this time?"

"Not everyone wears a manicure."

"I'll have to file that one away," Haskell said. "I was asking what brings you here."

"Start the day with some food, get my metabolism going. I'm taking pointers from you."

"You'd be a healthier man if you'd started sooner. I hear you're on the homestretch," Haskell said.

Zolly slurped the last of the milk from his bowl and began to sip his coffee. He might have to try this more often, now that he had met sugared cereal. "Yeah, they won't hold me after the grand jury's term expires. I've been studying what to do, but it doesn't give me a clue." Zolly had been digesting daily doses of *Ethics of the Fathers* instead of eating lunch. That was his habit these days, now that Darla walked with folks who liked to snort.

Haskell said, "You going to Israel when you get out?"

"I'm going home. But first, I have to learn the meaning."

"Learning the words isn't the same as learning the meaning. Even I know that."

"Rabinowitz said it would come to me."

"The grand jury is coming to you as well, or are you going to them? When does it end, next month?" Haskell sipped his coffee.

"Yeah, the week between Rosh Hashanah and Yom Kippur. Rabinowitz never covered that," Zolly said.

"So the end of the term is after the beginning of the term. Speaking legally and spiritually, of course."

"You could put it that way, if you want to mix your bullshit with religion."

Haskell said, "Take the Talmud and the Supreme Court cases you read for Solomon. They're both written by a bunch of graybeards pushing the same stone in different directions, looking to see how far it will roll. I'm not ashamed of being a Jew and all. I go to services, eat on the line. I don't mind being part of a race, a culture, a way of life, whatever. But when you start doing God on me, I lift my pants so my cuffs don't get dirty." Haskell stared at Zolly, his half cup of coffee forgotten.

"I've been straight with the guys at home, even though they didn't do a damn thing for me, but they're turning up the pressure. What do I do now?" He was weary of advice in bullet points. It came from reading the tout sheets.

"You do whatever you owe yourself. And your family. I draw the line at family. Friends are okay when you live in the area, but see what happens when you move on. They can't look the other way fast enough. I didn't get where I am today by living for anyone else." Haskell lifted his cup, as though making a toast. Before Zolly could respond, the millionaire left the table.

———————

BACK AT THE UNIT, ZOLLY PLACED HIS LAUNDRY IN THE DRYER and returned to make his bed.

"Are we sick, or what?" Maggiano was putting on the jogging suit he wore when he went to eat. The nap of the velour was raw from Charlie Chicken working on the kosher stains.

"I went to breakfast," Zolly said.

"Thanks for waiting."

"You were sleeping. I got up early to do my laundry."

Maggiano turned his back to study the movements of a robin outside the window. "Thanks for letting me save your ass."

"Thanks for your understanding. Anyway, I saw Haskell there and I asked his advice."

"You handing out a prize to the best opinion?"

"It's a coin toss, except I only see, 'Heads I talk and then I walk.' I don't see the other side of the quarter."

Maggiano's zipper snagged halfway up his shirt. He moved close enough for Zolly to see the acne that had scarred his face before Maggiano grew his beard. He put his fingers under Zolly's chin, his eyes holding the accusation that adolescents show and adults learn to hide. "I talked really close to Natron when I gave him the word. You're my roommate, so I'm giving you an easier message. I stood up for you. It's your turn to stand up for me." He bent down and kissed Zolly on the cheek. "I hope you left some food."

THIRTY-EIGHT

THEY CAME AGAIN THAT DAY AND SUMMONED ZOLLY DURING lunch. He passed Perez on the way.

"Our cameraman," Perez said. "Why you going to reception? No visitors come today."

Zolly wiped at the sweat that dripped in his eyes. He wadded the tissue and stuffed it back in his pocket.

Perez said, "Or did you arrange a private photo shoot? Let me tell you something fun. I got a card from Natron. He's having a good time now that he's free."

"Perez, fuck off. I got a delivery from the chaplain to the reception hack." It would be nice if Natron got busy enough on the outside to forget about Perez. Zolly, too, while he was at it.

"He invite the hack to do the sermon?"

"I won't be doing the camera much longer."

"You make a deal to move? Maybe go in show business? I bet I see you on the TV. Definitely, wearing a mask."

———

THE SAME TWO FEDS WERE WAITING, BUT THIS TIME BEHIND A desk. They were known to need one when things got serious. They had papers spread out before them, alongside a bag of popcorn, its open end facing Zolly. Cully was licking his lips while staring at the bag.

"I'll have this ready in a minute." Fallen was fiddling with a tape recorder, moving the switch back and forth with his thumb.

Zolly sat. "What's this all about?"

"We thought it would be a good idea to document the substance of what you're going to say ahead of time," Cully said.

"Ahead of what?" Zolly asked.

Satisfied with the switch, Fallen put the recorder down and reached for the top sheet on the pile. "We're not going to hang around long enough for bullshit, Berns. The grand jury's term ends in October, so we expect you there the first Monday. The day the Supreme Court reconvenes. You'll feel patriotic."

"Do I get to talk to my lawyer?"

"Gershom knew we were flying down. He said we should go ahead without him."

Zolly began to read the papers. As he'd expected, they were about his giving permission to hide a microphone in his booth. "There's no way I'm signing anything without my lawyer. I'm entitled to representation."

"Do you know the saying, 'A little knowledge is a dangerous thing'?" Fallen said. "The rule applies to criminal cases. So far, this is just civil. The judge sent you to jail to encourage you to obey his order, not to punish you. Next time, if you're dumb enough, it will be an indictment for criminal contempt. Your lawyer in that case will be with us every time we meet, running up legal fees. But that will be the least of your problems. We've also got you for tax evasion, mail fraud, violating the federal corruption statutes, and some other things we haven't thought of. We'll work hand in hand with the state and local authorities for your health and building code and any other violations. I have an itemized list of what we've got so far, in case you'd like to see." He pulled another set of documents from his briefcase and handed it to Zolly.

After five minutes, Zolly stopped reading and said, "You're asking me to lie."

Fallen pushed the popcorn almost out of reach. "Who the hell do you think you are? I put my life on the line so the scum won't choke us. You built yourself a nice business looking the other way." He studied the tile that covered the floor. "You ever go in your kitchen at night and turn on the lights, after they've been out a few hours?"

"What do I see?"

"You know damn well what you'd see if you looked. You've got tenth-generation cockroaches living in your place, but you refuse to look the first thirty seconds after the lights go on so you won't have to see."

"We had an exterminator service."

"Yeah, and you probably called the cops for any drunks your bouncers couldn't handle. But that doesn't mean you tried to find their nests." Fallen leaned back, looking over Zolly's head. "There were a few years I lived in the holes myself when I worked the Street undercover. I knew them all. Pushers who didn't give a damn if the customer had the money. Kids who got hooked and lost their future. Mothers who lost their kids. I swore someday I'd be the one who'd squash the roaches."

Zolly pushed the papers toward Cully and reached for the popcorn. "No one dealt drugs in my place."

"No, they just made the deals there."

"You think there was some mob of dealers who made their deals in my place?"

"Just your three go-betweens, Goldberg, Civiletti, and O'Rourke. Men who sold protection or made arrangements. Investment advisers who found a place to wash the money. If it wasn't for the suits, the sweatshirts and sneakers would starve. You know, like the roaches. They need crumbs on the floor to survive." Half an inch of cuff glared beyond Fallen's jacket sleeve.

"Good popcorn," Cully said, helping himself before he pushed the bag back to Zolly. "I told Mr. Fallen we had a better chance if we explained it to you instead of just telling you consequences. You can figure out those yourself." He was as close to the desk as Fallen, but his stomach no longer protruded over the top. His gesture was open and his face was friendship, unlike Fallen, who was the prosecutor whenever Zolly saw him. But it didn't matter that Fallen and Cully were flying different planes. They both had the same destination.

"You look like you lost some weight," Zolly said.

"I've been on a diet. Need to, if I want to squeeze in some tight places. In your case, it's the tight places you want to squeeze out of."

"It seems to me it's the two of you who are doing the squeezing."

"Let's start with the easy stuff. How often did they visit?" Fallen was relaxed now, confident in eventual gratification, leaning back in his chair, left hand flat on the desk and right hand fondling the bulb on the recorder that had turned from red to green when the popcorn got back to Zolly. Would the batteries last as long as they expected him

315

to talk? Or would Fallen turn it on and off, depending on what Zolly said? Cully ignored both the light and Zolly, fumbling among the kernels for a particularly puffy, buttered piece, while looking across the room at the vending machines. Zolly was tired of wondering. He decided to taste his answer. "Usually, once a week." His words tasted sour.

Cully put the bag down, brushed his hands, and leaned forward. Fallen pushed the recorder toward Zolly with his left hand while using his right to take notes on a yellow tablet of paper. The top sheet bore Zolly's name but last year's date and was even with the top, suggesting Fallen had reserved the legal-size pad since the first time they met.

"Any particular day?" Fallen asked.

"Usually Sundays. They came afternoons."

"Any special reason? End of the week, dividing things up?" The lines outside the corners of Fallen's eyes turned up.

"I think it was the beginning of the week. I never sat in, but it always seemed they were making plans."

When Cully asked, "Plans for what?" Fallen smiled again, Zolly's brand-new friend. When Cully asked how long they would meet, Fallen's eyes turned mean. "I'll handle this. Mr. Berns and I are getting along just fine."

"Sometimes all afternoon, sometimes just a couple hours," Zolly said.

"Depending on what?"

"I wasn't part of their get-togethers. I guess sometimes they had more to talk about, sometimes lots of visitors, people coming to the bar to see them, or they would be hungry and want a full meal after they were finished talking, or there would be a late-afternoon Bears game and they would watch the TV. They had all kinds of reasons. I think they liked my place." Zolly pictured Goldberg, waving his hands in welcome as his business friends approached, pushing the waitresses away when Civiletti was sharing secrets.

Fallen said, "You'd sit with them. You'd spend time. What did you talk about?"

"I had work to do. They wanted their privacy. We'd say hello, how about those Bears, what about the Cubs. Then I'd leave."

"Let's talk about who came to see them," Fallen said, and he began taking notes on the next sheet.

An hour later, Zolly's throat felt like four o'clock Sunday mornings in the old days. He sipped at the Coke that Cully had given him but had no appetite for the pizza. "I've told you all I know."

Fallen said, "We appreciate it. We're going to show you just how much when we meet with you and Mr. Gershom in Chicago. I'll have this session transcribed so you can sign it at the MCC. The other papers, too, about your consent to the wiretap we had in your booth. Then you do your part with the grand jury and you'll be on your way."

"What MCC? You intend to bring me back with the marshals?" Zolly asked.

Fallen hovered his hand over the recorder button, undecided whether to kill the fly or let it live. "Is this a concern? You might enjoy a nice drive through the countryside. You haven't seen the sights for a while."

"If I'm going to enjoy a ride, I want it on my own. You were nice enough to arrange to have me brought here in cuffs and shackles. If you want to be friends, I go home free."

Fallen returned his hand to the edge of the table. He tapped out the conditions a finger at a time. "If we knew you'd cooperate, we might be able to work things out. Of course, we can't have you self-report to the MCC. You have a place to stay? We'd ask Judge Dillon to put it in his order. We'd have to know your exact whereabouts every minute. We could get you a ticket to fly out the Friday before. What day would that be, Cully?"

Fallen's partner left the popcorn long enough to retrieve his wallet and extract a calendar. "That's October third. You could spend the weekend with your girl," he said, wallet returning to his jacket and his hand reaching back for the bag.

"Can I see that a minute?" Zolly checked the date. "What I thought, that's *erev* Rosh Hashanah. We'll have to make it the following week."

Fallen said, "Hair of what?"

"Not 'hair of.' *Erev.* It's the evening of Rosh Hashanah. The Jewish New Year."

"You don't have to translate; half the guys in our office take the day off. You want it off, too? Then we'll drive you up the week before, and you can celebrate in the MCC."

"If you take me up on the system or put me in the MCC, all bets are off. We can make it a different week."

"That's kind of you to offer, but Judge Dillon might have some other ideas on the schedule. Isn't that right, chief?" Cully licked his fingers.

"Enough of this," Fallen said. "You're going before the grand jury on Monday, October sixth. You want to come up to Chicago on your own, fine, if Dillon agrees. If you take off, you'll have the FBI chasing you for crossing state lines to avoid prosecution, plus the marshals on your tail. I'll be generous, let you see how we can take care of people who cooperate. You want to stay with your girl instead of the MCC, that's okay, too. Of course, we'll give you an immunity agreement, as well."

"That's not why I'm agreeing," Zolly said.

"Of course not. It's because of the roaches." Fallen returned his papers to his briefcase, after turning off the recorder. "We also recognize the danger you put yourself in. We are aware of your family background. We do offer protection."

Was this the way it had been with David? Was it hard to cough up names and numbers? Or was it easy, revenge for losing his slots? He had always imagined David giving up his friends, instead of picturing the moments David had experienced between the click and the blast. Maybe David had time to think of Zolly, regret the missed bar mitzvah. Did David shit his pants? Did he remember the Shema? "You going to give me a bodyguard?" Zolly asked.

"Nothing that dramatic. You know the witness protection program?"

"Where the snitches go to hide."

"You're being too harsh. As we see it, that's where the patriots live. We'll move you to a new town, set you up with a job, give you a new identity."

Zolly shook his head. They would never understand. Why would he want a new identity, when it had taken him all his life to learn his name was Bernstein?

THIRTY-NINE

ZOLLY USED THE TECHNIQUE HASKELL HAD TAUGHT HIM ALONG with stock market strategies. He joined the other prime-time callers who paid a quarter a pop to inmates who worked at the unit. He got the four thirty slot, which was always in demand because you could make your call, get to dinner before the kitchen closed, and have your whole night in front of you done with wife, kids, and creditors.

Her voice told him she was moving her ass the way she did for good news. "You'll never guess what happened."

"We only have the fifteen minutes."

"I've got a neighborhood job." She sounded as she had the night they opened the bar, counting the cash at closing time and weighing their success. "It's a sit-down job. I'm going to be a receptionist at the union hall."

Zolly said, "Sounds like Civiletti." The Chicago local was in the news whenever the papers did a report on clout, but as far as Zolly was concerned, there was nothing wrong with taking care of your friends. The challenge was explaining why you didn't.

"He apologized for the phone calls and all. He said it was a misunderstanding and that he wanted to make it up."

Zolly pressed the button that lit his digital watch, making his wrist glow green as the display marched to the end of his phone call. He pictured Fallen squeezed against the earpiece, picking up on every crime implied in Faith's recital. "Of course, this is all coming from you, so Goldberg can always deny it." He pressed the light-up button on his watch, this time more for reassurance than to know how much time he had left for the call. "The prosecutors came by to see me again today. They're calling me back at the beginning of the month, right before the Holidays."

Not being with her, he could see her any way he wanted. Faith was young again, trusting him to provide for them the way he had when they started off together. Not much of a payoff, after all these years, just a nine-to-five job where she didn't have to walk. He wanted to hold her, nothing more than that, and promise things would be okay. But he was tired of the lies.

———

SOLOMON'S BED WAS STILL EMPTY, AND HIS BLANKET WAS TAUT. He was hosting Haskell, the two of them occupying the client chairs. Zolly could get advice from two for the price of one. He stood beside Solomon, who was standing at the window, looking at the trees. When he met with a client, Solomon examined leaves the way a fortune-teller studies dregs in a teacup. He saw order when everyone else knew that chaos reigned.

"For you, my office is always open, even if it's closed. Who's hassling you these days? Your girl? Your former friends? Maybe the chaplains.

Or Perez? How about the feds? Lighten up. Otherwise, we can't make it through the day." He thumped Zolly on his back.

Solomon was a pain in the ass, especially on vacation, but it still beat going to Gershom. His lawyer in Chicago had more pockets than precedents and insisted on keeping them stuffed with cash from Zolly's bar. "I need some guidance," Zolly said.

Solomon studied him the way he considered a client with a sentence disproportionate to the crimes he claimed he was there for. He would nod to show he was paying attention, but otherwise would let the man continue until he had told enough of the truth that Solomon could throw the rest away. "You still take things too seriously," Solomon said. "I told you from day one, use the job for your own good. All you signed up for was to keep track of the records for the Welfare Fund. This religion stuff is extra duty that doesn't get you anywhere."

Haskell, who spent so much time with a telephone against his ear he was unable to handle a conversation more than five feet away, stepped across the room to join them. "I told him the same thing this morning. Take care of yourself."

Zolly said, "It gets your stuff typed." He wasn't looking for a thank-you, but an acknowledgment seemed in order. He typed his notes from the night before every morning when he got to work. By now, at least half the computer's hard drive was packed with motions and briefs. If it went on much longer, he would have to do the Inmate Welfare Fund books by hand.

Solomon said, "I appreciate the good work you're doing. There's a big difference between what you do for me and all your mumbo jumbo."

"Oh, so now stare decisis and res gestae aren't hocus pocus. Those are just everyday words everyone understands. It's only when we do religion that it becomes magic." When Solomon moved to thump him again, Zolly ducked away.

"I do Latin because I'm trying to do the right thing by my fellow man. To do that, you need to learn the words. I keep a dictionary in my locker." Solomon pointed to the open door to his locker in case they wanted to check it out. From where they were standing, they could only see the food. Solomon kept coffee, tea, dried soup, and crackers where Maggiano stored his college clothes.

Zolly had to redirect the conversation. They could do philosophy some other time, ideally with Haskell not around. "I'm leaving soon."

"In that case, you owe me coffee." Solomon measured a spoonful of instant into each of three cups on top of his locker. With the right music on the radio, it could have been Zolly's Place, where Bigman ejected the teenage crashers. Solomon held one cup between the forefinger and thumb of each hand and squeezed the third cup between them as he left the room for the water.

"I can travel on my own on a plane or a bus."

"How much does the ticket cost?" Haskell asked.

"I have to agree to testify."

Haskell rubbed his thumb against his fingers, feeling for the money that was never far from whatever he had to say. "That's a pretty expensive ride."

"I didn't think I'd make it back without spilling the coffee," Solomon said when he entered. "It would have been interesting seeing you two debate whose cup it was that fell."

Haskell said, "There would have been no debate; we both would have voted on yours."

Solomon replaced the mugs on his footlocker without losing a drop. Looking at Haskell, who was on his knees in front of the open locker, Solomon asked, "Find anything interesting?"

"Yeah, your dictionary," Haskell said, removing a book. He leafed to near the back, where he stopped and read aloud. "Here it is: 'Self-interest. Personal advantage.' Meaning your own, Zolly. Do you need me to look up advantage, or does this definition do it?" Without waiting for an answer, he put the dictionary back behind the food.

"That doesn't qualify as my word of the day," Zolly said.

"Because it's two words?" Haskell asked.

"Because I already know what it means."

"If you knew what self-interest meant, you wouldn't be asking advice," Haskell said. "You probably would never have come within a hundred miles of Lexington, unless it was for the Derby."

"Yeah, self-interest. That's why Solomon is always helping guys with their briefs hanging out. It's the same with me."

Haskell shook his head and walked to the other end of the room to stand under the Mickey Mouse clock. His back to Zolly, looking beneath Mickey's tail, he said, "Haven't you learned anything all these months? We don't always act to our own advantage."

"I don't have time for generalities."

"We work out of our perception of our own self-interest. That's different." Haskell was examining Mickey's toes for corns.

Zolly said, "You think we don't know what's good for us. We need someone else to give us our medicine."

Solomon spun around from the locker. "Would you like some sugar with your coffee?"

———————

AFTER COUNT CLEARED, THEY IGNORED THE CALL FOR DINNER. Zolly began his story with walking into the visiting room. He related the entire scene, including props and stage directions. His audience didn't let him act it out on his own. They improvised some dialogue that was mostly correct. What departed from the actual script still fit the scene.

"I figured if you really didn't know anything, they wanted something else," Solomon said.

"Did you think I made it up?"

"It didn't matter," Solomon said. "You could have been bullshitting us, you could have been bullshitting yourself, or you could have known the truth but not known it. I thought if you said anything, you might as well say everything. Now, even that isn't enough."

"I don't want to do it," Zolly said.

"You don't want to feel you're a rat." Haskell was done with his examination of Mickey and was favoring Zolly with the same degree of interest.

"That still doesn't tell me what to do. If I testify, what do I say? What I know, or what they want me to know?"

"What did you tell them?" Solomon asked.

"That there was no way I was going to go back to Chicago via the system."

"And they said?"

"They'll give me twenty-four hours to make it back to Chicago. I can even stay with Faith."

Haskell helped himself to some fruit from Solomon's bag. Munching on an apple, he asked, "You didn't answer the question. What did you say you'd tell the grand jury?"

"I told them I'd do the right thing," Zolly said.

"That proves my point. You satisfied them because they figure you'll do the right thing by yourself. Like I said, people think the next guy will do what they think is in his self-interest. They don't even bother to ask his opinion."

"You just said the next guy doesn't always know."

Hands clasped overhead, Haskell looked for the roar of the crowd. "There you have it. The next guy doesn't always know. Or agree. In your case, it's extra hard. There's your girl, she's got a job from them. That's one factor. And then, maybe they'll hurt you both if you talk. That's another consideration. If they offered you witness protection, I don't want to hear about it. But it would have to cover the both of you. Even I wouldn't leave my girl exposed." He cocked his head the way he did when he was about to short the market.

Haskell would probably have told Becky where his stash was banked and would have started the car with his family asleep. So far, all Zolly had proved was that he would not give up a friend at the expense of a lover. If he said anything to hurt Faith, he would be doing even worse than David. "I'm not leaving Chicago," Zolly said.

Haskell said, "Maybe that proves my point."

"You think I should?"

"You also have to worry about what the feds will do if you don't go their way."

"They can't give me my bar back," Zolly said.

Solomon said, "The time for miracles has passed."

Zolly smiled for the first time. "You should have gone to our old study group. Rabinowitz said the Almighty works in wondrous ways. He says we still have miracles, but that as we became more sophisticated over the centuries, the miracles also grew more advanced. These days, they're harder to recognize, but we still have them."

Solomon closed his mouth in deference to Haskell. Solomon knew how to treat a guest.

"Then maybe you'd better pray for one," Haskell said. "Maybe the miracle will be that you'll be able to recognize your own self-interest, if you pray very hard."

Haskell looked up at Mickey. No matter how many times a day you looked at it and how often you replaced the batteries, the clock kept moving slower. "Like Maggiano says, as though your life depends on it."

"Okay, Reb Haskell, which prayer should I say?"

"That's easy. First, say it to yourself. Just say the words, any words, say what they want you to say, then say what you might want to say, then say it every way you can, every different way, say all the words every which way. You'll finally get it right."

FORTY

On *EREV* Rosh Hashanah, the evening before he would leave, Zolly decided to skip services. It bothered him, considering all his practice, but he felt it would be harder starting the observance and then leaving in the middle. By now, he knew all the parts. He decided to say them on his own. He stayed in his room and started to pack in order to leave the rest of the night free for goodbyes. He piled his belongings on top of the mattress in order to choose what to take and what to leave with his friends. If you lived one box a year from home, limited to a list created by a bureaucrat who changed his clothes every day, you would be doing your laundry only once a week and reading a Scotch-taped copy of Mickey Spillane. You avoided that fate through the generosity of guys released ahead of you. Sixteen months earlier, his clothing had all fit in a single paper bag. Now, after repeated shipments from Faith and gifts from other inmates when they were released, his mattress held Jockey shorts and Guess jeans, polo shirts and Fila shoes, athletic socks and sweatshirts. He rubbed Gillette stick deodorant under his arms and cream aftershave on his face. His entertainment pile held the latest copies of the *Trib*, the *Journal*, *People*, and *Sports Illustrated*, as well as siddurs, Sidney Sheldon, and a pocket radio. The pile sagged his bed.

"Maybe we should put a sign on the door." Maggiano reached in his pocket, pulling out some quarters. "I got another roll in my locker, if this isn't enough."

Zolly didn't answer. You never knew what might set Maggiano off. Joey Philly would come in with the needle and Maggiano would hold out his arm, but if Zolly said a single word wrong, Maggiano would be on the attack.

"You trying to decide on a price?" Maggiano asked.

"I'm trying to figure what to pay for you to take some of this shit off my hands."

"Then I'll put my coins back in my locker." Maggiano sat on the spot on the edge of his bed that he wore like a saddle, his board balanced on his lap and swaying with every stroke of his pen. His finished work was next to him. It was still early, so there was only a small stack. "You got some stamps? Come to think of it, any stamps you got are extra. You can get as many as you want outside. In case you want to write me."

"You going to lick them, or should I?" Zolly asked. "You don't know where my hands have been."

"I been spending more than a year trying to see that you keep them clean. When they drag you before that grand jury, you'll be on your own."

"The first thing I have to drag is this stuff home with me. You got any extra sacks?"

Maggiano reached underneath his bed board. "You got to plan ahead, like I been saying." He removed several commissary bags and handed them over.

Maggiano was right. Regardless of what he gave away, Zolly should always save the bags. He could join the street people who lived on Lower Wacker Drive, under the street above. When the weather was warm, camping out along the river might not be so bad. He could use his bags as a pillow and sleep to the sound of the traffic that circled the Loop overhead.

"You going to wear those books when you get home? That's just excess baggage." Maggiano's words drove Wacker Drive away.

"Since when are you a reader? You're a writer," Zolly said.

Maggiano looked at the pile of handwritten sheets next to him that had now climbed as high as his lap. "I hear to be a writer, you also have to be a reader."

Zolly gestured at the books on his bed. "What I'm reading, I doubt you're writing."

Maggiano flexed his fingers. "Don't be so sure. My guess is your books and my letters cover the same thing. They're both about where we been."

———————

WHEN HE WAS DONE, ZOLLY WENT TO FINISH HIS FINAL rounds. He carried a checkout sheet that listed the departments he needed to clear in order to leave. Supply agreed he didn't owe them any government-issued clothing. The staff librarian's initials proved all his books belonged to him. The medical department had already confirmed he didn't have any surplus pills. Zolly was clear with the athletic department and even with arts and crafts, where earlier that day he had made his first-time-ever visit. The form was a one-page summary of life at Lexington, no grades given, needing only "course complete" to graduate.

The only boxes on the form that remained unchecked were for the lieutenant and the chaplains. The rules allowed him to skip work his last day, but his boss still had to clear him. Zolly saved the chaplains' offices for an evening visit, so he wouldn't have to be alone with Darla. He saved his visit to the lieutenant's office for a different reason.

The lights in Solomon's room were out when Zolly left the building. Solomon was probably walking around, letting everyone know his vacation was over and he would be back in business that Monday. He could find Solomon outside and avoid justifying his decision again. Wanting to remember it all, he made his way through the Yard and courtyard, pausing at the porticos and examining every door. He walked once around and then again, nodding at the strollers. Even those he didn't know by name received a wave. If he'd stuck around, he could team up with Manning. Instead, it was graduation day and he was leaving his classmates behind. He found Solomon and Haskell on the bench near Barnett. They watched as he passed the scene of Truman's crime without a single stumble. Zolly checked his Rolex. He was ready to measure by the minute again.

Haskell started up. "I didn't see you in shul, so I thought you might be out here with Solomon. I've got something for you." Haskell handed him a slip of paper with the same motion Zolly had used in the old days, when he palmed the maître d' at Kelly's twenty bucks for a table up front. "The first thing you do, open an account. You'd have to go through a lot of brokers before you'd find one as good as Bennie. Do a couple day trades. You won't even need money if you're a winner. You can cross checks. Or if it turns against you, just cover the loss. But the first few, you'll win. Bennie will put you in some new offerings until you have a bankroll."

"You don't get it," Zolly said. "I don't have any interest in playing the market. I appreciate the lessons, but I don't want any more. I'm moving in with Faith. If we're lucky, we'll have enough to eat and pay the rent."

"Then you'll turn into one of those collars," Haskell said. "The kind you swore you'd never be."

"I don't know what you're talking about."

"White collars, blue collars, all the collars. Nine-to-fivers, regular shifts. Not freelancers like you."

"Maybe I'll live a normal life. I'll put things together for the first time. I finally figured out how to live. First, I see the grand jury. Then, I get a job."

"If you give them what they want, be sure they help you get that job," Haskell said. He turned to look at Solomon, who was sliding away from both of them. Haskell turned back to face Zolly. "Don't mind this guy. You do what's best for you."

Solomon said, "What's best for you is take care of the ones you know. Do right by them."

Zolly reached across Haskell to Solomon while putting his other hand on Haskell's shoulder. "Before I go, I've got to say all of you gave me good advice. Maggiano says, friends or enemies, remember the code. You tell me, take care of my friends. Haskell says to take care of me. The hell with it, I think all three of you are right. I've finally put it together." Zolly stood. "I'll be leaving in the morning before you wake up. I'm catching the early bus. It's better than the plane. It will give me time to think. Maybe we'll see each other someday on the Street." He didn't look back.

———————

It was growing dark as Zolly made his way up the steps to the entrance of the main building. With summer about to die, the lights inside shone life. The lieutenant's office was the last door before the stairwell. It was the first time Zolly had visited when not summoned to take a piss. It was a bad idea to ever go to the lieutenant's office uninvited; people could get the wrong idea. However, this last night at Lexington, he needed the lieutenant's initials. Besides, ratting was exactly what he had in mind.

"What do you want, Berns?" The hack didn't look familiar, but he knew who Zolly was. "You don't need Lieutenant Johnson for that." He pointed at the sign-out sheet. "Any of us can initial it. If he had to see every one of you guys leaving, he'd never finish his work."

"I have to tell him something important," Zolly said. When he entered Johnson's office, the lieutenant was seated at his desk. There were filing cabinets lined along the wall to the left and right of the entrance, enough to hold the criminal records of every man and woman at Lexington going five years back. The desk was ten feet inside the room. Trying not to make it obvious, Zolly sniffed as he approached and found the air was clear. They must have moved the vials of piss. Lieutenant Johnson looked up at Zolly, as though he had expected his arrival.

"Took you long enough to get here," Johnson said.

"I didn't know you were expecting me."

Johnson rubbed his mustache. "Expected to see you every day since we got the order for your release."

"No one told me," Zolly said.

"You're supposed to come in on your own. That's how it works. What do you have for me?"

Zolly was uncertain what to say. He doubted that Johnson wanted him to talk about the grand jury. "You think I have something to tell you about the fire?"

Johnson nodded and motioned for Zolly to continue.

"I don't," Zolly said. "Like I told you that night, if I knew who started it, I would have told you then. Hell, some of my clothes still smell of smoke."

Johnson exhaled and shook his head. "Then why are you here?"

Zolly paused. It was difficult, even with Natron gone. He felt as though if he turned around, he would see Maggiano, Haskell, and Solomon on the chairs next to the cabinets, sitting as his jury. He doubted they would forgive him, even if no one were punished by what he had to say. "I came to talk to you about Mr. Truman. That time they caught him in the toolshed. He didn't do it. Those guys Natron and Perez trapped him with that female inmate. It was a setup."

Johnson began to laugh.

"He was innocent," Zolly said.

Johnson said, "I don't need an inmate to tell me that."

Zolly extended his arms toward the officer for absolution, or at the very least, an explanation. "You mean, you knew all along? Then why was he fired?"

When Johnson stood, he towered over Zolly. He moved his tongue between the hairs of his mustache as though pushing out the taste of piss.

"You thought we fired him because of what some inmates said? We took the word of an inmate about an officer? You really thought that?"

Zolly could barely breathe. "Why was he fired?"

Johnson paused, considering whether to say anything further. "We transferred him to Ashland because he let some inmates embarrass him. That was bad enough." He crossed his arms, considering further. "You liked him, huh? But you let a year go by thinking he got an unfair beef. I guess it figures," Johnson said, as he initialed Zolly's sheet.

––––––––

Zolly opened the stairwell door and walked downstairs. He passed the doors to the UNICOR courtyard for the next-to-last time and continued to the chaplains' offices. The reception area was full of inmates. Most of them were waiting to get their pictures taken. The others were walkies who were using the crowd as an excuse to stand close and fondle each other when the line surged forward. Zolly walked by Weaver, who was on duty alone and paying little attention to the waiting inmates. With a new cameraman and Darla handling the money by herself, Weaver was more bookkeeper than cop. As Darla collected each payment, she made a mark on the sales sheet, making sure of her tally before she deposited the coins in her box. She would open her hand to display the amount she held, a dealer in Vegas showing her take to the watchers. In this case, Weaver was the eye in the sky. Periodically, as the payments accumulated, Weaver descended on the collection table, counting the coins and handing Darla a scribbled receipt before he removed the payments for safekeeping in his office. Each time, Weaver commented to the cameraman on how business was doing, the status of the film supply, and whether he approved of the poses. If Burgess were in charge, he would have made the men stand at attention and the women, if seated, keep their legs crossed even when wearing pants. Weaver only insisted that their hands be in sight.

Beyond the group and deeper down the hall, the Rosh Hashanah evening services were already underway. Although the door was closed, and despite the conversations going on around him, Zolly could hear the chants. With Gabby and Adlai gone and Zolly a last-minute departure, the congregation had chosen a woman from Women's Unit to pinch-hit. Rabinowitz would never have allowed it. The pitch of her voice was distracting to the picture customers, but they forgot their annoyance when the audience repeated the prayers. If she was the seagull, their drone was the ocean's waves. When the membership prayed, it seemed to soothe the goyim.

The first time Weaver visited the table, he initialed Zolly's sign-out sheet. Each trip afterward, he took the chance to offer advice.

"Take care of yourself out there."

"I mean to. No offense, but I'd rather not return," Zolly said.

Then Weaver was gone until the next time, when he said, "Will you be going to your friend? As I recall, her name is Faith."

"I'll see her first thing. She's had a hard time while I've been in. I mean to make it up to her," Zolly said to Weaver's retreating back.

On his next trip, Weaver said, "Be sure you go to synagogue."

"I'll miss what we had here," Zolly said.

"Will you miss me, too?" Darla asked after Weaver left. She paused between her tallies. "When you didn't show up for work today, I didn't know where to find you. I thought of looking for you at dinner, but I didn't want to embarrass you in front of your friends."

"How would you embarrass me?" Tonight, she appeared as new as she had at the beginning, before Natron turned her on. It was the first time in months that she had looked straight at him. Ignoring her next customer, she reached out for him. He hesitated at her hand. *What the hell,* he thought as he took her fingers. They were cooler than he remembered, yet a comfort, nonetheless.

She said, "By saying goodbye, when we've forgotten how to say hello. By telling you I tried to get Natron to leave you alone and Perez to pass you by." She squeezed his hand. "By saying I understand why you backed away that night. By telling you that I was clean once, too." She covered his hand with both of hers, nesting his in her grasp. "To tell you that I'm sad to say goodbye. Tell Faith she's the lucky one." Her voice was like a lover's.

"I'm sorry about the way things turned out. I know what I have to do. I think I've been ready for a year, but admitting it took till now." He stepped back, tempted to touch her again, but determined to stand away.

Weaver was next to them again, but he didn't interrupt. He collected the inmate's money and entered the sale himself.

Darla picked up some papers from the other end of her desk. "I was looking at this while I was waiting for you this afternoon. This is the script for last year's High Holiday services, isn't it?"

"Yeah, this year's, last year's, next year's. The script stays the same, except we skip some of the prayers on Shabbat."

She leafed through it. "I see where you've marked it. I'm sorry you won't be here."

"I asked them to let me stay a few more days, but they won't. You guys will have to manage without me."

"I'm glad you're including me in the group. You're sure it's okay for a sinner to pray?"

Her eyes had a hint of tears. He almost reached out to her, almost told her that his drawing back had had nothing to do with her. It was the sounds, the sigh from the shul, what he could yet hear of David's departure echoing down the years. It was Faith calling for help, and Rabinowitz looking on.

BOOK FOUR

FCI LEXINGTON, SEPTEMBER 1986

MELODY

FORTY-ONE

ZOLLY HAD THE DREAM THAT REPEATED MORE FREQUENTLY AS every month went by, a dream with many colors in air so thick he could barely breathe. David was back from the road and recovering from the drive, reading the sports pages, pretending not to listen. Zolly was practicing his haftorah, a section from the Torah that bar mitzvah boys sing. There was a different passage every Sabbath of the year. Zolly's section was about justice, which still troubled him. His bar mitzvah was only a couple of weeks away. He hoped David wouldn't notice that his son's voice cracked every other line. Zolly was adolescence colliding with beauty. David put down the paper. He rubbed his eyes and provided a hint of a smile. "Don't embarrass me in front of Grandpa," David said, shifting over. "Get it right or I won't come." Zolly didn't answer. He forced his voice to a peak he had failed to reach ever before, intent on making his family proud. "Just kidding, kid. Your dad loves you, no matter what. Nothing could keep me away."

David faded into blackness while motioning for Zolly to follow. The air held an acrid smell. The smoke clogged his eyes. Zolly was barely able to see the ground beneath. He was minutes, months along before the air was slit by sun. The grasses parted to reveal a field filled with flowers, the green ringed with yellows and reds so fierce he cried. The sweetness fueled him as he raced toward the clearing. His destination shone as he closed forward, almost upon it, when the glow was pierced with pain.

He opened his eyes to the flashlight for the four o'clock Count. Passing across his face, lighting the corners of the room, the spotlight played on a bulletin board featuring Maggiano and family in happy times, his grandkids covering the entire board except for the empty corner that belonged to Zolly and showed the cork beneath. Then the light passed beyond, moving across the window, caressing the curtain, circling from the ceiling back across Zolly's body and out the door, letting the dream continue.

When it was morning, still dark outside but with the sky promising dawn and redemption, Zolly reopened his eyes and surrendered to the present, to the darkness and to the coming dawn. He swung his legs over the edge of the bed and felt for his slippers, before remembering he had given them away to Butterfly. Remembering his robe was gone to Grady, as well, Zolly took his towel and walked nude and barefoot down the hall to the shower. He stopped in front of the mirror before entering the water. The guy looking back was challenging him, asking if he meant to follow through on his resolve. *Sure I am,* he said to the mirror, and the image smirked as it mouthed the words back. *Sure I am,* he told himself as he soaped up. *This one time, I must.* That was for David. Afterward, he returned to the room and dressed quickly, careful not to disturb Maggiano. He sat at the edge of his bed, paper bag against his feet.

It was still dark when Maggiano awakened to the early shift making their way to the showers. Remaining in bed, he leaned on one elbow and said, "You ready?"

"It's my time. You know what they say, 'Everything has a season.'"

"Who says?" Maggiano was mumbling, turning over into his pillow.

"Solomon, I think."

"I never heard him say that."

"I'm talking Solomon from the Bible." Zolly kicked forward, getting up and reaching for his bag. "You could call him King of the Jews."

"Christ," Maggiano said. "We already got a King. You see this Sol, you tell him." More alert, he sat up in bed. "We had some real times together. Now, it's you alone. You know how I feel. But one more thing I got to say. Listen good when you go out the door. It's important to hear the click." Maggiano reached for Zolly, clasped his hand, and held it high in triumph.

The hall remained unlit, but several inmates, hungry for breakfast, were already moving about. No one said goodbye or even nodded. Foreign faces had repopulated Atwood overnight. The hack let Zolly leave with the kitchen workers before the morning call. This last time, Zolly chose the longest way. The sun was already beginning to show as Lexington leaned east, and the shadow of the cyclone fence sectioned the cindered walk. The air formed fog as it rose about him, not yet warmed by the morning or the walkies on their routes. When Zolly reached the archway, he gazed back through the mist at his unit. Across the Yard and up the hill, Atwood looked like home.

This first time he had ever been in the courtyard alone, he thought again of Darla. The pillars that supported the portico could have hid her, but he saw no movement in the gloom, heard no rustling in the dark, missed her scent among the flowers and couldn't hear her voice among the morning birds. The sound of his footsteps as he moved toward the administration building lagged in disbelief. He tapped on the glass entrance door once, twice, each time gaining reassurance from the sound. The sound of the buzzer that unlocked the door lasted beyond the time it took him to enter. The gap at the bottom of the control room window was a teller slot at a cautious bank. Zolly surrendered his sign-out sheet and exit pass to the hack inside, who checked the information against his list, slipped to Zolly an envelope with the bus fare, and pressed the button on his microphone. "You'll be back," he said, by way of welcome. Then he waved Zolly toward the door.

The signal announcing that he could leave was buzzing before Zolly reached the exit. Outside, he paused a moment on the top step as the door closed behind him. It didn't click like forbidden gum touching against one's teeth, or ring the release of a safety catch, or sound like thumb and finger snapping, or tick like the latch to the chaplains' john. For Zolly, it was the shofar, announcing the start of a new year. His time at Lexington done, it was as though Darla had never been. He said, "I'll be Goddamned," and entered the cab that would take him to town.

Riding down the drive to the road below, the headlights of the cars on the highway asked, "Who is there, who are you?" Zolly rolled down the window and leaned outside to display the answer. The force of the wind through the fog stung his face. As Zolly drew back inside, the driver said, "You weren't in that long, were you?"

"I look that young?"

"Not young, short. I drive this route a lot, delivering, picking up. When I take a man back to town, the more he hangs out the window, the longer he's been inside. I guess they're seeing how things have changed."

Although it was morning when they reached the city, the streetlights stayed on, fuzzy in the fog, the mist muddling the business buildings. The lights of the wakened homes nodded as they passed. Approaching the heart of town, the headlamps of the traffic blended in the haze. "We're almost there. Made good time, considering." The driver patted his fare box. The entire block was blank. The station was the only structure with its lights on. Downtown had long since moved. The buildings that had been left behind after prosperity passed had steel doors and barred windows. Zolly loved them, barricades and all. He took even steps walking toward the station, measuring the size of freedom.

Inside, there were occasional passengers and vagrants spread among the benches, but so few that they didn't have to sit close to each other. The walls were littered with posters that promised exotic destinations but peeled away from the plaster, as though exhausted by the effort. At the far end of the room, opposite the entrance, a man in a barred ticket cage drummed his fingers on the countertop. Zolly approached the clerk. "One way to Chicago, please." He opened the envelope the control room hack had given him when he left and handed the clerk the money. He had the exact amount of the fare and lots of time, according to the clock overhead. "And I'd like to make a call. Where's the phone?"

The clerk, who had watched Zolly as he made his rounds about the room, pointed toward the corner at Zolly's left. "You just passed it. It's that thing on the wall with its receiver on the hook. You'll need some money to use it."

Zolly turned away and reached in his pocket for what was left of his quarters. He awakened Faith when he called. "It's me. I'm at the bus station. I have to wait awhile. I thought I should let you know."

"I'm glad you called. Why aren't you flying in?" She cleared the sleep from her throat.

"They offered the airfare, but I wanted to breathe free as long as I could. Not that I'm not anxious to see you. When I get there, I'll stay with you. I won't leave you. I love you, Faith." There. Not so bad, after all. A little practice, he could even say it without his mouth going dry. "And I wanted the time to think."

"You've had sixteen months."

"The job okay?" he asked.

"It makes all the difference."

"Good," he said. "We'll work together. If not for them, somewhere else."

"Honey, you're not going to spoil things?"

"There's nothing left to spoil. No matter, we still would have lost the bar. Sometimes we can't control how things happen. But we can control how we react. That's what I've been working on."

"What are you telling me? What are you going to tell the grand jury?" She was awake now.

"The truth," he said, as much to himself as to her. His answer lifted his soul.

Faith didn't respond. Was it a gasp or a sob that he heard? He looked at the telephone a moment before he hung up. Faith would persevere. There was no other choice. There had to be some meaning to all this.

He sat on a nearby bench and waited for his bus. The early trips would run the longest, stretching out in all directions, Lexington the sun and their routes its rays. The room was filling with passengers carrying coffee and Dunkin' Donuts. Most of them were wearing work clothes and creased faces. Some had suitcases, but most, like him, carried their belongings in duffel bags and paper sacks. Neckties and Samsonite were for the airline terminal at the other end of town. Some of the travelers looked down as they sat on the benches, their hands crossed as though in prayer. A few punched their luggage into different shapes, none with satisfaction. One woman, by herself, rearranged her skirt about her knees. Her age was uncertain. These days, they all looked young. As Zolly studied each of them, he wondered about their stories. Then, far across the waiting room, he saw one person out of place, wearing dark clothes and a black beard. He could have been Rabinowitz, or that charity rabbi at his back door that time when he still owned his bar, or an Amish farmer or a hippie priest. Zolly smiled at each of them, all headed in the same direction. When the voice of the clerk making his announcement replaced the sounds overhead, Zolly realized he hadn't noticed the music that filled the station. The entire room rose.

The bus was shaped like a tube, its roof, sides, and rear rimmed with running lights, its sides plastered with ads. The vehicle was a neon sign selling better times ahead, its engine droning welcome. Zolly went to the rear of the line as the passengers boarded, hoping for an empty seat so he could ride alone, think more, sort things out, and work on truth. When he reached the top step and looked down the aisle, he saw several empty seats toward the rear. He passed riders who had already been on the bus when it arrived, as well as passengers who had just boarded. He walked by the bearded man, who bore a striking resemblance to David, although, this many years later, Zolly would have been unable to describe his father in words. He no longer remembered how tall David had been, or how he sounded or smelled, but the total image seemed clear. David as he was, or as Zolly wished he had been, no longer mattered. Zolly's truth was the truth, by emotional definition. Zolly nodded as he passed his memory of his father; the woman from the station relaxed her legs as he approached, shifted toward the window, and then stiffened when he passed her. Several couples sitting together looked only at each other, as though they themselves were the journey.

Zolly moved beyond them all until he reached the row in front of the bench at the back of the bus. There was a figure stretched asleep across the bench, but the seats in front were empty. Zolly sat next to the window and placed his bag alongside, rather than on the rack overhead, to discourage anyone from joining him. He was safe until the later stops, when the bus grew full.

It remained one of those days when the air fogs into autumn. Barely able to see the station as they pulled away, Zolly closed his eyes and tried to draw upon all he had learned at Lexington, who he had been when he arrived, and who he was in departure. He mourned for Truman. He reconstructed the shul and how he had come to help lead the services. He replayed his conversations with Weaver and relived his moments with the hack in black. He again said goodbye to Solomon, Maggiano, Haskell, and all the others, and a final, forever farewell to Darla. But Zolly spent most of his time considering truth.

Truth was the way it happened, not an artificial reconstruction. You married truth, till death do us part. The truth was a schedule of visits in his bar, nothing more. There were no overheard secrets in truth. No plots, no plans, no evidence. Truth was a solid tabletop from an auction house. No one would be happy with truth. Not Goldberg, Civiletti, and O'Rourke, whose chronicles he would tell. Not Fallen and Cully, whose deceit he would disclose. Not Faith, whose future would forever fade. He wondered, then, how could truth serve no one? It would not even serve himself. After this, even Faith would abandon him. He would be alone after he told the truth, denied by all he'd ever known. He would become another David. Eyes closed, hearing Maggiano, Solomon, and Haskell, remembering Darla, no longer having Faith, Zolly pondered truth.

While the bus moved onward, Zolly bounced against his bag. It was hard against his side. Mostly books, after all. He had left his other treasures at Lexington, parceling them out to his friends. He considered reading a novel, a short story, even his High Holidays prayer book, which were all inside his bag, but decided against turning on a light. In the dark, he could read with more than his eyes. He knew parts of the siddur by heart and decided to recite his favorite. Even though he was aware he should not recite *Ethics of the Fathers* when Rosh Hashanah came, he asked himself, "If I am not for myself, who is for me? If I care only for myself, what am I? If not now, when?" He whispered a line from the end of the High Holidays prayer book. "My God guard my tongue from evil, my lips from speaking falsehood." Eyes closed, head against the window, he heard snatches of melody above the engine's roar. Instead of a full poem, the fragments repeated as though trying to jog his memory. He knew it was important, but he was unable to make sense of the song. Zolly worked at it as the bus drove along. If the words came to him, perhaps that would help in recalling the melody, or if not, then the music might let him know the words. Perhaps he needed to join them together in order to grasp their essence.

He opened his eyes and looked across the aisle, searching for the source. Had the music come from the bearded man? Perhaps the woman in the seat by herself had been humming. As Zolly looked at her, she glanced his way and smiled. He turned and closed his eyes. Was it David who was finally singing? He stretched to hear the sounds that now seemed supplicant. Yearning to know them, he pressed his eyelids tighter still. He did not expect a miracle. He was resigned not to know the music that others heard for granted. Yet, he sensed that it might come to him, this one time, if he prayed very hard, as though his life depended on the outcome. *Our Father, Our King, may it be your will that I be able to put the sounds to words.*

Then there was movement behind him. The sleeper said, "Mind if I join you? That backbench ain't got no cushion. You don't need to move. I'll put your bag overhead." Zolly did not open his eyes. He could always recognize a speaking voice, particularly a man who slurred his words from a high pitch to the even growl with which Natron ended his sentence as he moved to sit next to Zolly. Through it all, Zolly did not respond, his whole body straining instead to hear more of the melody that now suffused the bus.

When the vehicle stopped, its engine idling at a traffic signal, Zolly opened his eyes, his forehead still against the glass, and once more looked outside. They were opposite a store whose dim interior had transformed its display window into a mirror. As Zolly felt Natron shift against him, as the pain cut between his ribs and the blood surprised his mouth, in that moment he put words to the song and saw the image of the bus in the showroom window, defined by its running lights, etched as though by a laser. Like a laser light, it glowed.